A LADY CYCLIST'S GUIDE
TO KASHGAR

A Lady Cyclist's Guide to Kashgar

Suzanne Joinson

BLOOMSBURY

LONDON · NEW DELHI · NEW YORK · SYDNEY

First published in Great Britain 2012

Copyright © 2012 by Suzanne Joinson
Map on p.viii © 2012 by John Gilkes
Chapter opener illustrations © 2012 by Sarah Greeno

The moral right of the author has been asserted

Endpapers: Anonymous, American, active 19th century Strobridge Lithograph
Company (printer), American, active 19th–20th century Martin Wells Knapp
(author), American, 1853–1901 Wrecked or Rescued – Which? (Preaching
Diagram), 1898 Colour lithograph poster $27^3/_{16}$ x $21^{15}/_{16}$ in. The Fine Arts
Museum of San Francisco, gift of Eleanor Dickinson, 2006.83.6

Extract on p.vii is from 'Here the Birds' Journey Ends' © Mahmoud Darwish,
The Butterfly's Burden translated by Fady Joudah (Bloodaxe Books, 2007)

Bloomsbury Publishing, London, Berlin, New York and Sydney

50 Bedford Square, London WC1B 3DP

A CIP catalogue record for this book is available from the British Library

ISBN 978 1 4088 2514 3 (hardback)
10 9 8 7 6 5 4 3 2 1

ISBN 978 1 4088 2520 4 (trade paperback)
10 9 8 7 6 5 4 3 2 1

Typeset by Hewer Text UK Ltd, Edinburgh
Printed in Great Britain by Clays Ltd, St Ives plc

MIX
Paper from
responsible sources
FSC® C018072

www.bloomsbury.com/suzannejoinson

For Ben

Here the birds' journey ends, our journey, the journey of words,
and after us there will be a horizon for the new birds.
We are the ones who forge the sky's copper, the sky that will
 carve roads
after us and make amends with our names above the distant
 cloud slopes.
Soon we will descend the widow's descent in the memory fields
and raise our tent to the final winds: blow, for the poem to live,
 and blow
on the poem's road. After us, the plants will grow and grow
 over roads only we have walked and our obstinate steps
 inaugurated.
And we will etch on the final rocks, 'Long live life, long
 live life,'
and fall into ourselves. And after us there'll be a horizon for the
 new birds.

'Here the Birds' Journey Ends', Mahmoud Darwish

A bird of the air shall carry the voice, and that which hath
 wings shall tell the matter.

Ecclesiastes 10:20

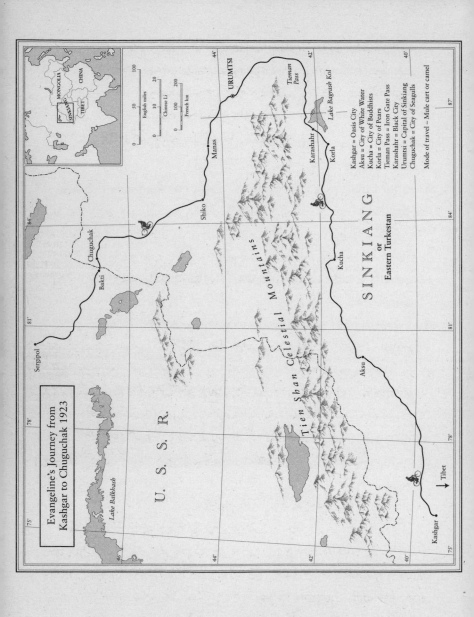

Evangeline's Journey from
Kashgar to Chuguchak 1923

U. S. S. R.

Lake Balkhash

Sergipol

Baktri

Chuguchak

Shiko

Manas

URUMTSI

Lake Bagrash Kol

Karashahr

Korla

Kucha

Tien Shan Celestial Mountains

Tieman Pass

SINKIANG
or
Eastern Turkestan

Aksu

Kashgar

Tiber

MONGOLIA

CHINA

SINKIANG

TIBET

0   50   100

English miles

0   10   20

Chinese Li

0   100   200

French km

Kashgar = Oasis City
Aksu = City of White Water
Kucha = City of Buddhists
Korla = City of Pears
Tieman Pass = Iron Gate Pass
Karashahr = Black City
Urumtsi = Capital of Sinkiang
Chuguchak = City of Seagulls

Mode of travel – Mule cart or camel

A Few Things to Remember: *Study the country you are to travel and the road-surface, understand your map, know your route, its general direction, etc. Always observe the road you cover; keep a small note-book, and jot down everything of interest.*

Maria E. Ward, *Bicycling for Ladies*, 1896

A Lady Cyclist's Guide to Kashgar – Notes

Kashgar, Eastern Turkestan. May 1st, 1923

I unhappily report that even *Bicycling for Ladies* WITH HINTS AS TO THE ART OF WHEELING – ADVICE TO BEGINNERS – DRESS – CARE OF THE BICYCLE – MECHANICS – TRAINING – EXERCISES, ETC., ETC. cannot assist me in this current predicament: we find ourselves in a situation.

I may as well begin with the bones.

They were scalded, sun-bleached, like tiny flutes and I called out to the carter to stop. It was early evening; anxious to reach our destination we had travelled, in the English fashion, through the hottest part of the day. They were bird bones, piled in front of a tamarisk tree and I suppose my fate could

1

be read from the pattern they made in the dust, if I only knew how to see it.

This was when I heard the cry. An unholy noise, coming from behind a gathering of dead poplar trunks whose presence did nothing to alleviate the desolate nature of this particular desert plain. I climbed down, looking behind me for Millicent and my sister, Elizabeth, but could see neither. Millicent prefers horseback to carts, it is easier for her to stop at will to smoke a Hatamen cigarette.

For five hours our path had descended through a dusty basin, its lowest part dotted with tamarisk trees emerging from mounds of blown soil and sand that had accumulated around their roots; and then, these dead poplars.

Twisted stems of grey-barked saksaul clustered between the trunks, and behind this bracken was a girl on her knees, hunched forward and making an extraordinary noise, much like a bray. In no hurry, the carter joined me and together we stood watching her, he chewing on his splinter of wood – insolent and sly like all of his type – saying nothing. She looked up at us then. She was about ten or eleven years old with a belly as ripe as a Hami melon. The carter simply stared and before I could speak she fell forward, her face on to the ground, mouth open as if to eat the dust and continued her unnerving groans. Behind me I heard the crack of Millicent's horse's hooves on the loose-stoned pathway.

'She's about to give birth,' I said, guessing.

Millicent, our appointed leader, representative of the Missionary Order of the Steadfast Face – our benefactress

– took an age to extract herself from the saddle. Hours of travelling had evidently stiffened her. Insects vibrated around us, drawn out by the slackening heat. I watched Millicent. Nothing could be a more incongruous sight in the desert than she, gracelessly dismounting, with her dominant nose cutting the air, and a large ruby ring on her hand at odds with the rest of her mannish dress.

'So young, just a child.'

Millicent bent down and whispered to the girl in Turki. Whatever she said provoked a shout and then came terrible sobs.

'It's happening. We'll need forceps I think.'

Millicent instructed the carter to bring forward the supply cart and began fumbling through our possessions, looking for the medical kit. As she did I saw that a group of women, men and children – a large family perhaps – were coming along the track towards us, pointing and nudging each other with astonishment at us foreign devils with hair like pig straw, standing as real as anything on their path. Millicent looked up at them, then used her preacher voice:

'Stay back and give us room, please.'

Clearly shocked at her accurate words, repeated in both Chinese and Turki, they arranged themselves as if positioning for a photograph, only hushing when the girl in the dust leaned forward on hands and knees and screamed loud enough to kill trees.

'Eva, support her, quickly.'

The crying child, whose swollen stomach was an

abomination, looked to me like a dribbling wildcat and I did not want to touch her. None the less, kneeling in the dust in front of her, I pulled her head on to my knees and attempted to stroke her. I heard Millicent ask an elderly woman for help but the hag shrank away, as if contact with us would contaminate her. The wretched girl's face buried against my legs, I felt a wetness from her mouth, possibly she tried to bite but then abruptly she heaved away, back on to the ground. Millicent wrestled with her, turning her over on to her back. The girl let out pitiful cries.

'Hold the head,' Millicent said. I tried to hold her still as Millicent opened her knees and pushed them down with her elbows. The material around her groin came off easily.

My sister still had not arrived. She too prefers to travel by horseback so that she can go at whim into the desert to 'photograph sand'. She believes that she can capture sight of Him in the grains and dunes. *The burning sand will become a pool, the thirsty ground bubbling springs. In the haunts where jackals once lay, grass and reeds and papyrus will grow . . .* These and other words she sings in the peculiar high voice she has acquired since being fully possessed with the forces of religion. I looked round for her, but it was futile.

I can still hear those screams now, a hideous anguished noise, as Millicent pushed her finger into flesh, creating a space for the forceps until a combination of blood and some other liquid came out, streaking her wrist.

'We should not do this,' I said. 'Let's move her into the town instead, there must be someone more experienced than us.'

'No time. All merciful Christ look upon us and preserve us,' Millicent did not look at me, 'thy servants, from fear and evil spirits, which hope to destroy the work of Thy hands.'

Forceps pushed in and a scream that was white-pitched murder.

'Lord, alleviate the hardships of our pregnancy,' Millicent said, tugging, pulling as she incanted, 'and grant us the strength and fortitude to give birth and enable this with Thine all-powerful help.'

'We should not do this,' I repeated. The girl's hair was damp and her eyes were panic-filled, like a horse in a thunderstorm. Millicent tipped her own head back so that her eye-glasses retreated along her nose. Then, with a quick movement, as if pulling up an anchor, a blue-red creature came slithering out along with a great swill of watery substance and was caught, like a fish, in Millicent's hands. Blood from the young mother quickly formed a red crescent in the dust. Millicent put her knife to the umbilical cord.

Lizzie came then, Leica camera in hand, wearing our uniform of black satin trousers covered with a dark-blue silk skirt and a black Chinese cotton over-coat. Her skirt hem was blotted with the pink dust that engulfs everything here. She stood, staring at the scene before her like a lost girl at the edge of a fairground.

'Lizzie, get water.'

Millicent's knife separated for ever the baby from its mother who shuddered, her head lolling back as the fish-baby loudly demanded to be let into heaven. The crescent continued to grow.

'She's losing too much blood,' Millicent said. The girl's face had turned to the side; she no longer struggled.

'What can we do?'

Millicent began a soft prayer that I could not hear very well beneath the cries of the baby.

'We should move her, find help,' I said, but Millicent did not respond. I watched her lift the mother's hand. She shook her head, did not look up at me.

'Millicent, no.'

I spoke uselessly, but I could not believe it: a life disappeared in front of us, down into the desert cracks, as simple as a shift in the clouds. Immediately, there was uproar from our gaping spectators.

'What are they saying Lizzie?' I shouted. Blood kept coming from between her legs, a hopeful tide looking for a shore. Lizzie stared at the red tracks on Millicent's wrist.

'They are saying we have killed this girl,' she said, 'and that we have stolen her heart to protect ourselves from the sandstorms.'

'What?' The faces in the crowd dared to come close to me, rushing against me, placing their hands with black nails on me. I pushed the hands away.

'They say we have taken the girl to give ourselves strength, and that we plan to steal the baby and eat it.' Lizzie spoke quickly, in that odd, high voice. Her ability with this impenetrable Turki language is much better than mine.

'She died in childbirth, natural causes, as you can all very well see,' Millicent shouted uselessly in English, and then repeated it in Turki. Lizzie set about bringing water in our tankards and a blanket.

'They are demanding that we are shot.'

'Nonsense.' Millicent took the blanket from Lizzie and they stood together; a lady and her handmaiden.

'Now, who', Millicent held the screeching baby high up as if it were a severed head, an offering, 'will take this baby?'

There was not a sound from the disbelieving faces watching her.

'Who is responsible for this baby girl? Is there a relative?'

I knew already. No one wanted her. None of that crowd even looked at the girl in the dust, just a child herself, or at the blood becoming earth. Insects walked on her legs already. Lizzie held the blanket out and Millicent wrapped the furious, wailing scrap of bone and skin into a bundle. Without saying anything she handed it to me.

We were then 'escorted' by the family elder and his son to Kashgar's city gates where, through whatever magical form of communication, notice of our arrival had already been received. The Magistrates' Court was open, despite it being early evening, and a Chinese official brought in, because, although this is a Moslem–Turkic area, it is ruled by the Chinese. Our carts were searched through, our possessions examined. They took my bicycle from the back of the cart and it, as well as us I suppose, attracted a large crowd. Bicycles are rarely seen here, and a woman riding one is simply unimaginable.

Millicent explained: 'We are missionaries, entirely peaceful. We came upon the young mother as we approached your city.' Then, 'Sit as still as the Buddha,' she whispered. 'Indifference is best in situations like these.'

The baby's skull was a curious hot thing in my hand, not soft, but neither hard; a padded shell filled with new blood. This was the first time I had ever held a baby so new, and a baby girl. I wrapped her in the blanket, tight, and held her against me in an effort to soothe the angry fists and the purple-red face of a raging soul howling with indignation and terror. Eventually, she swooned into an exhausted sleep. I checked her every moment, fearful that she would die. We struggled to sit as still as we could. There were murmurs and discussions in the fast local dialect. Millicent and Lizzie hissed at me:

'Cover your hair.'

I quickly adjusted my scarf. Like my mother's, my hair is a terrible, bright red, and in this region it seems to be a sensation. Along the last stage of our journey from Osh to Kashgar in particular men stared with open mouths as if I were naked, as if I were cavorting before them with wings on my back and silver rings in my nose. In the villages children ran towards me, pointing, then moved backwards as though scared until I was done with it and covered my head with a scarf like a Mohammedan. This worked, but it had fallen off during the scuffle in the dust.

Millicent translated: due to the accusations of the witnesses we were to undergo a trial, charged with murder and witchcraft (or the summoning of devils). Or rather, Millicent was. She was the one who had held the baby aloft and had used her knife on the girl.

'We will have to bribe our way out of this,' Millicent whispered, her face was as hard as the sun-charred desert earth.

'We will give you the money,' Millicent said, her voice quiet, but clear, 'though we have to send a message to our supporters in Shanghai and Moscow, which will take some days.'

'You will be our guests,' the official responded. 'Our great city of Kashi is pleasured to host you.'

We are, therefore, forced to remain in this pink, dusty basin. Not under 'house-arrest' exactly, though as we must have permission to leave the house, I confess I fail to see the difference.

•

London, Present Day

Pimlico

Lighting the scented candles had been a mistake; now the room smelled like a synthetic pine forest. Frieda blew them out with an excessive puff-puff at each one. It was 1.20am. She closed the window, pulling the sash-frame down with a bang, and looked in the mirror. Her silk vest was the colour of the inside of a shell – cool, silver, shivery – and its pearl-shade faded and melted her down. She glanced around for a cardigan and tipped the bottle of wine she had opened – to let breathe – down the sink, watching for a moment the blood-swill of it drain away. It could breathe as much as it wanted now. From the smell it was rough stuff anyway. *At least I didn't cook for him*. She looked at her phone on the table. Not a call, a text, anything.

She deliberated, vaguely, over the thought of running a bath, but didn't have the energy for submergence, or the decision of when to get out. Mascara came off with a cotton pad. The last time she was in bed with Nathaniel, several months or so earlier, he had said, 'I can't believe you let grubby me lie beside you'. She rubbed her face with a towel. She couldn't believe she let him, either. Three cacti stood along the windowsill like tired soldiers waiting for instructions. She put a finger against a yellow spike of the largest one and pushed on to it to get the sting but the spike was soft, and fell off at her touch. The cacti had anaemic patches all over them. They were in need of tending. She went to the kitchen.

Children come first. That's how it is. If there were a contest or a selection process or a ranking system then children would always win. Top priority: the boys. Afflicted, apparently, with disrupted nights, perpetually waking up to check that Daddy is there, to make sure he is breathing in the room, that his hand is near to their head and that they will never be left alone in the dark. Their dreams come scarily – monsters, pirates and loneliness – as do thoughts they can't control or articulate properly, yet. The last thing they want is for him to disappear to the garage for cigarettes for a few hours in the middle of the night.

Her palms were itchy, hot then cold. It had all worked well with Nathaniel for a while, the balance of freedom and intimacy. *You're a free spirit, Frie'. You come. You go.* The travelling and the landing; the hot, profound, close impulsiveness of him. It used to leave her body light and her daily existence unreal and immaterial, so that it did not matter that he wasn't in much of it. She was in control, back then, when Nathaniel suggested that he leave his wife to come and be with her, but she refused. She did not want three little boys' battered hearts upon her conscience. Though there was more to it. He was one of those men who needed tending, like her patchy cacti. She wanted none of that.

She stood at the kitchen sink. *Her first night back and he'd missed it.* Cool fingers of September air came in from somewhere. Outside a train appeared, heading for Victoria Station. Electrical lines above the tracks linked and flashed, creating a line of light that sliced Frieda's face and neck like a laser so that she was exposed for a second, a hung x-ray in white light, and then thrown immediately back into darkness. It was a relief to be home. That last trip, the last hotel, was not at all fun: a four-star, but with no room service and an empty mini-bar. Police and military vans moving around the square outside the hotel and loudspeakers booming instructions. The internet had been turned off by the authorities across the entire region and the streets were empty apart from packs of soldiers jogging in groups of eight holding riot shields. She had stood at the window staring at her phone as if it were a broken heart in her palm. It flashed up disconnect every time she tried to make an international call. Some sort of civil unrest, but she had no way of knowing what was happening; she just knew she wasn't meant to be there. Where? It didn't really matter.

The cities were blending into one, now. It was just yet another place that was no longer safe for her to be in, being English, being a woman. Actually, it was the English part that was the problem. In taxis she always told drivers she was Irish. Nobody hates the Irish any more.

She had booked the first possible flight home and all through the long journey had thought of Nathaniel. In the airport lounge – that existential zone for the lonely traveller – it occurred to her that lately the balance of control was ambiguous. Nathaniel's unreliability brought out a brutal, almost paralysing frustration in her. She was feeling something new in herself and with horror realised that it was neediness, or worse, a craving for consistency. For the first time, her work was not enough.

There was a cough at the door. Damn. Just as she had taken all of her make-up off. She walked towards the door, but stopped. There it was again. It wasn't Nathaniel. She waited several moments and then walked quietly to the spy-hole. The night light was on in the stairwell and a man was sitting on the floor just outside her door with his back against the wall, legs stretched out in front of him. His eyes were closed but he did not look asleep.

Frieda jumped backwards with her heart whacking against her chest, but she could not resist peeping out again. He was facing her now, as if he could see right through the door. She thought he was going to stand up, come towards her, but he glanced down at his hand and did not move. He was holding a pen.

She went as quietly as she could back into the kitchen. There was a number on the pinboard for the City Guardians, a group of volunteers responsible for cleaning up streets and clearing off the homeless; she could always phone that, or the police? There was the double lock on the door, but if she put that on now he would hear it and she would only draw attention to herself. She moved into the living room, instead, and returned to the window. In the street the group of kids with their mobile phones had gone and there seemed to be nobody left out there, just the rain, and the concrete swelling in the wetness and the shake of trees sagging under water. At intervals she heard the cough from the stairwell. A city fox, scrawny and barely coated, flashed underneath the skip bins. Frieda looked down the empty, wet street and made a decision. From a cupboard she pulled out a pillow and a blanket. She took another look. He was curled up on the floor now; she could just see his bent back, his leather jacket, the black scruff of his hair.

It was undoubtedly inadvisable to let him know that there was a young woman living here, probably alone, but she opened the door anyway. The man immediately scrambled himself up into a sitting position and looked at her. He had a moustache, and sleepy-looking eyes, not an unpleasant face. Frieda didn't say anything, didn't smile, but handed him the pillow and the blanket and quickly closed the door. Five minutes later she looked again through the peephole. He was sitting with the blanket wrapped around his legs, leaning against the wall with the pillow propped behind his head, smoking a cigarette.

In the morning she found the blanket folded up with the pillow balancing on top of it, and on the wall next to her door was a large drawing of a bird: long beak, peculiar legs and a feathery tail. It was not a bird she could identify. There were some words in Arabic and although she actually had elementary Arabic, she wasn't up to understanding what it said. Below, in English, was written:

> As the great poet says you're afflicted,
> like me, with a bird's journey.

Next to the bird was a swirl of peacock feathers, and alongside that an intricate drawing of a boat made out of a flock of seagulls, the seagulls floating off and forming a sunset. Frieda walked out of the doorway to have a proper look. She touched the black marks with her finger, then leaned over the railing to look down the spiral of the receding staircase. The cleaner was on the ground floor, with his mop. He looked up at her and nodded.

For Beginners: *Mount and Away! How easy it seems. To the novice it is not as easy as it looks, yet everyone, or almost everyone, can learn to ride, though there are different ways of going about it.*

A Lady Cyclist's Guide to Kashgar – Notes

May 2nd

We have been put up in a Moslem inn because we are considered too unlucky for the Chinese to house. We are 'guests' at this Inn of Harmonious Brotherhood and I am minded of the words of Marco Polo about this heat-crushed city:

The people of Kashgar have an astonishing acquaintance with the devilries of enchantment, inasmuch as they make their idols to speak. They can also by their sorceries bring about changes in the weather, and produce darkness, and do a number of things so extraordinary that no-one without seeing them would believe them.

I can believe it. It would not surprise me to see the devil lurking in every corner of this courtyard to which we are confined.

This morning as we waited for Millicent, Lizzie and I strained to see the women in veils and drapes as they fluttered back and forth. They wear gaudy scarves over tunics and vibrant headscarves and though faces are covered it is possible to guess who is handsome, and who less so, from the artfulness of the headwear arrangement.

'They are more colourful than I expected.' We were seated on the floor, on bright bolsters and cushions, in a reception-area room that led on to the courtyard. Lizzie sat opposite me, flicking at her precious camera.

Outside the main entrance to this inn is a wooden sign with the words 'One True Religion' painted across it in red. Tin pots line the shelves in the cramped kitchen and embellished, ornamental teapots with complicated handles made from bone are proudly placed in the divan room. Our host, Mohammed, pours green-coloured bitter tea for us himself, holding his curious teapot high above the cups, allowing the stream of liquid to lengthen like a twinkling rope. Breakfast is served on large copper trays, arranged so that we can look out towards the centrepiece of the house, a small fountain whose running water falls into a shallow pool that is decorated with a scattering of rose and geranium petals. Carved columns of poplar wood lead up the rafters, and a colourful balcony encases a second floor of rooms. The running water, in this thirsty desert area, is, I suppose, an ever-flowing symbol of this Mohammed's personal wealth.

'There are so many of them. Millicent says it is a combination of wives and daughters.'

'Lizzie, I want to ask about the baby. Do you think she is alive?'

Lizzie shrugged.

Mohammed returned and methodically covered the table with pitchers full of the juices of peaches and melons, plates of wobbling, slightly cooked eggs, flatbreads, rose yoghurt and tomatoes sprinkled with sugar. Next came blue earthenware bowls containing honey, almonds, olives and raisins were placed in a row along with bowls of thick, worm-like noodles. Beneath his peculiar beard, Mohammed's face is thinner and younger than one first suspects, and although he only has a small amount of English, I noticed that when Millicent said grace quietly over her food last night he turned his head and snorted through his nose, like a horse pulling at its reins.

Lizzie and I both started slightly, and looked up as Millicent emerged from one of the dark rooms, dressed in a blue cotton coat. Her rebellious hair, a frizz that strains against her attempts to control it with wax, was as usual in a cloud around her head.

'The bribery money from the Inland Mission will take several weeks to arrive, which means we have no choice but to remain here in Kashgar,' she spoke as she knelt down at the breakfast spread without smiling, poking her chin upward as if she were trying to reach a ledge to rest it on. Millicent's body has the contradictory look of a woman of a certain age who has not borne children: surprisingly girlish about the hips and waist, as if the milk of womanhood has passed her by, though she is not mannish either, despite operating outside of the usual restraints of femininity, which is at odds with her woman's mouth, laugh and her high voice.

'And the baby, Millicent?'

'They have found a wet-nurse for her. She will be returned to us shortly.' Millicent took a sip of peach juice, and licked her thin lips. She looked at me.

'The question of the baby is unresolved, but for the time being, you will be responsible for her.'

'Goodness, Millicent, I have no comprehension of how to look after a baby. I merely wanted to reassure myself that she is not dead, or being burned on a pyre.' She ignored me and lit a Hatamen.

'Remember, he is tolerating us infidels in his inn because we are women, the undangerous sex – we should not waste this opportunity. I've discovered that one of the middle daughters, Khadega, speaks Russian and so we have been able to communicate very well. It is arranged that we will begin phonetic lessons for her. She is keen to "practise her English".'

Millicent aspires to capture young women in a holy net as a fisherman catches a minnow and what a catch this would be: directly from inside the false prophet's house, to be guided into the arms of the only true Prophet.

'How can you be sure she wants to "practise English"?' I said. 'She might actually want to *learn English*.'

'Might I remind you', Millicent stood up from the table, pushing her eye-glasses up her nose, 'of Matthew 28:16–20, and of the eleven disciples in Galilee who doubted Jesus. What did he do? He turned to them and said: "All authority in heaven on earth has been given to me. Therefore go and make disciples of all nations, baptising them in the name of the Father and Son and the Holy Spirit, and teaching them to obey everything I have commanded you".'

I finished the next line for her: ' "And surely, He said, I am with you always, to the very end of age." '

She made a light hissing noise. It irks Millicent that I know my scripture, and recently, she has been opting for the more obvious of texts. Lizzie's eyes, always large and wet, grew larger and wetter: *don't Eva.* I would hardly have thought it possible.

'Well, I suppose this is as good a place as another to set up a Mission.'

Lizzie looked at me. It is many long months since we left Victoria Station (where I picked up my glorious, green BSA Lady's Roadster bicycle). Our luggage was labelled with fantastical words: BERLIN. BAKU. KRASNOVODSK. OSH. KASHGAR. Before we came, the Reverend James McCraven talked of our destination (such as we had one) as the least-visited place on earth. His craggy fingers poked invisible blisters in the air as he raved of barren deserts full of evil idols and beings no better than animals, his look implying that I was in some way responsible for such barrenness, such empty, heathen terrain. I lay in the stiff, uncomfortable bed at the Inland Mission's Training School in Liverpool holding a stolen, illicit, and for that reason much-treasured apple underneath the blanket. As my finger scraped the shiny red skin of the apple I tried to picture a desert, conjuring vast, empty spaces full of refractions of light and an infinite variety of shades of sand. I pierced the skin so that juice came out and with the tip of my finger burrowed a hole such as a worm might make into the apple's flesh, longing to reach an empty place, thinking of the peace and stillness that must be inherent in such a landscape. I have yet to find this blissful void. Instead, there has been an eternal lugging: railway tickets and strange hotels, holdalls full of quinine and sticking plasters, the rolling and unrolling of a Jaeger sleeping bag, arguments with the dragoman, trunks being loaded on and off and sorrowful headaches. Then, once past Osh we were confronted with the appalling jangle of travelling by postal cart; such a clattering of the bone and an incomparable torture of muscle. There is nausea, too, as we recoil at much, if not all, of the food available and the endless trouble with fleas.

Still, perhaps, after weeks of tramping, Lizzie and I have arrived at the thought that we would travel to the end of the world and round again. I don't believe either of us ever expected to stop. I was thankful for that look from Lizzie. Lately, it seems to me that Millicent has stolen her, spelled her away from me. Our proximity through travel has annihilated any sense of intimacy so that I am left alone, watching the two of them, but I saw that she, too, does not want to remain here. We are together, at least, in that.

London, Present Day

Victoria Station

Tayeb watched Roberto disappear into the rush of commuters like a fat fish, a bottom-of-the-sea grazer, looking exactly like what he was: a short, squat, Portuguese chef. He didn't look back once.

So that was that, then; another segment of his life pulled off and discarded like a sour piece of tangerine. No going back to the Hackney flat now.

Tayeb had waited two hours for Roberto, sitting at a table in the café on Victoria Station concourse, stretching out one cup of tea for the duration. As he waited, he drew dead-straight lines in a grid across the interlaced feathers of a falcon's wing he had sketched on to a napkin, using a fountain pen stolen from a charity shop. Stealing was easy in this country, unlike in Sana'a, where ancient grandfathers sit in the corner of shops and stalls watching fingers, their cataracts cleared by qat. When Roberto finally did arrive, at first he'd seemed concerned:

'You OK, brother?' He spoke through his green-toothed smile, not much of an advertisement for a life in the kitchen.

'Yeah, yalla. I'm OK.'

'Well, I hate to say this, Tay', but I think you're right to be paranoid.' Roberto spread his hands across the sticky table, spanning his fat fingers out.

'Really? Why?'

'They came again,' Roberto squinted down at Tayeb's doodles on the napkins, wings, talons, bones.

'The police?' Tayeb leaned back in his chair.

'Yeah.'

'Two of them, in normal clothes. No police gear, which is probably a bad sign, wanted to speak to you.' Roberto scratched at his face leaving three pink trails across his greasy cheek.

'Anwar was out, thank Gods,' he continued, 'but they had a list of names, read 'em out and Anwar's was on it. Me too, but it was you and Anwar they wanted.'

'Did they say anything else?'

'They asked if you had a visa. And if you knows about . . . Al . . . Al . . . Al . . . jazz, or something.'

'Al-Jahiz?' Tayeb sat up straight, his foot accidentally kicking a pigeon that was pecking at the plastic stirrer on the floor under his table.

'That's it.'

'What did you say?'

'I said I ain't got a clue what they are on about.'

'Al-Jahiz – "Book of Animals".'

Roberto had shrugged then looked at Tayeb, thinking to ask, 'Where did you sleep last night?'

'Outside a door in a housing block in Pimlico.'

There was a pause. 'Listen, mate. I don't think you should come back for a bit, if your visa's a bit, you know – dodgy. Could get us all in trouble, yeah? I think Nidal is very worried.'

Tayeb thought of Nidal in their kitchen, tutting at the KFC cartons and Diet Coke bottles. Nidal's quietness always agitated Tayeb's skin. The way he arranged his food, eating certain colours first and a fastidiousness about the contents of cupboards, endlessly checking that the attic door was closed firmly; it made Tayeb itch just to watch Nidal simply exist.

'Look. Tell Nidal not to worry. I'll stay away. I have some leads.'

'Good.' Roberto did not look as if he believed him, and although his face had moved into the shape of a smile, it was not one. Roberto stood up then and all but ran away, with a last 'take it easy', quickly becoming one of the people filtering through the station on their way to wherever.

The pigeon continued to peck near Tayeb's feet as if looking for something in particular. It seemed impossible that so many people should have somewhere specific to go. To calm himself, he drew, circular lines, into dots into dashes. No point in being angry with Roberto, or Nidal or Anwar. Betrayal is too large a word for the flushing away of an inconvenience.

The ink bleeding into the napkin calmed him as he talked to himself in his head: if you find yourself lost then the best thing to do is to select a point of focus and keep your eye on it, to steady yourself, to keep yourself from falling off.

Last night, when Tayeb knew he couldn't go home, with nowhere to sleep, he had picked a woman, not quite at random – she was a woman after all, and looked youngish – and followed her. She was pushing a red bike along the pavement on Buckingham Palace Road in the rain. He didn't really see her face, she was looking down at the ground as the rain came hard at a vicious angle. National Express coaches crunched the wet tarmac, buses and black cabs wrestled for road space. At a set of traffic lights she'd turned a corner into Ebury Bridge Road and immediately, like a spell, the transient, frenetic atmosphere of Victoria Coach Station disappeared. This steep, hilly road already felt like a quieter London backstreet. The hill was a railway bridge and through a gap in the wall Tayeb saw a great spread of railway tracks laid out like metal roads leading to nowhere, and in the distance Battersea Power Station's four white towers stood surreal and pointless in the dirty city sky. He winked his right eyelid, like a camera shutter, as if to photograph them.

At the end of the bridge the woman opened a metal gate and entered a closed housing estate. He watched as she locked her bicycle to a rack against the wall, disappearing into the first entrance of a residential block. There was a sign on the wall: Peabody Estate. Below it someone had scratched into the brick a skull and crossbones. As he entered the building he heard keys. Door. Then he went up, his own footsteps making less of an echo. When he reached the top there was a blue door. Number 12. He sat there for some time. He simply had nowhere else to go.

Then, much later, she'd given him a blanket; a small miracle.

He needed another miracle now. Where should he go? He did not belong with the 'exile' community. He was not a refugee. He refused to associate himself with 'immigrants' from Yemen. The Yemeni social clubs made him feel guilty and guilt made him angry. He did not miss home. He was as adrift here as he had been reluctantly following his father around with a bucket of water to clean out the bird shit at the bottom of his cages. There had been a time when he'd had an identity: he used to film, to be a filmmaker. He used to document and witness, but, since arriving in England, he had not picked up a camera.

A fresh wave of people swelled through Victoria Station, many of them almost running, everyone important in their own universe.

This was all Tayeb's own stupid fault. It had happened in a public toilet on the Strand, the one situated just outside the Zimbabwean Embassy: On the wall above a stained urinal Tayeb had painted a long-necked bird using matt acrylic. It was supposed to be identifiable as an ostrich but he wasn't sure it was. It sat on top of five eggs. To its left he'd attempted a long spindly flower, to its right, wandering foliage. The expression on the ostrich's face was supposed to be one of stupidity but this, he discovered, was surprisingly difficult to capture. Below the ostrich he'd written:

The ostrich is the stupidest of all the birds; this is because it ceases to brood on its eggs when longing for food; meanwhile if it sees eggs belonging to another ostrich which has gone away in search of food, it broods these eggs and forgets its own.

He was about to write more when he heard the stamp of feet coming down the staircase. Before Tayeb had time to do anything, even to put the lid back on to his pen, two men entered the toilet. They looked at Tayeb and Tayeb looked back; they all remained silent. One was tall and his face was ragged with skin trouble. He walked towards the wall and looked at Tayeb's script.

'What is this?'

'A quote.' Tayeb spoke quietly. The shorter of the two men read it out, looking over at his friend and winking. They didn't look like police, but who knows what police look like these days? The taller man pulled out a packet of red Marlboros and lit one up.

'Very artistic. May I ask where it's from?'

Before Tayeb could answer the smaller man, who, Tayeb noticed, had thick sprouts of hair covering his fists, began inexplicably to giggle:

'You're a bit dishy with your dark eyes. Do you work this area?'

'Excuse me?' Sharp giggles bounced from one dank wall to another. Tayeb instinctively ignored him and looked towards the older gentleman, perhaps in his fifties, about ten years or so older than Tayeb.

'He is asking if you offer more services for public consumption than just your artistic ones. Ignore him. He has a filthy mind.'

Tayeb looked at the unclean tiles on the floor, hoping his shock wouldn't show. He arranged the muscles in his face so that it looked confident, relaxed and smiled, looking at the two men.

'I do not *work*. No.'

'Shame,' the hairy one said in a high voice, 'I like a bit of exotica.' The tall man was examining the ostrich.

'It is a quote, my friends.' Tayeb decided that friendliness was the best approach. 'From the great Al-Jahiz' masterful work, "The Book of Animals". Although I am sad that my painting does not do the ostrich much justice.'

The tall man threw his cigarette on the floor, crushed it out with a Cuban heel and stood facing the urinal. He undid his zip. There was the sound of liquid hitting the urinal, then a smell, a metallic tang filtered through the air. As he pissed, the man looked at Tayeb.

'Would you like to join us for a drink?' Tayeb focused on the buckle on his bag, flapping it up and down, aware that the man was still holding himself in his hands, taking his time to put himself away. When he heard the zip Tayeb looked up and nodded. If they were police, he figured it was best to go with them.

As it was early Friday evening the ground floor of the Coal Hole on the Strand heaved with red-faced city types. High-voiced women passed glasses of wine from the bar to each other, great round glasses like bowls on stalks. The downstairs basement bar was cooler, much less occupied. Introductions were made – Graham, the hairy one; Matthew, the tall – and Graham was dispatched to the bar.

'So, are you some kind of graffiti artist?'

'No.' Tayeb stroked his moustache. His fingers twitched for a cigarette. The scars on Matthew's face were patterned, deep and coherent, as if they told a story.

'I prefer to see myself as a messenger.'

'Oh. And what is your message?'

'I like to remind people of how their actions have ramifications.' He pronounced the r of ramification with a long-drawn-out rrrr.

'I *like* the way you say that,' Graham sat down with three glasses of red wine.

'Yes,' said Matthew, 'I once nearly had a tattoo on my buttocks: *action* on one cheek and *consequence* on the other.'

Graham said, 'Now that would have got the message around.'

Tayeb had smiled, he had been magnanimous. Was this a hustle? He moved his feet under the table, confident, thinking that queers should be easy enough to handle. He took a sip of the wine and winced. Free food and drink for a night.

'Have you got a piece of paper?' Tayeb asked Matthew. A piece of yellow lined paper was fleeced from a well-handled Filofax. Tayeb took out his calligraphy pen and began to draw.

'Now, this', he said, as he sketched a squat-legged bird, 'is the Qurb. A legend of my home country says that when the bird says *qurb amad* this means it is safe for a ship to land.'

Graham ripped his beer mat into very small pieces. Matthew smiled at Tayeb as if he were a winsome puppy.

'There is a second bird.' He drew a round body and long, stick legs. 'The Samaru speaks when a traveller who has been away is about to make a return.' Tayeb looked at Matthew, but his grooved, scarred face was dead still and difficult to read.

'What is your favourite bird?' Tayeb asked Matthew.

'A pigeon,' said Matthew. 'Scuzzy, dirty, common and vicious: like me.'

'Just like you,' said Graham, sulky.

'I thought so. Samaruk in Persian means pigeon and pigeons carry messages. They indicate a return.'

Matthew laughed, 'You're saying it's a sign. We're meant to meet? You fruitcake,' he said, 'I think we shall get on fine. What a pretty, funny little thing to have found in the bog.' He finished his glass in one gulp and squinted. He jabbed Graham in the leg.

'Let's order a whole bottle.'

Stupid, foolish Tayeb; he hadn't read those messages clearly enough, had he? Look at him now. A Sudanese-looking café-worker was hovering, waiting to take his cup away. There was no point in being angry with Roberto, Nidal or Anwar, he thought again – it was not their fault at all.

Tayeb kicked at the pigeon beneath his table but missed. It hobbled away. It had one damaged foot, he noticed, but it seemed unperturbed; off it went, pecking without concern.

Difficulties to Overcome: *There is the mounting difficulty and the steering difficulty and the pedalling difficulty; and then there is the general difficulty of doing all these things together.*

A Lady Cyclist's Guide to Kashgar – Notes

May 3rd

Mohammed's first wife Rami mimed a cradle gesture indicating that we should follow her. The skin under her eyes is layered and creased like the sugared pastry baklavas we were presented with in Osh. Finally, after two whole days of tea-drinking with Mohammed and a stream of visitors, we have been shown into the interior of the women's quarters, much welcomed after endless greetings with men wrapped in turbans, wearing coloured shirt-gowns and soft leather boots, offering services, blacksmith, carter, cook and tailor and asking questions: Where are your husbands? Where are your children? Why has your father allowed you here with no men?

The upstairs room was dark, with slants of light coming through uneven windows half covered with blinds. Various women of different ages sat about on low cushions and bolsters looking at us as we three stood awkwardly in the centre of the room, not knowing whether to sit or stand. The floor was made up of thick felt rugs dyed red, indigo, blue; there was a bright strip of yellow across the centre of the floor and the woodwork of the room, the blinds and wooden columns were all painted a bright, stimulating blue. The air was soporific and two infants scuttled across the floor; one of them had his genitals completely exposed, and what's more, one of his testicles was swollen as big as my hand.

Rami pointed us towards some cushions. My eyes adjusted in the dark and there it was, the baby, in the corner of the room, on the breast of a wet-nurse who was not young. This was the first time I had seen it since our arrival – so it had not been burned, or thrown away or left to die in the desert dust. The nurse's face was sour and she seemed much too old to be providing milk. As the baby suckled she looked neither at her, nor at the women or children but stared into a distance before her, as if dead.

Millicent and Lizzie sat together on the cushions, but as I moved to join them a woman came behind me and held my arm. She pointed at my hair and would not let me go. Once, in Southsea, a gentleman with a cruel smile had whispered to me as he blew cigarette smoke in my face, 'You have the hair of a Burne-Jones beauty, but sadly not the face,' and I had wept all night because of the truth in his words.

32

We were approached by a young woman. 'This is Khadega,' Millicent said, and they greeted each other in Russian. It was the first time Lizzie and I had met her. She is not the prettiest of Mohammed's daughters (I'm not surprised that she was one of the last to lower her scarf from her face in front of us). Her mannish-wide face has a repelling effect and she has what Mother would call an unfortunate manner. Khadega nodded at Lizzie then took a handful of my hair, pulled it roughly and held it in her palm as if feeling the weight. She rubbed an individual strand between her thumb and finger and seemed to be providing some kind of commentary because whatever she said made everyone, including Rami and Millicent, laugh. She saw me looking at the baby.

'Halimah! Huh?' pointing at the wet-nurse. Confused, I looked to Lizzie for help.

'Halimah, halimah!' and then a discussion – or argument, I couldn't tell – began and the women all shouted and waved. Khadega was loudest, her voice stealing the air around me, until Rami shushed them, slapped Khadega's hand away from me and directed me once again to the cushioned floor. Khadega seated herself next to Millicent and immediately they began to talk in Russian. I took my place next to Lizzie.

'Apparently, the Prophet Mohammed had a wet-nurse called Halimah,' Lizzie said. As drinks and honeyed nuts were served Rami introduced us to Lamara, Mohammed's youngest wife. Lizzie and I could not look at each other with the shock of realising that they are both his wives. Lamara smiled, liquid-eye pretty, and caught up the smallest, crawling child, not the disfigured one, whooped it into the air with a laugh and pulled it to her chest.

We sipped tea. I was embarrassed by the closeness of the room and by the examination we were enduring. I held each mouthful of tea for as long as possible to contain my hysteria. The violence of their language filled the air and as usual I understood nothing. Nor could I read their codes or signals. What I could see, however, was that these women weren't friendly. One or two of them looked at us with open hostility.

Eventually, the foul-looking wet-nurse pulled the baby away from her chest, wrapped her roughly in a blanket and stood up, her leaking, flaccid breast exposed. Rami pointed to me. For the first time all of the women stopped talking and stared. I am inexpert at handling babies and as I tried to cradle her in my arms a frown flurried across the sleeping face. I stood up: ridiculous, big and ugly-footed in that room full of graceful women. I nodded to Rami, trying to communicate a thank you, and that I would leave, and I took the sleeping bundle out of that dark, scented room. Lizzie, who had said nothing but, with slanted eyes, had watched Khadega, stood up and followed me. Millicent spent an eternity shaking hands with every woman in the room and joined us. The second we walked out of the door we heard a burst of lively talk and laughing.

The wet-nurse apparently sits and waits in the kitchen. I am to take the baby to her whenever it needs feeding. She is asleep now, and I sit here with this journal, fearful that she might stop breathing. These rough, scribbled notes are as far as I have got with my guide for Mr Hatchett though I have grand, blazing plans for my book. It will be a new kind of book. 'A Lady Cyclist's Guide to Kashgar' is the current title I am labouring beneath and I shall sub-title it, 'How I Stole Amongst the Missionaries'. It shall be my own personal observations, filled with insights about the Moslems. I intend to spy upon the women, fascinating in their floating garb; and the landscape, these great, monotonous plains; and I shall sit upon my two wheels and feel the grit of the desert and move about the streets as if flying. For courage, I recall the conversation I had with Mr Hatchett before leaving:

'A bicycling guide for the desert,' he smiled. 'How curious.'

Two years ago my little sister Lizzie, incandescent-eyed, with a touch of otherworldliness, declared at the dinner table in Southsea, in front of Mother and Aunt Cicely and the dust lying in heaps upon the walnut-cased clock, that she had succumbed to what she termed a calling. Her new friend from St Paul's in Portsmouth, Miss Millicent Frost, had guided her towards this calling and helped her to arrive at certain understandings. I truly could have died with shock.

I remember it was raining outside but uncomfortably warm in Aunt Cicely's parlour as Lizzie elaborated upon her plan to train as a missionary with a view to travelling East. It was imperative, she insisted, that she save the wretched souls of the lost, diseased and the destitute. It was her duty to help the unfortunates, cruelly condemned by geography and ignorance and I recall thinking how dismal that the rain kept coming and sensing the certainty that Father would now die soon.

We had returned to England for him. He had a need to return, he explained, before he grew faint, white and dry as paper. He wanted to see his sister and to sit beside an English fireside and eat Dorset-grown potatoes. So we returned from Geneva to Southsea. Only, for Lizzie and me, it wasn't a return. Despite our being English, despite our names – Misses Evangeline and Elizabeth English – despite learning our Bible from King James, and singing *ring-a-ring-of-roses-a-pocket-full-of-posies* in the nursery, we had never, in fact, lived in England, nor even visited it. As children we followed Father to Alger, Saint Omer, Calais, Geneva, but never dull, ghastly England.

Mother, quite a name in Geneva, with her red hair and committees and pamphlets, was as unprepared as Lizzie and I for our first sight of the desolate Southsea tea-houses closed for the winter, and the pier asserting its futile defiance against the interminable unfriendliness of the grey, spitting sea. How that clock ticked on like a metronome. Mother said nothing as Lizzie, slight and beautiful, sat with her face obfuscated as if she were covered in gauze. My sister is, and has always been, like the feeling in a room from which someone has recently left. I watched her twist her handkerchief into a rag, stretch it with anxiety, and I wondered, who is she, this Miss Millicent Frost? I could see that Lizzie was serious and my immediate thought was this: there is not a chance I will stay behind in the damp, phlegmatic dreariness of an English winter whilst unadventurous Elizabeth travels to Babylon! Mecca! Peking!

Just three or four weeks before leaving, by chance, our cousin Alfred had invited us to a luncheon in Hampstead. We were curiosities, to be shown off, so that he would look somewhat interesting to a publisher whom he was in the process of flattering. He had hopes for his own book of verse.

The publisher, Mr Hatchett, we had been warned, was a stiff old fish. We were to tell him of our forthcoming travels and give off the air of frightful intriguing adventuresses, or similar. It was a surprise, then, when Mr Hatchett sat next to me, not at all a stiff fish, rather courteous, with an encouraging smile. It was even more of a surprise when I found myself telling him my plans to write a guide of the area.

'I have this idea, you see,' I said.

'Go on,' he responded, clapping his hands together lightly.

So, I talked, and was impressed that off-the-bat he knew my reference, Egeria – the astonishing woman who travelled in the fourth century from Gaul to Jerusalem – indeed, he told me the story of her book being discovered (possibly 1884 or 5?) and I admitted that it was reading her descriptions of the candles and lights and the mysterious glittering interiors, the tapirs, silks, the jewels and hangings that had inspired my desire to travel.

'I understand,' he said and again, that generous smile. He looked as though whilst he dreamed of travel for himself, he did not a bit resent my imminent adventures, rather, he admired me for them.

'You really must tell me more about this Guide. I should be very interested to publish it.'

I did not tell him that I was hunting for something distant, something terribly unEnglish; something that would obliterate Southsea.

Oh – now Millicent calls me.

May 4th

'I'm scared of Mohammed,' Lizzie said, watching me hold the baby up on to my chest and rub her calm as I've learned to do.

'Why?'

'He hates us.' Before I could reply, she had gone.

The sandstorms are oppressive. They consume the air like an agonised howl from the earth's heart. Every afternoon they whirl and blow up, flinging huge volumes of sand around the city, accompanied by a mourning sound.

Steadily, I am beginning to understand the rhythm of this inn. We are all three of us, Millicent, Lizzie and I – well four, if I count the baby – sleeping together in one room with the kangs lined in a row like coffins. The kangs are strange beds made of hard mattresses resting above a small brick stove area built underneath. The fires keep our bodies warm at night but strangle the night air of oxygen. I have created a crib from one of Millicent's Bible trunks which I half-emptied and padded with paper and blankets.

In Millicent's trunk I found the presents we have collected to use as gifts or bribes. Six packets of Russian lump sugar. Five jars of caviar and at the bottom of the trunk several packets of candied jujube fruits, like dates, but redder, to hand out to children. Underneath were Millicent's two maps. I unrolled them and laid them out across the numerous turquoise and golden satin-covered pillows. The first is a Map of the Great North West. There is a vast area, coloured black, and at the bottom left of it I find it: Kashgar. The black area below it is the Takla Makan desert, famous for blizzards that freeze men on their feet, leaving only the bones to be picked by the insects. Indeed, the words Takla Makan in Turki mean, 'If you go in you shall not come out'.

This map is a none-map; rather, it is a hole in a map, an ink stain against the bright turquoise of the wadded quilt below it. I am reminded of the great explorer Burton's opening words from his *Personal Narrative of a Pilgrimage*:

> *In the autumn of 1852, through the medium of my excellent friend, the late General Monteith, I offered my services to the Royal Geographical Society of London, for the purpose of removing that opprobrium to modern adventure, the huge white blot which in our maps still notes the Eastern and Central regions . . .*

Our current location is the sin-filled other side to Richard Burton's white emptiness. It is Millicent's destination, her pilgrimage. From Baku, then Osh, she pushed us further on, further East even though we were warned of bandits and Moslem brigands, and of thieves and soldiers hungry for loot and violence. Millicent's determination to reach the great strip of blackness untouched by Christian mission, where no Churchmen (nor even many white men) have visited over-rode her fear. As far as she is concerned, where the Mission has not been, a wild, unfettered and heathen hole resides, a hole Millicent intends to fill with her own limitless goodness.

The second map is not geological. It is a Missionary Map, rolled up in the same scroll. A river of sin runs like a course of blood through the desert of Eternal Despair. At the bottom is a quote from Bunyan: 'Know, prudent cautious self-control is wisdom's root.'

In my mind's eye I conjure up Sir Richard Burton's crackling eyes (I once saw a photograph of him in *The Times* dressed as an Arab, with a machete in his hand and a long-nosed saluki at his side). Give me courage, Sir Richard! I have convinced Millicent of my missionary calling. I have convinced a publisher of the worth of my proposed book. I have even tricked my dear sister who believes that I am here in His name, to do His Good Works. I should be feeling clever. I have escaped England, but why, then, always this apprehension? To my surprise, despite a childhood of examining maps and reading adventure stories, I realise that I am quite terrified of the desert; of its insects that grow louder with the dusk; of its relentlessness; of becoming simply bones, left in a desert to petrify.

London, Present Day

Pimlico

'Now that's what I like to see,' a voice from behind an enormous bunch of lilies, looking like a stage prop in their opulence. 'A half-dressed girl waiting for me at the top of the stairs.'

Frieda pushed her glasses up her nose and watched the flowers as they consumed the corner of the stairwell.

'Before you say anything,' the voice continued, 'I do know that wild moor grass and rare Alpine tulips are much more your thing than these hideous lilies, but it was the best I could do and I know I will remain unforgiven, but . . .' Nathaniel's head twisted from behind the bouquet, his hair pushed up from his face as if betraying the after-effects of a recent argument with himself. He reached the top of the stairs.

'But,' he went on, 'I have got some poppies on order from the Kirghiz Pass. Until then . . .' he held the flowers towards her, arranging his face into a carefully raffish mode. Frieda looked at the creamy, preposterous petals without smiling.

'I won't even explain,' he said. 'Just make me coffee and I will try my hardest to thaw that chilly, frozen expression on your forehead.'

Frieda turned away. 'Oh come in,' she said, finally, leaving him to squeeze the foliage that accompanied the lilies through the doorway.

As always, when he visited, Nathaniel made Frieda's flat seem reduced and cramped and in all senses inadequate. His six-foot frame and general expansiveness monopolised the limited space in seconds as he nearly knocked over the coatstand, shifting himself about with soft grunts, giving it all the smile of an adult surveying a Wendy house: marvellous. Terribly sweet.

'Would you like some tea?'

'Coffee.' He grabbed her hand, tugging her towards him. 'Come here, you sulky thing.'

Frieda allowed him to pull her. 'I am sorry,' he said, making eye contact.

'Full marks for earnestness.'

'Oh, come on, that's not fair.' His hand pressed on the small of her back, and then he pulled it away and rubbed it through his hair, sighing. 'There was no way. I just couldn't get out.

Kids crying all over the place. Margaret crying. It was a disaster area, last night. A war zone.'

Frieda almost asked why Margaret was crying but stopped herself. She had long since forbidden herself to think about Margaret, forcing herself not to analyse her, nor think about their marriage. If uncontrollable thoughts did occur they would be in terms of an empty house, or, more often, a disused church: mouldy, uncomfortable and full of empty sounds that shift uneasily, making a visitor wish to be invisible but rendering that invisibility impossible. Regardless, despite herself images came, hallucinatory, like blown-up balloons: Margaret in a summer dress in their rose-bedecked garden, smiling at the children. Nathaniel on a sun lounger, quaffing wine. Their four-bedroom house in Streatham with its antique furniture, piles of curios (stuffed waders, mounted antlers) and collections of antique bicycles in the shed. Margaret, dead-heading the roses, no doubt wishing she could dead-head Nathaniel. Frieda tried not to care. It was not her concern. She wasn't going to be one of those sordid losers who meet up with their lover's wives in cafés to lament his lovable flaws. She clanged about, pulling out coffee things.

On her kitchen table was a yellow pamphlet. It had been left outside her hotel room whilst she was on her last trip, but whoever left it had scurried away. One of the waiters, perhaps? Or a bell-boy. It was odd to see it here, in London. Written in English, it stipulated amongst other things the rulings concerning the removal of body hair of women, as instructed by the Prophet and interpreted by Sheikh Abdul:

43

1. *Removing the hair from the armpits and private parts is Sunnah (part of the tradition).*
2. *As for the private parts it is better to shave them.*
3. *Removing hair from the eyebrows on request from the husband (or without it) is not allowed because the Messenger of Allah said: 'Cursed is a woman who removes (or cuts) the eyebrows of other women and a woman who has it removed (or trimmed) for her.'*

In the hotel room she had wondered about this Sheikh and his specific rules, this intense consideration of women's personal hair. On her table the pamphlet was surreal, or rather, hyper-real, and incongruous, like looking at a shopping list on a wedding day.

She could hear Nathaniel in her living room, pacing about like a polar bear in a cage, pretending that he was relaxed and at home. She was still a little jet-lagged and a little wired. On the floor was her carry-on bag containing the knickers she had changed for fresh ones in the cramped toilet on the plane, magazines and one of the crinkled 'ethnic' scarves she always wore in Islamic cities, as if a scarf draped across the shoulder and paired with complicated earrings made her sympathetic and sensitive to a cultural and religious manifestation about which she knew nothing, really, despite her fellowship, her Ph.D, her Government-sponsored paper entitled *The Youth of the Islamic World*, et cetera. Her current research job was a thankless, limitless task: to interview the 'youth' of the Islamic world, to surmise their concerns neatly and to present ideas and 'solutions' to a European-funded think tank (no, sorry: 'think-and-do-tank') with a secret name. This is why she had been away for months, travelling, moving and dissolving.

She was such a fraud.

'So.' Nathaniel took up the entire door frame. 'How was it? Did you get to the bottom of the veils? Did you unpick the Muslim Brotherhood?'

The lines on his face joined and folded. She did not mind his age, but she did mind that he looked unwholesome, not merely unwell but seedy, as if his seams were undone. How to begin? The soldiers? The strange looks? The woman in the mosque who hit her across her calf with her walking stick?

'You have an hour to spare, I guess?' She looked at his face, which was frowning.

'What? Less?'

'Well, I . . .'

'What?'

'Got to be in Brixton for ten to open up.'

She said nothing.

Nathaniel groaned, 'I don't know what you want, Frie'. Things aren't going well. The shop's struggling and Margaret's been banging on about me going back to teaching again. I would rather barbecue my own spine.'

'You don't know what I want?' She said it quietly.

'No, Frieda darling, I don't know what you want, but I do know I'd rather drown myself than teach the vile children of London.'

'I'm not the one telling you to teach.'

This wasn't quite the reunion she'd imagined. There was a five-week bundle of mail on the table. Junk. Bills. An official letter. She'd been to fifteen countries in seven months, and by now most of her friends had given up calling. Standing in her kitchen, swaying a little, it was as if she were only slightly connected to the floor. So much of this year had been spent in trans-border international zones, a blur of boarding passes, CNN, free drinks. The hotels had all become indistinguishable, televisions showing American films dubbed with Egyptian Arabic, and water features in identical lobbies where she was eternally checking in, or out, or eating hummus for breakfast, or smoking shishas or being looked at by black-suited American oil-company workers. Or sitting alone, for too long, in a lukewarm jacuzzi, trying to remember why she was there.

Why, indeed? Usually on an assignment. Reporting on the *Bibliotheca Alexandrina* (magnificent library, a shame it has no books) or interviewing the young women along the corniche (To veil or not to veil? We are so tired of this question). Writing a report for a government-funded scheme brilliantly entitled, 'Belief in Conversation and Exchange Between East and West'. Frieda's rudimentary Arabic and a willingness to jump on a plane at any time, any day, has taken her to these places.

Nathaniel had launched into a complex anecdote involving his neighbours, bicycle thieves and local councillors. She murmured as if listening and looked at the junk mail. The offer of loans, pizzas, and cleaning services (let Agnieska clean for you, only £9 per hour!) felt reassuringly local. Frieda held up the official-looking letter and examined the envelope. It was postmarked yesterday, SE1 stamp.

Dear Ms Blakeman,

We offer our condolences regarding the recent death of Mrs Irene Guy. According to our records you are the next-of-kin of Mrs Guy. One of our key workers tried to contact you by telephone regarding the funeral for Mrs Guy, which took place on the 31st August but we were unsuccessful, we are sincerely sorry.

We request that you contact the Deaths, Marriages, Births department as soon as possible to organise a time to visit her accommodation at 12A Chestnut Road to remove her belongings.

Demand for Council properties is extremely high, therefore we can only give you one week in which to complete a full clearance. As of 21st September we will be authorised to enter and remove all remaining property. Please contact us at your earliest convenience to make arrangements.

Yours sincerely.

R. Griffin

Deaths Manager

'You don't understand', Nathaniel was saying, 'what it is like for me.' He walked towards the door rubbing his forehead with vicious thumbs. It was something he did when really he wanted a drink.

Irene Guy? She didn't know the name, she was sure. She looked up at him, this man she had been implicated with for many years now and he was looking back at her with an odd expression. It took her a moment to work out that it was the expression of a father who acknowledges for the first time that his child is not beautiful, or clever, or funny.

'I know,' she said to the closing door, 'you've got to go.'

She touched the lily stamen and let the bright orange pollen stain her finger. Presumably that was some kind of incident, though God knows what about. Nathaniel could create an argument with an empty portion of wordless, soundless air. She could always follow him. To be fair, it was true that almost all of the time she didn't know what she wanted. *I must be less . . . absent.* Instead, she looked again at the letter in her hand. Irene Guy? Outside, a train screeched past, giving the foundations of the building a thorough shake. On the other side of the tracks was a similar residential block to Frieda's, housing association, red-bricked, Victorian Gothic with its chimneys and peaks. It was dull enough outside for her reflection to be layered on the window. She looked at herself. In that awful hotel room she had cut her fringe snip snip snip with nail scissors – a bad idea, her fringe was left wonky – and it occurred to her now that she looked like her mother, as much as she remembered her. Frieda blinked to break the memory before it came, but couldn't stop it: the tickle of her mother's long hair on her arm, a low voice saying, 'Don't cut your hair, baby, it's your power.' A pair of scissors in Frieda's hand digging grooves into her little fingers.

She stood up and went to the door. Nathaniel was walking slowly down the stairs, obviously stalling, waiting for her to call him. He looked up at her but she flattened herself against the wall and said nothing. She turned and looked at the drawings on the wall, the seagulls floating, wings touching. She liked them, though Peabody probably wouldn't.

The Art of Wheeling a Bicycle: *Steering is a subject for serious consideration; a sharp eye, quick determination, constant care and a steady hand are needed.*

A Lady Cyclist's Guide to Kashgar – Notes

May 6th

I write this by the light of a linseed lamp accompanied by the tapping of too many insects throwing themselves against the paper windows like souls struggling to be allowed in. Or out. Millicent's sleeping breath is fast, Lizzie's is soft and dull; they are so close, these days, that even their breathing seems to call to one another. This heat hangs like a dead weight over all of us and still we do not know when the trial will be, or, indeed, what it means. Officials from the magistrate visited tonight, there were whispered meetings between Millicent and Mohammed but she explains nothing to me.

I am watching her, Millicent. I need to understand why my sister worships her so. She is always in an agitation. There is no humility to her, interesting, for one who is supposed to be humble in the Lord's name, she rubs her heel to the sound of her own ambition. Her neck shows the strained length of a person in a hurry to achieve a personal quest. She will do anything to achieve it. Her fingers are bony, and untrustworthy.

Dinner was on the floor in the reception room. We sat tailor-fashion on the large rug in the central room to eat and were served mountains of knotted meat bones, spiced yoghurts and almond breads. Rami arranged small pieces of mutton skewered on to long pokes of metal on trays before us. I dipped them into a thick, brown, fruity sauce, and then a spicy red one. Lizzie ate almost nothing and I remembered the day Mother brought home a baby sister, Nora. Appalled at our mother's evident fresh love for this imposter, Lizzie and I made a pact to be together for ever. We believed this as children do, with our hearts complete and true, our eyes wide and clear. I now watched as occasionally, she put the camera up to her eye, as if to take a photograph of the scene before her, although she never did.

The skinny, dark-skinned slave girls, to whom we are not allowed to speak, brought out dishes of baked figs in a red sauce and another impressive tray of meat. I ate what I could with the baby asleep behind me in a bundle. Millicent turned, suddenly, from Mohammed and Khadega and leaned towards me, pointing at the baby.

'She needs a name.'

'Is it our place to name her?'

'The Lord has placed her in our arms as a gift,' she amended herself. 'She is a symbol of His bond of love and so I suggest we call her Ai-Lien.' Millicent put down her metal poke of kebabe meat. 'Which means Love Bond.'

Mohammed was smiling at the great spread of food surrounding him and the women attentive like sparrows. The older women wear dark abayas and brown conservative veils.

Millicent lowered her voice, 'Christians are not wanted here. Mohammed is making arrangements.'

I was alarmed, thinking that we were to be arrested.

'Are we leaving?'

Millicent nodded, 'Mohammed introduced me to a Suchow merchant, Mr Mah. He has a house we can rent very cheaply outside the city. A good one, built as a pavilion. It stands in a beautiful, cool garden.'

'Outside of the city? Where?'

'Just outside the Old Town city walls. We will remain under house-arrest.'

I was silent. My sister sat on the other side of the room like a fulgurite, her eyes fixed on a point in the distance, refusing food, cradling her camera on her knee as though it were her own babe, looking as incongruous as I felt. I wanted to lean across to her, as we did when children, at night across the ocean of the nursery floor so that we were not alone and our fingers would touch.

'Regardless of the house-arrest I believe that there have been a number of powerful signs indicating that we should set up a Mission in Kashgar.' Millicent blew smoke into my face. 'Don't you agree?'

'What signs do you mean?'

'Well. The child delivered directly into our arms, for one.' She blew smoke again, away from me.

'But to be stuck in this terrible desert. Surely there is a better spot?'

'Have you looked around?' Her voice grew louder. 'There are immense possibilities for our missionary work here.'

I coughed, trying to get Lizzie's attention, but she would not meet my eye. That Leica! I should like to stamp on it, that box of images, its trickery. I am still appalled that she used it to photograph Father as he died. I remember raging at Mother in the drawing room: why should she be allowed to photograph him? What about dignity and peace? Poor Mother sighed and stroked my hair, agreeing with me, but said that this was Lizzie's way of coming to terms with death and we could not take that away from her.

As Father grew weaker she talked of capturing the transformation of his body from flesh into spirit and then Mother even agreed to a dealer visiting from London. In he came, with his cases, an elderly German gentleman, placing his various photographic models across the dining-room table as if precious jewels, emitting a long-drawn-out whistle-wheeze each time he exhaled. His assistant, I remember, was a squat piggish man called Jones (I don't recall the name of the dealer) who winked at me as he polished lenses and pointed to each model as the elderly man talked through the various components of the folding vest cameras. The Leica was a limited edition, a prototype, extremely technically advanced; needless to say the most expensive. Lizzie pretended to be interested in the inferior models, but she had already seen it, already wanted it. Aunt Cicely was mortified, and not just at having a German in the house, but Mother was too faded and shrunk with exhaustion at that stage to argue so agreed, with a wave of her small pale hand, to the purchase of the most expensive model on the table that had the advantage of being used with or without a tripod – the perfect thing for a traveller.

I remember watching this new zealous Lizzie fluttering about Father's bed, examining the quality of the light, impervious to his pain.

'Where did she catch it?' Mother asked the room at large in Southsea. Ours is a family of gentle Anglicans with a strong Fabian streak of educationalist reform; Mother is a believer in suffrage for women and progress in general.

'An Anglican is one thing,' I remember her saying, 'but an evangelist is another.'

The day Father died the afternoon light was thin, as if worn down in anticipation of his departure. Or perhaps it was a trick to be played on Lizzie's photography. Aunt Cicely cried unprettily into her handkerchief but Mother had more restraint, simply holding his hand and rubbing at his gold wedding ring with her finger. I stood at the door as quietly as I could, leaning my head against the oak panel. Lizzie fretted with the aperture on the camera at the end of the bed and the shutter click-clacked as her finger repeatedly pushed at the button. Father was barely there. He hadn't spoken for a fortnight, he certainly hadn't recognised us for perhaps a month; for weeks he sang to the stars and the nurse gave him laudanum. What made me the angriest was that it was just like Lizzie to steal that moment from him and make it her own.

Millicent called out to me as I moved away with Ai-Lien. She had obviously asked me a question. She repeated it.

'You do not like the desert, Eva?' She was staring at me and I blushed.

'I know it's obvious to say,' I said, 'but the immensity of it can be –'

'Yes,' Millicent said, patronising and dismissive now, 'it has that effect.'

'I think Lizzie feels it too, I don't think we expected the desert to quite –'

'Oh, I think Lizzie understands the fertile nature of the work we can achieve in a Mission here. She herself has mentioned the signs to me. These wretched Moslem women huddled in their back-rooms for one.' She said it loudly, fearless of being overheard. Ai-Lien's cry grew louder, a plea to an unknown god; these cries pushed through me and were impossible to ignore.

'Are you sure this is where we should stay?'

'It is here that our desert pathway to God must be laid.' Millicent sat upright, her voice pompous. 'It is our responsibility, Evangeline, to find and root out the hidden wells of ignorance and superstition. This house will suit us, I am sure. We will set up our Mission here. There is just one problem.'

Millicent glanced at Mohammed who, along with his male companions, was smoking a long-necked pipe.

'Oh?'

'It's believed to be haunted by djinns.' Millicent smiled her smile reserved for the mention of idols, idolatry and witchcraft.

'Djinns?' The baby – Ai-Lien – abandoned herself to her crying, her small head growing hot. I shifted her on to my chest; it was like embracing a cat that simply wants to die.

'Yes. Mah believes it is haunted by a troublesome spirit who gives a twisted face to everyone who lives in it. But he said that as we are Christians we are not afraid of evil spirits, so we might consider it.'

'I see.'

'Apparently the landlord and his sister have crooked faces. I reminded him that God is stronger than their spirits, more powerful than their numerous idols.'

'I shouldn't like to wake up with a crooked face.'

Millicent smiled at me, as if she had reached out and taken something I had offered her.

'Oh, I think the chances of that are very remote.'

May 7th

This morning a strange incident: Suheir, Mohammed's third wife, a sulking, brooding woman of about thirty years old who hasn't spoken to any of us directly, and wears dark, covered abayas, suddenly ran towards Ai-Lien just as the wet-nurse had finished feeding her and attempted to pull her out of the old woman's arms. Rami was carrying a vat of vinegar through the courtyard when this happened. She put the vat down and began to shout at Suheir, who then collapsed on to the floor, sobbing, and pushing her hands out in front of her. I ran over and took Ai-Lien who began to cry.

Rami shouted at Suheir who continued wailing. She crawled across the courtyard floor towards me, pointing at Ai-Lien, and actually began to rasp at my feet with her hands. Then, in front of us all, Rami struck Suheir across the face with her hand, and along with one of the daughters, pulled her away. Millicent later discovered that Suheir has been unable to bear her own child with Mohammed. I haven't seen Suheir since, I don't know what they've done with her.

I hold Ai-Lien very close. Strange, vulnerable creature. I wish I could feed her milk myself. The repetition is wearing: Rami helps me to bathe her – she has taught me how to spread warm oil on her, how to rub Ai-Lien's skin all over with it and squeeze her limbs until she is lulled into sleep – then all too soon she is awake. I feed her, clean her, wipe her, dab-dab with water, rub and sway her to sleep. It runs in a loop, through the day and night and the tiredness I am feeling is very different from that of travelling fatigue, it's a rocked-in sleepless hypnotism of the bones. We speak through mime, like children, and it works well enough.

Lizzie is suffering. Millicent is ignoring her. For the first time, since leaving Victoria Station, Millicent's eyes are focused elsewhere. She is like a queen, the way she conveys her attention and withdraws it. Now Millicent sits with Khadega, speaking in Russian.

May 8th

At last – an outing for my bicycle. Preparations are under way for our move to the Pavilion House and a visit to the souq was permitted. We took the Roadster to carry our supplies and what a caravan we made: myself, two Chinese guards, Millicent, Lizzie and one of Mohammed's men whose task it was to guide and protect us. Khadega wanted to come but Mohammed forbade it. Ai-Lien was left safely in the house with Rami.

The streets are wide and dusty at first but quickly become narrower. Birdcages hang in many of the doorways, with red and yellow chaffinches inside singing for their lives. There are birds stripped of their feathers and rammed on to spikes for roasting, and swarms of starlings living in crevices in the rooftops, and leather-skinned men selling falcons on the streets. Lizzie and I tried to minimise attention by covering our hair with light brown veils given to us by Rami, but despite using pins to secure them, neither of us could stop the veils from slipping about our heads. Our 'disguise' is therefore useless.

'Smell it, the rancid stench of these wasteful lost souls,' Millicent shouted out as we passed men hacking into mutton carcasses. To Millicent, the inhabitants of these foul bazaar alleyways are stinking in their own skin and a disgraceful waste. It is our role to save and clean them. I looked away from them, these clusters of men squatting outside dark entrances to copperware shops with moulded basins and cut pieces of metal under their feet. They did not say anything to us, but stopped their work to watch as we passed, their eyes on the wheels of the bicycle as I pushed it.

We timed our arrival with the lessening of the afternoon heat and as we moved deeper into the maze, the bazaar came to life. The Chinese guards weren't particularly concerned about watching us and agreed with Mohammed's man that they would remain at a tea stall until we returned. Our sullen guide then led us into the sand-coloured alleyways, walking quickly so that it was a terror for us to keep up with his pace. Mutton carcasses hung in a row along most of one street. I watched a boy dip chunks of the meat into a bowl of yellow paste and then poke the pieces of flesh on to a kebab spike, just as Rami did in the inn. Beside him was a vast clay oven with a giant lid which greedily devoured a constant flow of wood and dung into its flames.

As we wound along the streets Millicent gesticulated and pointed at the dark-eyed men watching us from doorways.

'Look,' she said, 'they are ripe for our taming!' A gaggle of small boys had accumulated behind us and ran around our ankles, tugging at our clothes.

'What are they saying?'

Lizzie answered, 'They are calling us "red monkey, red monkey face".'

A thin road led us past the impressive Id Kah Mosque with its gardens full of glorious yellow roses. We crossed the square in front of the mosque where a fruit market was in full fettle, its stalls precariously piled with yellow globe melons, and pyramids of onions and apricots. Donkey carts were laden with glittering-green water-melons. We entered an even narrower complex of roads, eventually arriving at the bakery quarter where ancient brick bread ovens glowered from walls and the sticky smell of sweet dough filled the air. Our guide took us to the stall that sold flour in sacks of varying sizes. The merchant was a large man, in contrast to most of the natives here, and white flour dust coated his untidy moustache. He looked nonplussed at the arrival of us European women.

How unreal it felt, to be standing in the middle of the hustling bazaar as Millicent began negotiations. Lizzie nudged me and pointed into the crowd. A European man, dressed in clerical black robes, with a large, thick belt and a felt black hat, was pecking his way through the crowds, carrying a pile of papers under his arms. He cut a queer figure, with a rough-looking beard, and a moustache like an animal upon his face. When he saw us he stopped and looked shocked. He must not have known of our presence in the city because he hesitated before running towards us in a chicken-like flap, shedding papers and calling greetings in Italian. Millicent turned round and there was much clapping of hands and kissing of cheeks as Lizzie and I stood waiting, like children, until Millicent finally thought to introduce us to the city's only other European resident, the Italian priest, Father Don Carlo D'Antoni.

'Father lives in the centre of the old Mohammedan city,' Millicent said, 'where he is working on a significant translation work. I have heard of you Father, but I did not know whether you were alive, or here, or gone.'

'Oh, as you can see, I live on,' Father Don Carlo bowed and smiled at Millicent, and then at us.

'Father dear, it is such a pleasure to meet you,' Lizzie said. I nodded too. His narrow face examined us as we examined him and if one can get past his alarming moustache then one can see that his eyebrows are thick and much blacker than his beard which is patched here and there with grey. Underneath all of that hair it is just possible to glimpse that he has quite the dirtiest face imaginable, with grooves of dust well settled into its creases.

'You must come to my house now,' he said in heavily accented English. 'It is humble, but there will be peace from these hands and these eyes.' He shooed at children who were jumping at Lizzie and me, trying to reach our hair. In fluent-sounding Turki he negotiated with Mohammed's man who unwillingly crept away. We followed the priest through the crowds, excited to have found a fellow European in this sea of natives.

Father Don Carlo's home is a single room above a knife souq where the tables are covered with blades, swords and small sharp knives with handles carved from bone. It is a simple bachelor room with a stove for cooking, a bed for sleeping, a bucket for his toilet, an upturned crate for a writing desk, and an altar made out of a stool covered with a rag of red cloth, topped with two candles, a rosary and a very filthy framed picture of the Madonna. There was no water, tea, nor refreshments, just several bottles of his self-brewed communion wine, and for want of something wet in our mouths Lizzie and I each accepted a dirty, slightly broken cup of wine. We were forced to sit on the floor as we sipped. Millicent and Don Carlo began to talk in fast fluent Latin and then French.

'Look at them,' Millicent said, switching abruptly to English, standing at Father Don Carlo's papered window, 'terrified souls.' The priest nodded, smiling.

'Father Don Carlo informs me that he has achieved many conversions. He is doing magnificent work for the Italian church.' Millicent's curled hair had mostly released itself from her usual tight bun and was illuminated in the light, as if illustrating her thoughts externally. The wine was rancid. I put mine to one side but the priest and Millicent drank cheerfully, and continued to do so. Before long, their conversation became a performance for us, as if they were long-acquainted dance partners, waltzing about the room as they spoke, waving arms, flipping through languages like fishes in a stream.

'It is not easy, we have many enemies,' the priest said. 'Marshall Feng is rallying trouble. This region is always close to flames.'

'Who is Marshall Feng?' Lizzie asked as she picked up the empty wine cups and went to place them on the altar, seemed to think better of it, and set them back down on the floor.

'A native Christian, converted as a child by American

Protestants. Famous', Millicent said, 'for mass baptisms with a fire hose.'

'Mohammedan feeling is growing stronger these days, as the General knows well. This is why he has banned the publication of Turki-language materials,' the priest said. He was standing next to his crate which was covered with papers and books arranged in unreliable-looking piles. 'Come.'

We followed him out of his room along a tight, foul-smelling corridor to a staircase at the end of the ancient building which seemed to be half made from the pink adobe clay, half from rotten wood. We climbed the Jacob's ladder and emerged like a miracle on to the roof of the building, from where we could see a spread of rooftops stretching out across the Old Town. It was like rising from hibernation, into the full pelt of the powerful sun. A shelter had been erected along the south edge of the roof terrace and underneath it were a number of cages made from poplar branches. The priest walked towards them, and we followed, keen to get out of the glare. The cages were filled with pigeons. They rustled and chucked and as the priest came close, their cooing grew deeper and louder.

'The atmosphere is not unlike the build-up to the Boxer Rebellion,' Father said, but almost more to his pigeons than to us.

'What beautiful birds, Father.' Lizzie knelt down and began to whisper softly into the cages. As children, Lizzie and I avidly studied our father's *Guide to Pigeons and Doves of the World* and had taught each other the specific voices: the quiet but far-carrying *kor-wuu* of the cuckoo dove, the *kroookkrrooooo coo-coo-coo* of the mourning collared dove. Lizzie and I looked at each other and smiled.

'Can you remember any of it, Lizzie?'

'The Chinese spotted dove and its "mournful croo crook croo" is the only one I remember,' she said. She whispered, 'coo coo cococo' into the cages and was rewarded with a hustle and a warbling response.

'The diamond dove has a doodle-doo-doo,' I remembered.

'When I first came here,' the priest said in English as he opened one of the cages and carefully brought out a delicate-necked grey pigeon which sat well-trained on his arm, 'during the Boxer times, I kept hearing a sound in the sky, a beautiful strain, like a harp.'

He stroked the wings and ran his fingers along the shimmering-grey neck. Millicent lit a cigarette. Spread below us was the vast, pink-dust Old Town. It looked like an insect mound, or a child's city made from clay or earth.

'I did not understand what this melodious sound was,' Father Don Carlo continued, 'but after being here in Kashgar for perhaps a year, I realised that the sound came from the air and would fade away, like heavenly music.' His hands gently continued to stroke the feathers of the sleepy pigeon on his arm.

'I even began to wonder if it was a celestial crowd singing to me, but then I met a man who explained to me the unusual Kashgar tradition of breeding pigeons. They tie light reed-pipes to the longer tails of some of the bigger pigeons, so that when they fly, when they swoop suddenly up or down in the air, you can hear these strange tunes come from the sky.'

'How lovely.' Lizzie had walked to the edge of the roof which had no wall, but simply a drop. She held the Leica to her eye to take photographs of the toy-town below us. I felt it imperative that I understand the political situation, for the purposes of my Guide, but I was struggling. The bicycle was left at the back of the souq and I was also worrying about thieves.

'So, this Marshall Feng, why does he cause you trouble, Father?'

'He has been given official sanction for the Christian Church on the borderlands, but it is not a comfortable arrangement.' Father Don Carlo's face grew blotches of purple red as he spoke.

'Why is that, Father?'

'The natives here resent his ways and are suspicious of his motives, making the work of conversion even more difficult for me and no doubt for you, too, when your Mission is established.'

'Who is suspicious of him, Father?'

'Everyone. He takes a *political* approach you see,' the priest spoke in a calm, soft voice, as if lulling the pigeon on his arm. 'He is less concerned with souls than with halting the opium trade which has been by far the most fruitful export trade in this area.'

Millicent scratched her cheek; she couldn't have been less interested in the discussion.

'He converted local farmers, encouraged them to sow wheat instead of opium in their fields,' the priest continued.

'But surely that is a good thing, Father?' I said. On our journey here I have already seen what the hated opium pipe could do to men, making them useless, sleepy, unable to work.

'No. The Christian farmers refuse to pay the opium tax, so the levy was raised for other farmers. The natives resent it.'

He leaned forward and put his pigeon back into its cage.

'I ask for nothing,' he said. 'I make wine for Mass which I undertake to read by myself each day, without fail. But I know things! I travel about the city and I talk and I discover. The General is feared. He beheads people without trial. He isolates people. They disappear. The postal, wireless and telegraph offices are all under the control of his censors. He pretends to tolerate the Islamic religious and cultural identity amongst the Turkic people here, but it is only enough to avoid sparking a revolt. He hates the Universal Mission of Christianity from the West.'

'That does not sound very optimistic – for us, I mean,' Lizzie said.

Millicent stood up, 'He cannot do us harm,' she said with confidence. 'It would be too much of a diplomatic scandal. Come, I want to talk alone for a moment.' She took the priest's arm and they left us on the terrace and went back inside. Lizzie pointed down to the narrow street below.

'Look: Mohammed's man.' He was waiting for us, skulking near a wall. She whispered to me, nodding towards the priest as he climbed down the steps. 'Do you think he's a bit touched?'

'Perhaps.'

Lizzie looked back at the birds once more before we made our way down the ladder to join Millicent and the priest. Our departure was protracted as our new friend repeatedly congratulated us on our imminent new house and promised to visit.

Back at the inn Mohammed was waiting, severe with the news that our new house is ready (he might as well have said *riddance!*). Thus, we are to be cast out on to the wrong side of the city walls. Lizzie whispered to me in the kang room that it is official that Millicent is to be charged with murder. The date of the trial is set for a month's time, but I wonder how it is that she knew that, and I did not.

London, Present Day

Google

A search for Irene Guy brought up Guy + Irene Wedding 6 October 2009, Irene Guy Dr GP, consultation in 53 Railway Avenue, 6111 Kelmscott and Irene M. Guy Obituary Cleveland. None of them seemed to apply so Frieda picked up the phone, holding the letter in her hand and called the number. Her palm on the window created a black starfish against the sunlight as a man answered, 'Hello, Deaths.'

Frieda hesitated for a moment, then, 'Can I speak to Mr Griffin please?'

'Speaking.'

'Hi, yeah, I have received a letter about Irene Guy who is
. . . who died recently.'

'Yes?'

She took her glasses off. She was about to say that there had
been a mistake, that she didn't know who Irene Guy was nor
why she was listed as next-of-kin, but she didn't. Instead she
said that she wanted to arrange to visit the flat, to clear it.

'Can I have the reference number please?' Frieda read it out
to him.

'Looking you up on the system . . Yes. OK. The address is
12A Chestnut Road SE27. We will be there at 2.30pm today
with the key. You have one week to clear your belongings.'

'Right. Thanks.'

Why on earth had she done that? She pulled at the bad
job of her fringe and put her glasses back on because without them she was mole-blind. Once Nathaniel had said, 'You
look stoned when we're doing it, your eyes all glazed, amazing,' and she had not wanted to disappoint him by letting
him know that astride his torso she simply couldn't see as far
as his face.

She couldn't quite say why. A chance to look around a
stranger's house appealed. Irene Guy. She was curious. She
would call work and tell them that she was jet-lagged and
exhausted.

She was aware, for a moment, of the innumerable flight
paths above the ceiling of her flat, above the roof of the building, up in the sky. She could hear, now, as she listened, the
engines (at least two of them, simultaneously) zinging along

invisible paths in the sky. It was the wrong way round, her being on the ground. Usually it was Frieda up there, knees squeezed behind plastic trays, head resting on a grubby window looking down at a view half-obscured by a wing, at the mini-lives being lived in toy houses, wondering how she was meant to be a part of it.

Perennial ryegrass. Cock's foot. Couch and sedge. Crossing the cemetery she began to fear that the sound of her wheels on gravel was disrespectful to the great stretch of dead laid out all around her so she pushed the bike on to the grass instead. Up in the highest part of the cemetery, grandfatherly oaks stood nodding like village elders. Reaching the exit, Frieda pulled the letter out of her bag to double-check the address and looked again at her A–Z, squinting at the confusion of red, yellow and blue stains.

Out of the gate. Twenty yards. Immediate right.

It was local authority, a red-brick ground-floor flat. She D-locked her bike to a post and looked up and down the street. There was no sign of an official with a key, just an unwelcoming stairwell leading to a front door. She decided to wait on the street and she pulled out her phone and looked at the time. An elderly man cycled past, wobbling across the road, right into the other lane and then back again, his wheels wheezing with each turn. Her dad answered just as a bin lorry consumed the entire road like a tank, lights flashing, its skip-carrier at the back wide open like a ravenous mouth.

'What? What?'

'Dad, it's me.' Frieda turned away from the lumbering truck as it pulled off and looked down the street into the sun instead.

'Oh, you. Listen to this,' he said. There was a thwacking noise. *Thwack thwack thwack.*

'What do you think?' He sounded nasal, as if his nose was stuffed up. She wished he would blow his nose, clear it, or not sound so . . . congested; she would much rather have an uncongested father.

'What is it?' She placed both of her feet so that her heels touched the kerb and her toes met the yellow lines.

Thwack, thwack, thwack.

'What do you think?' he repeated, nasally.

'Well, it's a little difficult to tell over the phone. What is it supposed to be?'

'What do you think it is?'

'No idea.'

'Delicious isn't it? Satisfying. Doesn't it sound brilliant? Best hundred pounds I've ever spent.'

'On what? What is it?'

'It's a divining rod, made out of beech. Beautiful, really beautiful.'

'You paid a hundred pounds for a beech rod?'

He let out a sigh. 'It doesn't just *divine*, it can also be used as a wand, a drawer down of energy, a phallic energy courser.'

'Right,' Frieda said, holding back a sigh. 'Listen, Dad, have you ever heard of someone called Irene Guy?'

'Don't think so, why?'

'Because I am outside her flat now and apparently I am her next-of-kin.'

'Hold on,' he said, 'aren't you supposed to be in Egypt or Jordan or China or somewhere?'

'Yeah, I'm back now. I am on some Council list as being connected to her.'

'You could have told me you were home. It would be nice if you could let me know which country you are in, at the least. And when are you visiting?' A disingenuous question, she was sure, because he doesn't actually want her to visit. It would ruin his cosmic alignments, made all the more cosmic and aligned with his new girlfriend Phoebe, an aromatherapist. Or physiotherapist. Or masseuse, or something.

'Dad! Irene Guy?'

'OK. I don't know. Maybe you had a teacher with that name? Or we had a neighbour?'

'Really, or are you just guessing?'

'I'm guessing.'

She sighed. The same sigh that dated back to that unhappy day when it occurred to her that everything he believes in, she does not.

'Are you just totally making it up?' She could hear him whacking with his cane. 'Do you think it's a mistake?'

'I don't know.' He sounded weary now. Frieda leaned down and picked up a chipped brick from the edge of the kerb.

'Do you think it is something to do with Mum? They seem very sure, on their system, I'm down connected to her.'

'A possibility.'

'Do you think? Have you any idea where she is?'

'Last heard of on a commune in deepest Sussex – and I am not even joking.'

'Come on. It's a bit surreal.'

'I'm serious. She sent me a letter asking for money. Communes are expensive, it seems.'

'Do you know how I can get hold of her?'

A young woman with an overloaded buggy walked towards Frieda. Three children appeared to be stuffed uncomfortably into it and numerous supermarket bags weighted the handles; she scowled as she passed. Frieda tried to smile at the young mother but was demonstrably ignored.

She surprised herself by asking, 'Have you got the address, Dad?'

'You want to contact her?'

'Maybe.'

She waited for him to find the address, listening to the sound of him rustling about, her toes resting on the kerb. She remembered an instance when, as a child, she had trapped a caterpillar under a glass, one of those black and orange hairy ones, and watched it concertina back and forth. She recalled that behind her the caravans had been full of divine brothers and sisters, there for satsang. Satsang was a meeting but what it really meant was *don't make a noise Frie'*, *we're meditating*. A divine brother had come up to her in the garden.

'Hey, Frie', what you doing?'

'Nothing.'

He had an enormous beard, enormous forehead and enormous glasses. He looked like God, according to the Seven Days of Creation illustration.

'Nice caterpillar,' he'd said.

'Thanks.'

'So, tell me . . .'

'Yeah?'

'What kind of boy do you think you'll marry, hey?' Frieda had stared at the caterpillar and not answered.

'Maybe you're ideologically opposed?' He was laughing at her. He lit up a rolled cigarette. If he was God, would he smoke? It seemed unlikely. She had looked up at him, his head was gigantic against the sharp blueness of the sky.

'With those pretty little dark eyes you will have the pick of the world, sweets.' To make him go away Frieda had started to hum, then sing: *Put your hand in the hand of the man who stilled the water. Put your hand in the hand of the man who calmed the sea. Take a look at yourself and you can look at others differently. By putting your hand in the hand of the man from Galilee.* She had heard her dad say that the brothers were allergic to Christianity. It had worked. He'd gone away, laughing to himself, smoking.

Thwack thwack thwack.

'I can't find it, Frie'. I'll have to keep looking and call you back.'

'Oh, OK,' Frieda said into the phone.

'I'm holding it now', he said, 'over the kitchen floor and it is – literally – dragging me to the left, towards the sink. It knows the water is there.'

Frieda listened as her father hit the floor with the stick and she tried to ignore a gawky man who was standing near her, despite the fact that the entire pavement was empty. Frieda realised that he was saying something to her, waving his hand at her, flapping it near her face as if to scare off flies.

'I'm going to have to go.' She hung up.

'Here for the 12A flat?' The man said, squeaky, petulant. His jacket was much too big, he seemed incongruously young. Frieda had an urge to pat his head.

'Yes. I am, yes.'

He nodded, held out keys and a brown envelope. Without a smile. Without asking her for ID, for anything.

'We need the keys back and the flat empty by the twenty-first,' he mouse-squeaked. 'You can post them into the safe box at the town hall, or you can bring them into the office. If you haven't cleared by then the salvagers will be in.'

'OK.'

He pulled himself up, as if to leave, and Frieda asked, 'Can I just check, am I down on the system as Irene Guy's only next-of-kin? Is there anyone else? Does it say who I am exactly, in relation to her?'

'Don't you know?' He looked at her, frowning. There was a pause, long enough for a car to drive past, a Jack Russell's snout poking out of the passenger's window. It yap-yapped as the car passed. A cloud moved, exposing the sun.

'Of course,' Frieda faked a laugh. 'I was just curious to know what is on your system. It is always interesting to know . . . what information is held.'

His fingers stroked the keys on his mobile phone. He looked to Frieda as though he only ever ate homemade sandwiches, and perhaps occasionally soup. 'I don't know,' he said, squinting at her, 'your name just comes up as the main contact.'

'Right,' she said, 'cheerio then.' Frieda watched him walk away from her in the direction of the cemetery. The young mother with the buggy was just up ahead, and looked back once more at Frieda and at the young man in his misshapen jacket, shaking her head, as if disgusted with all these strangers on her patch. Written across the envelope in red biro it said GUY. DEATHS. REF 1268493.

Possibilities: *Instead of a few squares, you know several towns; instead of an acquaintance with the country for a few miles about, you can claim familiarity with two or three counties; an all-day expedition is reduced to a matter of a couple of hours; and unless a break-down occurs you are at all times independent.*

A Lady Cyclist's Guide to Kashgar – Notes

June 7th

I must attempt to get this down – our new home: Pavilion House, which is in fact two houses, separated by a track. The Eastern side is where we sleep, all four of us in a single room, with a kang built into each recess. As glass is rare and expensive here the windows are covered with paper. The Western part is what Millicent calls 'the business side' and consists of a large, attractive courtyard with two rooms leading off it, and a third leading off one of those. The courtyard has that mysterious element, as if the walls are turned inward and are intent on protecting inhabitants from the desert outside. There is a simple fountain in the centre, not as striking as Mohammed's, but pleasing none the less, as the sound of water is welcome in this land of dust. Pots of fig trees have been tended by a previous owner, as has jasmine growing finely along the walls. Two Chinese guards are on permanent station at the house gates to 'protect' us. Behind the house is a large garden that leads to an enclosed, unkempt orchard.

Lizzie and I traipsed like children behind Millicent, whose movements are always impatient, as she instructed us: the large divan room is for entertaining guests; the second room is for scripture study and the housing of our books and materials; and the final much smaller room is the kitchen. Millicent met the landlord alone. Lizzie and I were disappointed – we were keen to see the crooked face. He lives in Hami and so leaves a representative in the city for our liaisons. Millicent, whether through canny and mischievous insight or coincidence, I don't know, has assigned me a most challenging of tasks: I am to be in sole charge of the kitchen, if kitchen is what one can call the cramped corner with a hodgepodge stove made from some old paraffin tins and no windows to speak of. The rules of the house are thus: Lizzie, garden; Millicent, all things cerebral, spiritual and conversational; and me, kitchen and baby, and the momentous task of procuring meals, three times a day. But – with the kitchen comes a cook.

The cook's name is Lolo and he is a Tibetan. He is supremely exotic looking with long, white eyebrows hanging in drapes and a matching white beard and numerous liver-spots on his face and hands. His skin is a leather. He smiles at Ai-Lien whenever he sees her, and he didn't whatsoever mind posing for Lizzie to take photographs of him.

Our Home. I repeat it in my mind. Two men stayed into the night last night, Mr Mah, the merchant whose eyes have the look of a person who has relinquished something precious a long time ago, and the priest who brought us a welcome gift, a mimeograph machine from Eastern China. It comes in a hinged wooden box, complete with printing frame and screen, inking plate, roller and a tube of waxed paper. Together, they and Millicent spent the night in the divan room, the three of them, drinking wine and smoking. Lolo made tea in a metal samovar and dough strips which he prepared, sieving the flour, turning out the butter, measuring the salt, and Lizzie and I served them the tea, which they drank between wine courses, but we were not invited to join them.

Mr Mah seems to have taken it upon himself to be the prominent person for our arrangements. He is a mysterious person, neither Moslem, Tundra, Chinese, Russian nor Tibetan, but some form of hybrid. Unlike most native merchants, it appears that he is unconcerned with the scandal of dealing with us *twei-tsu*, foreign devils. He watched as Millicent and the priest searched the Bible for appropriate sections to translate into Perso-Turkic.

I continued to supply them with drinks and on my last visit to the room noticed that the priest had laid out his calligraphy sticks in a row next to him, and I saw on some paper examples of his beautiful Arabic script.

'Eva,' Millicent said, as I moved to leave, 'we've decided on a section to translate.'

Mr Mah was smoking a long-handled black pipe, he did not look up at me, but puffed and stared into the distance as Millicent handed me a piece of paper. In her crabbish writing she had transcribed Ezekiel 37:

The hand of the LORD was upon me, and carried me out in the spirit of the LORD, and set me down in the midst of the valley which was full of bones, And caused me to pass by them round about: and, behold, there were very many in the open valley; and, lo, they were very dry. And he said unto me, Son of man, can these bones live? And I answered, O Lord GOD, thou knowest . . . So I prophesied as I was commanded: and as I prophesied, there was a noise, and behold a shaking, and the bones came together, bone to his bone.

'What do you think?' Millicent said, letting the smoke out of her mouth.

'What is it for?'

'To distribute about the bazaar and to announce our presence.'

The priest smiled at me. 'I will translate it into Arabic and Turki,' he said.

I read it and wanted to say this: that I have reservations regarding the wisdom of talking of bones rising up in the desert and dancing in a place where bones should be left alone. Millicent herself taught us that this is a place where you are expected to rinse your hands three times from water poured by a host before entering a home; where you are asked to stand, hands together, palms upward, as if holding the Quran, then pass them over your face in a religious gesture of blessings; where the salaams are serious and the older men stroke beards as a sign of courtesy. It seems dancing bones would not be welcome, but I said nothing and returned to Lolo.

Millicent demands English meals but does not explain what this means. Lolo knows nothing about English cooking, but then neither do I, so we have gone about our kitchen together labelling and naming things in a mish-mash of languages, English, Russian, Turki and a little Hindustani. The bottles we managed to get from the bazaar for Ai-Lien's milk are called the *botties*. Lolo pulled from a sackcloth several huge, disc-like flatbreads and a dozen small, flower-shaped rolls and we settled on *bibi* for bread.

Very ceremoniously, Lolo gave Lizzie and me a tour of the garden which is laid on two levels, the lower part being the orchard grown wild. It is indeed very charming, and abundant and one would not guess we are in a desert. All in all, there is too much fruit. It is almost obscene the amount of fruit growing and fermenting: baby pomegranates and peaches, not yet ripe, and there are nectarines, apricots, figs and apples. At the orchard's heart is a wooden pavilion, next to which is a very curious tree with petals that look like handkerchiefs draped from its branches. Lizzie holds the cherries in her palm in wonder, a fruit from home in this strange place. It is her role to help Lolo with the garden but so far she has simply cut the pomegranates in half to photograph them. Nor will she help with Ai-Lien. When

I pass the baby to her she holds her uncomfortably, away from her body as if carrying something that needs to be disposed of.

Arranging food for Ai-Lien is a difficult business. The wet-nurse could not be convinced to join us in our new house although Mah has found us a nursing mother, four li away, who has agreed to supply us with four bottles of her milk each day. It is a tedious arrangement: in the mornings, before it gets too hot, I am to walk with Ai-Lien strapped to my chest with a swathe of Kashgari silk, accompanied by either of the guards whose names we have discovered are Li and Hai. We are to meet the mother's son half-way at the dry river to exchange money for milk.

So, I am expected to keep the infant alive and to feed them all English food when the only thing I know how to cook is a cake. Sir Richard Burton disguised himself as an Andalusian and a Moor. He dressed as a Balochi and travelled with tribes-men to study falconry. He journeyed to Mecca disguised as a Moslem. He would have thought nothing of pretending that he had a devout religious calling in order to reach the wildest, most remote edge of the desert for the purpose of recording his observations. I have no doubt that he would have positively relished donning an apron if his disguise required it and acting the part of a Hindustani cook, or a Ladakhis in the garden or a Kashmiri in the marketplace. Why, then, do I find it so diffi-cult to inhabit my own disguise?

Kashgar opens its secrets to an English lady cyclist. The guards agreed to me leaving the house.

I see things. I see rooms of girls asleep at their sewing machines and a filthy hovel they call the hospital, with two metal-framed beds and dirty sheets. Streets far removed from the Chinese style, streets full of Allah and donkey carts, mutton and bread echoing the steppes, a whole universe away from Peking. I see traders, bazaar men and I hear many languages: Altaic, Uzbek, Qazakh, Kyrgyz, Turki, Chinese, Russian and Arabic. I have learned that the script is a modified form of Arabic, that the religion is Islam inside a mystical Sufi, and, well, it seems to me that the mysticism overrides the Islamic. Mosques are numerous, their steps swept clean at all times. Chants of Quranic passages can be heard. The priest told us that people who are suffering are beaten with dead chickens to rid them of evil spirits (but I haven't seen this). Eyebrows joined in the middle are considered a sign of beauty in the women. I saw the herbs used for enhancing eyebrows.

My wheels bump over the tail of something dead, forcing me to swerve in front of a donkey pulling a cart full of spring onions and small oranges. The carter spits, the men sharpen long knives at kebabe stalls and laugh at me. The road that leads from the Apak Hoja tomb, down past the Sunday market stalls, is sleepy and content during the weekday. Small girls in torn dresses play on the edge of the road. What are they crowding round? A yellow chick, quivering, a vulnerable ball of yellow-feathered fluff, they are poking it with a stick.

Birds, everywhere.

Winding through the labyrinth, behind the Id Kah Mosque, two skinny kid goats stand without a mother, their backs covered in sores and bones poking through their skin. Faster, now, my bicycle almost floating, and the feeling of being chased although I am not; no one is very much interested in chasing me. The smell of mutton fat and excrement. A small boy holds out his palm as I pass, in it, a terrapin moving in circles.

The wind begins as if it were a signal and the heat is about to strangle everyone and everything, but as I float and fly I can almost trick it. The middle of the morning is the beginning of the terrible part of the day. Down I go, through the Old Town, out of the city gates where the guards sit up from sleep to look at me. On to the long, winding track that follows the dry river bed and eventually reaches Pavilion House. Too much strangeness. Faster still, back to the baby whom I have left with Lolo. This morning I handed over a small sum of money in exchange for bottles of milk. It is precarious that Ai-Lien's food must be dependent on the dirty hands of this small, native boy and I am determined to find an alternative milk source. So far we can only get sheep's milk which Ai-Lien refuses. To make matters worse, I have learned from Lolo's mimes that this mother is an opium taker and I fear that the milk is infected. Millicent has cabled the Inland Mission for an urgent supply of Allenbury's dried food but how long it will take to arrive I do not know.

June 15th

My sister came to me, in my kang.

'I had a dream about the crows,' she said. I had to think for a moment, the crows, and then I remembered. Ah, yes. As children we called the Sisters the crows. Sister Marguerite. Sister Eunice.

'What on earth made you dream of them?'

'Do you remember me standing on that wall, being a bird?'

'Yes.'

'I remember green. The trees, and behind me the school building, the outhouses, the chapel. How much I wanted to fly.'

We, the only two Protestant girls at a Catholic school, suffered during the month of May. This was when the first communions began, when excitable girls sat in groups making paper flowers and stripping roses for their petals. The increased religious instruction around us left Lizzie and I removed from the festive feeling and to cheer ourselves, we resorted to speaking to one another in the bird-language of our own invention.

'I haven't thought of Sister Eunice for a long time.'

'That baby will love you if you rock it to sleep like that.' Lizzie looked at Ai-Lien. I said nothing, just stroked the fine black hair.

'She seems to bring you a sort of peace.'

'Yes, I suppose she does.' She was asleep, I stood up to put the tiny baby in the crib. We were alone in the kang room; Millicent was with the priest, attending to their pamphlets.

'It has returned,' Lizzie whispered to my back. For a moment I did not know what she meant, and then I realised.

'It's very painful?'

She calls it the honeybee inside her head, buzzing in the night when the dead silence of the desert hangs over us like death itself. Like a bee, dancing in her head. I should have guessed from the lines around her mouth and the squint of her eye. Her eyesight goes in and out when the buzzing in her head rings louder than life outside. Both of us listened to Ai-Lien's gentle snores for a moment.

'When it is bad I can't even see through the camera view-finder. Mostly though, oh dear me, it's a bore.'

'Have you told Millicent?' I asked. 'How much medicine do you have left?'

'Don't tell her.' She looked down at her dirty feet, tapping in the sand that coated the floor after the most recent sand-storm, rippled like a beach with the tide out. 'Promise me?'

I was surprised. Millicent and Lizzie's friendship was so thick and tight, like old cardigans put together in a trunk these past two years, and more so, with each mile slogged over to get here. How could Millicent not know about this? Or about what inevitably comes after the headaches? I confess here that I almost felt glad that Lizzie will suffer, just as I have suffered with loneliness as she and Millicent read their Bible together, heads knocking in the candlelight. Then I was ashamed of my thought. I turned to Lizzie, want-ing to get her hand and remind myself of the realness of her, but she had gone.

I should hide this book. Millicent has warned me several times not to write. She quotes John: *If I bear witness of myself, my witness is not true.* But I do not write it for truth (what good is truth to me?). Perhaps, I write it for sense. I write it for cohesion, I suppose, to understand the progression that must occur in the layering of different selves that create a life. I am aware that meaningful, straight-forward progression simply will not happen in these pages. It is not a very straight-forward Guide, nor am I straight-forward. It seems imperative that I keep it hidden.

London, Present Day

Buckingham Palace Road

It was sunshine that Tayeb needed to stop the itching. The doctor had told him to expose his skin to UV rays, to let them eat up the scales and the dry patches that break off and bleed. Well, he wasn't an actual doctor, but a medical student at UCL, a friend of Nidal's. Beneath his shirt, Tayeb's skin raged.

He walked and walked and the urge simply to return to the flat in Hackney was strong. He could just turn the key, walk in, kick Anwar off the Xbox, drink tea and slip back into what, until yesterday, was his life. Yesterday, he had been examining the damage in the mirror in the hall: a small cut above the lip and the kiss of a bruise on his cheek. He had thought it would be worse, actually. When they kicked him he had managed to shield his head, but his ribs were sore. Those queers weren't policemen, but they certainly didn't want to hear the words 'No thanks' at the end of the night. He had been hungry and part of him enjoyed the game, letting them buy dinner and drinks, but he was a good Muslim, usually, he did not drink – well, much – and wine was followed by whisky then cognac then more wine. Then to a bar off Oxford Street then another on Dean Street, then came a suggestion that they all take a walk down along Embankment. Tayeb had been polite. *Must go now.* Best smile.

'Come with us, come with us,' a jokey mantra until Tayeb tried to slip off down a side alley near Charing Cross Station. Graham came behind him and with surprising strength pushed him roughly against a wall, twisting his arm into a painful lock behind his back. Matthew was close, his mouth almost touching his face:

'I know you are an illegal, you should not go fucking about with me.'

'Au contraire, you should go fucking about with him.' Graham's hand weaselled into Tayeb's pocket and found his wallet. He read out his name. *Tayeb Yafai.* Then he forced Tayeb to face him and gave two vicious punches into the stomach.

The pain sang an opera around Tayeb's bones as Matthew whispered in a lover's voice, 'Last chance.'

'No.'

One last twist on his ear. 'Then you're going home sweetie. We're reporting you.'

Tayeb had woken with a hangover, aches and a very nasty sense of dread, but it was not until two in the afternoon when, back in the Hackney flat, as if summoned directly by his self-pity, there was a bang at the door. Two diminutive persons, a male and a female, both with blond hair sticking out from under their official hats looked at him with eyes that needed kohl to bring them alive. The spidery white lashes on red rims made Tayeb think of pigs, blanched, squealing and ready to be killed. It was a shock to see such feminine forms in uniform, the man included. Were they twins? Tayeb registered their uniform and prepared his face into a smile.

'We are here to speak to a Mr Tayeb Yafai, please,' the woman spoke.

'He's not here at the moment, can I help?'

'Does he live here?'

'He sometimes passes through but not always. He is away at the moment, and I am not sure where.'

The white lashes floated up and down. A small frown appeared between the white-haired eyebrows. The twins looked at each other gravely.

'But is this his permanent residence?'

'He uses this as his official address, yes.'

'Right. Well I need to issue a summons to him, and I need it signed.'

'I can do this for you, I can pass this on.'

'Right.' The woman coughed. She took out some notes and began to read from them.

'Hereby notice is given that Mr Yafai is being issued with an appearance notice to answer charges of vandalism of the toilets on the Strand on the fifth September. He is required to attend court on the thirty-first October. Failure to do so will result in immediate arrest.'

Tayeb signed the paper as Ali Cherabo and handed the policewoman back her pen just as Anwar heaved up the stair-well carrying a pile of International Development Studies books in one hand and a battered guitar case held over his shoulder with the other.

'Tayeb,' he said, glancing at the policewoman. 'What's going on?'

The policewoman looked at Tayeb. 'You are Tayeb?'

Anwar stared at the floor. 'Shit.'

'You realise that lying to a police officer is a very serious offence?' She had a grave look on her face, as if compensating for her girlishness by looking intentionally cross. Tayeb opened his eyes wide, shining all-innocence, but saw immediately from her expression that this was the wrong approach. He tried the flirt instead, a cheeky glint, a wide smile.

'Look, I'm sorry,' he smiled at her. 'I was going to tell you who I am, I just wanted to hear what you had to say.'

Her cross features flickered with indecision. Her twin was silent and still, as if he were her shadow. She looked up at Tayeb quickly, and this time, he was sure she was not immune to his smile. He let out a laugh, an everything-is-fine laugh.

'And who are you?' She turned towards Anwar who was tapping his fingers on his guitar case, his right leg vibrating.

'I don't have to tell you.' His too-loud voice reverberated around the corridor and the policewoman looked over Tayeb's shoulders, into the flat.

'What do you think you'll find?' said Anwar. 'A handbook on how to bomb people?' At this she flinched. Tayeb touched his own bottom lip and pulled at it. The policewoman spoke into her radio again and then got out a fresh form and held it out to Tayeb.

'Your real signature this time.'

Tayeb walked along Buckingham Palace Road. A siren welled up sudden and fierce and then evaporated. Across the street was a billboard saying, TYPE IN YOUR FUTURE AND PRESS GO and below that, a smaller poster with the words, *Seat. Pint. Decent View* printed over the silhouetted shape of a woman's body. Anwar's cosy upbringing in a five-bedroom house in Norton had clearly not prepared him for a policewoman's questions, much as he currently enjoyed touristing in the immigrant's life. Tayeb wasn't actually sad to be gone from there. The place stank. It would have been comfortable if five men didn't live there – Nidal, Roberto, Nasser, Anwar and himself – holed up above a self-service launderette on Mare Street called Stars and Spins. It was a thrill for Anwar to be fed greasy garlic chicken by Roberto, rather than be fed by his mother at home, while the rest of them were always trying to get money together and some of them were endlessly trying not to get thrown out of the country.

Soon, that piggy little policewoman would sit with her fat buttocks on a chair, drinking her tea, looking Tayeb up on her enormous database. Her chubby fingers would press the keys and up he would come: arrived on a three-month English-language student visa fifteen years ago, meant to go home but never did. How was he supposed to get sun on his skin with all this rain? More importantly, what was he going to do? *This country*: it had given him a plague that he never knew in Sana'a. Soon, the dry, itchy patches would spread on to the back of his hands and face and that was when getting a cash-in-hand job in a restaurant was not so straight-forward.

As he walked, he remembered being on this road before, when he first left Eastbourne, saying *so long* to the English Language School which had provided him with a room in a family house and to the woman who was supposed to feed him as part of the fees paid to her, but no food ever came. *Goodbye to Quality Cod! Fish Restaurant* where his only question at the interview was what football team he supported. A week later he had a job as a fish-fryer and in his hand his first pay-packet of several five-pound notes in a chip bag. Nodding *peace be with you* to the seagull he watched every morning hula-hooping like a fool against the threat of rain. He'd left all that behind and headed to London.

Tayeb had travelled by coach, for most of the journey watching the ladder-straight neck of the woman who sat in front of him. The title of her book, *Heresies. A Journal of Feminist post-Totalitarian Criticism. A Russian/English Bilingual Edition* had excited him enormously. Here was a woman, he thought, who might be open to unusual events, a sort of Russian–French-style public transport encounter, perhaps, whatever that might be. He ached, then, for a woman. The coach had pulled in at 8pm and he watched her walk away, pulled heavily to the left by her rucksack. He had learned enough about English people by that time to know that she would not appreciate an offer to help with her bag. Tayeb had turned around and around, looking for Buckingham Palace, but could not see anything like it and here he was now, on exactly the same road.

These circles. They were unbearable. He turned on to Vauxhall Bridge and walked towards the river and it was happening again: the ground around his feet cracking, sand coming up. It is harder than one would think to escape a desert.

He sat down at a table outside a Lebanese café. His legs were aching. He pulled from his bag a paperback, Graham Greene's *England Made Me*, not to read, but as a prop or an aid to keep his hands steady. When he left the flat he had packed all of his calligraphy and drawing materials and his notebooks, some books, some T-shirts and emerged into the living room with the satchel over one shoulder. He had tripped over Anwar's guitar case which was left lying across the floor and had given the case a boot.

'Hey,' said Anwar, 'watch it.'

'Why do you carry around a case with no guitar in it?' Tayeb had felt like kicking the case again; actually, he felt like picking it up and smashing it across Anwar's skull. Anwar laughed without taking his eyes off the screen.

'Gets the girls. Pulling magnet. Works every time. Off out?'
Nidal was sitting next to him, hypnotised by the high-definition contorted images on the screen. He didn't acknowledge
Tayeb. Tayeb didn't answer Anwar who, with a cup of tea on
the floor next to his red-socked ankle and his rolled cigarette
fuming in his hand, looked young and stupid. Tayeb didn't
hate him. He walked out without saying anything.

A waiter came out to take his order but Tayeb stood up
and moved on, heading slowly towards the river. The traffic was a violence around him. He should have just done it,
what they wanted; it would have been over now and he could
have continued his life, drawing his tattoos on the city. He
crossed the road. The river-path was wide and breezy. Tourists
walked in small groups, tall men walked small dogs on thin
leads and women pushed prams. Tayeb's brain circled in on
itself: there was Marcus and his wife Audrey, but he couldn't
impose on their north London terrace and their forever trying
to conceive a child. Anatole from Dalston? No, he had his
own troubles. Some of the men from the casino? No.

At the entrance to a waterway taxi opposite Tate Britain
he looked down the ramp to a swaying boat. Paying for a day-
return even though it was expensive, he made his way to a seat
at the front of a boat so that the full expanse of Westminster's
finest arranged itself before him. The movement of the boat
unbalanced him; it was like viewing a painting through the
rain which had started up. A person could disappear into a
scene so desolate and never return again. Tayeb imagined a
camera in his hand. If he were filming he would not go for

the obvious panoramic shot, instead, he would focus on the boy sitting on the seat alongside him with hair as orange as oranges. The boy was holding his mother's hand and looking anxiously at her face. Next, a close-up shot of the mother: in her thirties, with the melancholia that comes from mother-tiredness. She was not looking at her son but thinking about something else and as the boat began to move on the water, the boy continued to look up at her, for reassurance perhaps, but her eyes remained on the water outside.

Tayeb was from a desert, he was uncomfortable being adrift. He could identify with the small boy's worries. At some point during his first year in London, Tayeb had walked across Lambeth Bridge at night just as a man, about twenty yards in front of him, had pushed himself off it. It was not so much a jump, more of a lean. Tayeb rushed to the side of the bridge and saw the body fall into the grey–black swirling water. It disappeared immediately. Tayeb had uselessly shouted, 'Hey hey, hey!' into the wind. The body re-emerged momentarily, corked up on the swell of water like a cormorant, but very quickly down it went again. Tayeb knew he should phone someone, or do something. The body did not bob up again and then it occurred to him that he could not give his name to an official and that he could not be witness to anything in this country.

The anxious-faced boy with the orange hair was closer to his mother now, his fingers touching her hand and Tayeb was relieved when she looked at him finally, not smiling, but with the territorial confidence of the one in charge. What power she must feel at being able to ease him, even if temporarily.

The boat pulled in at Greenwich and the sulky young black girl with the ticket machine round her neck asked him if he wanted to get off.

'No. I'll go back.' He showed her his return ticket.

This time nobody got on. The boat turned round and the journey was repeated in reverse, as if he were being sucked through a mirror. He rummaged through his satchel, through the empty envelopes with stamps but no addresses on them, the poems of Darwish, a cheap notebook with the cover ripped off, something he had written in English on the back of an Oxfam request for money envelope – *red-hot blood runs fast, like rivers. I have seen too many injuries for one person. Bodies are fragile, they are meaningless dust. At Victoria Station: the gateway, place where ~~life in England begins and ends~~. The pigeons are pecking at my toes and I can't smoke in here. This country has stopped smoking at stations which is barbaric, really* – but there was no sign of his fountain pen. It was lost and that fact seemed unbearable, emblematic: that he had lost himself again. Back to the blue door where he slept last night. What else could he do?

Dress: *The outfit may be completed with a number of hats – a light straw for summer, a soft felt for touring, and a small and becoming hat for the park.*

A Lady Cyclist's Guide to Kashgar – Notes

June 19th

The baby breathes magical air, her skin is mole-skin soft. The tips of her fingers pat against my arm, it is the softest feeling, like a butterfly walking. Lashes are black insect legs, sticking to a cheek. Skin hangs around the knees, waiting for bones to expand inside. She likes to be folded in against me. Her toes spread wide, large gaps between each one. Her ears are oyster pearls, sweetness. There is a terrifying translucence of the skin. I have night visions now, of her falling into a river and being taken away. Nightmares filled with floods coming, waves washing over her. Sometimes she is caught up in a tree, tangled in its branches and I must get to her, but can't.

Or she is a cat, fur falling off in patches and uttering a pitiful cry. She is slipping away from me, falling away, or I have been careless, and lost her. I wake up convinced that she is gone; I reassure myself by touching her flat, uncurled fingers and put them in my mouth and suck them. She seems to like it.

'Eva, come, look,' Lizzie said.

I followed my sister to the back of the house where Lolo was standing with his hand resting on the flank of a white cow and its calf. The calf stood trembling between its mother's bony knees. Lolo was gently patting the cow's back, looking pleased with himself.

'Millicent bought it at the cattle market and it transpires that Lolo is a charmer of cows,' Lizzie said, and giggled. 'Aren't you pleased?'

The cow looked philosophical, flicking its tail at the flies which were persistent in bothering it.

'She's beautiful.'

'I've named her Rebekah,' Lizzie said. Then I realised: our own supply of milk. No more opium-scented yellow milk. I can now feed Ai-Lien directly. It is fascinating to watch Lolo and the milking process. The calf tugs at the udders and suckles on his mother, then, once the milk is flowing, Lolo gently moves the calf aside so that it is still standing next to the mother, nestling about her, being licked, and Lolo squeezes from the teats six or seven pints of milk before allowing the calf to return and drain the rest. As he pumps the udders he sings, softly and soothingly to the cow and its calf.

Ai-Lien enjoys it – both the singing and the milk. Her eyes close and her lips swell. She seems to have grown in size almost immediately, but I am sure I must be imagining that. She sleeps on my chest, breathing softly, and often I hold her on me all night. I happily forgo my sleep for her comfort. Such a distance I have come since the day I journeyed alone, by tram, to the China Inland Mission in Stoke Newington, to stand in front of a panel of four men and two women to defend my calling. I memorised my speech so intently it is still with me now:

'Members of the Council, my Direction is never illuminated to the degree at which I fully understand the nature of the path I tread, or indeed, what I will find along that path; but by a small flickering candlelight of faith, that gives off only enough light for the next, immediate part of my journey.'

Pausing, as rehearsed.

'And with each step, I grow stronger. I am steady.'

I hear the rattling rain, watch the grey faces of the Council conferring, the bonnet – worn on Millicent's advice – slipping. I had decided against a description of mystical swooning, or an emulation of Lizzie's wet-eyed devotional face, thinking rational argument would be more convincing. Lizzie had already been selected to accompany Millicent on overseas missionary work. I could not be left behind, and to my great relief, rationality won out. Signed, witnessed and welcomed a missionary. I did not expect to come to know a baby.

It was a surprise to see Khadega in the courtyard at midday sitting amongst the potted fig trees along with a chaperone, a minuscule elderly lady swathed and mummified in brown material. I came in with my bicycle and leaned it against the courtyard wall.

'Here is Eva,' Millicent said, poking her small, black leather Bible towards me. The chaperone made a clicking noise in her mouth as she sat down, squatting on her heels with her back against the wall in what looked like a terribly uncomfortable position. I looked around for Lolo. I had left Ai-Lien in his care.

'Eva, good, you're back. Mohammed has agreed that Khadega will visit each day to learn English, as he has no sons. We have convinced him that English will help him when it comes to trade negotiations.'

'I'm surprised.' Apart from her eyes, Khadega's face was entirely covered. It seemed excessive in the privacy of the courtyard. A lizard flickered past my foot.

'I spoke to him last night. He could not resist in the end.'

She smiled at Khadega, and then glanced at me. 'You will be her teacher.'

'Me? But Millicent, I have the kitchen and the food to oversee, as well as Ai-Lien, of course.'

She looked over at me. 'I have noticed that you find time for your bicycle rides and your little writing sessions in the pavilion. I am sure there must be an opportunity to teach Khadega some vocabulary.'

'Writing in the pavilion?' Lizzie said, putting down the teapot and looking at me.

'Yes, through the hot part of the day I am . . . I do make notes.'

'But you should sleep,' Lizzie said.

'I can't in this heat.'

The writing: it calms me, makes me feel as though I am exploring. Actual movement, in the heat, in the day, is too difficult. I must somehow – I hesitate to use the word pretend . . . I must believe I am keeping these notes for some reason.

'Yes,' I said then to Lizzie, apropos of nothing. She was looking at me strangely. Lizzie's blue clear eyes look like chips of glass standing out from the eyeball, like marbles at the bottom of a glass of water.

'Khadega will be a conscientious learner,' Millicent said.

My sister twisted her hair into a rope on her shoulder and moved away, reversing backwards, a light-touch eradication of herself. She did not look at Khadega.

June 24th

My student and I have not successfully achieved a rapport. Our problem is mostly one of communication. I rummaged in my trunk and found the book I had optimistically acquired in London before departing, A *Sketch of the Turki Language* by Shaw, but as soon as I sit down to read it the usual feeling returns: this great battle with language, the unending task of learning the name of everything: bowl, spoon, wheel, tree, road and river. I immediately want the specifics, I want to know the name for each curled, dried root on the market stand, each strain of tea, each type of animal foot hung up to dry. I want to rush past the basic words, house, door, horse, and find the word given to the moment before the sandstorm arrives. In my haste, though, I become very quickly muddled. Whereas Lizzie wanders the world collecting words like stones and linking them together quickly into conversational chains, for me it is like trying to hold sand in my palm and my inadequacies infuriate me. What did Burton say? It took him twenty-two days to master a language? Without language, infiltration into another culture remains impossible.

Khadega speaks – as well as Turki – colloquial Russian, some Manchu and some Chinese, but I struggle with all of these. With the Turki instruction book in hand, I tried again, recalling Millicent's words: 'Turki, stretching its complex structures all the way to the Turkish of Constantinople, though less changed, perhaps, purer, by virtue of existing in one of the most isolated areas of the world.'

'Turki is like a great, ancient tree', Millicent taught us in the acclimatisation centre, 'with a thousand branches growing from one trunk. Imagine this and it will help.'

My tree spreads its roots along the floor; it grows up, poking through my feet, extending through my spine, shooting upward. I try to conjure life into new words and grow them. I draw shapes, Turki is an alphabetical language in the Arabic script, and it is pleasant to draw the curves, but then the grammar comes and drowns me. Whatever is hearsay-present or future-potential? Vocabulary rests briefly in my mouth. It is as if each word has been polished down, smoothed to an almost perfect sphere, and then dropped, lost. Everything has a name: the carter, the dusk, the birdsong. But the names won't stay in my mouth.

'How can I teach her when I can't speak to her?' I complain, but Millicent only answers, every time, 'Ask, and it shall be given'.

I keep on knocking but it does not open. I sit opposite Khadega, both of us cross-legged on a suzani rug. I continually fail to understand her, or to be understood. The expression on her ill-formed face grows ever darker as I painfully try to extract words from her until I want to pull up the suzani threads, unravel the images of pomegranates and leaves and use the threads to wrap around her neck and half-strangle her, she is so insolent. It is an immense relief when Lolo brings refreshments and I am released so that Millicent can spend the remaining hour with her.

After luncheon today Millicent held a makeshift service in the courtyard, and telling Khadega that this is our normal practice she invited her to join. They knelt together and bowed their heads. *Dear Lord.* I watched Khadega's mouth move over the sounds as Millicent incanted the lines. When the prayers ended Millicent picked up Khadega's hand and rubbed it, pressing the surface veins on the top of her hand like violin strings.

Afterwards, they came into the small kitchen and Millicent instructed Lolo to 'do something domestic' with her. They stood at the table and she 'helped' Lolo. They cut the wild garlic and the grasses Lolo uses to flavour our food and, as they cut, Millicent asked Khadega questions, only the simpler of which I could understand. Does your father respect you? Does your mother understand you? Are your sisters kind, or cruel? Khadega was not forthcoming, particularly about her family, but eventually she answered: my mother hates me, Rami also, and my father only loves Lamara, the pretty one.

As the questions continued I noticed that Lizzie had left the courtyard. I went down into the garden to see if she were there. Despite the dead-heat of the mid-afternoon, Lizzie was walking towards the small native outhouse at the bottom of the orchard. I ran behind her.

'The conspiracy has set in somewhat, hasn't it, darling?' Lizzie said. She was wearing a long blue Chinese smock without the satin trousers and her hair was untidily gathered at the back of her neck. A blue convolvulus flower was poked behind her ear; it was wilted. She snapped a small branch off a jujube date tree and hit it, gently, on leaves of the small shrub-like trees that make up a hedge, not looking at me.

'Where are you going?'

'For a walk.'

'She's monopolising all her time, isn't she?' I said.

Lizzie stood upright, as if shaking off an unwanted thought and flicked a leaf with irritation.

'What?'

'Millicent. She's focusing totally on Khadega. It leaves us out, rather.'

'Oh. That. All in the name of evangelism.' She was squinting in the sheer light.

'Yes.'

Lizzie turned away from me. I stumbled after her; the heat was ferocious, and the fabric of my satin trousers began immediately to soak with my sweat.

'Shall I come? Let me get Ai-Lien and we'll come with you.'

'No. It's too hot for the baby out here.'

'Oh, she won't mind. She'll sleep.'

'No.'

'She is a native after all.'

Lizzie backed away from me as if offended by my presence, then turned, and when I called out her name, she didn't look back. She opened the gate at the bottom of the garden.

'Take a hat at least,' I shouted pointlessly, 'or a scarf.' She walked out despite the sun, each strand of hair looking as though it might at any moment be set on fire, her long cotton robe flapping about her legs, the camera held on its leather strap around her neck.

I watched her go for a moment, puzzled as to why Millicent asked Khadega so many questions and why they spent so much time in the kitchen, but as I write this now it occurs to me that she intends to infiltrate Khadega's home and convince her that there are better alternatives. Home, after all, is the central province, the base of power. If Khadega's conversion is to be successful then she will be cast out from her family, and it is likely that she will be isolated, condemned, despised and rejected. The only way to persuade a young woman to undertake such an experience is to convince her that where she currently abides is oppressive, and to offer her an alternative, better sanctuary. Entry to the home represents, for Millicent, the ultimate missionary goal of entry to the heart, gateway to the soul.

These are her techniques, now I can see them, and this, I presume, is how she cast her spell on Lizzie.

London, Present Day

Chestnut Road, Norwood

Whoever Irene Guy was, she was certainly a hoarder. The room was carpeted with a well-walked-on beige shag and in the air was the distinctive smell of old lady. A suggestion of skin, pieces of person everywhere, hair, flakes, scalp and nails, all become dust and settled, now unsettled by Frieda. Once, Frieda remembered now, she had looked up the constitution of dust and saw that it was dead skin cells and the dried faeces and desiccated corpses of dust mites. Lovely.

The room was a heap of indistinguishable matter, so much of it that Frieda had the sensation of being ingested. A nut-brown sofa commanded the centre of the lounge, covered in magazines, papers, books, knitting needles and endless piles of debris. Hanging above a faux-marble mantel that rested over an alcove where once a fireplace might have been was a large print of a map. A river ran through the centre, leading off to a heavenly, celestial horizon. The tributaries were all labelled: 'The River of Death' running towards 'The Desert of Eternal Despair'. Along the bottom was a quote: 'Know, prudent cautious self-control is wisdom's root.'

Frieda walked slowly around, both wanting to touch everything, and not to. She had asked a friend, Emma, to come with her, but she was busy, and so alone, like an absurd burglar, she began to look for clues as to who Irene Guy had been.

In front of the window she realised that there was a large brass birdcage and was disconcerted to see that inside it was an owl. Frieda looked at it, assuming it was stuffed, and then looked again. No. It was possibly breathing. Its eyes were closed. Tufts of feathers around its ears – were they ears? Its wildness was a shock. Tawny feathers. It was odd enough, to be allowed into a strange house, a stranger's house, and Frieda felt peculiar, a trespasser, but she was not sure what she was supposed to do with a live bird.

The owl did not move and so she backed away from it and walked over to a bureau and opened a narrow drawer. It was stuffed with old Christmas cards. *To Irene, Merry Christmas, love George and Rini, Xmas 1981.*

The bedroom was a rush and clash of colour. There were throws, rugs, cushions and very bright purple curtains. Several rugs layered each other on the floor, with felt patterns and appliqué motifs edged with crouching stitches. Frieda sat on the bed, slightly oppressed by the burden of a stranger's intimate space.

In the corner of the room Frieda saw a dusty glass dome. She bent down and swiped at the dust on the glass. Inside was an entire street scene in miniature at the centre of which was a temple, complete with a monkey on its roof. There was a shop with a hanging sign saying 'money counter' and a row of red flags with Chinese characters imprinted in gold. Next to the stall was a doorway labelled 'opium den' and in front of it a market stall where three upside-down chickens hung, tied at their feet, Peking style. At the end of the street were two figures in Chinese dress standing next to a donkey. There was a key lodged into a thick wooden base and when she turned it, clicking it round, gently, twice, a mechanical version of an oriental tune played out and the figures began to move, wonkily. The donkey raised its head up and down, in and out of a miniature water trough. It's charming, she thought.

She wiped away more of the dust with the sleeve of her black woollen cardigan and, as she did so, a grumble came from what she assumed must be the airing cupboard in the hall. The heating seemed to be on. She walked back into the living room. A strip of late-afternoon light striped the carpet, cut across objects scattered all around the floor and climbed the wall at an angle.

The owl's eyes were still closed. Only once, previously, had she seen an owl this close and that was in the foyer of a hotel in Moscow. That had been a tawny thing, magical, mainly because of its Russianness. She had looked into the eyes of that Russian owl before going to bed in the small, chilly room and dreamed all night of spiders and leaves. This owl was bigger, with more white feathers layered amongst the brown ones. It still did not move, though it seemed to be alive. Frieda began to calculate. If the funeral had been on the thirty-first of August, then it must have been at least a few days, or even a week, before that when Irene Guy died. The owl must not have been fed for – well over a week. Could that be possible? And what did owls eat, anyway?

Frieda wrapped the entire birdcage, complete with the owl inside, in two bin liners that she had fished out of one of Irene Guy's kitchen drawers. She strapped the cage into her bicycle basket – luckily, an old-fashioned large one – using string found in the same drawer. She had looked through endless books, cards and picture, but was still unclear as to who Irene Guy was. Trudging, invasively, through a lifetime of ephemera proved to be tiring, and eventually Frieda decided to come back the next day to look for photographs. But how could she leave a living owl?

Rain came at her like small knives. She cycled carefully along the route that went past one of Nathaniel's favourite pubs in Brixton. London traffic has neither heart nor compassion for a cycling woman and particularly cruel are the screeching black cabs that skirt up against her wheels. Glowing ahead was the pub, shining potently like a castle on a hill in a fairy story, and Frieda knew that there was a high chance that Nathaniel would be in there. The poor owl hadn't made a noise and she could only presume that a detour at this stage wouldn't hurt it. Dripping with rain, she poked her head through the door.

'Is it OK to bring my bike in?'

The barman nodded. Balancing the bike against the wall, Frieda left the cage in the basket covered in its bin liner and stood damply at the bar examining the wine list. Within a minute a hand pressed flat against the small of her back.

'Frie',' Nathaniel said, 'naughty of you but marvellous.' He was several glasses in and less conscious of onlookers than usual. He grabbed at her hand and pulled it towards himself.

'I'm exhausted to my core, no help in the shop, just me,' he said, holding out his oil-stained fingers. 'What do you want, Pinot Grigio?'

Frieda smiled at him. 'I'd love one. Yes.'

'Good girl,' he said. She was about to tell him not to good-girl her, as if she were a Girl Guide leader, but didn't bother. He had some difficulty balancing himself on the bar stool next to her, but once done he immediately put his hand on her knee and gave it a squeeze. The pores on his nose were open and more visible than usual.

'You're looking delicious,' he said. 'Windswept.'

'Hmm. You're not.'

He put his hand up towards her lips, as if to shush her, but lurched forward and accidentally jabbed her cheek instead. She pushed his hand away.

'What brings you to my humble office?' He cast his hand around like an estate agent demonstrating the width of the kitchen. He put his hand back on her leg, this time further up her thigh.

'Know anything about owls?'

'Only stuffed ones. Taxidermy. Tried it once, pretty gory.'

Frieda very much wanted to talk to him about the letter, the flat, the owl, the hotel and the estrangement of being back here. She had a list in her head. The police and military vans, for one. The rules from the Sheikh. The cutting of the hair, already a lifetime away and also, a growing frustration with her job and a sense of wanting to do something else. Just the thought of the fluorescent-lit boardrooms aflutter with earnest interns caused Frieda a migraine. From unfortunate sandwiches eaten under an umbrella whilst wandering along the Strand to losing hours to an inadequate phone system, Central London office life with its persistent slipping away of time was gently barbaric, and this barbarism was highlighted by the surreal contrast of the assignments abroad: she came back sun-blinded from foreign colours to sink down into English grey.

She looked at the grey in Nathaniel's black hair and realised that she had not noticed it before. When did that arrive? Everything she had to say, about where she was currently, slipped on to the floor beneath the bar stool. She sipped her drink.

She had met him, Nathaniel, five years ago now, as they both stood droopily in a dripping marquee at a folk concert. A young woman was singing terribly as she hacked at violin strings. He had turned and said, 'This is one of the most awful things I have ever witnessed. You must have a drink with me in the beer tent, now.'

Cider with chips followed and the night ended in his tent, both of them trying to squeeze into one sleeping bag, he miraculously discarding her clothes as she wriggled in. Rain on the tent all night, and in the morning Frieda awoke naked except for a pair of woolly socks, with him running his finger in circles around her belly button saying, 'You're like something from a film.'

Breakfast was an extortionately priced omelette and bacon baguette and, as Frieda ripped open a packet of white sugar and tipped it into her tea, he had said, 'This is the kind of breakfast my eldest loves.'

Of course. Children. Wives. All of that.

Nathaniel coughed loudly, banging his fist on the bar with each bark, in time, as if the force of his banging contributed to the dislodging of whatever solids were causing the blockage in his internal system. Frieda turned away until he had finished coughing. She wanted so much to explain to him how she'd been feeling – dislocated, rootless – but here he was, drunk, so it was pointless. She kept looking at her bike, worrying about the owl, but it wasn't making any noise.

'Margaret's been re-filing all of her payslips in plastic wallets and, for some totally unknown reason, bulk-buying bikinis off the internet – about fifty different versions of the same ones, at twenty quid a pop – and the house has been full of those hideous NCT women waving organic celery sticks at me.'

Frieda stared at the bottles on the wall behind the bar. Nathaniel looked at her, catching her hand in his.

'What?' he said.

'I didn't actually want domestic details, funnily enough.'

'I know, I am sorry. You are right.'

It used to be that the thought of his wife heightened it. The visits to his bicycle shop on Broadway Market. Frieda popping in, pretending to be a customer, and sometimes, there she was, Margaret, on the phone. She was always inordinately well groomed in an earthy, functional sort of way with short hair and homespun clothes, a casual, arty tastefulness. Frieda running her finger along the handlebars of a Pashley bike, smiling a small smile; hearing the sounds of his blood shooting and smelling his skin from across the shop floor. The bell of the door ringing. Looking in from outside, a slight nod. Coming back later when she was gone. It was vile. They were disgusting. Hands up her skirt in the back room, thumb circling her, thigh pushing between her legs. A wife could come back in at any minute; the twist and tug of a nipple and Frieda, slowly kneeling in front of him, breathing on him, not looking up yet, mouth close.

Frieda had been taught that all love was valid and boundaries were for the sullen, the half-dead and the half-wit. Marriage was an anachronism, outdated and dead. It was her duty to pull it apart, unpick its edges and bring out the real. She had, after all, walked in on her mother, when she, Frieda, was what, aged six? A year or so before she left. In bed with the American Arthurian specialist who was living in one of the caravans: Frieda's mum's legs sticking out of the bed and American Bill's legs wrapped around them. Later her mum said, 'Love is free, Frieda sweetheart. It's better that way. I love Daddy too.'

This was when Frieda had first discovered that it was possible to run away on a bike. Cycle, wheels fast, move fast, keep moving, go go go until you are far away. She had been taught that she should be above the crass rules of those who troop along in lines, getting married, pretending at monogamy, falling apart, getting divorced, starting again. Her mother and American Bill and her father's subsequent collapse had fully illuminated the important life lesson that marriage was a farce. Frieda remembered answering the phone, standing barefoot on the cold kitchen lino early in the morning, everyone else asleep and a woman's voice: 'Who's your mum in bed with?' But there was something unconvincing about this free love idea, and Frieda was left with a feeling that they were all in a wilderness somewhere, and it seemed important – her survival depended on it, in fact – that she get away from it, to find some shelter.

Keep riding, riding away. If you cycle fast enough you fly.

Frieda locked her bike to the railings next to the Peabody entrance and untied the string. It was sevenish in the evening. Gently, she pulled the birdcage out of the basket and holding it in front of her, arms wrapped around it, she walked towards her building. Wine-warmed and flushed, she had let Nathaniel kiss her just outside the door of the pub,

116

even though the distance between them was getting as swollen as the Thames.

Now, at the top of the staircase, she wondered what she was doing with this owl. She had things to get on with. Her career; reports; expense claims. When, at the age of eighteen she had told her dad that she was going to university to study International Relations and Politics he had looked at her in horror.

'But surely you would rather be a poet in Paris?'

She had seen something in his eyes that looked distinctly like shame. It didn't even taste so good in the end, to have become so proper, her own pathetic rebellion. But she was stubborn, and she kept at it. Working hard for years at real and concrete and meaningful things, understanding issues that were important and relevant, embracing various causes (the Kurds, the Palestinians, the Tibetans, the Saharawi tribes and so on) with the full vigour of the ardent young, leaving her parents' cosmic radiations behind. She did not need to be rummaging through an old woman's memories. She should hand the owl over to someone, the RSPB.

The swirls and seagulls were still there, of course. She opened the door, leaving her bag on the step and put the cage on the kitchen table. She pulled the bin liner off and two enormous, disconcerting eyes looked at her. Clear eyes. She peered into the cage.

'Hello owlie,' she said, 'what do you eat?'

From the fridge she pulled out a cold sausage, cut it into pieces and tried to poke it through the bars, but it was too big so she opened the cage door. A draught curled around her ankle, and she realised that her bag was still holding the front door open. She went to kick the door shut but it resisted. A sharp pain shot through her toe and she hopped back into the kitchen and pulled off her boot to examine the damage. As she did, she felt a flap and a whoosh near her head: a flush of brown feathers, a flutter against the concrete wall. The owl was out the door before she could even think. She ran to follow it into the hall, spotting it perched up near the ceiling on an exposed pipe. It seemed entirely unconcerned, blinking once, twice, then once more.

What the Bicycle Does: *Mounted on a wheel, you feel at once the keenest sense of responsibility. You are there to do as you will within reasonable limits; you are continually called upon to judge and to determine points that before have not needed your consideration, and consequently you become alert, active, quick-sighted and keenly alive, as well to the rights of others as to what is due yourself.*

A Lady Cyclist's Guide to Kashgar – Notes

June 26th

Great excitement this morning: two Kashgaris on horseback arrived carrying three sacks of mail. Our first post since Baku. Even Millicent sat happy as an infant, tearing open the packages. They were in a pitiful condition, ripped or emptied and some nearly destroyed. Most date back at least three or four months and I marvel to think of the journey they have been on. There are such complexities, limits on weight, additional costs, not to mention censors at various points. Bibles emerged, along with posters, books, newspapers, Inland Mission reports, articles. Lizzie held up a number of copies of *The Times*, completely out of date, of course, but a joy to read none the less. I held the paper to my nose and fancied I could smell England.

A good many packages had nothing inside, their contents long-since looted. A letter from Millicent's friend in Moscow had been so brutally censored with scissors that it was now an unreadable paper-doll chain. Lizzie sorted everything into piles and I was pleased to see that there was a small pile for me.

The first parcel contained uncontaminated Allenbury dried milk and dried food packages for Ai-Lien, an estimated eight months' worth, although a handful of the packages appeared to be destroyed and milk powder covered everything. Equally importantly, I saw that Lizzie has received her supply of medicine. I watched as she carefully put the medicine tins to one side, so that Millicent, who was engrossed in a long letter, did not see them. I hope this will mean an end to the vagueness that has come over her.

Joy: two letters for me, one from Mother. I stood up, leaving the others to sort through the enormous pile for Millicent and went to the courtyard and sat under the shade of one of the knotted fig trees. The paper is thin, ripped in places, but mostly intact. She writes of Father and of the terrible weight of missing him; of Elizabeth, her health, her medicine, her strength. *Unlike you, Eva, dear, I do not think that Lizzie has the constitution for travel.* In the spaces between the words it is possible to see Mother sitting with Aunt Cicely, a widow of thirteen years – two women with nothing in common living together next to an unfriendly sea.

Poor Mother. Even after the liberal and continental child-hood we enjoyed – the artists who came to stay, the anarchists, suffrage women, painters, musicians – two of her three daughters have chosen the Church, and a life of service. She expected something different, that one of us might bring poetry into the world, art or music. She wanted beauty, always more beauty. Perhaps this is why she agreed to buy the most expensive camera for Lizzie? Or why little Nora, our youngest sister who stole our mother's love, has been allowed to live in Dublin where we hear that she has become a liar who cavorts with artists and consumes gin.

Just before leaving I almost confided in Mother about my pretence, the real nature of my so-called faith, but ultimately I decided not to. She wanted so very much for us not to go that if she had known my secret I am sure that she would have convinced me to stay. My supposed calling was my only weapon. As we prepared for our journey she looked at me, puzzled. Lizzie she could understand, she had always had a transcendental element to her personality, but me? She was suspicious, but I pushed on, to be away, to keep running. Those men who visited her, contesting for her attention, who brought her gifts, who listened to her talks at the university in Geneva, none of them would be with her now.

'Could you not', I remember her saying, 'simply go to Umbria?'

'No, mother; Umbria would not do at all.'

I folded the letter and placed it on the low wall that surrounded the fountain in the courtyard. As we left Geneva for England she'd said to me, 'It is still my time, Eva.' A curious thing to say.

The second letter was from Mr Hatchett:

Dear Ms English,

I hope that this letter finds you well settled and comfortable in your Great Eastern outpost. I have thought of our meeting and conversation often. I do hope you will be understanding about this, as I could not reach you to confirm that this course of action is preferable to you, but I endeavoured to formally put a proposal to the board here at Hatchett & White for the publication of your Lady Cyclist's Guide to the desert. I am very pleased to inform you that we would very much like to publish your suggested Guide and impressions of this unknown region. With great pleasure we offer you an advance of £150 for the Guide and, although we are unsure as to your return date, we look forward to receiving the manuscript in due course.

May I also add that it was a very great personal pleasure to make your acquaintance and I hope that we shall become good friends. I pray that you remain safe in your chosen location.

All kind wishes,

Francis Hatchett

What do I remember of him, this Mr Hatchett? His beard was gingerish, lightly trimmed. Cousin Alfred described him as an Oxford man, uneasy in Cambridge company. This, of course, is how Alfred assesses the world: one college versus another and everyone else in the mire. He had an uneasy way of sitting as we talked, his hands a little shaky, yet, at the same time, a confidence – the sort that comes with breeding and wealth. Or, what I mean is, I suppose, he did not have the unbearable atmosphere of the English middle class about him: the dowdy, the greedy, the endless concern about what others think, the ghastly parochialism. Yes, he is beyond all of that, though certainly I could not imagine him comfortable in the cafés of Geneva. Despite it being April, it was cold and blowy in that house in Hampstead. I crouched near the fire in the green, book-lined room and looked up at him, smiling. Where was Lizzie? Over with Alfred and that friend of his, the one who talked relentlessly at a woman all looped in lace and froth whose name I forget. I daresay Mr Hatchett was polite. I don't recall his words, but I do remember his encouragement, which was charming, and I remember him picking up my glove and that he is not at all old.

I watched several small lizards disappear into the courtyard wall behind a white, fragile flower that was so pervasive it seemed it must have been responsible for the dry, bitter cracks in the earth. It smells far too strong and sweet for its colour. I returned to Millicent. Packages and envelopes were in a mess across the room and then I saw that Millicent looked grim.

'What is it?'

Lizzie looked up from reading her letter from Mother.

'It's the Inland Mission,' she said. 'They are refusing to provide funds for our release. We must "talk our way out".'

Millicent looked round the room. I picked up what she was looking for, her Hatamens, and handed them to her. She put one in her mouth and took out a match to light it, turning to Lizzie whose face had become blotchy.

'They won't provide the bribe?' Lizzie asked. Millicent leaned against the wall. Lizzie put the letter down, pushed aside the papers on the floor with her foot and walked over to Millicent. I was astonished to see her pick up Millicent's hand and hold it.

'I should send a telegram to Mr Steyning in Urumtsi at once. He will help. He is the senior representative in the field, more aware of the reality than those in the Mission houses.'

Millicent glanced down at Lizzie's hand holding hers, then looked away into the distance. Lizzie was looking at her face, directly, but Millicent avoided returning the look. She coughed, as if all were absolutely normal, and so on we all go, like a ship, drifting hopelessly.

This evening, I wrote a letter back to Mr Hatchett. Here is a copy:

Dear Mr Hatchett,

I write to you from the shade of a pavilion in the centre of a garden that seems like a jungle. The heat here is something you could not even imagine, and I hope for your sake, that it is something you never experience. From memory, at any rate, I think you have pale skin (you are of Irish descent, perhaps?) and I am quite sure that the sun here would not suit you. It made me extraordinarily happy to have received notice from your board regarding my book and I shall be forever grateful. Thank you for your support. I very much look forward to meeting you again on our return. I cannot thank you enough.

June 27th

Millicent is in the kitchen, reading from the Bible as Khadega cuts segments of fruit and puts them into a clay bowl. Apricots, apples, figs. Side by side with their backs to me. *God's intimate friendship blessed my house.* Millicent's hand rests on Khadega's shoulder, her thumb rubbing a specific place as the questions continue: *Do they love you, at your home? Do they need you? What is your value to your family?* Millicent takes up pieces of Khadega and opens them up, like prising open a shell. She places her fingers into them and pulls them open.

I'm writing this now – fast in the pavilion. The heat seems intent on crushing me today, droning on and in, suffocating like a blanket being unfolded and placed upon the earth. The courtyard, usually a shelter, is too opulent and over-bearing. Roses grow out of walls and hang heavily like crepe-paper decorations. Jasmine spreads as if it intends to smother.

Watching Millicent and Khadega it occurs to me again that this must be how Millicent bewitched Lizzie, with this tight female intimacy. All the flattery and prayer and the talk and the tea and the attention. I suspect Khadega has never felt so central, so important and seduced, in all her life, ignored as she is in her home of so many women because she is ugly.

Millicent smokes and asks questions, smokes and asks, and I can see now that real conversion can only begin when secrets are surrendered. She is trying to find a secret, a pearl; the one thing that would make Khadega vulnerable. Khadega's unpleasant, square face nods and smiles, and parts of her rise up to the surface like stolen items hitherto concealed in a pocket. Witnessing this, I am left wondering what Lizzie's secret must be? What is the soft pearl inside Lizzie that gave Millicent the key – and ultimate control – to her soul? Poor Lizzie.

Then, tonight, witnessed, an argument between my sister and Millicent, in the garden, beneath the curious handkerchief tree. I saw them from the top of the garden, but couldn't hear what they were saying: Millicent holding on to Lizzie's wrists, Lizzie shouting, and then her head dropping, her hair hanging down, Millicent letting Lizzie's arms fall and walking away, and me left saying to the air: come back to me, Lizzie.

June 29th

I came through the gate into the courtyard with Ai-Lien strapped native-style against my chest and walked into a very unusual scene. The altar was upside down, candles were on the floor, and Khadega was crouched in front of the fountain. Millicent was beside her, stroking her back. They were talking fast in a blur of Turki and Russian.

Khadega's body was shaking. Millicent took her hand and began to pray, her hands traced circles around Khadega's bent spine. Irritation came over me, like water, as if I were submerged in it. Why should Millicent take this young girl away from all she knows? Where is she taking her? To total abandonment by her family. To the breaking of all the sacred codes of her community. If Millicent succeeds she must then provide her not only with a physical haven (will she come to live with us here?) but a moral one. Millicent, in realising her evangelist ambition, will create the ultimate dependant. Perhaps this is her way; she thinks herself a collector of souls.

Khadega looked wretched with her black hair hanging damp with sweat and free and I could not help but think of the layers of her life: the Holy Quran ringing its laws, the words of her prophet and father, then Millicent, spelling her away from all of that. Millicent continued her prayer. It was sung in a rhythm, but I could not hear the words.

I pressed myself against the courtyard wall and felt the prick of a rose thorn on my thigh. The sting of it kept me still, even though I wanted – powerfully so – to take Khadega's hand and deliver her back to her father, to put her in his total possession again. I wanted to rush to Mohammed and tell him of the perils here, that he should take his ugly daughter away from us, but I couldn't move. It was as if the roses themselves pinned me still, as if Millicent had magicked them to do so.

When I looked again Millicent was holding a piece of paper. She put it into Khadega's shaking hands. I guessed it was a pledge of some sort but Khadega was not immediately ready to sign it. The prayer continued, soft and repetitive, like a lullaby. Khadega began to whimper. The prayer and the crying connected rhythmically and Millicent ran her hand along Khadega's neck, pulling her hair back to expose a vulnerable part of skin behind the ear. She offered Khadega the pledge, again, and her pen and this time, shaking, her head bent low, as she crouched towards the courtyard floor, Khadega signed it. She then dropped the pen and her whole body collapsed into the dust. Millicent stopped the lullaby-prayer and bent down next to her and kissed her neck, then, and as if sensing suddenly that I was here, she turned round and looked at me. Her eyes narrowed and then she looked past me. Lizzie, emerging through the doorway, was also watching, with one hand on her cheek and her camera in the other.

London, Present Day

Pimlico

Lying flat like this on the concrete floor, looking up at the talons, she could watch it with her eyes half closed. A line from Dr Seuss came to her: *lots of noses smelling owls' feet*. Perhaps the owl was happy to be free? Frieda had no idea. In her hand was a tea towel, although in what way a tea towel could help her catch the owl was unclear. The window in the hall was open a little. If the owl were determined enough it could squeeze through to a new life in the wild woods of Pimlico, fashioning a comfortable home in the golden-topped trees of Battersea Park. Frieda had often seen escaped parrots and cockatiels up above the Peace Pagoda, looking dolefully across at indigenous crows.

It hadn't moved for more than an hour now. She had only left it once, to go to the toilet, but she ran straight back and it hadn't moved. She was fearful of losing it. Whoever Irene Guy was, she'd owned this owl, perhaps cherished it, and now Frieda had carelessly let it out. It was one of those actions that could never be undone, and now she was left with the question of whether to leave the bird or not. The responsibility of this owl that was not hers was making Frieda weary.

She had once made an owl from plasticine during what her dad termed the 'Plasticine Era'. It began with a Noah's Ark, with two cows, two sheep, and two blue whales, then quickly expanded into a zoo. It became an obsession, this caravan full of stretched-out figures, hooves and wings moulded in reds, blues and greens, and she remembered her mother, always wary of Frieda's tendency to stay indoors and make creatures out of Play-Doh substances, poking her head into Frieda's caravan:

'Come on, out into the sun.'

'I don't want to, Mum.'

Her mother, stepping round the door, grabbing hold of Frieda's hand and pulling her away from her plasticine wilderness, saying, 'Don't call me Mum. Come on!'

'Why?' Everyone else said Mum. Mum. Dad. Me. Brother. Sister. Dog. Fish.

'Call me Ananda, Frieda, baby, you know that. Get your jeans on, come on . . .'

Her mum swaying in the door frame, singing a stupid song, something to do with looping and loo, barefoot, with painted red toenails, wearing a long blue skirt, her black

130

hair shimmery, and her dark eyes shiny and laughing as she stuck out her tongue at Frieda. She was trying hard to be infectious.

'Where are we going?'

'Come on!'

Jump. From bottom step to beach, then out towards the sea. The tide far out past the rock pools, far enough that a skin of sand comes up, like a lick of stomach, or a flash of back.

'Come on, to the sea.'

Frieda skittered across slimy rocks, eventually letting the soles of her feet recover in the relief of flat, wet sand.

Don't call me Mum. Don't call me Grace. I am Ananda Amrita. Divine Sister.

Ananda Amrita pulled her black vest off in front of Frieda, throwing it into the sea and splashing about. The sun was getting up in the sky. Ananda's long skirt clung to her legs, her small breasts were exposed, nipples saying hello to the sky, her arms flapping like seagull wings.

'Come on – look at the light!'

Frieda waded through the shallow water until it was deep enough to bend knees, lower her chest, and flipper into the cold of the sea water. Ananda was going further out, not looking back. A grey coral of fish eggs bobbed past, along with a cigarette butt, and Frieda's feet could no longer touch the floor.

'Mum,' she shouted out, lifting her chin up like a turtle, swallowing the salty water, and then there was a splash behind her. It was her dad, wearing all of his clothes, coming fast towards her and scooping her up, pulling her out of the water and holding her. Shouting, 'What do you think you are doing?'

Ananda Amrita was swimming, half-walking through the waves, saying something, but Frieda couldn't hear. Her father said, 'You don't deserve her, this child.'

Frieda hung upside down over her father's shoulder, like one of her plasticine bats, looking at Ananda who stood still and half naked and wet in the sea. It was her mum's fault that Frieda had eyes that were black and dark and different from her dad's. That she wasn't right.

Nostrils: wide and deep and she could see right up them. Above them were eyes, looking down at her, below them a moustache. Frieda didn't move, for a moment, and then jumped up, pushed her glasses along her nose and coughed.

'I have forgotten my pen.' The man had an accent. Frieda blushed at being found lying on the floor, so oddly, and stood up, feeling that she ought to apologise, even though he was the one intruding, but she said nothing.

'Ah, there it is.' He pointed at a green and silver fountain pen that was poking out from underneath her welcome mat. Frieda bent down and picked it up. As she turned towards him she saw the drawings on the wall.

'You must have been working on that all night.'

'Yes.' He did not look sheepish, or apologetic. In fact, she saw him smile at his work appreciatively. Frieda was about to ask him what the Arabic said, but didn't.

'I like it,' she smiled, 'although I might get in trouble for it.'

There was a pause. What was it about, this lurking about in her stairwell? Was he following her? She was about to ask him, but he spoke first:

'Why were you on the floor?'

'I was trying to work out how to get the owl back, but I must have fallen asleep.' He looked up in the direction of Frieda's glance, to the owl.

'Ah.'

Frieda watched the man move until he was exactly below the owl, which sat impervious on a pipe. He held his hand up towards the owl and made a gentle cooing noise. It didn't respond.

'He escaped,' Frieda said, redundantly. With his pen still in her hand she watched the small, wiry man as he continued with his cooing.

'It is very stubborn,' she said. 'It has been there for hours. I don't know what to do.'

The man laughed. 'That is the way it is with owls.'

'Al Salaam a'alaykum,' she said, shyly.

He turned and wrinkles appeared around his eyes as his smile grew with surprise and pleasure. 'Wa aleikum ah Salaam . . . you speak Arabic?'

'A teeny bit. Very, very badly.'

He offered his hand, moving closer to Frieda and she took it, a formal handshake, much like a child in a play. His hand was small and smooth and he was shorter than her, by about an inch. After shaking her hand he rubbed his palm over his black, springy hair, as if to calm it, and tidy himself for her.

'It is very nice to meet you,' he said, speaking as though in an English lesson, and introduced himself. Having introduced herself back, Frieda held on to the door frame. She still did not give him his pen.

'The problem is, I don't know if by letting it out I'm killing it or setting it free.'

She looked at the Arab man's face as he looked up at the owl. She caught herself thinking *Arab man*, as if he was the sole representative of a race. She should know better with her training. He did not seem to be surprised by events, her lying on the floor, or an owl on the pipe. In fact, he looked rather as if he were enjoying himself. He raised his chin, considering the bird, and turned to look at Frieda.

'Do you want him back or have you let him go?'

The question took residence in the air between them and it had surprising weight. Frieda, as well as feeling suddenly rather cautious about this man, surprised herself by thinking that she might cry, contemplating it. To cover her confusion she said, 'It was let out,' and then, 'I didn't mean to.'

'So you want it back?'

Frieda looked at the owl. 'Yes. I want it back. Do you know how I can get him? Is it a "him"?'

The man put his hand on the rail and leaned back with an air of leisure, with an expansive sense of having endless time to ponder the problem. His rumination took the mode of meditation and Frieda, unsure whether to speak or not, moved her foot back and forth on the mat. Finally, he said, 'Yes. It looks like a male. The females are larger, I think. Food is the only way. You will have to . . .' he paused, '. . .. *lure* him back.'

'Do you think that will work?'

'Well, it could, but it might take some time.'

'How long?'

'They are in no hurry, owls. My father had one that escaped and sat in a tree for three days before we got it back. It depends how hungry it is.'

'Oh, I am sure it must be hungry.'

They both looked up at the owl. Its eyes were closed.

Six rashers of Waitrose Essentials range bacon lay in strips across the floor. The man who had introduced himself as Tayeb was squatting calmly against the stair-rail. He sipped from a cup of tea in one hand and held a yellow pillowcase in the other. Frieda repeated the word after him, in her head: Yemen. What did she know about Yemen? Nothing. Almost nothing. Once a British colony. Desert. Muslim. Home of terrorists. Everyone owning guns. In all her travels, this was one country she had not been to. She would have liked to ask him about his home but there was something in the way he sat, self-contained and taut, that didn't encourage further enquiry. Instead she said, 'Have you any . . . experience with owls?'

'Some. But I know the bigger ones, the Siberian types. This is a British type, smaller.'

Frieda, standing drinking her tea in the doorway nodded, as if familiar with Siberian owls. She ran a finger along the shape of one of the feathers he drew last night.

'This tea is good,' he said, smiling. 'We could be here for some time.'

He had an interesting smile. He was actually rather good looking.

'If you don't mind me asking,' Frieda said, her hand still on his drawings, 'are you homeless? You don't seem like a . . . homeless person.'

'I like this, the English way of getting permission to ask a question. I am in trouble,' he said. 'I was about to be arrested, which means I will probably be deported. So I have had to leave my home, so as not to get my friends into trouble.'

'Arrested for what?'

'Vandalism.' She looked at the bird drawing on the wall.

'Do you mind if I smoke?' Tayeb half pulled out a cigarette from a packet and looked at her with the question on his face. Frieda nodded. He offered her one and she declined.

'I was drawing on a toilet wall and some men caught me. I wasn't sure if they were police or not. I thought the best thing was to be friendly. They wanted me to do things I didn't want to do and then the police arrived at my door.'

'Oh.'

'It was an unpleasant night, and now I am trying to work out what to do.' He drew on his cigarette in a contemplative way and touched a scar on his chin. Frieda put her cup up to her lip to hide her face. He had not moved from his squatting position for a long time. It was an exotic pose, she supposed. It made her think of lepers on the edge of the street in Delhi or of Chinese cooks. She was appalled at her own inner-Orientalist, but she couldn't stop it. She remembered girls in her school, not being able to work her out, asking her, 'Are you Turkish? Are you Spanish?' They would run around her in circles calling her a bloody i-ti, a bloody dago. Nathaniel once told her, 'Your eyes are too black. They are unnatural, and unnerving.'

Tayeb reminded her of a man she had watched on the promenade in Alexandria, one trip, not long ago. Or Alex, as she liked to call it, like a local. There were men everywhere, in clusters, leaning back to watch her walk, as self-conscious as a tourist, past them. They shouted, *Hallo, Hallo*, or, *Tsssst. Hey: how are you? Talk to me.* Frieda had let her head droop down, averting her eyes from the leather jackets and the slicked-back black hair, the laughing brown eyes. The men – boys, actually, most of them, teenagers – were simply being Mediterranean men, she said to herself, but still, it was overwhelming and tears welled up in her eyes as the whistles and calls followed her flip-flopping footsteps along the seafront.

For years she had dreamed of visiting this famous city, expecting something decadent, full of beautiful people luxuriating in the sunshine, drinking coffee. She laughed at her own idiocy, her own Western buffoonery when she discovered on arrival that the city was not unlike some of the more clapped-out, dishevelled English seaside towns. A bizarre concoction of shabby European-style hotels and tramlines, and a smell at once African and Arab to Frieda (whatever that is, whatever scents those could be, trammelled into one essentially non-European root, she supposed, part-seductive, part-repulsive, part soporific).

Her flight had been delayed due to security issues and problems at the airport and rather than fly to Cairo she had walked around Alexandria, accidentally finding, she remembers now, a Jewish cemetery, protected at its gates by vicious black dogs chained to the rocks on the path. She couldn't get into the cemetery; the gates were locked. Nor could she get near, because of the dogs, but through the iron bars of the gates she could see a chipped marble mausoleum, and some unloved gravestones. For a while she had stood and watched the dogs who intermittently barked at her, before returning to the mauling of a small carcass, a dead rabbit or rodent, from what she could tell. She had wandered off, overcome with the familiar hopeless feeling of being an unwanted stranger, but she was pleased with herself none the less: for keeping herself together, securing a salary that would make her father shiver, managing the minuscule matters of each day. All in all, a patchy yet valid holding together; that is, until the men on the promenade undid it all with their calls. Eventually, a man who looked a little like Tayeb had shushed them all with a *tsssst*. Whatever he said, she didn't hear, but it helped. They all turned away, to look at something else, something more interesting. She had scurried past, back to her hotel, and didn't go out again until it was time to catch her plane.

'What do you do?' Frieda drank the last of her tea, which had gone cold in the cup.

'I had a job at a Turkish restaurant in Dalston, but I had to leave. By a bad coincidence I now have neither job nor a home.'

Tayeb was not looking at Frieda any more, but at the owl, addressing it with his musical, swinging accent. Clouds must have shifted in the sky as the quality of the light coming through the window in the hall changed. If Frieda could reach up, high enough, she could close the window so the owl couldn't get out. But that still wouldn't solve anything; it would still be there and now, she had the additional problem of a homeless Arab man on her stairs. In a quiet voice, he whispered, 'Don't move.'

Frieda looked up. The owl had shifted a considerable way along the pipe and was now wide-eyed and looking directly at the bacon on the floor. It hopped one, two, three hops along the pipe. Then there was a flurry and it flew towards the bacon, a talon ripping effortlessly into one of the strips. The pillowcase was over it with a whoosh and Tayeb flicked the bird up, twisting the pillowcase so that the owl could not escape. There were a few bulging movements and then it went still. It was neatly done. Frieda swung the door open, pointing to the cage in the living room. Tayeb leaned over the cage and Frieda could not see how he manoeuvred the bird in, but the next second there it was, ruffled and disgruntled-looking.

Frieda returned to the corridor and picked up the rashers. She took them in and poked them through the bars for the owl.

'Poor owlie,' she said, looking at Tayeb, who was now standing in the centre of the room, smiling, nodding as if in agreement, though she did not know with what. There was indeed something odd about the fact that he had sat outside her door last night and now he was here again: why was that? Nothing is accidental. He was scratching, scratching at his wrists so much that she wanted to pull his hands away from themselves and something about this movement prompted her:

'It seems only polite to offer you another drink as you have been so kind as to catch my owl for me,' she said, wary – he was a stranger, after all – but propelled to invite him nevertheless.

My owl: how ridiculous. She pulled her hair over her face slightly, feeling shy.

Training: *The only thing alive about bicycles is the persons who propel them; and if they are only half alive before attempting to mount, they will become very alert and keenly appreciative of all that concerns them long before the sport has ceased to be a novelty.*

A Lady Cyclist's Guide to Kashgar – Notes

July 2nd

A visitor blew through our house like a hurricane, but not for long. It was Mr Steyning from the Inland Mission. He arrived on horseback yesterday afternoon entirely unannounced, was gone by nightfall and his visit is already like a dream. It is as if he rode on his horse from the sky, and returned that way, cloud-ward.

He appeared at our gate alone, although we found out later that he does have a boy who carries his supplies, but for some reason this boy had stopped further down the track. News of the arrival was imparted in the usual way. The wily, skinny boys move faster than snakes, they are like carrier pigeons.

They whispered to Lolo that a visitor was nearly upon us and Elizabeth and I rushed and scrambled about to tidy both ourselves and the guest-room, although, in fact, we did not have enough time to do either.

I looked at myself in the mirror for the first time in a while to see how I might seem to a stranger. My red hair has grown blonder in the sun and dry-straw looking as a consequence. My eyes are red-rimmed. I am beginning to look sun-beaten, the creases now remain. I don't know why I was concerned about my looks, but I flattened my hair down and replaced my Chinese cotton smock with a European skirt and blouse, made from sea-green silk. The particularly English shade of green, bringing to mind moss and hedgerows, seemed immediately out of place here in this land of bright yellows and dusky pinks. I felt garish and conspicuous, but it was too late to change. Lizzie remained in her Chinese smock and looked surprised when she saw me in European wear.

'What are you wearing? You look ridiculous.'

Lizzie stood appraising me, her frail bones buffeting beneath the cotton blue smock, her eyes sticking out, her hair twisted up, standing ornamentally still. I wanted to both bite her and stroke her, little Lizzie. Contrary as ever, she now became the perfect, beautifully presented parlour-room daughter, whereas sweat was already dotting my silk shirt.

Mr Steyning stood in the garden wearing a full black suit despite the heat, and shoes that shone like spectacular jewels in the immense dust of the road. He is a large man, expansive and big-framed, with a very black, clipped beard. I could not look away from those shoes, wondering how they could possibly be so clean. I can only conclude that he stopped, just before arriving at the Pavilion House, and changed from his riding clothes into a smarter outfit. It was a pleasure to see and meet a fellow countryman, especially one so at home in these distorted, wild surroundings and fortunate that we had the opportunity to meet him without Millicent here. She was visiting the priest, or Khadega.

'Did you come in response to our telegram?' Lizzie asked.

In fact no, was the answer. He has been travelling. The telegram was sent to Urumtsi and he has not been there for weeks. It is luck that he came to find us.

'We must tell you', Lizzie said, 'we are under house-arrest.'

'I am so relieved that you are here,' I said.

Mr Steyning is a gentleman, and fascinating. He has lived in Turkestan for seventeen years, having arrived in 1906 with the Inland Mission. Elizabeth sat with him as I served tea and dough-bread biscuits. He glanced frequently at Ai-Lien, though was too polite to ask any questions, and so I sat down and quickly told him our story. He absorbed my words calmly, asking the odd question here and there about the trial, and of Millicent's great danger and the accusation of murder. He took out a small notebook and wrote several lines and nodded.

'I see,' he said. 'I must talk to Millicent about this.'

Then, encouraged by his smiles, we asked him question after question, poor man. He did not seem to mind, answering with magnanimity. Geography, distance, religion, social issues, and the women of the region, the Moslem question, the Chinese question, the Russian question, and the state of the Empire, all discussed in great and lively spirits. He spoke of his acquaintance Mr Greeves, with whom he lives in Urumtsi, a world-renowned specialist in Turkic folklore and language, a specialist of Manchu and who is at their home at work on a great dictionary and various important translation works.

'Ah,' Lizzie said, 'we know a priest, Father Don Carlo, who is also at work on a dictionary.'

'At least – I think it's a dictionary,' I added. At the mention of Father Don Carlo, Mr Steyning frowned slightly.

'You must visit us, Miss English,' he said. 'We too have a small mimeograph and have taken some of Mr Greeves' translations of the Gospels and printed them into Turki, Manchu and Qazak. We are currently working on "The Pilgrim's Progress".'

We passed a pleasant afternoon. Elizabeth led a tour of the garden, with me trailing behind and Mr Steyning was immediately in raptures. It turns out that he has a wonderful knowledge of botany of the area. He gave us the names and I noted them down for my guide book: *Acer griseum*, with cinnamon-red papery bark. *Dipteronia sinensis*. *Lonicera tragophylla* in full flower, and *Schizophragma integrifolium* is the name of the mass of white that clambers over all. Flowers: *Lilium giganteum*; *Ilex Pernyi*; a sort of cowslip called *Primula sikkimensis*; and he pointed out a dark-red Tibetan lady's-slipper orchid (*Cypripedium tibeticum*) that grows in abundance in our garden.

Lizzie invited him to follow her into the small adobe outbuilding where she spends much of her time. I have not been into it myself, I could tell she was hesitant about letting me in, but I simply followed. It is a sort of hovel built into the ground, presumably previously used as a cellar, or similar. Lizzie lit a linseed lamp. Clipped to a piece of string tied along a wooden pole was a series of photographic prints. I sniffed at the smell of chemicals, glad to see, however, that they were being put to use having travelled so far. Apart from one of a cluster of pigtailed native children, the prints were mostly self-portraits – one next to the handkerchief tree, or near flowers in the garden – and they were layered with images, gauzy and indistinct, ghost-like. I had not seen them before and looked at them with interest.

Mr Steyning looked closely. 'These are very impressive,' he said.

'Oh, they were mostly accidents. I have difficulties with the chemicals, with the light. I cannot control the conditions adequately here and can only shut out the light using several blankets over the door. I long for a dark-room.'

'You seem . . .' Mr Steyning paused for a moment, scratched at his chin. 'In this one, well, you seem light, as if you have lightened yourself and released yourself from the gravity of this earth.'

'That is insightful of you.' Lizzie was smiling. 'I am very interested in heavy things made light.'

We walked back into the garden and I lingered behind as he and Elizabeth chatted about the bark, the colour of the wood and the details of the garden. I did not know she had taken such photographs. There certainly is something about Mr

Steyning that inspires private confidences. Later, I told him of my endeavour to write a guide as one of the first English women to visit this region (apart from the wife of the British Consul) and to my delight, he was sympathetic to the idea, offering his study and resources in Urumtsi if ever I should need it. He gave me his card with the address embossed in silver in English, Chinese and Turki. It has a picture of a hummingbird in the corner.

Millicent still did not return, even though we had sent a scout to inform her of our visitor, and so I took over the organisation of the evening. I instructed Lolo to prepare some Tibetan thenthuk stew (when Millicent is away we abandon English cuisine, Lolo's native concoctions being profoundly superior). Mr Steyning insisted on joining us in the kitchen as we were preparing the evening food for him.

'Do excuse me, Mr Steyning, as I attend to the baby.'

'Oh, Miss English, I would much prefer to sit here and chatter. I am an incorrigible chatterer as you can tell.'

Elizabeth offered to arrange his room, but he insisted that he would leave that night. Lolo prepared the food, humming as he cooked. I tended to Ai-Lien as Mr Steyning conversed with Lolo in what he said was a broken form of Tibetan dialogue. Mr Steyning patted Lolo on the back as he mixed the flour, pressed the dough with his wide hands and chopped the vegetables into strings.

'Oh don't lay the table, English-style', he declared when he saw Lizzie begin to bring out the tableware items. 'Mr Greeves and I normally eat local-fashion, it is much more convenient, much simpler.'

So we sat on the divan with the food laid out on plates, using the bread to sweep it up. As we ate, he began, for the first time, to ask about our Mission. Do we have any converts? Are we of much interest? Under suspicion? I let Lizzie talk on Millicent's behalf at this point and she certainly demonstrated conviction. Her blonde thin hair fell over her face as she talked of our great plans for a Children's Service – this was news to me – and of our distribution of the translated pamphlets.

'But have you any converts, yet?' Mr Steyning persisted.

'Mr Steyning, you may disapprove, but we have a rather *female* approach to spreading the Gospel,' Lizzie said.

'Oh, do elaborate, Miss English.'

'We talk, Mr Steyning. We call it – well, Millicent calls it *gossiping the gospel*. We infiltrate the female elements of society, the harems, the inside of the Moslem women's quarters and families and it is there that we begin the process of conversion. Slowly, but surely.'

Mr Steyning nodded, smiling.

'The daughter of one such house has come to us and although she is just one, she will surely be a conduit for more.' Lizzie looked pleased as she spoke.

'And you, Miss English, do you gossip the gospel?' I blushed across my face and neck and Mr Steyning, to be kind, changed the subject.

We finished eating the stew followed by one of Lolo's sweet rice puddings, a simple and delicious dish with traces of apple and a delicate honey saturated through the rice. After dinner we talked of the Moslem situation in this area. I had not realised it was quite so devastating. According to Mr Steyning, all of the cities of the North West are now in the grip of terror as Moslem Brigands maraud through the desert, raiding cities at will, warring with the Chinese.

'Goodness,' Lizzie spread her toes out in front of her as she spoke, 'but they are not furious with us?'

'Foreigners are always treated with suspicion,' he said. 'We are not welcome here, particularly our Mission, which reminds people of the violence of the dreadful Boxer era.'

'Do you mean it is very dangerous for us?' Lizzie asked.

'It is always dangerous. But more so at the moment. Tensions are very high, suspicion is rife. This is why I am here, to talk to Millicent. To suggest that she –'

'You want us to leave?' Lizzie sat upright and pushed her hair behind her ears. 'I don't think we can, we are still under house-arrest, in effect.'

Mr Steyning continued, 'These Moslem bands are terrifying. They are not your usual bands of thieves and beggars. The area is profoundly militarist. City gates are shut up at night. Soldiers are permanently mobilised. There is an atmosphere of war.'

'Mr Steyning,' I said, 'we feel quite removed from all of this, here.'

Mr Steyning smiled an intelligent smile, if a little foxy. He looked at us with a concerned expression.

'Evangeline, you are on the outside of city walls, under no protectorate. There is suspicion of Christians at the best of times. We offend the ancestral spirits. The Moslems have usually been more indifferent to us than the Chinese, but now, suspicions run high. I should warn you, too, that all correspondence will be censored.'

We were silent for a moment.

'I don't want to alarm you,' he said, stroking at his wrist with his long fingers as he spoke, 'but during this time of high tension our methods do rather need to be amended and our profile reduced.'

I was not sure what this meant. There was a pause and then we heard the clang of the gate and Millicent's voice instructing one of Lolo's boys to take her packages. There was a scuffle and the sound of running, and then Millicent walked into the room, glancing first at Elizabeth, then me, then fully at Mr Steyning. I do not know why but I felt rather guilty, and could tell from Lizzie's expression that she did too. Millicent's hair was wild and she had a rakish expression. Mr Steyning stood up quickly, gracefully, and held out his hand. It was a clever gesture, at once a hello, but also, he had seen that she was swaying slightly, and as he shook her hand he steadied her.

'Dear Millicent,' he said, with warmth, 'I have been wonderfully looked after by your protégées.'

Millicent opened her mouth to speak and then closed it again.

'Perhaps we should talk in the courtyard, Millicent.' Millicent concurred and I was astonished to see that she allowed him to steer her by her arm, out into the cooling night air. They remained there together, being served coffee by Lolo.

Once Ai-Lien was asleep, I stepped out from the kang room into the courtyard. The scorching heat of the day gives way at night to a sharp chill which seems to come up from the ground and take a standing person by surprise. I heard the strike of a match and its hiss as the cigarette took light. They were sitting together on the garden chairs and had not seen me. I leaned against the cooling wall and listened.

'Millicent, it has fallen to me to impress this upon you immediately.'

Millicent said nothing, just smoked. Mr Steyning's voice was lulling, not unkind:

'You know, Millicent dear, that your services to the Church, to the overall work of the Mission, and your outstanding contribution to the development of Illumination of His Will amongst the dark, heathen and closed corners of this Earth are not without noting and are deeply appreciated by the Mission community, and beyond, both here, in the East, and back home in England.'

'If that is the case then why are my methods criticised by the committee?'

'You mistake criticism for concern, I fear.' There was a squeaking in the air, bats carousing for their supper. 'There have been some serious changes to the political situation in the region. To be frank, Millicent, I fear for your safety and that of your two companions and I – and the Committee – insist that you amend your approach immediately.'

'What do you mean, John?'

'I mean that you have been distributing pamphlets that are provocative. The locals don't like your approach, your taking up with the Mohammedan girl. It is very tense, as you no doubt know. We need to maintain a low profile at this moment.'

'That is what I am doing. Exactly what I am doing.'

'You are not. You have been talked about, striding around the souqs. There is much hostility. In addition, I see no evidence of your educational proposal, the school for children, the Sunday school. Your stipend is entirely based on this information.'

'You want me both to maintain a silent presence, a trouble-free presence, but also to set up educational facilities for the children?'

'Our Missionary policy is to provide a useful service as well as spiritual guidance and currently I do not feel, and the Committee agrees with me on this, that you are offering any such service. If I feel this, then, undoubtedly, the Chinese officials and the network of leaders, tribal, nomadic and otherwise, feel the same. As such, you are under threat.'

They were quiet, I could see from the tilt of their heads that they were both looking up at stars, almost shockingly clear and bright.

'What of this trial, Millicent?'

'I know as much as you. We are accused of killing a girl, the mother of the baby Evangeline is caring for. She died in childbirth as we were trying to help her. We are not allowed to leave the region. Your Inland colleagues have refused to provide me with the funds for a bribe. Is there anything you can do to help in this regard?'

'Well, of course, I have the funds to support you if such a trial should come to pass, and we will defend you fully, without question, but this is entirely dependent upon one specific condition, in addition to the points I have already raised.'

'That is?'

'You must sever all contact with Father Don Carlo. He is entirely disconnected from the Mission and has been disallowed to operate under any auspices, including the Italian Missions. He is not a suitable contact, nor is it beneficial to your reputation to be considered in communication with him. I am extremely firm on this subject, Millicent.'

She said nothing.

'Finally, I cannot emphasise enough how imperative it is for you to heed these issues not just for your own safety, but also that of Misses Evangeline and Elizabeth English. I am sure that together, we can navigate this Mission back on to safe terrain.'

On his departure, long after nightfall, Mr Steyning handed me a present that sits beside me now: a small booklet, handmade on beautiful paper. It's a copy of Mr Greeves' translations of Mongolian folktales.

'I wish you the best with your book,' he said. 'Work at it. Just keep working and I shall pray for your safety.' He did not mention Millicent. He smiled at Ai-Lien in her cot and then it was time for him to go.

What I was unprepared for was that his presence should bring my father to mind. As a consequence, I felt his loss viciously, like the injustice of a puncturing wasp sting. We watched, hopelessly redundant, as he mounted his horse and we stood like three ghosts, waving him goodbye.

July 3rd

I might have dropped down dead and died. In fact, I did drop down, my heart beating, a shiver and a sweat came up all about me, and I shook my head.

I really do not know how I shall write this – but – I shall.

Start where I can. Well, it has become my habit to leave Ai-Lien with Lolo during the early-afternoon hours when the heat bleeds through skin and bone. He entertains her and then they lie and sleep together in his cubbyhole behind the kitchen. She seems to like it in there, and more often than not she is tucked into the corner of his elbow, sweet as a pea. During these hours everyone is asleep. Lolo's messenger boys sleep in a tumble, a jangle of limbs at the gate, even Rebekah sits her great legs down and sleeps.

More often than not, I cannot sleep at this time despite the heat. I write in here, or I read. Today, though, restlessness bewitched me so that I was useless. I could not get a certain thought out of my head: that Ai-Lien loves Lolo more than she loves me.

Could that be? Certainly he can stop her crying in an instant with his low singing. He charms and lulls and those brown spots on his hands stand out from the rest of his skin; he carries a leathery smell and his eyes glimmer. I simply cannot work out if he is a person I can trust or not. Ai-Lien looks at him in a way she does not look at me.

I headed to the kitchen. (I am avoiding writing it, but I must.) The air was afternoon-heavy with heat and insects. The earth in the courtyard scorched my bare soles so that I was forced to hop.

In the kitchen I could already hear the snores from Lolo and, as I peeped around the corner into his cubby, I saw Ai-Lien with a light sheet over her, sleeping face down next to him. They were serene and I was ashamed of my jealousy. Why, after all, shouldn't they love each other?

I decided to take a peek at Lizzie and Millicent asleep. I was still greatly concerned for Lizzie and her secretive, removed manner of late. I crept, wanting to be invisible, to the kang room and instead of approaching the door I bent down so that I would come to the window unseen. Then stretched up and peeped through the window.

As I said, I could have dropped down with shock, though I could not help but look again: my sister Lizzie lying on her kang, wearing Millicent's dragon kimono. Only, the kimono was mostly undone and hanging off her and she was lolling, one moment on her side, saying something, then on her back, looking up at the ceiling. Then Millicent stood up, she had been crouching near the floor, arranging something, and I saw that she was naked, apart from her black satin trousers. Her breasts are small, boyish, and her pink nipples almost square-shaped. There appeared to be a moon-like scar, quite vivid, across her stomach. They were talking, though I could not hear what about, and then Millicent began to laugh, sat on the kang and leaned on to Lizzie's knees. Millicent extinguished her cigarette by grinding it on the floor, and then – Lord – she pushed my sister, in a playful way, back down (she had risen slightly in conversation) so that she was flat on the kang and actually pulled her legs apart a little, and then bowed forward.

I dropped down below the window. Ants disappeared into a hair-crack in the ground. I crept on my hands and knees across the courtyard, praying that I would not be seen and then I stood up and ran into the kitchen. On the table was a chicken carcass which Lolo had ordered, left there by one of the boys, and I picked it up. Quickly, I dunked it in the bucket of water and began to pluck. The feathers came out easily enough, tug tug tug. I picked up Lolo's carving knife and hacked it, chopping through tendons, quartering it. I ripped the thighs from the body and, as the flesh came away from the bone, my heartbeat finally began to steady.

London, Present Day

A flat by the railway tracks near Victoria Station

Knowledge sleeps dormant in the bones until an opportunity comes for it to flourish again. It's a long time since Tayeb has handled a bird. His father would have coaxed that bird down with ease and much quicker. At least he had remembered that it's all about food with birds. Tayeb stood in the small living room listening to the woman make noises in her kitchen. He was not sure what to do, whether to sit or move or remain where he was. He looked at the owl in its cage and it occurred to him that she might know that he had followed her last night. She had put the pillows out for him – why had she done that?

‘Would you like tea or coffee?’

'Tea. Please.'

He walked over to a large bookcase that occupied an entire wall and picked up a glass – blown paperweight – rubbed the dust off it and put it back on the shelf. *Mill on the Floss*. Proust's *Swann Way*. Dostoevsky. Trains screeched past every few minutes and each time one passed the entire building shook, gently, as if in complaint. A loud beep resonated from Tayeb's duffel bag. He pulled out his phone and glanced at it. Finally, a message: **A being questioned by police. Nidal gone to Manchester. Won't text you again. Don't come back to flat. Keep Safe. R**

As he read, the woman who had introduced herself as Frieda came into the room with a tray, tea, biscuits, chocolate bars.

'Help yourself,' she said, putting the tray on a low table. Then, pointing at the sofa, 'Please, sit down.'

Tayeb sat on the leather sofa and gestured to the owl.

'I haven't seen an owl for a long time. It brings me memories.'

'Thank you so much for helping me to catch it.'

She had dark hair and dark eyes and the element about her that had made him follow her, originally, a daintiness combined with hardiness. She was like a vine.

He should offer to go, he realised; he should not be in her house. He scratched his moustache and looked at the owl again, sitting as if dazed at being back in its awful cage. Some nights, even now, he still dreams of his father's cages. Each one stacked one above the other with all of those terrible, blinking eyes looking out. He hated those birds as a child. He had wanted to run and unlock them, not to set them free, but so they would die.

One summer he had been instructed to accompany his father on a trip into Wadi Dhahr. They were supplying the birds for a hunting party. An Omani Sheikh and his family were visiting Yemen and they all travelled the twisting steep road North West out of Sana'a, eventually stopping near Amran. The Sheikh and his sons tried to shoot an eagle but missed and Tayeb was told to bring all the boxes of birds off the cart and put them in a row. The Sheikh and his sons demanded that the bustards be released and then their competition began: to see who could shoot the most birds in the quickest time.

Two hours later, the twitching, mostly-dead bustards had been pushed into a pile, but one of the sons, about twenty years old, still wanted more. The Sheikh had asked for Tayeb's father to bring as many birds as possible and so more cages came out: curlews, a white owl and two falcons, both of which had infected feet.

'Open them, Tayeb,' his father said.

Tayeb knelt and opened the cages and each bird emerged in a flap, into the sunlight, to be immediately killed by the shotgun. But one of the falcons, despite its impaired foot, flew away, fast over the dune. The men shot and shot but missed and then were outraged. They took their fury out on the other birds. Two more cages and the dazed, brutalised doves flew up just high enough for the men to shoot them. Blood and feathers flew all around Tayeb and the carcasses dropped, thudding dead weights to the ground. He paused, looking at a small white owl in a cage. His father shouted, again, and Tayeb opened the door, wishing that they would let the owl live. It did not move, even when the door was open. Tayeb made no move to force it out. His father angrily leaned forward, scooped up the white owl with his hand and threw it into the air. The Sheikh's son shot at it just inches from Tayeb's head, the feathers stuck in the sand.

When it was over, his father was given a thick wad of money. The family drove off in their Land Rover, leaving Tayeb and his father in their small Ford truck. Together, saying nothing, they piled the cages on to the back of the truck. The bloody little bodies were mostly still now. Tayeb did not look at his father on the long journey home, knowing that he would be beaten for crying over the death of a bird.

'Are you all right?'

The woman was smiling at him. He was rather dumb-founded at her kindness. He had not actually met anyone this kind in England for the whole fifteen years he had been here, but he did not want this to show on his face, not least because it would make the past years a waste; a sad waste. He peered at his phone and read the message out to Frieda.

'I'm sorry,' Tayeb said then, 'I don't know why I read that out to you. You don't need to know my troubles.'

She was sitting cross-legged on the floor, looking both old and young simultaneously.

'Who is R?' Frieda asked.

'My friend Roberto.'

'And who is A?'

'My friend, too. Stupid Anwar. I always knew he would get us into trouble.'

'Questioned by police? That sounds rather heavy.'

'Anwar is a bit zealous on the anti-American and anti-British websites. Plus, you know, he's living the Muslim Brotherhood dream these days.'

Tayeb could imagine what she was thinking: bomb plots and jihad. He sighed. She was the type of English girl to wear the Palestinian flag on her T-shirt, but still think he might blow her up on the tube.

'Anwar is just a big mouth. He doesn't know what he's talking about. He spends his days in his boxers playing video games. He's just playing at it all. I myself am just trying to exist. I am not interested in all of that. Nor is Roberto or Nidal. They are all just trying to stay in this country.'

Tayeb wished he would stop talking. This woman didn't care. He tried very, very hard not to scratch at his wrists.

'The problem is, what is a game, a phase, a bit of as he would say, head rush, for Anwar, is dangerous for me. If I get deported, things will be very bad for me. Anwar's parents live in south London. He does not have the same worries, you know?'

'I can imagine. Have you tried explaining this to him?'

'He's too lost in his visions of the victimised East. He hasn't even been East. The most East he has been in Plaistow.'

Frieda laughed. 'You seem to know your London geography very well.'

Tayeb raised his eyebrows, tugged on the edge of his moustache and again touched the scar on his chin.

'So if you don't mind me asking,' she said, 'why do you draw on walls?'

160

'A difficult question to answer,' he smiled. 'Where I come from, a child caught writing on walls will have his fingernails removed by security police.'

He looked at her reaction; her eyes widened slightly, but she did not look surprised.

'Still, despite this, people write on walls all the time. We write what we cannot in newspapers or books. There are Arabic words sprayed everywhere but without an artistic feel to them. Usually with a political message.' He paused, how would he explain it to her? He had never actually explained it to himself. He carried on.

'In Yemen, where there are many crumbling walls and empty spaces, the words are political or religious. I have always wondered why the Kufic forms could not be extended into drawings, jokes, tags?'

He stopped. She was nodding, listening, but he couldn't explain it to her further. Why he has this compulsion to write out sections from 'The Book of Animals'. Because it is ancient, scientific, anecdotal and funny? Because it is not a slogan?

'For my own amusement, I suppose.'

'So, if you don't mind me asking, are you now officially on the run?'

'Yes.' He smiled again at her asking permission to ask. 'I suppose so. Now that Anwar has made me look more glamorous and exciting than I am, the idiot. Or if not that, then the immigration people will want me.'

'What will you do?'

He shrugged. That was the question. There was a buzzing, this time from Frieda's thigh. Tayeb watched as she pulled her phone out from her pocket and looked at it. She turned to Tayeb.

'I don't mind if you smoke in the kitchen,' she said, 'near the window.'

'Allah was wise when he guided me to you. You read my mind as well as give me refreshments.' He pulled a packet of cigarettes out of his pocket.

Five trains passed each other simultaneously below Tayeb as he blew smoke out into the dull Victoria air. Two trains in one direction, three in the other, then, suddenly, it was dead quiet. He could hear her talking in the other room, she was trying to keep her voice low, but it was clearly an argument. What must it be like to own this flat? To have a room above a railway line to keep for ever? He had been hounded out of his own country for writing obscenities in classical calligraphy: an unforgivable sin. And for filming the police; it was not advisable to make marks and to witness. He threw his cigarette stub down towards the silvery fence that lined the track. He should go, he knew. The image of the two men – Matthew and Graham – came to his mind, and then a white-sweat feeling of dismay.

He had once been approached similarly in Sana'a, a lifetime ago. He had been standing with his camera, filming a piece of graffiti on the wall behind the small alley that was used as a toilet by tea-house customers, just inside Bab-al-Yaman. Running his camera slowly along the wall to catch the words painted in rangy Arabic. As he did so, a short man, his head wrapped up in his somata, his sandals almost devoured by dust, hissed at him. Tayeb had immediately put his camera into his inside coat pocket and walked off, entering the silver souq quickly. The man followed, though. He thought Tayeb a homosexual, he supposed.

Tayeb walked fast towards the Great Mosque. He had heard from his brothers of men approaching other men in the souqs and, if refused, they would threaten to announce that person as a homosexual to the world, or they would demand enormous bribes. The sentence for such actions in Yemen was the death penalty. Sana'a is a maze, a hive that can protect. It is an alphabet city, words on the walls, and lost letters everywhere. The walls are layered with continuous scratches of ancient and new handwriting. Tayeb could have filmed and photographed the walls of Sana'a for a decade, if he hadn't been forced to leave. He had started to believe that the messages on the walls were for him: come this way. Left. Right. Down here. That's it. Come with me.

The man had followed him through the vegetable market, but tripped over the old qashshamah, crashing into her produce: bundles of ansif, parsley, tomatoes, fennel and herbs. From the ground the man shouted to him. Several women halted their shopping, looking through the gauze of their niqabs at him. Tayeb ran into a vein-like passageway that passed below tall, disjointed houses all leaning into each other like old friends. He kept going, without looking back, running like a dog following a scent for food past closed doors, abaya stands, past the medical souqs, until he looked up and saw that he had lost the man, but he was also lost himself.

163

His mother always told him that he had lucky bones and no djinns in his shadow but he didn't imagine this is what it meant to be lucky.

'I have an idea,' Frieda said, standing behind him in the kitchen, leaning against the door. He turned and looked at her, hoping he hadn't breathed cigarette smoke into her kitchen. She was thin, attractive, though she seemed nervous. Or perhaps, if not nervous, then ill at ease with herself. She acted confident, but it wasn't very convincing. She smiled at him.

'Of somewhere you can stay, just for one week. But it might help.'

'Oh? I can't stay here, you are very kind, but I cannot intrude.' Tayeb stood up straight, in truth he was a little shocked at her suggestion.

'No, not here,' she said. Her voice was quiet and delicate, yet she was curiously unfazed by a strange man in her kitchen. 'Another flat, there is another one. I have it for one week, well, five days now. I am . . . clearing it out. You can help me maybe, in return for the favour of staying there?'

Tayeb looked at her quiet, wide face and thin lips. He was hot with relief. His psoriasis rose up as if trying to take him to the end of his own endurance.

'Five days will give me time to work out what to do. I am so grateful.'

'Good,' Frieda said, and to avoid the awkwardness of discussing what he would do about sleeping somewhere that night, she said, 'Why don't we go there now?'

164

How to Make Progress: *The oftener discouraged, the oftener the opportunity to hope again. The art of bicycling is a purely mechanical attainment; and though its complications may at first seem hopeless, sufficient practice will result in final mastery.*

A Lady Cyclist's Guide to Kashgar – Notes

July 9th

I must record the last three days but I shirk from the task. Then – think of myself at fifty wondering, what was it like? Was it really like that? – Think of Mr Hatchett who awaits my Guide. I am a disgrace.

According to Father Don Carlo a man may lose his life by crossing the street at midday in July, so it was a surprise when Millicent insisted we go into the desert to see the travelling theatre troupe.

'It's the opportunity I've been waiting for,' she said, hopping about the courtyard like a chaffinch. 'The performance runs for three days; I will request permission for us to attend from the General.'

'But Millicent – the heat.'

To my dismay, we were granted permission to go, as long as Hai and Li accompanied us. Now I cannot help but think that we would have been much wiser to have remained in our home.

Just beyond the boundary of Kashgar's Old Town, on the other side of the disease-breeding River Tooman, a track runs into the desert. It appears desolate, but like most of these seemingly unused pathways, there is a destination. It is, in fact, the beginning of a long tramp to a temple in the desert: the Temple of Red Rock Ladder, so named because it is situated at the base of a wide plateau of curiously staggered cliffs. Their formation falls in such a jagged way that they create the perfect silhouette in the bright, empty sky, of a staircase, or ladder, leading up to Heaven. Presiding over the temple is an ancient abbot who has never once cut his beard or hair. His head hangs with twisted rope-like hair giving him an unreal look of a medusa. Indeed, he is affectionately known as Abbot Snakehead.

By the time we reached the plain of the Temple of Red Rock Ladder throngs of families were in full festival regalia. We were forced to set up camp in an exposed patch, close to the main thoroughfare that stretched down to a makeshift theatre built in front of the temple. Father Don Carlo joined us and together we set up a table and arranged bibles, some translated quotes and his beautifully decorated pamphlets in a fan.

The first afternoon we simply waited for the actors to arrive. Lizzie darted about with her Leica, trailed by children.

Millicent and Father Don Carlo distributed the pamphlets to passers-by, many of whom stopped to peer at us. Drumming came from every direction, and every now and again natives would begin to dance with alarming, spontaneous movements. I held Ai-Lien wrapped and close to me as the crowds flew around us.

Eventually, in the full blaze of the afternoon, the actors came, looking more like prisoners than a theatrical cast. They carried trunks on their shoulders and they spilled over with stage properties and costumes. Musicians followed, even more unsightly and haphazard than the actors. They seemed to be made up of a whole range of nationalities, some of them – the ones carrying pipes and cymbals – had the pointed chins and the pigtails of the Mongolians, others were Turkic-looking, some barely Eastern at all. They came with huge drums, and flutes and several long-headed stringed instruments with wide bowls. They waved shakers made from sticks and nails and jangling bits of metal, and primitive tambourines. Lizzie was like a sprat, flitting here and there. When the animal handlers came she went as close as she dared, photographing a wretched-looking tiger attached by a great chain to a man with a long pigtail; several yaks; and the five or six donkeys laden with cases and packages and bundles tied up Kashgari-style in scarves of bright colours that followed.

It wasn't until the light began to fade in earnest, and torches were lit around the edges of the stage, that there were clear signs of the show actually beginning.

We took it in turns to man the tent and to watch the perform-
ances, but it was almost impossible to understand the thread of
the narrative. A minuscule Maestro character made jokes, in a
fluid range of languages, slipping from Turki to Chinese to various dialects, nodding and curtseying, charming the audience.
We ate well: lamb kebabes, cucumbers with red peppers, jiaozi
pancakes, steamed bread and rice. Occasionally, unfathomably,
the crowd laughed at the creatures on the stage. The sights and
sounds and lights and songs and clashes of drums and cymbals
and storming out of Emperors and lonely warriors left me dizzy,
almost hallucinating. I returned to our makeshift tent to add
water to the dried food for Ai-Lien, and had an uncomfortable
night's sleep. When we awoke at dawn there was a crowd of
people standing and squatting around our tent watching us.

By the second evening, our supplies were proving inadequate. We had finished all of our bread and were reduced to
making a paste of flour mixed with oil, pulled into strips and
boiled in water. At dusk I returned from a scavenging hunt
amongst the food vendors who had all increased their prices
enormously, and was surprised to see Khadega in the corner of
our tent talking to Millicent.

'Eva,' Millicent called, 'Khadega needs to come and live
with us for a time.' Khadega was sitting in a squat position,
with her face covered.

'Will Mohammed allow it?'

'It is no longer safe for Khadega to be in her home.' Lizzie
came in then, tired-looking. She glanced at Millicent with
Khadega, holding her hand.

'What's happening?'

'Someone has informed Mohammed that we are attempting to convert Khadega.' Millicent pulled out a Hatamen. 'It is not safe for her, he is angry. Rami has sent Khadega to us, asking for a haven.'

'Is he here now?'

'Yes, but Rami heard that we are here, deposited Khadega, and has steered him away.' Millicent laughed. She seemed to be enjoying herself.

'Millicent – this is not a situation that you should be amused at. She will lose her family,' Lizzie said.

'She has chosen a new family, a new way.' Millicent squeezed a territorial grip on Khadega's hand and translated her words into Russian. Khadega sat next to Millicent with the atmosphere of a rescued cat: at once shivering, in recovery with wet fur, yet sitting like an Empress awaiting a party in her honour. Lizzie slumped on to the floor on the opposite side of the tent and focused on the business of pulling off her boots.

'Lizzie, can I leave Ai-Lien in your care while I go and see the temple?' I had a strong impulse to leave our tent. Khadega remained covered and cowed, but through her veils it was possible to see her eyes, too emotional and swilling for good sense. I rebuked myself. Khadega deserves freedom as much as the rest of us. Lizzie stretched her arms up for the baby and, as she did, I saw flashes of her younger self: Lizzie in the school room at the convent, refusing to say mass and Lizzie climbing a chestnut tree in Saint Omer, waving; Lizzie listening to a recital in Geneva. Hold my hand. A secret language: a cooo coroco pigeon song. Do not stop laughing in my ear. She took Ai-Lien to her chest and held her sweetly. This was the first time I have seen her do so.

It was almost dark. Various shrines were dotted about the temple grounds, each with a line of people queuing to light incense and receive their blessing. I wandered, watching the people solemnly light their sticks. The monotonous drone of the chanting priests created a confusion of sound in the air and the clapping of their oyster-shaped instruments provided a pulse. Worshippers flung themselves prostrate, cast down their money and sent prayers out.

The immense jagged, stair-like cliffs were in front of me. Before them, I felt that my own prayers, such as they might be called, were but dead leaves in a dying wind, achieving nothing. Through the flickering light and the gnats and the flies I saw Mohammed. His head was down, his hand on his beard, he was talking to several other Mohammedans. As I somehow knew he would, he looked up and directly at me.

I moved backwards and I saw him draw away from his company. Then, he was next to me. There was no choice but to acknowledge him as he swung round and stood in my path. He spoke quietly:

'Khadega?'

Father Don Carlo was in the tent, sweating, smelling of his wine, his wide lips parted and spitting and muttering.

'There has been a clash. Shots. A Tundra man killed, two Moslem men stabbed.' He was rambling. 'I think it would be wise for us to leave immediately.'

'If you think it is for the best,' Millicent said. She was rolling up the Jaeger sleeping bags and putting them into the holdall. Lizzie was singing softly to Ai-Lien. Father Don Carlo had his back to me and so did not see my companion. Khadega did however. As if hypnotised, she rose and stood still. Millicent and Lizzie looked at her. Saying nothing, she walked towards Mohammed and together they left, without glancing back at us, or touching each other.

Dusty bodies, woeful children, weary fathers, all on the long walk home. A stoat-sized man jumped into our path waving one of the pamphlets that Millicent had distributed, spat on it and ripped it up in front of us.

'Just keep walking,' Millicent said.

'What was that?' Lizzie asked.

'Some resistance to our message,' Father Don Carlo answered.

'You should be careful,' I said to Millicent. I remembered Mr Steyning's warnings and Mohammed's face in the flickering light.

'He doesn't like your methods. I don't think anyone does. Don't send out these pamphlets any more.'

But Millicent didn't hear me. I had spoken to a moth, instead.

July 10th

She fell into the river they say, though of course everyone knows it was Mohammed who drowned her. Perhaps she was dead before she touched the water. His fury was bright. It could be that she was beaten to death, strangled, shot? The news came through the dust and I looked at Lolo's face as he looked to the floor.

'Tell me, Lolo, what is it?'

'Memsahib –'

We had been making a cake, using the remains of Millicent's funds. Churning cream to make butter, sifting flour and crushing Russian sugar lumps in the mortar. We shelled, blanched and pounded the almonds. As we worked, I taught Lolo nursery rhymes – *Little Mary Esther sat upon a tester eating curds and whey* – which he repeated with great seriousness, stroking his long, extraordinary eyebrows. A dust-covered boy sidled in and whispered something to him.

'Memsahib –'

It falls to me to tell Millicent and Lizzie that Khadega is dead and Millicent's conversion experiment has gone dreadfully wrong. They have been out all day. I hold on to the knowledge like a secret tattoo.

Lolo is uneasy and asks for Ai-Lien but I refuse. I respond to a death by holding on to a life. I call her my tiny bird and keep her close, in the folds of the fabric of the sling her little hands squeeze me. Loving her and being her mother, which is what I've become, is like a private waltz between the two of us.

A dance of soft touches, fingers underneath her chin, a stroke of the softest place below her ear, and the dance moves faster until I am spun completely, lost to a love that will be life-long.

Ai-Lien's hair is the same colour as Khadega's. Khadega sank into a fetid river to become part of the desert and her unhappy face lies at the bottom, staring as if to make something out that is blurred around her, but she can't quite see it.

Later: Millicent did not cry. She smoked, and said not a word about Khadega's death and her complicity in it. She comes in, pretends to be calm and serene, she acts the Missionary. It is a great act. Is this my problem? And who am I, to be accusing another of acting? The act and the demonstration, the tedious putting forward of opinion: I do not like any of it. I do not find it nourishing or pleasant. I counsel myself: be polite, but really, I cannot bear it. Her motivations are suspect, the way she controls Lizzie is suspect. It occurs to me that she is harsh with Lizzie. *You haven't done this right, Elizabeth. You are not adequate as an assistant to my work, Elizabeth.*

Lizzie came in finally, looking battened down, holding three feathers. They were brown with white tips and lightly speckled. She held them out towards Millicent.

'Eagle feathers, I think.'

Lizzie's smock was stained and rumpled, and her hair in knots. Altogether she looked somehow undone. I wanted, very suddenly and in a rush, to protect her, but what a word – protect – how does one sister do this for another? Stars and fishing lines decorate the inside of my eyelids as I write this.

I want to steal her back. My sister knows things that I have
yet to learn; that terrible thought, of Millicent and her – yet,
Ai-Lien is here, close to me, with her nostrils defined and
breathing steadily. If I put her to sleep on my chest my dreams
might be sweeter.

I told Lizzie about Khadega. She dropped the feathers on to
the floor and glared at Millicent.

'Now we have the blood of too many dead on our hands,
Millicent. They will kill us.'

'You are talking nonsense,' Millicent said, squinting in her
own smoke, rubbing a hand through that atrocious frizz of hair.

'Why do you think they will spare us? Why don't you tell us
what is happening with this trial?'

It was a shock to hear Lizzie speak to Millicent this way. Yet
Millicent simply turned, presenting her back, like a shutter,
and said nothing.

London, Present Day

Norwood

Materialism is Evil. This was the mantra of Frieda's childhood, living in a cluster of stationary caravans with her father who made a sort-of living as the caretaker of a Blue Seas Holiday Park in Sheppey. First lesson in life: possessions are meaningless. People spend their lives chasing bigger cars, bigger houses, bigger TVs, Frieda, and where does it get them? What does it mean? The answer is nothing! Nowhere! Look at the sea, at the sky, see: we are the same as them.

Secretly, in her caravan, Frieda had prayed to an actual God rather than a manifestation of sublime energy. She prayed specifically for an actual house with carpets. She had been to other people's houses. She had witnessed drawers expressly designated for lunchtime sandwich boxes consisting of recognisable branded goods such as Club bars, Wagon Wheels and Hula Hoops. Frieda prayed to an illicit God for these things. Our Father who Art in Heaven, please may I have a normal lunch and carpets. She did not pray to her father's Guruji. She did not Sun Salute with her mother at dawn. She suspected Guruji of being responsible, somehow, for the unorthodox meals she was subjected to, the bean-sprout salads and the beetroot goulash and the ghastly celery soup.

Looking at Irene Guy's things, she thought she understood these little collections: the melancholy cluster of ceramic dogs, the hopeful stones; the rubber bands and faded envelopes. Still, though, she had found nothing that explained exactly who Irene Guy was and it seemed peculiar, given the level of paraphernalia, that there were no photographs.

It was chilly in the flat and Frieda now regretted spontaneously offering the place for Tayeb to stay. His strangeness had grown as they had come by cab with the owl cage between them on the back seat. Leaving it behind had felt like leaving a child, a curious feeling of guilt, and so she had decided to bring it; perhaps to leave it in the flat, again. It was an expensive crawl – she insisted on paying – across Battersea Bridge, with the Thames reflecting the orange–black of the city at night.

She gave him a tour of the rooms: bedroom, living room, kitchen, bathroom, and he had nodded and smiled and did not ask who the flat belonged to. She pointed to the bed.

'That is for you, until Friday.'

Now, he was in the kitchen, opening and closing cupboard doors. He seemed obsessed with the little old-fashioned pantry and its contents. Frieda felt a need to explain:

'I'm going through the things, to see if there is anything I want to keep. Everything else is being salvaged.'

'OK,' he said, still not asking. Tayeb carried the birdcage into the living room and spent some time putting it back on to its stand. The owl endured the wobbles and waves with a stoic expression.

Tayeb turned to her, 'I can prepare it some meat.'

'Wait.' Frieda pulled out of her pocket a printout about owls that she had downloaded.

REASONS NOT TO HAVE AN OWL

1. Human-imprinted owls become strongly attached to their owners and they don't like change. This makes it very hard for you to go on holiday or leave it with someone.

2. Owls have an instinct to 'kill' things. They will shred towels, knick-knacks, socks, toys.

3. You are 100% responsible for every need of a captive owl: what to perch on (to avoid infection), what food to avoid, how to care for talons and beaks.

4. Mating season involves all-night hooting or tooting and for a human-imprinted owl the noise will be directed at you. You are expected to hoot with the owl and if you don't it will hoot even louder. Mating season can be for up to 9 months.

5. Owls don't like to be cuddled and stroked, but they do like to play and can be rough!
6. There will be poo, feathers and pellets everywhere.
7. You need a consistent supply of adult animals for your owl to eat. You will need to cut them open and extract the liver, intestines and stomach, otherwise you will find yourself collecting intestines and stomach off your floor and walls. Owls have an instinct to hide their left-overs. If your owl is not cage-bound then you will find, several days on, stinking meat secreted into hiding places.

The ready-roasted chicken they had brought suddenly didn't seem alive, bloody or fresh enough. Frieda watched as Tayeb pushed parts of the chicken carcass into the cage and this act of poking meat into the owl's cage dispelled the awkward-ness between them. She began to think that she might even like being in this unfamiliar house with an unfamiliar person and that perhaps it was where she wanted to be, currently. Ostensibly looking at Irene Guy's things, she kept glancing at Tayeb. A curious moustache and the sort of physique which folds itself up, neatly, like a dog in a passenger seat. His shoes were very clean. She tried to guess his age: around forty.

In the bedroom she picked through the once-loved posses-sions, taking up from the windowsill a shiny, almost perfectly round pebble with a hole through its centre. She held it to her eye and looked through the hole. It was exactly like the one her mother had left the night she went, leaving no real explanation. Just a postcard held down by the pebble. The postcard was of a painting entitled, 'At the Dressing Table'. It was a self-portrait by a young Russian woman, brushing her hair. Frieda could not understand the significance, then or now, and years later it was a shock when she saw the painting itself, in the Tretyakov. The woman was preparing herself for a sacrifice, she had thought. The note on the back of the card was quite incoherent, saying that she had to go, to work on a cruise ship, that she would be IN TOUCH, and here is a pebble with a hole in it; it is magical. How the pebble was meant to replace her mother, she never knew.

'Look!' Tayeb's voice called from the living room. 'Look, yalla.' He was pointing at a camera on the bookshelf.

'Do you mind if I have a look at that?' Before she answered he had it, holding it up to his face, looking closely at the back of it, rubbing it, flicking the winder, and examining the lens.

'Very nice.' His face was flattened and serious. 'Actually, this is *very* nice. It is a Leica. A very early Leica. Could even be a trial model, as I don't think they went on the market until a little later in the twenties.'

Frieda watched him hold the camera up to his eye then rub his finger along its back. They both jumped as a metal square sprung up, suddenly, on the top of the camera body.

'One of the first 35mm. Interesting, is it yours?'

'I don't know,' Frieda said, 'I just . . . I just found it here yesterday.'

He lined up the viewfinder to his eye and moved the camera around the room as if running a film.

'You found it?'

Frieda didn't answer but took the camera from him and held it in her palm, feeling the weight of it.

'How old do you think it is?'

'Nineteen-thirties,' he said, without hesitating. 'No. I think, actually, twenties. One of the very first.'

'How do you know this?'

'I am a filmmaker. Or –' he coughed, 'I was a filmmaker and at home in Yemen I collected cameras, whenever I could.' They both stared at the camera for a moment.

'Could there be a film in it, do you think?' He ran his hand over the camera, looking at the back, looking all over. He found a small lever and triggered it. The back sprung open but there was nothing inside but dust.

The door to the kitchen opened and Tayeb walked in having showered, wearing a different shirt. He was spruced and had obviously had a shave. He stood in the doorway rubbing his damp hair. There was a vanity to him, she guessed, watching him stroke his thumb along his eyebrows as if to press down rogue hairs, and open his mouth to stretch the skin of his face. He folded the towel up neatly, put it on the back of one of the chairs and looked at the objects she had placed on the table. Incongruously, Frieda blushed at his presence. To hide it, she looked down at the camera, the Chinese musical toy in its glass dome and a wooden box that she had found at the bottom of a cupboard in the living room. Inside it there seemed to be some sort of printing apparatus.

'Look at this.'

'It's like a smaller version of the transportable printing press we have in Sana'a.' He pulled a chair out and sat down. 'I used to work in a printing room . . . for a while.'

He examined it for some minutes, and Frieda stood back, leaning against the kitchen sink, watching him. She thought about Sana'a. She could imagine visiting. She has always been more flexible than others in her office, more ready to jump up and fly to wherever is required, unfazed by stop-offs and stop-overs and long-hauls. The further, the more unusual, the more distant and *other* the better. For a long time now there has been nothing to hold her back, or down. No gravity or grounding in her own day-to-dayness that would encourage her to remain still, even for a short time. After spending a week or more in Sana'a she would realise that the narrative of the city would forever remain unfathomable to her but she would work hard to ignore that realisation. She could see the paper now: *UK Opportunities for Emancipation in Yemen: the New Sana'a*.

'I should try to see if I can get it working,' he said, 'I wonder if there is any ink?'

Five minutes later he had laid out various items from the machine on the table: a roller, an inking plate.

'The printing frame is missing the screen,' he said.

'Are you hungry?' Frieda pushed her glasses up her nose and looked directly at Tayeb.

'Always.'

'Let's have fish and chips. Do you fancy them?' She didn't wait for his answer. 'I know, I know, they always make you feel sick as an after-taste, but the first mouthfuls are glorious, aren't they?'

He nodded.

'There'll be somewhere still open,' she said. 'Bound to be. I'll go.'

Frieda returned with the fish and chips and a bottle of white wine. She poured each of them half a beaker-full and began to talk as she ate. She told him about the letter, about Irene Guy's death and the flat, as much as she knew.

'Hmm, what a mystery,' he said, as he gently worked at pulling off the orange batter from the cod.

'I know. At first I thought it was a mistake, but now I'm not so sure. I asked my dad; he said I should talk to my mum.'

'Have you done this?' Tayeb asked.

'It's not that easy. My mum abandoned me years ago.' She said it lightly.

'Oh.'

'Would you like a glass of water?' She got up and moved to the sink.

'No thank you.'

'I wonder who she was,' Frieda said, looking round at the belongings in the kitchen. 'An explorer, perhaps?'

'A traveller? She was quite educated, I think,' Tayeb said. 'Whoever lived here had taste in books. A surprising range. Texts on Sufism and Afghan literature. I am amazed to see a book on pre-Islamic Arabic poetry.'

'It looks as if she could speak several languages. She was obviously clever.'

'Do you think I can smoke in here?'

Frieda paused, looked around. 'I don't see why not.'

Frieda's phone on the table in front of them flashed. She took no notice. It flashed again. Then a third time.

'Someone is really trying to reach you,' he said, but she ignored him.

Frieda walked into the bedroom and pulled open the top drawer of a Victorian chest. It was crammed with papers, stencils or transcripts of some sort. Thin, waxy paper with a curious foreign lettering on them. Her pocket began to vibrate. This time she answered.

'Baby. Baby! Don't hang up.' She said nothing. 'Baby, I've got to see you.'

'No, Nathaniel.'

Oddly, she'd forgotten him. For perhaps the first day in years she hadn't thought of him at all. In the pocket of his leather jacket Nathaniel always carried two items, a blue marble and a crystal tip stolen from a chandelier he once dealt as a sideline to the bicycles. As long as the two items were together and on his person they balanced the universe and were perfectly complete. That he should believe so magnificently and wholeheartedly, like a child, in the talismanic power of objects, had shown her a glimpse of another world, a world where objects came with inherent stories, and had led her to love him.

'No, listen, seriously, this is it. I've done it. I've done it.' His voice was hysterical; crackling and vicious.

'What? What have you done?'

'I told Margaret.' Nathaniel said this in a quieter voice.

'What?' Frieda stared at the page in her hand. The paper was magically thin, like a layer of skin; the script seemed to be Arabic.

'I told her. I just said it. I said I'm not in love with you Margaret. I'm in love with Frieda Blakeman.'

There was something, a slight whine in his voice, a tone he used when waiting for praise, exactly like a child, that made her press her nails into her own palms.

'I said it exactly like that.'

She was cold; her skin seemed to shrink and tighten around her bones and it seemed to her that she was thoroughly lost again, as though she had just woken up in a scrambled, mossy, English wood, with no possible knowledge of how she'd got there or how to get out. She continued to pull out the Arabic-scripted paper from the drawer. Underneath them was a thick black notebook with a leather cover.

'What?'

'I need to see you – now!' Nathaniel shouted.

'Oh – OK.' She was stunned. Margaret. The Boys. The bloody Boys.

'Are you at home?'

'No. No. I'm . . .'

Frieda gave him the address and he hung up. She refused to think about the boys; she would not let herself think about the boys. Those blond-haired, milky-faced nightmares she had only seen in photographs, or once, getting into their Volvo, a tangle of untied shoelaces and petulant voices. Nathaniel was his own, determinable person, entirely responsible for his own fate, his own equations, she reminded herself. Her mouth was dry. She walked into the kitchen holding the notebook and one of the sheets of paper. Tayeb spun round to her, cigarette in his mouth, several parts of the machine in his hand.

'It's a mimeograph,' he said, 'a sort of early photocopier.'

'Really?'

'Yes. You could probably sell . . . or give it to a museum. It's interesting.'

'Do you think it's linked to these papers I've found?' She held one out to him, aware that her hand was shaking.

'Ah,' he said, looking at them, 'this is Arabic.'

He sat down on a chair at the table and held a page close to his eyes; he must be short-sighted, she thought. Then: the bloody boys. Tayeb took the paper and went to the mimeograph machine. He placed a piece into the screen frame.

'Yes,' he said. 'Look, it fits.' He smiled at Frieda and she was tempted to catch one of his hands. To squeeze it. She had better not drink any more wine.

'What does it say?'

He continued to squint, and then read: وذو الجناح يخبر بالأمر، 'لأن طير السماء ينقل الصوت،

'Can you translate?'

'A bird of the air shall carry the voice . . . and,' he pulled the paper away from his eyes and then back close again, 'and that with wings . . . which has wings shall tell the truth.'

185

He coughed, then read again, 'Not truth, exactly. Tell the story. Ecclesiastes, ten twenty.'

There was a noise from the letterbox being slammed up and down and a voice, 'Frieeeeeda'.

Tayeb stood up, alarmed. 'Oh God,' he said.

'It's OK,' Frieda said to Tayeb, whose eyebrows were shooting up. 'I know who it is.'

At the front door Nathaniel's top and bottom lips did not fit together properly and his chin seemed more pronounced than usual. He blinked into the light of the room, looked at Frieda, then Tayeb, the mimeograph machine, then back to Tayeb. He started to say something but the swaying overtook him and he clutched forward to get hold of the door, but it swung back and he staggered with it.

'Woah. Steady girl. Who's your friend?'

'Tayeb this is Nathaniel, Nathaniel, Tayeb. It's a long story why we are here, but please be careful because none of this stuff is mine.'

'Well, this is a cosy little scene,' Nathaniel said, sinking in a heap on an armchair as he blinked around the room. Frieda resented his arrival immediately; she had been stupid to give him the address.

'Is this a house clearance? There any good stuff here then? Good enough to flog?'

Tayeb stood up and put his hand to his chin, looking to Frieda as if for a signal. When she didn't give him one, he said,

'If you excuse me.' He tried a smile and began to walk towards the kitchen.

'Oh no, Tayeb, please don't go anywhere.' Frieda looked at him, trying to apologise with her expression. 'I'll make us all some coffee.'

She had brought supplies in a carrier bag: tea, coffee, milk and bread. She began to make coffee in the kitchen and Nathaniel came up behind her, blasting whisky smells into her neck and grabbing at her; he turned her round and tried to kiss her. She pushed him away.

'Come on, baby. I've done it!'

Frieda pushed his face away from hers and looked at him. He looked old.

'Well, what am I supposed to say? Congratulations?'

'Fuck me, Frieda, you've been on my case to do this for years.'

'That's not true.' The kettle hummed.

'Do you know what it means?' He grabbed her hand and put it up to his forehead as if acting the part of a patient with a doctor.

'I have some idea, yes.' Frieda pulled her hand away.

'Do you realise it means we can be together, now? Properly.' The kettle finished its boiling and Frieda tried to listen beyond its steam, beyond Nathaniel's drunk monotone voice, to Tayeb. He was still and quiet and probably extremely uncomfortable.

'But what about the kids? Edward? Sam?'

'Yes, I know the names of my own kids, thank you. You forgot Tom.'

She undid the coffee jar and spooned its golden seal savagely. 'You know what I mean.'

'They don't know yet. I will have to tell them, have to talk to them.' There was silence as Nathaniel looked around the kitchen.

'So, who's pretty boy in there, anyway?'

'Shush,' Frieda said, jabbing at him. 'He's a friend.'

'Right.' A cuckoo clock pinged on the wall and a desolate-looking bird on a stick poked in and out. Nathaniel wandered back into the living room and Frieda spent a moment putting cups on a tray, aware of the murmur of their voices. When she walked in Tayeb was standing awkwardly, rubbing his hands.

'We've just agreed, haven't we mate, that your friend here's going to hop it so we can have a bit of . . . space.'

Frieda glared at Nathaniel. 'What?'

'It's OK, Frieda. I'll just get my bag,' Tayeb said and he smiled at her and began to walk towards the door.

'No. Nathaniel, who do you think you are? He's not going anywhere. He's got nowhere to stay at the moment.'

'Nowhere to stay? So you're helping him? Well that's sweet. Did you pick him up from a bar?'

'Just shut up. I think you should go. We can talk tomorrow.'

'Go? Frieda, baby. This is a big night, a big time.'

Tayeb, looking anxious, leaned forward, 'Really, I will go.'

'No, Tayeb. You are staying. Tayeb is helping me sort through this stuff, helping me get to the bottom of this flat, Nathaniel. He can read the Arabic he can . . . understand. You have to go, Nathaniel. You're drunk.'

'Listen babe, tomorrow when I tell Margaret, that will be it. We'll be together.'

Frieda stared at him. 'What do you mean, tomorrow? Haven't you told her?'

Nathaniel swayed. 'That's what I mean. Yeah, I mean I've told her. Tomorrow it all unravels.' Nathaniel turned to Tayeb, swinging his arms in a wide gesture as if addressing a lecture hall. 'I bet you've got no idea what it is like to have your whole life unravel, do you?'

Tayeb smiled, 'Actually I do.' Nathaniel looked as though he wanted to hit him.

'Who are you? Have you picked little Frieda up or has she picked you up? Lost souls together?'

'Shut up Nathaniel. Please go.'

'Don't cry, baby.'

Frieda flinched away from him and Tayeb stood with his back against the wall scratching his wrists. She picked up Irene Guy's pebble and turned it from one palm to the other. The night her mother left, her father went to bed and didn't get up again for weeks. Frieda took him tea and toast each morning because they were the only things she could confidently make. Whilst he was in bed, she took a bag of flour from the cupboard and made glue by mixing the flour with water. She diligently made up bowls of the gloopy, sticky substance and then dabbed it on to the back of cut-out images from catalogues, various material items that she coveted: tin openers, duvet covers, lawn mowers, garden sheds, night lights, shoe horns, lampshades, secateurs, coasters, blinds, curtains, shelves, doorknobs, light switches, shower heads, wellington boots, ice-cube trays, lemon squeezers, fairy lights, lava lamps, toilet roll holders . . . She glued them all up on to the wall of her caravan and did not stop until the walls were entirely covered. Here it was again in this room with these two men, much like her dad refusing to get up, a feeling of dislocation; as if some part of her was left behind on a pavement.

Difficulties to Overcome: A difficulty early experienced is uncertain steering and an uncertain sense of direction.

A Lady Cyclist's Guide to Kashgar – Notes

July 12th

Her face had a tilt and the mouth was wet. More than a little wine, I suspect. Lizzie and Ai-Lien were asleep. She balanced on my kang, lit a Hatamen, saying nothing for a moment and then, the talk came: those plants, have you seen them, Eva? The sand jujube? With small, silver leaves and golden flowers. The people of Turkestan associate the scent of this flower with a story of home. When prisoners of war were carried from Kashgarian lands to Peking in the eighteenth century a beautiful Kashgarian girl was amongst them. The Emperor Chien Lung saw her and loved her. He gave her everything she could want, but she was homesick. He built a mosque for her and a

Kashgarian landscape in the grounds of the palace, and eventually a pavilion called the Homeward-Gazing Tower.

Millicent blew her smoke over me. ' "Why aren't you happy? What more could you want?" the Emperor asked her and she told him: "I miss the scent of the trees with silver leaves and golden flowers." So his men were sent to pick some trees and they were brought back to Peking and planted. For a moment she was happy as she smelled the fragrance of home but the plants would not hold, they all died.'

Was I supposed to answer? For the first time ever she offered me a Hatamen and I took one. She lit it for me and my mouth filled with the foul taste immediately.

'Are you constructing your own Homeward-Gazing Tower, Eva?'

'I don't know what you mean.'

'In your pavilion, Eva. I read what you wrote: "real conversion can only begin when secrets are surrendered".'

She has found it, then, this book. It was difficult to hold myself steady. I sat up in the kang and looked over at Lizzie, but she was still asleep. Millicent's face was full of a strange energy, as if she had too many thoughts to control, as if the thoughts she had kept shifting under her skin and jostling for room. I pulled the blanket up, calculating: she knows about Mr Hatchett.

'Why did you read my personal things?'

'Does Lizzie know your own little secret?'

'What secret?'

Millicent removed the paper from the window, the light outside was beginning.

'Your non-faith.'

I held the blanket tighter to contain myself, as lines from this book came to my head.

'You have violated me, Millicent.'

'They want the baby back you know,' she glanced at Ai-Lien, 'you don't think she's yours, do you? The natives want her back.'

'What for? They kill baby girls all the time. Why would they want her?'

Ai-Lien was in her crib in a deep sleep, lying on her front with her head to the side, her palms facing upwards in a fan at either side of her body. She was snoring, lightly. Millicent has read that I am growing to love Ai-Lien and now she wants to take her away – it's a punishment.

'Lolo told me,' she said. 'They want her back.' A surprise, to think that Lolo talks to Millicent. I rather thought he didn't. It occurred to me that Lolo is in and out of the pavilion regularly.

'Millicent, about Khadega –'

'Poor Khadega, drowning.'

'Yes, but obviously Mohammed killed her. She brought disgrace on her family, by associating with us.'

Millicent's eyes narrowed. 'She drowned.'

'Mr Steyning thinks it is dangerous for us to stay here. Is it possible we can negotiate leaving?'

'I shall defend us.' She stood up. Ai-Lien rustled, turned her head. I crouched down close, partly to see that she had moved sufficiently to breathe, partly to avoid Millicent's gaze.

'Three men dead because of us, Ai-Lien's young mother and now Khadega,' I said, directing my voice towards the baby.

'What did you say?'

'Father Don Carlo, he mentioned that three men were killed at the festival. He inferred that the distribution of our pamphlets had something to do with the rising tension.'

Her eyes were laughing at me, and at once I could not contain my anger. Without checking myself I spoke:

'There may have been no grieving for Khadega. No mourning. Lizzie walks around quickly, as if a splinter has been taken from her foot and you are unconcerned, but there is one thing I know, and that is that Khadega was killed because of us, because of you, Millicent.'

Millicent moved quickly, then, and pulled Ai-Lien out of the crib, roughly, waking her up. Poor Ai-Lien started to cry, a soft, still-asleep cry. Millicent held her in her arms as if she were a log being carried in for the fire. I jumped out of the kang, I did not like Millicent's expression.

' "As for Ephraim, their glory shall fly away like a bird, from the birth, and from the womb, and from the conception." '

She said it darkly. I did not know the quote nor what it meant. I wanted the baby back. Her crying grew louder.

'Millicent,' Lizzie said, waking up, 'whatever are you doing?'

Ai-Lien was crying fully now, Millicent was holding her too tightly, and shaking. I moved forward, ready to fight her but Millicent pushed Ai-Lien into my arms.

'Do not forget,' she said, 'that she is not your child. You have gone a-whoring from your God. You will suffer.'

She walked out of the room. I held Ai-Lien to me, kissing and singing to her to stop the crying; to stop myself from crying. The vulnerability of Ai-Lien – indeed of all babies – suddenly seemed to me to be unbearable: the defenceless bodies, the skin, breakable bones. I could simply leave her in the sun for one moment too long and she would die. Fury, on Ai-Lien's behalf, made my hands shake and I closed my eyes to control myself. Then I looked over at Lizzie.

'Millicent is your voice of authority,' I said. I was burning, hot in the ears with temper. Lizzie pushed her hair behind her ears, looking confused,

'What do you mean?'

I wanted to ask her, why Lizzie, why do you obey her? But instead, I said, 'What was she quoting?'

Lizzie thought for a moment. 'Hosea, I think.'

It took me some minutes to shush Ai-Lien. Millicent has since been away for the whole day. I do not know where she is. This afternoon I looked up Hosea. I am not familiar with it. Her quote comes from a vicious, vitriolic passage of revenge for betrayal. I write it out here:

Though they bring up their children, yet will I bereave them, that there shall not be a man left: yea, woe also to them when I depart from them! Ephraim, as I saw Tyrus, is planted in a pleasant place: but Ephraim shall bring forth his children to the murderer. Give them, O LORD: what wilt thou give? give them a miscarrying womb and dry breasts. All their wickedness is in Gilgal: for there I hated them: for the wickedness of their doings I will drive them out of mine house, I will love them no more: all their princes are revolters. Ephraim is smitten, their root is dried up, they shall bear no fruit: yea, though they bring forth, yet will I slay even the beloved fruit of their womb. My God will cast them away, because they did not hearken unto him: and they shall be wanderers among the nations.

Hosea 9.

London, Present Day

Norwood

She was in the bathroom now. Tayeb could hear her crying and he did not know whether he should do anything or not. He had fairly limited experience with women. There had been one girlfriend when he was in Sana'a, a French PhD student studying Arabic. Her name was Sandrine. She had once said to him, 'Don't you feel anything when I cry?' and he had answered her honestly, 'No'. There was something insincere about her. She was so in love with Yemen. In love with him, a real, authentic Yemeni man of her own. Through her he understood that some European women collect Arab men like stones. Because she was foreign she could move through the city with relative freedom and she was skilled at not drawing attention to herself. She lived in a European compound and would pay for a taxi to sneak him in through the barriers.

'It's called cultural tourism, the thrill you get from bringing me here,' he said to her once.

'Maybe.'

She was sexually forward, so much so that it was a shock to him, but exciting at the same time. It was part of her game to wear not very much under her abaya, her skin rubbing against the black fabric. She lay about her room, shocking him with her exposed flesh, so casual and meaningless. He gave her blankets to cover up, but she always managed to drop them and then she would cry and expect him to comfort her without explaining why she was crying and he would close his eyes to stop himself from hitting her. Rich and free as she was, she had no reason for tears.

Now, though, Tayeb was surprised at his concern for Frieda. He stood on the other side of the bathroom door, listening. His hand rested on the door handle but he was unsure whether to open it or not.

'Frieda,' he called out softly, 'can I come in?' There was a sound of a tap being run, and the door opened. Her face was temporarily rearranged by sadness and wine and her eyes were red.

'I'm very sorry about all that,' she said.

'I know what English girls need when upset: tea.'

She smiled, holding on to the door handle as though it were the greatest support to her in the universe.

Tayeb could not get used to the insipid tea in bags. He preferred his tea Yemeni style, boiling the water with sugar and cardamom before adding tea and pouring the mixture into glasses. Now, however, he made it the lazy English way that Anwar had taught him, putting a bag into each of two mugs, pouring the water on to the bags, adding a blob of milk, mixing it round to create a grey swill. He took the two mugs out to Frieda. She had stretched herself out on the sofa, and was lying on her side with her hands under her face like a small child in prayer. He placed the mugs on the low glass coffee table and sat in a chair opposite.

'I don't think I've got the strength to go home,' she said. 'I'll just stay here, tonight.'

'You have the bed, I'll have the sofa.'

'OK.' Her small, smooth face was patchy, and her hair stuck to her forehead. Within a minute she had fallen asleep on the sofa without touching her tea. She began snoring, very lightly.

Tayeb lit a cigarette and looked at her. He stood up, moving his feet softly so that he wouldn't wake her. There was a hole in one of his socks and a toe poked through. It depressed him, this toe showing. He moved around the room and it occurred to him that he could sell some of this stuff. He needed money; what he had left would run out fast. He could take that Leica camera, now, walk out the front door and get some not-bad money for it. The owl was watching him, but in a detached way, as if meditating. He could sell the owl, even. He needed to work out what to do. Where could he go? Nikolai in Eastbourne? Delilah, the Spanish chef in Southwick? He needed a job, a home, actually, he needed to disappear into the cracks of the city again like an earwig. He pictured his father at home in his chair after a meal, chewing qat. Tayeb remembered sitting cross-legged on the floor in front of him as a child, incredulous at his father's ability to be comfortable in his own skin, to relax anywhere and to sleep standing up.

His father had said, a long time ago, 'Do not do it, you will regret it. Be anything else. Not a filmmaker.' This was a man who lived by birds, who could teach Tayeb all of the bird lore he should ever wish to know, but Tayeb did not like the talons and wings, or the awkward way birds had to be held. For years, Tayeb sat smoking in a rudimentary editing suite in a back room of an office that during the day dealt with complaints and procedures around parking restrictions in Sana'a's growing city centre, whilst at night it transformed into a primitive but functional film suite. From the age of eighteen, Tayeb worked alongside Sana'a's greatest filmmaker, Salah Salem. First of all, his job was to bring him coffees and cigarettes. Then he moved on to running errands, hunts for light bulbs, wires, radios and sandwiches. After a year of this, Salah finally allowed Tayeb to sit next to him and watch him edit.

Hours of forwarding and rewinding, like two disgruntled djinns they sat in front of Salah's shots of the great wastes of qat crops and thirsty scrubland in the north. Reframe. Cut. Reposition. Tayeb learned the art of the eternal reduction so that in the end, the results were barely recognisable from the original takes. Funding for the film came from the Ministry of Information and Culture who approved of its Nationalist, anti-British, anti-Colonial message. It was sent to the censors for clearance and returned four times. Each time it came back with notes and suggestions for change and Salah threw his coffee cups into the air in rage so that the sticky coffee spattered on to heads, and chairs and equipment.

Eventually, it was finished. Salah and the censors agreed a version and then Tayeb submitted an application of his own to the Ministry. After his long apprenticeship, it was finally his turn. A code of honour amongst the filmmakers meant that when one person received the rare funding, he would employ the other filmmakers and so Tayeb's boss and mentor was suddenly his assistant. Tayeb shyly gave instructions and began to resist any editorial suggestions. Contrary to everything he had learned about cutting and editing he proceeded to put everything he could into this first film of his. There were the sleeping men on the kerbs of the marketplace and the waste of qat; Kalashnikovs against the back door and the taste of bread. The melancholy of the mothers' eyes, the smell of his sisters playing in the street. Scenes of a cracked, thirsty and ever-growing desert, the Palestinian neighbour, a broken-hearted cousin whose girlfriend was one of the New Islamic believers. He included shots of stacks of Islamic books at the book fair, the Soviet army bases, the legacy of the English, the gulls of Aden and the letters on the walls.

His film was to be long, and winding, and rich. With Salah's help he cut it down to four hours. At first he had resented Salah's powerful intrusion, but steadily, he gained confidence and his vision grew and he could see that Salah had begun to respect him. Despite himself, he caught images of birds and tried to capture the sense of freedom that comes with watching a bird in flight. Birds carry messages, he wanted to say, but it is up to us to have the skill to be able to decipher those messages. Wasn't the invention of writing inspired, in China, by the flight of cranes?

The censors considered the film anti-Yemen. It was too 'pan-Arab and regional'. He was given a list of over a thousand changes to make. They were suspicious of his portrayal of the fervently religious young girl; they wondered, was he mocking? Through it all, he was leaving his father behind. Each hour in the editing suite was an hour pushed between them, a new distance grown. Salah was supplanting his father, and, likewise, his father got a second wife, and with her had two more sons. He forgot about Tayeb. The other sons grew up fast and held the falcons' claws. They learned the bird lore. They did not creep behind the mosque to photograph the graffiti on the old city walls.

Once, Tayeb made the mistake of describing a dream to his father. He had put it in a language he thought his father would understand: I want to be like a bird, Father, and fly and see from the sky. See the way the world works and record it and shape it. His father was silent for such a long time that Tayeb thought he was asleep, but then his cheeks swelled out as he chewed his qat, a slight green froth on his lips.

'Why am I cursed with children making irrelevant choices? You need a wife. Children. Food. Home. You will see later, that without these things you are lost. Homes don't just come to you, you have to make them. Work for them. Plan your life around them.'

How desperately infuriating that he was right.

Really the only person who might possibly help Tayeb was Nikolai. The day he'd left Eastbourne, his boss, Nikolai, with his Cypriot smile said, 'You've got to go, I can't have you here any more mate. They are checking all the restaurants on this road for illegals.'

'Of course. I understand.'

This was his only choice, he realised. He would go to Eastbourne and find Nikolai.

The air in the bedroom hung low. Tayeb returned to the living room and flicked on the TV. A weather woman with a horsy face was talking about a squally wind. He did not know this word, *squally*. He found, on the main bookcase, a dictionary as heavy as a rock. The pages were thin and slippery and seemed expensive. *Characterised by brief periods of violent wind or rain. Storms or commotion.* As he flicked the pages, the words and definitions showed themselves to him, important in their exactness, their precise placing in language, their specificity. His eyes began to water as he looked at all of the words.

He was weary. He was tired of the thought of having to find somewhere else to live, of this impermanence; of pushing an unnatural language through his head; of being in rooms belonging to others. All around him people sat in their own homes, getting fat, like his father. Tayeb had never had a home. Instead, just a series of rented rooms borrowed for limited periods of time, and himself alone, scratching marks on the walls. It exhausted him, it was ageing him. Most of all, though, he was tired of himself.

The horse-faced woman on the TV finished up the weather and was replaced with jarring music for a quiz show. Tayeb picked up the Leica again, and gently held it in his palm. Just holding a camera gave him a surprising ache. Nostalgia? More like regret. It had certainly not been a conscious decision to avoid cameras over these years, not allowing himself to even touch one. The last film he shot was standing on the corner of Zobairi and Shari' Ari 'Abdul Mughni Street filming a street-scene panoramic. As he filmed, a Ford bus – those little white death-traps – had crashed into a car in front of him. The bus skidded and flipped over. The children, women and exhausted men inside were crushed like beans.

Tayeb filmed it, the whole thing, the cracked windows and a girl who no longer had an eye. A policeman shouted at him to get away and then another policeman grabbed his camera, and threw it on to the floor. He then stamped on it, to ensure that it was destroyed. Without thinking, Tayeb punched that policeman, a firework crack of his fist on the face. He put the Leica down on the table, gently. It was his eldest brother who said to him, 'You'll have to leave now.'

For the first time, Tayeb allowed himself to look properly at Frieda's body. She was thin, with short legs. Her face did not look peaceful, but neither did it look anguished. It was something else, sorrowful, perhaps. He imagined her hair would be very soft to touch. She looked a little Spanish, a little Turkish perhaps, not the mottled meat-coloured grey–white of most English girls.

After finishing his cigarette he sat down on the armchair opposite her. It let out a wheeze, like a gentle protest. He knew he would not steal the camera, or anything else. From this position it was impossible not to notice that one of Frieda's breasts fell down on to the other, creating a light groove. Released from shyness by her unconsciousness he allowed his eyes to follow the shape of her breasts like fingers and he could see that they were small. To redirect his thoughts he took his pencils out of his bag. Loneliness can be assuaged, he had discovered, by drawing. First, an imaginary grid, fix the main object into the middle of the page, then use the two-point perspective. Pull vertical, horizontal and oblique lines together quickly – don't hesitate – then vary the thickness and thinness of the lines. Look at the light: *be accurate, what do you see?* But, instead, what came out was a swirl: her hair, her cheek, her neck in a slope. He glanced up and saw the owl looking at him with the yellow bird-eyes of his father. Guiltily, he got the rose-coloured duvet from the bedroom and gently covered Frieda's body with it. He returned to the bed and lay down flat on his back, fully clothed; within a minute he was asleep.

Tayeb had made coffee for breakfast and was sitting at the kitchen table when she came in. He was drawing on a piece of paper, an intricate web around the words *kitab al-hayawan*. The smell of coffee was pleasing. Frieda pulled out a kitchen chair and sat at the table.

'I'm really sorry about last night, the crying, Nathaniel.' She looked tired. Her eyes, when she pulled her glasses off and looked at him, were red-rimmed and did not seem to open fully.

'Oh, don't be sorry. I hope you slept well.' He handed her a coffee and pushed the sugar bowl towards her. Frieda quietly put two spoonfuls of sugar in her coffee and looked at his drawing.

'You're very good,' she said.

'I won a prize at school for my calligraphy.'

'Really?'

Tayeb had taken the prize home to his father announcing his intention to be a master calligrapher. His father simply ignored him, but for some time afterwards, when in the souq, Tayeb lurked near the sign-writers' stall, crammed with its bottles and turpentine and brushes, and watched the men and their apprentices draw the calligraphy signs. Their roughness disturbed him; they were not how he imagined artists to be.

Then, deep in the souq, he'd found a calligrapher's stall. An old man, bent over his work, his room filled with copper pots of bamboo reed pens, animal skins and the jet-black gum arabic crushed and smelling of rose water.

'It's strange, isn't it?' she said.

'What?' He was smoking a cigarette and looking out of the window.

'I feel like I've known you for longer than a day.' He turned towards her, but blew the smoke in the other direction. He was thinking of the old calligrapher, the concentration on his wrinkled face as he moved the reed in quick, smooth motions with his hand resting on a piece of gazelle skin. Tayeb had thought the old man was unaware of him but he'd turned suddenly, looked at Tayeb and said, 'Scram, it is not your destiny to be a messenger.'

'Yes. I know what you mean,' he said.

'I guess we've become friends?' Her red cheeks smiled at him.

'Yes,' he said, finally looking right at her, 'although I don't think your friend from last night likes it.'

'Oh, him,' Frieda sighed. 'I don't want to see him ever again.' She drank a mouthful of Tayeb's coffee; it was strong, exactly as she liked it.

'It all became clear in my head,' she said. 'It all righted itself, and I could feel the poison draining away, so I know it's right –' She stopped herself. 'God, I sound so tawdry.'

'Listen, you can talk about anything you want. I am so grateful to you for letting me stay.'

'Have you worked out what you are going to do?'

'Not exactly.'

'Hmmm. Me neither. About this place. I suppose at the end of the week I will just tell them it was a mistake, or not say anything, just give them the keys back. They can deal with all this stuff.'

'You are going to let it all go?' He looked at her.

'Well. It's not mine, is it? I don't know what I'm doing here. I keep saying to myself, what am I doing here?'

Tayeb laughed. 'That's what I say too.'

'Maybe Irene Guy wouldn't have minded us here?'

'Maybe.'

'I'm going to the shop to get us some breakfast, and you can . . . you can . . .'

He smiled at her. 'I can decide where I am going and what I am going to do.'

'I suppose so, yes. What shall I get for the owl?' The owl was turning into a constant worry, like an errant son off travelling in South America. This concern was a taste of responsibility, she supposed. She couldn't bear it if the owl failed to thrive because of her.

'Any raw meat, I guess,' he said as she walked towards the door, and then he stopped her.

'Look,' he said, holding out a photograph.

'Is it a picture of Irene?' She took it from him.

He shrugged, 'I found it in this Bible.'

Frieda looked down at the photograph and he returned to the page in the Bible he had been looking at, then read aloud the English words: ' "The words of his mouth were smoother than butter, but war was in his heart." '

The woman in the photograph was in full seventies beatnik garb, standing in a long smock dress, her hair long, heavy and black, parted in the middle. She was in front of a caravan, squinting at the camera. Frieda turned the photograph over. On the back in pencil it said, *Golden Sands, pregnant with F, 1974.*

'Where was this?' she said.

Tayeb held up the small, black Bible. 'I was reading it . . . in the bathroom,' he said, 'and that photograph fell out.'

He continued reading the quotation from a passage, ' "His words were softer than oil, yet were they drawn swords." '

It was her mother, pregnant, standing with her long, hippie hair hanging down. Seventies hair. A seventies smock. The brown sepia tinge of time. A great big stomach and there, inside it, Frieda.

Possibilities: *There is always novelty and the possibility of excitement, for it is unusual, on a bicycle trip, that everything happens as it is expected or has been planned for.*

A Lady Cyclist's Guide to Kashgar – Notes

July 16th

I took Lolo's hand and pulled him towards the door.

'Lolo, look.' I showed him the black pillar on the horizon, swaying and moving. His leathery face dropped and the air was curious, like held breath.

'What is it?'

Lolo's long white beard seemed dirtier than usual, I noticed.

'Buran,' he said. Then Millicent came up behind us in a rather crumpled condition, shoving into me. 'He means a storm.' We rushed, then, all about, closing things up and bringing things in.

'Where's Lizzie?'

Of course, she was out. I held Ai-Lien tightly, tucking her head under my chin. Lolo smacked Rebekah on her flanks and urged her forward. The kitchen is the deepest room in the house, the only room with no exposure at all to the outside, its door opening on to the divan room rather than the courtyard. This has often been to my chagrin as I have sweltered over a boiling pan, but now we huddled in the small space, a hungry baby, a grumbling cow, a Tibetan cook, a surly missionary and me.

'I've got to go out and get her.'

'No,' Millicent said, 'you'll be killed, stay here.'

'That means Lizzie will be killed,' I shouted. 'I must go and look for her. I can go on the bicycle.'

'You will not go anywhere.' Then, as if to placate me like a child, 'I'm sure she will have found a burrow or a crevice to hide in.'

'I don't think so. She doesn't even normally wear a veil to protect herself from the dust.'

I am not a pretty crier. My blue eyes quickly look bloody, my pink eyelids swell becoming sore and unsightly and the red of my cheeks blur with the red of my hair. Millicent was shouting but I couldn't hear what she was saying because then the storm bore down upon us proper and all the air was sand. Even though we were secluded in the most sheltered room, the sand found its way in, into our eyes and hair and mouths. I crouched forward on my knees, sheltering Ai-Lien as much as I could in the well of my stomach. When I did look up I briefly managed to see Lolo clinging to Rebekah who was snorting

211

and stamping and moving backwards and forwards in distress. It continued like this for hours, not gusting, but one continual pressure. I lay curled on the floor and poor baby Ai-Lien finally gave up her sobbing and collapsed into an unhappy sleep against me. I almost slept myself, despite the noise.

Some time later there was a slackening in the air and a drop in the ferocity of the storm. Opening my eyes, I saw Millicent kneeling in prayer. Sand covered her entirely, coating her hair and face. Then the air lost its magnetic feel and it all stopped.

July 18th

Lizzie has been missing for two days. Millicent insists I stay here while Lolo and a team of men search local villages and the houses that are dotted like pearls along the edge of the dry river, but to remain here is intolerable and I make jam from the garden fruit to control my fidgets. Peach jam, plum jam, jujube jam. I sent one of Lolo's toothy, sinister little boys to the bazaar to get sugar and hence have been peeling, pitting, plucking and pulling off the furry skins, ripping out the seeds. A large vat of hissing juice and sugared fruit fat churns on the paraffin kitchener.

I know my sister better than anyone here. Who, exactly, is more likely than me to guess which tree she might have sheltered behind or which hovel in the desert she might have hoped would protect her from the storm? Oh – but my mind is a scramble and a jumble, crowded and rushed with memories of Lizzie and I as children in Saint Omer, crawling like mice through the remains of the old fortifications in the jardin public. Our old English family is filled with eccentric survivors. Our strong roots in Calais render them torn, their minds in France and their hearts in England, or, what might otherwise be termed, belonging nowhere. At any rate, we were told enough family legends to sustain the belief that we are of a race of tough-skinned curiosities. As I chop and chop at this fruity flesh I think of Captain Stanley and his cats, his ancestral shadow reaching as far back as the Norman Conquest. Of a distant relation who kidnapped a mistress of King Louis Phillipe II, demanding a ransom. Ours is a family at war with itself for more than 200 years as various members served Spanish, French and English kings and hopped left and right between Catholics and Protestants.

Why Lizzie, lost in the desert, should lead me to think of these ancients I do not know, only, when I think of us replaying family legends with black soil behind our ears it occurs to me that in our games, always, the central motif was one of survival.

No news. The way Lolo takes up Ai-Lien as if she is his own irritates me. And the food he is producing is dismal at the moment. It is all insufferable. I chop the blood-red flesh of the plums into small chunks and put the stones into a pile of tiny, bloody skulls.

Later: I caught Lolo allowing the boys to sit beneath Rebekah and take milk from her just as a calf would. The little faces sitting suckling upward, really – too much. I took him to task, but though he nodded and mumbled the insolence was there. Really. He is in Millicent's pay; it would do me good to remember that.

July 19th

They brought her back covered in pink dust. In her hand was her camera. I took her arm and led her past Millicent who looked up from her reading, thinning her lips as if she intended to say something, but then was silent and looked away. In the kang room Lizzie simply looked down at the floor like a guilty child. I tried to prise the camera off her but she wouldn't let go.

'I must develop the film.'

'Of course, darling,' I held her arm, 'but first you need to get clean, and eat, and sleep.'

I began to remove her clothing, all dusty and damp, and bits of wood and stones fell on to the floor.

'Have you had a terrible time? Where did you shelter?' She closed her eyes, said nothing.

'Lizzie, are you in pain?' She put her hand to her ear and tipped her head to one side as if draining out water. Then Lolo coughed outside the kang-room door, from which I understood that the bath water was ready. I covered Lizzie with a long robe.

'Come in.' Lolo slopped the water into the galvanised bucket we use as a cleaning tub – not that one could bathe in it, one can simply slurp water all over, it provides a pitiful dowsing. Steam curled up and displaced across the room like smoke. I thanked him. He left smiling, nodding at Lizzie.

'Gosling, my baby oiseau,' I whispered. 'I will help you to clean then you must get some sleep, take your medicine and you will soon be much recovered.'

My sister stood listless and submissive in her robe as I placed her camera on top of one of Millicent's trunks, returned and handed her the cloth. She dipped the cloth into the hot water and began to rub her face.

'Did you shelter?'

'No – I didn't . . . I wanted to photograph inside the cyclone. Did you see the pillar?'

'I did.'

'I stood next to a tree, and then I had an idea. There was some rope near a fence, used for tying down the gates, and as I saw the pillar come towards me I took the rope and tied myself to one of the low branches.'

'I am speechless.'

'I tied myself to a branch so that as the storm came upon the tree I should not be flung about but should be able to control my camera and capture the photographs of the inside of the storm.'

'Oh, Lizzie,' I said, looking at her as she held the cloth up so that the water dripped into the bucket, 'why?'

'I thought, if Khadega has died, I should at least pay homage to her.'

'But how is photographing the inside of the storm homage to her?'

'I was looking for . . . a centre, for her.'

She wasn't making sense. This is the element that always frustrates me about Lizzie: her perversity. I wanted to scold and shout, 'But you disliked Khadega', but I stopped myself; what good would it do? It seems to me that Khadega is a presence on our consciences, but not Millicent's. The room felt constrained, airless.

'Where is your medicine?' I stood up, looking around the kang room.

'There is none.' Her head looked large on top of the bright thinness of her body.

'Pardon?'

'I destroyed it. It stops me.'

'It stops you in what way?' Annoyed, I took the cloth from her, turned her around and removed her kimono. Water fell in streams along her narrow back but she barely seemed to notice.

'It stops you in what way, Lizzie-gosling?'

'The medicine stops me talking to God. Without it, I can talk to Him directly.'

'He speaks to you directly?'

'Yes,' she said, stretching her neck, 'with Millicent, in prayer.'

'What does He say?'

'We have questions for Him. Sometimes they are answered directly, and sometimes He has other words, other signs.'

'Millicent is usually there?'

'Yes. She agrees, without the medicine the communication is clearer. She has always assisted me in reaching Him. Well, until recently, or I could say, until Khadega.'

I held my breath as the water rained on her pale skin. I trickled it on to her hair and watched the blonde strands matt and knot as they turned wet.

'But Lizzie, you know what happens if you don't take the medicine.'

She shifted and looked at me over her shoulder, 'I knew you wouldn't understand, leave me.' She took the cloth. 'I can finish this alone.'

I don't know what to say to my sister. That sense we once had that the world was ours to take and reduce and make of it what we would is lost. My scatterbrained, robust sister of old is evaporating in front of me and I am witless, incapable of holding on to her.

Listen (to whom do I speak? Myself, I suppose), I have just understood the recurring dream of a lighthouse in the desert. It is Father's story, but also mine. In our bed-time tales he told me that I began in Algiers; that I was born during a sandstorm the size of Spain, big enough to cover a town like a curse. Father, a diplomat, said that after I was born he went out to look for a French doctor who lived in the Jewish quarter, shielding himself from the sand with a turban wrapped twice around his head. He feared that Mother would die, or I would, or both. He ran along spiral stone stairways of the Mellah district, hardly wide enough for a single person and searched amongst numerous subterranean rooms, becoming quickly lost. It was so hot that even the French officials in the Arab Bureau slept through the afternoons with their dusty boots up on the desks; meanwhile smugglers and tradesmen crept under the window, pockets and bags bulging with kif and skins and knives and gold. By the time he returned with a medicine man my mother was unconscious and it was two whole days before she would look at him with recognition. Her eyes became right finally, just as soon as the sandstorm abated and the native midwife who had kept me alive handed me to her, wrapped in a sheet.

After that he wanted to leave Algiers. It took weeks of negotiation, but he finally got the permission to relocate to our new home, Le Phare du Cap Bougarou. The Lighthouse of Bougarou. My cot was next to the window, the air was sea-fresh. My new ears were open to the sad swish of the Mediterranean sea, shifting itself around, as if perpetually searching for a more comfortable position. Every night the lamp-light of the lighthouse reached the ships and in the morning Father held me up against the pane of our watchtower, waving my arm over at unhappy Europe, whose glory was already fading on the other side of the sea. Living in that lighthouse may have brought Father some rare comfort.

He loved lighthouses. He told us that as a young boy, each week his English governess would walk him to the market square in Calais where they would stand and admire the new lighthouse which had replaced the ancient watchtower.

How impressive it must have looked, presiding over the busy market, over the hauling of the fishermen's boats, sending its signals across the channel as if looking for something lost.

Lizzie was born in Calais, and another baby who died. Later, in Saint Omer, Nora came. Later, in Geneva, I would lie on my back in the neat Swiss park, listening to chaffinches and sparrows, belonging not quite here, nor there; lying next to my friend, Vera, who smoked cigarettes and spoke of Bolshevism and Anarchism and Libertarianism, our bicycles laid out next to us, the pedals digging into the green grass. Then, 'home', to an England that did not want us. Now, all this distance passed, these long, vast train and sea journeys and I find I cannot see her properly. Lizzie is like light, she is like water.

July 25th

Today Lolo informed me that Rebekah has stopped producing milk. This is connected I am sure to the milk-thieving children.

'But why, Lolo?'

'I don't know, Memsahib.'

'Please don't call me Sahib, Lolo.'

Lolo has changed; he no longer smiles at me, he does not even pretend to take my orders, though he takes care of Ai-Lien. He moves around the gardens and rooms with a heavy presence and the language gulf between us makes a casual enquiry impossible. I cannot begin to articulate the questions I want to ask him in our crude jumble-language. Frustrated, I followed him and pointed at the cow who stood, despondent-looking and sad.

'Where's the calf?'

He shrugged, picking at his teeth and I felt sure that he knows more than he is saying. I put my hand on his elbow and looked directly at him.

'What? Lolo, what?'

Finally, his demeanour shifted. 'Grey Lady bad. Kill Mohammed daughter Khadega.'

'Lolo, I don't understand, come.' I took him to find Lizzie, with her clever tongue. She was in the kitchen drinking water.

'Lizzie, please ask Lolo to find out what is happening here.'

After several minutes of broken, animated chatting and arm waving, she turned to me.

'He thinks, as do all of these errand boys and the neighbours and villagers, apparently, that the ghost of Khadega has put a curse on us as revenge for her murder and that is why Rebekah has lost the calf and why her milk has dried up.'

I stared at my sister nonplussed, but she simply shrugged and turned back to her drink, as if what she had just said was mundane and normal. Ai-Lien began to cry. I went to pick her up, and to find Millicent.

As usual, Millicent was with Father Don Carlo and they were heartily engaged in the consumption of his wine. They were crowing over their mimeograph machine and for some time I let them explain to me its workings and the implications of what they could now achieve.

'Mr Steyning mentioned that he has something similar, am I right?'

'Indeed,' said Millicent, 'Steyning does have a press, a little larger than this one.'

Father Don Carlo took out a fountain pen, wiped off its leaking ink, and began to write in Arabic script. I took the translucent page from him. For a shaky, ancient man his hand is remarkably steady and his calligraphy surprisingly skilful. I said as much and he smiled broadly in response. I held it for Lizzie to see.

'I studied both Arabic calligraphy and Chinese,' he said.

'I am impressed, Father. You are a man of great knowledge. Millicent,' I said, 'would you mind if we talked to you about something?'

She looked up. 'Of course not,' she pushed the lever of the machine up, running her finger along it, then pushing it down again.

'It's about Khadega's death.' Millicent looked up and glanced at Father Don Carlo, and moved her head, slightly,

'I do hope you don't mind me interrupting you, Father?'

'Not at all, not at all,' his red-skinned hands patted his cadaverous cheek.

'I think that people in the town will see us as responsible for her death, and for causing trouble more generally.'

'Not at all,' Millicent looked dismissive, 'she drowned. We weren't anywhere near her. Besides, not many people really knew of our association with her.'

'Rebekah has stopped providing milk and they all think that she has put a curse on us.'

They both stared at me for a moment, gaping like calves themselves and then Father Don Carlo sat forward, and slippery lipped said, 'Don't listen to the soothsayers of the East, Eva.'

I agitated my feet on the floor and shifted Ai-Lien up on to my shoulder. Millicent stood next to the priest as if she were his helper and said:

'Well, something must be done about the milk situation. For Ai-Lien's sake, if not our own.'

The curious thing about the priest is that he never quite looks at one directly. The eyes meet, then flicker down and sideways, unless there is wine and food about and then out comes a flurry of greed, champing and taking and not thinking about whom else might need to eat. I don't like greed, particularly when it is accompanied by eyes that won't rest still and reasonable whilst in conversation.

'I do not know, Millicent, if Lizzie has ever actually told you this, and I tell you now in greatest confidence because I am concerned for her.'

The priest made busy work of examining his papers as I spoke.

'But Lizzie has an illness. She has had it all her life. A doctor in Geneva finally diagnosed it, much to my mother's relief. It can be controlled, with a ketogenic diet and her medicine. It is a form of epilepsy. She is shy and does not usually let anyone know.'

Millicent pushed her eye-glasses up her nose impatiently. 'Of course I know of it, Elizabeth has spoken of it often.'

'Oh. Good,' I coughed. 'It is manageable; it is greatly helped if she eats foods rich in cream and butter, and avoids stressful situations. I am worried that here . . .'

Father Don Carlo rubbed his beard, 'Ah, Lizzie, divine Lizzie, her soul is delicate. *Ella cammina con gli angeli.*'

There was silence, I continued, 'Lizzie hasn't been taking her medicine.'

Millicent pushed the lever of the machine down, quickly, so that it made a vicious sluicing noise, her nose shining. She glanced down at Father Don Carlo's delicate script.

'The paths of their way turn aside, they go nowhere and perish.'

'Yes, yes,' responded Father as if they had been in the middle of a theological discourse.

'Job,' he turned to me, 'the directions we take, the pathways are sometimes mysterious. In Samuel: "you enlarged my path under me; so my feet did not slip." '

I was determined not to be derailed.

'Were you aware, Millicent, that Lizzie has barely been eating? That she is not taking the medicine? Are you aware of the consequences?'

Millicent looked up, cross and out of balance, like a half-trodden-on beetle.

'Most of us are mortal. Most of us walk this earth with anchored feet that hold us down, narrow and blind and stumbling. That is you and I, Evangeline,' she continued, 'but some of us walk with angel feet, some of us can fly like birds.'

Father Don Carlo's teeth were stained berry-red so that his smile looked painful. He watched us both carefully.

Millicent carried on, 'Some of us who talk in the manner of birds have the capacity to talk to God. Modern medicines do not always understand this and can interfere.'

Millicent turned to Father Don Carlo, pointing at the transcripts and I understood that I was being dismissed. As I walked out, Millicent said:

'I am surprised at you believing the evil superstitions of the natives.'

So: I am at a loss. I think of poor Mother. I have hunted about the kang room for the medicine package but nothing is there; I don't know if it truly has been destroyed or not. Meanwhile, we have no milk, only ghosts. Millicent and the priest plan an entire day of distributing pamphlets tomorrow. They intend to hand them to people who gather at the Id Kah Mosque.

London, Present Day

Norwood

A photograph can do this, unpick at time.

In Irene Guy's kitchen was a back door that neither of them had thought to look out of previously. The key was in the lock and Frieda discovered that it opened up on to a tight, contained courtyard that had clearly been tended with care. Buckets were filled with flowers, there was a Victorian park bench and a proliferation of ivy encouraged around the walls. A medium-sized maple Acer tree stood in a sun-baked terracotta pot and several rose bushes were coaxed upward by means of bamboo sticks as support. The ivy, and the pieces of slate and rocks on the floor which were interspersed with natural-growing moss, gave the sense of a trapped piece of wilderness, or a secret grove. Still holding the photograph, Frieda breathed in the sticky city air, and felt slight dots of hesitant rain on her hand.

Looking again at the picture she almost physically fell back-wards: Family photographs are slips of time, trap-doors to the past, and she wasn't prepared for confronting her mother. Not here. Despite desperately trying not to, she was falling, all the way back to the Isle of Sheppey where the seaweed looks like dead hair and dogfish are tangled up in fishing nets, back to Frieda at fourteen: her father, leaning over the plastic table so that his shirt cuff dips into spilled coffee, saying, 'Happy fourteenth'. Two plates of chips, veggie sausages and beans slammed on to the table by a girl with electric-blue mascara. Breakfast in the supermarket is a tradition, *so glam*, and the breakfasting shoppers surrounding them, each marooned on plastic-table-islands with their individual food trays. Poor Arthur left in the car, in the lonely car park and Frieda know-ing without looking that his wet, black nose will be pressed up against the window in the pose of heartbreak.

'It always rains on your birthday.'

Frieda doesn't answer because she is thinking about her mother, thinking that this is what lost or displaced mothers do, they hang over your birthday, making it rain, making you want to cry. The café is full of tired old people and she can hear all the conversations separately but also at once, a morning orchestra: this tea is cold. Such a windy day. What a horrible colour. Her Karen's got the kids up at the dad's. I do hate the wind.

Frieda at seven: her favourite book is *In the Beginning –
Creation Myths from Around the World*. Although this was
not quite what she had asked for, in fact, she'd specifically
requested the Bible (and not a children's annotated version)
but her mother had given her the *Creation Myths* instead,
saying something like this way you can read all of them and if
you still want the Bible rather than the Up-Ani-Shads then,
well, we'd better concede.

The book was beautiful. Indians believe in the mountain lion,
Nigerians in the stream of life. There was an old spider, a Viking
god and the Seven Days of Creation, under-earth people from
Australia, the dance of life, the Japanese twins. From this Frieda
learned that she began somewhere. She was created and begun,
named Frieda because her mother thought it meant freedom.
Her mother in the caravan kitchen spooning up the green lentils
saying, 'Well I can't be free, so you may as well be'. Slop. Slop.
Slop. But as Frieda knows, you only have to take the time to look
in a book to find out that Frieda means peaceful, not freedom. But
where is the peace? She should've been more careful with names.

Frieda at seven: sitting in the garden, next to the swing.
From the house the intermittent sound of a low, soft
ommmmm. It was called the Knowledge, with a capital K, and
if you ate enough seeds, went to enough satsangs, touched the
Margarine's hand and grew your hair, you got it, according
to Bill the Arthurian specialist who was living in a caravan
along with his wife Stacey. They had been learning about the
Knowledge for much longer than Frieda's mother and father.
Bill had even met the Margarine twice.

'Maharaji, Frie', not margarine. Guru Ma-ha-rah-ji.'

There was a picture of the Guru in the kitchen: black hair, Indian, young. He didn't look like God, the Devil, or Krishna, none of those. He looked normal, like Raj from the shop. Stacey, whose hair reached her arse when she let it down, said, 'When you've touched the Margarine's hand, then you get the techniques, and when you've got these, you become God.' But then Stacey was what Frieda's father calls a Fantasist and so difficult to believe. Stacey didn't stay too long; she went to Australia to learn about wine and the agricultural industries, but Bill stayed and Frieda's mother said the rent would put us right. Him and his wife were on a sab-bat-i-cal.

'Go and do something, Frieda, we need quiet.'

Frieda at fourteen again: she is moving the HP sauce bottle in front of her father as he lights a cigarette. He sucks on it, then sends the smoke out away from her, towards the other people.

'It's lovely out there, isn't it?' Frieda says, for something to say. Sarcasm's not nice. When he smiles he looks like he is in the process of injuring himself.

'I'm sorry I haven't sorted anything better out for your birthday.'

'That's OK.' Sometimes, he still looks invincible. Other times, he seems folded up on himself or as if he's been turned inside out.

'Frieda . . .'

Oh oh. She blanks him out, turns teenage on him again, like it's a script she's following. She doesn't want to hear any

228

of it, these confessions. She closes her ears to his, 'I made it happen' and all this looking to her for validation. Especially as, since Christmas of this year, he has taken to coming into Frieda's room in the night, drunk, swaying everywhere, knocking over her books, leaning on and breaking her papier-mâché globe of the world and on one occasion (that she doesn't think he can remember) opening his trousers at the end of the bed and pissing: a long stream of his urine reaching as far as her writing desk, hitting the metallic bin on the floor. She doesn't want to hear again, 'Frieda, forgive me for making your mother leave,' like she is a judge who can release him or redeem him.

Every seven years we get new cells. There is a poem about it but she can't remember who by. This means that every seven years we are a new person and seven-year-old Frieda has gone. One night, when that long-gone seven-year-old Frieda was down, deep under the covers, the long unfurling sound of her father's voice came up through the floorboards, and lifted her from a dream in which she had been cornered into a section of the garden and told to stay there for ever. His voice was angry. There was Bill the American Arthurian specialist. They were all involved.

Frieda's mother shouted, 'Why do you care so much, I thought you were all for free love, anyway?'

Her father shouted back, 'It would have been decent to let me know.'

The voices began to mix with the sound of the moving trees outside in the wind so that it all became one noise, like a sound-kaleidoscope. Frieda rolled up against the wall and fell asleep as if she and the wall together made one person. The next day, all the arguing noises seemed to have disappeared.

There are certain things Frieda can remember about her mother if she chooses to. Here she is walking over the rock-pool stones towards her, the sun shining into her black hair, making it brown-red, shouting, 'Hello little bookworm'. Or in the kitchen singing, 'Today I am making a tangy meringuey soupey de la roupey. Want some?' Or walking behind her on the beach, fitting her own small foot into hers in the sand: one flat foot, followed by one flat foot. Keep the balance, a perfect line. Frieda pressing her feet down harder. I am here. I am here. Toes, arches, heels, pushing down into the cold sand, but always an immediate closing over, no trace. Sandwiches. It was alfalfa and tofu sandwiches for lunch. Al.fal.fa. strog.a.nov. All the way back to her mother's sandwiches, alfalfa and honey, nutmeg and cottage cheese. Holding a hand.

The creak of the door and it is Tayeb, behind her. For a moment, Frieda does not know who he is: he's an Arab man and he is looking at her, eyes large and brown and concentrating on her, then a frown on his face. Where is she? She is entirely disconnected now, the balloon string has finally been cut, and up she goes.

'Ah, I did not realise this was here,' he said.

'I know,' Frieda answered. 'It looks as though she really looked after it.'

He nodded, agreeing, and leaned over to smell the yellow roses.

Watch and Cyclometer: In coasting, sit well in the saddle, letting that take the whole weight, and do not push too hard with the feet on the coasters.

A Lady Cyclist's Guide to Kashgar – Notes

July 24th

Something has happened to Elizabeth. She is in the kang room and Millicent won't let me in, claiming she is infectious. Lolo described it like this:

'She was all crazeee, Memsahib, she was in the garden and she did this . . .' He put his hands to his head and began to spin around like a madman.

'What do you mean, Lolo? What was she doing?' He did it again, hands gripping his own head, spinning like a dervish and I understood that she has had one of her fits. I pushed him and ran up to Millicent at prayer in the study room.

'Millicent,' I said, daring to interrupt her prayer. Her head turned quickly with the shock of the interruption but when she looked at me it was with calm eyes.

'Evangeline, your sister is infected, you must not go in.'

'It is not an infection, Millicent. There are certain things we need to do. We must get a doctor from Urumtsi, and most importantly, she must have her medicine. What have you done with the package?'

Millicent sighed, 'She is infectious and must be quarantined. Eva, leave it to me, you will be most helpful by continuing to run the household.'

'But Millicent, she is my sister. I must see her.'

'No –'

'I insist. If she is really ill, I must inform our mother.'

'No.'

Millicent rose slowly, with creaking knees, so that she was facing me. I made a move to walk past her, towards the kang room, but as I did she took my wrist with her thin, surprisingly strong hand. Her grip was very tight. Then, a peculiar thing. She slackened her hold, slightly, and ran her thumb slowly along the purple trace of one of my veins and it was as though she had drugged me. I was still, and stood pathetic, looking at her. Then I heard Lizzie call. I pulled my wrist away from her and was about to run into the kang room when Millicent pushed her face close up against mine. Her eye-glasses were so dirty that it must have been almost impossible for her to actually see through them. I tried to lean back, away from her until I felt wetness: her saliva on my face.

'Millicent. You –' Her mouth was tight, her white-edged lips had thinned so much that they almost disappeared.

'Elizabeth is consumed with a fever, Satan himself has her. You are not to touch her.' She walked away.

The door is locked. I did not realise there were even keys to each room, but it seems there are. I have seen Millicent take water in, but no food. I could push through the paper windows, but they are too small for me to crawl in and I cannot pass anything through because Millicent hovers about the room constantly. I asked Lolo but he has not been asked to prepare anything for her.

July 25th

I cycled across Kashgar to the postal exchange centre in the Chinese section of town and without Millicent knowing I have sent Mr Steyning a telegram asking for help.

July 28th

I lay Ai-Lien on the floor in the divan room and began to tend to her, looking round for Lolo to bring us drinks.

'You won't find him.' Millicent was standing behind us, her eye-glasses still filthy. Her Chinese smock had several small tears in it which she had not yet repaired.

'Where is he?' It occurred to me that the errand boys were missing too.

'They've all gone.' Millicent looked down at me, her eyes small, as if reduced to red sores behind her eye-glasses.

'I had a message from Father Don Carlo,' she said. 'He is arbitrating on our behalf. The Magistrates' Court is demanding money now. They say otherwise the sentence at the trial will be death.'

'Death?'

'Yes, mine. Possibly yours, too.' The afternoon light was strange, it held her skin to ransom, bringing out the years in her and walking them to the surface.

'Can we telegram for some money?'

'The Mission have declined to offer, but Mr Steyning was going to help. I have heard nothing from him.'

I did not tell her of my recent telegram to him, paid for with the last remains of my own money.

'I instructed Father Don to offer them the baby. A gift back to them to do what they will with. I will defend myself in the court.' She looked at Ai-Lien, who was lying, naked, legs cycling in the air. Catching Ai-Lien's foot and squeezing it, I concentrated on keeping my face as unreadable as possible.

'Come with me.' Her eyes rolled, pushing out against the edges of themselves and she walked towards the entrance to the courtyard. I gathered Ai-Lien up and followed her, letting Ai-Lien hold on with the surprisingly tight grip that babies have, an instinct to stop them from being left behind.

The floor of the courtyard flickered with shadows from the fig tree and roses and the bright afternoon sun fought for space to burn. Next to the fountain I was surprised to see that Millicent had placed Ai-Lien's crib on the floor and that she had tied red ribbons on it.

'They want her,' she said, nodding towards the crib. This was clearly some prearranged demonstration.

'Who?'

'The natives, out there. We need to offer her back.'

'They don't care about Ai-Lien,' I said. 'It's the pamphlets you have been distributing that are causing the trouble, nothing to do with the baby.'

It was clear from her face – its awkwardness – and the awful vein on her neck, that she was more than a little off-balance, and not from the wine this time.

I must be careful. Lizzie and I are vulnerable; as is the baby. It is as if the thinnest areas of our skin is exposed, our wrists and the backs of our necks and our temples, all for her to cut.

'There was an effigy of me,' she said. 'I saw it, hanging in the main street.'

'How did you know it was you?'

'The hair, it was grey. Made out of goat hair I suspect. It was hanging from a piece of string on the tamarisk tree just outside the gate. I was meant to find it.'

'Ridiculous, Millicent. You're imagining it, why would they do that?'

Millicent stared up at the sky and blew out her smoke which did not disperse. I pulled Ai-Lien close, tucking her against me and, saying nothing, picked up the crib with its red ribbon decoration and brought it back into the kang room.

She still won't let me near Lizzie. I must remain calm and wait for a return telegram from Mr Steyning. I do not know what to do. I will not put Ai-Lien down.

London, Present Day

Norwood

She sat on a kitchen chair with the light splashed out at her feet, her face in shadow. Tayeb was surprised at the intensity with which he had a desire to feed her, and not fish and chips. Laid out on the kitchen table were small piles of paper, the Bible he had found, two books, the photograph and a thick black notebook that she was reading. He hesitated at the door. He had tried to be useful by putting all of the magazines and old newspapers in one big pile in the living room, pulling out items that looked interesting or putting into a black bin liner those that were obviously rubbish.

She was reading that notebook with total concentration. He could see the bone of her skull beneath her skin and the corner of her jaw. She had black marks under her eyes. As far as he was concerned, she was too thin. He came into the kitchen but she didn't look up. Without saying anything, he began to investigate the cooking possibilities. In the cupboards there were spice jars, peppercorns, caraway, cardamom, turmeric, even saffron. Cooking would calm him, help with the flash of itches across his back and his arms. Whilst cooking, he could think and work out a plan.

'Shall I cook?' he said, twisting at his moustache.

She looked up at him from her notebook, 'You want to?'

He nodded. It was eleven in the morning. He wasn't hungry, but he wanted to make something luxurious to taste, something with depth. Tayeb ran his finger along the spices. Yes. There was enough here to make something good. He would feed her the most delicious thing he could think of, 'akwa, if he could remember how to do it.

'Is there a butcher round here?' His voice emerged with too much force for the quiet air in this strange flat, but she did not seem particularly affected by it. She was difficult to read and he began to wonder whether she wanted him to leave, whether she might be frustrated by his presence, but probably, she was thinking about the drunken man from last night. Her boyfriend, he supposed. But then she seemed, in fact, mostly concerned with the notebook.

'I'm sure there must be.' She smiled at him.

It was good to have a purpose. There was a long queue of unhappy-looking people at a bus stop, shuffling to keep out of the rain. Most of the shops along the parade were boarded

238

up, and at first he could only see a Seven-Eleven which was unlikely to sell what he needed. But then as he walked further on in the rain he saw a red sign, HIGH CLASS FAMILY BUTCHERS.

They had it, oxtail. They even chopped it for him, and not too expensive either. He cooked as Frieda read, occasionally stopping to make tea, or to smoke a cigarette. He extracted a casserole dish from a cupboard. He brought the oxtail to a boil. He added the spices, then the tomatoes and onion. He put a lid on and he left it.

'Three hours,' he said.

'Wow. That's a lot of simmering.'

'Oh, that's just the first stage.'

'Really?'

'Yes, then I take the lid off and it has to cook for another five, maybe six hours.'

Tayeb looked at the cuckoo clock. 'It'll be done by nine.'

The smell of cooking meat brought the flat to life. It was as if by opening her spice jars and by heating up her pans, Tayeb had voodoo-summoned the old lady back to life. He felt her around him, thought he could sense her approval.

It was good to have his hands working. There was perfectly fine rice in the cupboard that he would serve with the meat. Being in a kitchen, or, more precisely, cooking for someone else rather than just himself, brought to his mind the taste of hurs and tawa, and he found himself wanting these childhood breads.

Frieda looked up, sniffed the air and smiled. 'This is unbelievable.' She waved the thick black notebook at him.

'What are you reading?'

Frieda stretched her back in the chair, held the notebook about five inches from her face, flicked to the front and read out: 'A Lady Cyclist's Guide to Kashgar – Notes. It's someone's journal, or diary,' she said, 'a missionary.'

'Oh? The Irene lady?'

'No, it couldn't be her, the dates are 1923 . . . She couldn't have been old enough to write this diary then.'

She read out sections as he cooked:

I am beginning to understand the rhythm of this inn. We are all three of us, Millicent, Lizzie and I – well four, if I count the baby – sleeping together in one room with the kangs lined in a row like coffins.

He was enormously hungry by the time the food was ready, late in the evening, and to watch her eat it was a pleasure. Despite her thinness and seeming lack of interest in food, she ate with lush delight. Tayeb could see her enjoying the saturated flavour of the meat.

'Tayeb,' she said, as they sat opposite each other at the kitchen table, 'this is the most delicious meal I have ever had.'

Oh, he was happy, but he hid it. 'I am sure it is not.'

She pushed her hair back behind her ears and her glasses up her nose. 'It is! I tell you. The juice of this stew is divine.'

He couldn't stop himself from grinning.

'That photograph you found.' She looked at him.

'Hmm.'

'It's my mother.'

Tayeb nodded, still simmering himself in her praise of his cooking. But then he frowned, 'Why would a photograph of your mother be here?'

'That is exactly what I've been trying to work out.'

Tayeb felt a flicker of heartburn, but dismissed it. 'You say you don't know Irene Guy?'

'No. Never heard of her.'

'But there must be some connection.'

She was concentrating. He was not sure if this was the right time, but he decided he should talk about what he intended to do in case she might think that he was . . . after something; a hustler.

'I have worked out what I am going to do.'

'Oh, really?' She leaned back in her chair.

'Well. Just immediately, I have no idea in the long term, you know.'

She smiled. 'I can imagine.'

'I'm going to find my old employer in Eastbourne, he will help me.'

'Eastbourne.' She repeated. She moved her hand towards his cigarette packet. 'May I?'

'Of course.'

She looked older, as soon as she smoked. Watching her lips move around the cigarette he saw the ghost of nights full of drink, conversation and cigarettes. He could see a decade

241

of talking and drinking in the faint lines around her lips and although it made her look a little ragged and less contained when she smoked, he quite liked it. He liked that the smoke from her mouth mingled with his.

'I think I need to go and find my mum,' she said. 'She's in Sussex on a commune or something.'

He nodded. There was something about her dark, contained stillness that made him conscious that they operated in parallel spaces. It seemed impossible to cross into her space. Perhaps because of the strangeness of being here, together, in this flat, and both of them a little lost, it was as if they were each talking to themselves, really. Then she sat up straight and smiled at him.

'We'll go together. You need to go to Eastbourne, I need to find my mother in Sussex. I'll borrow a friend's car and drive us.' She blew smoke into the air, as if to direct it away from Tayeb, but it didn't work, some of it crossed his face like a whisper.

'What about this place?' he said.

'I feel like a trespasser. I'm not supposed to be here.' They both looked at the camera. 'But I am going to take some things.'

'Oh?'

They made a pile on the table: the mimeograph machine in its wooden case, the dome toy, the notebook, Bible, camera, some books that Frieda had found all piled together and tied with a piece of fabric that seemed to be a kind of embroidered flat-weave.

'We'll take these books,' Frieda said, 'and the notebook and the photograph, of course.'

She did not tell him how curious she was, about the ink in the notebook. They looked at each other.

'Difficult to know if this is stealing,' Frieda said. 'It feels odd.'

'I don't think so. It is almost as if these things are waiting here, for you to rescue them, take them.'

That seemed exactly right. It was as if each item left in this flat sheltered its own imprint of memories but was left listless and doomed without its curator, Irene Guy. If Frieda were to take and resuscitate them, the embedded memories might then be released. It was as if everything in here might be a witness, watching them navigate the furniture of someone else's life. She turned to say this, but Tayeb had drifted off and seemed to be engaged in a private conversation with the owl.

Solving a Problem: *When choosing a wheel, you should know what you want and why you want it.*

A Lady Cyclist's Guide to Kashgar – Notes

August 1st

They came for her and this is how I discovered the names the natives have for us. Millicent is the Grey Lady, I am the Red Lady and Lizzie is the White Lady. I know, because at dawn, in a manner of speaking, my prayers were answered with a kerfuffle at the gate, two Chinamen shouting loudly:

'Grey Lady, Grey Lady!'

They hustled through the gate and a dog on the track began to bark. Millicent appeared, wearing her faded cotton nightgown, her hair on its ends around her head. I ran out. A Chinaman came forward and pointed at Millicent.

'Millicent, what's happening?'

'I'm being summoned, presumably to the General,' she said, and then began to cough, a wracking cough that threatened to bring up blood.

'Do let her sit down,' I said, but both men stood aggressively. They talked in a fast, thick Chinese to Millicent directly. I could not understand what they were saying. She sighed, then turned to me.

'I have to go with them.'

'Don't, don't take her.' They pushed her unnecessarily, as she was walking with them, then each of them gave her another harsh shunt forward, more vicious than before.

'Don't hurt her.'

They forced her to walk fast towards the gate. Millicent has disturbed me of late, but I was suddenly terrified of them taking her away. I stood redundant, an imbecile, paralysed.

'What should I do, Millicent?'

As they reached the gate her eye-glasses fell off and the guard to her left trod on them, cracking the glass. She turned to me, blinking. 'I will get a message to you as soon as I can,' she said. She threw the clutch of door keys over to me and leaned down for her eye-glasses, but the men moved her, roughly, through the gate.

I picked up the keys and gestured to the glasses. 'Please,' I said, 'she is very blind – do take them.' They ignored me. I gathered up the broken frames.

'Millicent,' I called. She twisted and looked round, but her face oddly blank. She could see nothing I realised. A lizard

245

flickered past my foot, and I stood at the gate with the eye-glasses in my hand, thinking now everyone had gone.

Lizzie lay on the kang under one of the thick, silk-covered wadded quilts that we carry for the winter months. Each papered window was covered with a kashgari silk scarf so that the room had an underground feeling, with light filtering through patches of clashing colours.

'Lizzie, Millicent wouldn't let me near you. She's been taken away. Lolo's gone.' I bent over to look at her, talking too fast. My poor sister's lips were dry, cracked, she had the beginning of a sore in the corner of her mouth and her skin was pallid. I went to the kitchen to get her water.

'Drink.' She shook her head and would not look at me. Instead she was staring at the Missionary Map on the wall, at the river and the tributaries.

'I am fasting,' she whispered.

'For Ramazan? That is a Moslem tradition, not a Christian one.'

'No. To be clean.'

'Well you must drink water.' I held the cup to my sister's mouth and she let me tip the water in.

'Why are you fasting?'

'Millicent is helping me.'

'But she is starving you,' I said, confused. 'Is she at least giving you water?'

'Yes,' she answered once she had drunk a little, 'I simply want to hold it: love.'

'I don't understand.'

246

'Of course you don't.' She turned away from me then as if she was weary of my company but I took her hand regardless. I thought of us as children, walking along the Rue de Thérouanne on a spring morning and the devastation we felt at the sight of our favourite trees felled. They were chopped down to prevent a disease from spreading, leaving bare, brutally cut stumps. Little Lizzie took my hand, *Don't be sad, Eva, look, it is in fact easier to see the river without them.*

'Of course you don't understand,' she repeated. She began to talk, rambling, and it was difficult to follow, about Khadega in the river; that she should have found her and photographed her, because there should be something to remind us that she was real.

'But you didn't like Khadega.'

'No.'

I knew we were both thinking the same thing, culpability. In the dense heat of the room I was nauseous and weary.

'It is important to keep the images, to hold them,' she turned in the kang, away from me, but continued to talk:

'I can print it on exquisite paper. Monochrome. Take the print and nail it to the wooden frame, the weightlessness of the paper. The edge of the paper rising up like an insect's wing. A simple powder cover, the light and the shadow. I can handwrite it on the print.'

'I don't know, Lizzie, what you are saying.'

She sat up, becoming very alert. 'Millicent says I am lovely and sacred, like Saint Wilgefortis.'

Again that image of Millicent and my sister together in the kang room. Then I remembered long afternoons in Southsea when Millicent was hard at work convincing Mother of the importance of our journey. Maps were laid out, and books, and endless talk of travelling, of it being more than a physical journey, it being a pilgrimage. Talk of conversion, persuasion, of an ambassadorial role, of making strides for England and the Church. Talk through the night until eventually mother was brow-beaten into agreeing.

'Millicent has been taken away,' I said again. Lizzie simply looked at me. 'And Lolo has gone.'

'Gone?'

Ai-Lien, whom I had carried in with me, bundled in her shawl-wrap and left on the floor, began to snuffle and snort. Lizzie sat up, pushed herself upward and forward, like a teacher waking up from a daydream to a room full of pupils, aware and bright suddenly.

'I loved a baby too,' she said. She was facing away from me. I stood completely still. Was she feverish?

'It never had a chance to grow, but it was inside me. Millicent helped me to send it back to heaven. That's how we met. I went to the Church for help.'

The heat overcame me then, for a moment, as I looked at the back of my sister's head and at her angel-white hair gone dull. I longed for rain, or greyness. The flat grey of Geneva, or Southsea, even. I was homesick for a place that wasn't even home. I wanted Lizzie to stop talking, but at the same time I needed to know because even though I wanted to dismiss it as feverish talk, I knew that I couldn't.

'You want to know who the father was?'

'Well. Of course.'

'Mr Wright.' It took a moment for me to recall him, the tall, curly-haired gentleman with a guttural face and the overloud voice of a publican-man, who had been keen to visit us as soon as we arrived from Geneva. He was an acquaintance of Aunt Cicely's.

'You remember when we went to Kew to photograph the palms?'

'Yes.'

'He managed to lose the chaperone. He forced himself upon me, against a sycamore tree.'

I held the cup of water up to my mouth, not to drink it, but to cover my mouth, to have something to rest my lip against. I had been jealous of her friendship with Mr Wright. He never noticed me, he made me feel ugly. When he did look at me he appraised me viciously, his expression turning to pity before refocusing on Lizzie. She began to cry; my gosling.

August 5th

I am nurse and mother and sister, attentive to Ai-Lien and to Lizzie. Wipe, clean, feed them and with each action I hollow myself out. I am a vessel for their requirements and this relentless giving has begun to hammer a new shape inside of me. It is the selflessness of mothers and wives, I suppose, carving rooms inside oneself and allowing love to come running into them like water. The danger is that the water could engulf and erase me entirely. Even so, I pity those who have not felt such reconfiguration from a simple self-serving do-as-thou-will soul. It does not bring me peace, however.

There has been no message from Millicent yet. Each time the gate clangs I jump. The heat is up, thick in the air and deadening. The natives milling in drones along the track are dirty and evil. I cannot think of where to go or whom to speak to. Lizzie sleeps for most of the day but I barely sleep. When I do, it is in short exhausted bursts with my head on my knees and I dream of Khadega, her body dragging and buffered at the bottom of filthy water.

Ai-Lien cries through the night, she holds my hair and pulls it, sucks on to the skin on my neck. She wakes every hour or two at night now and exhaustion leaves me dull and stupefied. The only way to calm her is to sing, and my singing voice is terrible. There is no one else to hear it, though.

It is August and much of the fruit in the orchard is turning. The walls of this house sag and groan, suffering with the heat. The leaves in the courtyard and garden have grown large, the tendrils wander unchecked, the climbing plants are strident, shifting through the yard, strangling whatever they can as they progress. The pavilion is too hot. The insects are shrill, louder than usual, and I think about the sensation of life in the womb, flickering like a candle. These things – and others – my sister has tasted, meanwhile I become dry as bones in the desert sun. I take dumplings or dough strings to Lizzie hoping to thwart her starving herself in her kang but, despite her frailty, jealousy creeps over me, perverse as it is. I fear that Millicent will take Lizzie or that Lolo will take Ai-Lien but then I remember that they have all gone. I must sleep. I do not know what to do.

The A21, Present Day

En route to Sussex

The owl was quiet. It did not seem to mind the car journey, or at least, it hadn't protested, though quite how owls would go about protesting Frieda was not sure. The cage was next to her in the back seat of the car. Tayeb had offered to drive and Frieda accepted, surrendering to passenger status, letting the grey lines of the road's edge and scrubland wash past in a blur. She read the notebook. In fact, she could not stop reading it. The handwriting was mesmerising, slanting as it did ferociously to the right. Mostly, it was written in black ink, but sometimes in pencil, though the pencil sections were faded. There were dates at the beginning, and quotes from Marco Polo, or Bunyan.

Reading it was like being submerged, a ducking into another realm, though not into water; instead into a dry, hot place. The description of the desert's heat consumed Frieda's mind so much so that it was a shock to look up finally, after an hour or so in the car, at the English sky outside, layers of grey working through steel and iron hues to silt. A voice in her head said: you are in a car with a man you barely know on your way to meet your mother whom you have not spoken with since you were seven. This voice combined with the sonorous tones of the Radio 4 gardening expert who spoke of geraniums and slugs and the problems of growing broad beans in snow. The leather notebook in Frieda's hand smelled powerfully of elsewhere.

At the service station she queued to buy water and thought of Nathaniel, in particular of his thumb on his bottom lip, pulling it down absentmindedly when talking to her, a habit of his which always annoyed her. Back in the car, she counted the trees, allowing herself to return to the motorway slipping past, the rain and the moustachioed man in the front seat. There were things she would like to ask him, such as why he was here. Why this country? But it was difficult to ask such personal questions. What, she wondered, would he think of her recent project for the think tank, 'Belief in Conversation between the West and East', and how could she bring herself to admit to that title? She wasn't sure she could stand it much longer, this work, this scratching of the surface, the vulgarity of it, and the ongoing colonial power assertion under the guise of dialogue. It was like the time in Saudi, once, when the young women students invited her into their part of the café, the back part, or the family room, and as there were no men they all took off their abayas and she willed them to put them back on. Surfaces are often preferable; sometimes we don't want to look underneath.

'That's it.' Tayeb turned the radio down and looked over his shoulder at Frieda. 'That road there.'

He was going too fast to make the turning so pushed the brakes quickly and Frieda was shunted forward. She put her hand on the back of his seat to steady herself, then sat back, pulling a piece of paper out of her bag. Her father had given her the address, some sort of a 'village' in rural Sussex.

A sign indicated the A21 to Battle and Hastings and underneath it was a smaller sign saying, 'Prima Village'. They turned into the road and drove at a slower speed along its winding country contours. The hedges were thick and heavy with dipping clusters of elderberries. The road veered to a sharp left and they emerged facing a triangle of grass surrounded by a row of toy-house cottages. At the peak of the triangle sat a vibrant-looking pub and on the opposite corner was a neat, Norman church.

'Yalla,' said Tayeb, 'this is the kind of England I imagined as a child. So it does exist.'

'Oh yes.'

These white-washed cottages were a long way from the caravans of Sheppey. Here, window boxes did not contain a single dead plant. The complex arrangement of recycling bins on driveways, all with significantly different coloured lids, indicated that the rules for rubbish collection were strictly adhered to in every household, and in every window net curtains hung with perfectly weighted hems.

'It gives me the heebie-jeebies.'

'What is this?' Tayeb asked, 'the heebie-jeebies?'

'Oh, you know,' she put one finger against the car window pane, ran it slowly down the glass, 'the willies.'

'The willies?'

'It's terrifying, Tayeb. Look at it. Can you imagine living here?'

Tayeb pulled the car to a stop at the junction.

'I think it is beautiful. Tranquil. Peace. I could happily live here until old age, drink tea and die happy.'

'No you wouldn't. You'd go insane. Imagine all these people, knowing your business, looking in your windows.'

'I would smile graciously at them all, be friends with them.'

'But they wouldn't want to be friends with you, Tayeb; you're way too foreign and scary.'

Tayeb laughed. 'I could live here for ever, even if the neighbours all hated me.' He patted the steering wheel twice.

'Where now?' Her father's directions said: edge of the village. Prima Foundation. Tayeb slowly followed one edge of the village green.

'I don't think we can go any further this way.' He flicked his cigarette out of the window. 'Dead end.' He began to reverse, nearly hitting the back of a parked grey Citroën.

'Careful, Tayeb, or they will come after us with their knitting needles.'

Tayeb drove in triangles, two more times around the village green, each time taking a turning off and meeting a dead end.

'It's like a maze,' he said, 'bigger than it looks.'

'Maybe we should ask someone?' Frieda lowered her window and leaned out, slightly. Tayeb slowed down alongside two elderly ladies walking so close together it was as if they were holding each other upright.

'Excuse me,' Frieda called to them. They looked at Frieda as if she were an abomination to their sense of reality.

'We are looking for the Prima Foundation. Do you have any idea where it is?'

One of the ladies whispered something to the other and then looked directly at Frieda, before, in unison, the two scowled and turned their soft white curls away and walked off in a rustle of tutting.

'Okaaay.' Frieda sat back. The car cruised on a little further.

'Let's try him,' she said, seeing a middle-aged man wearing long green shorts, walking along with a small dog on a lead.

'Excuse me.' She was all smiles. The man looked up at her, unsmiling, and raised his chin up as if to fend her off with it.

'Hello, we are a bit lost. I wonder if you could help?'

He stepped nearer to them. 'Where you going?' he said, yanking the straining white dog back towards him.

'Thanks. We're looking for the Prima Foundation. Any idea where it is?'

The man frowned and then shook his head. 'Nah.'

'Right.' Frieda sniffed.

'Oh, hold on, is it the commune?'

'That's it.'

The man's face shadowed. He looked at Tayeb for the first time, then back at Frieda, then at the owl in the cage. Frieda's breath rose in her throat and for a slip of time, she was tempted to jump out of the car and abandon Tayeb. The familiar and the unfamiliar crossed into one, like light on water and for an instant she had absolutely no idea who she was.

The man coughed. 'The weirdos,' he sneered.

'Hmm, I bet they are,' Frieda said, trying for complicity. The man was checking Tayeb out again, his nostrils flaring as he did so. Begrudgingly, he pointed back in the direction they had come.

'You have to go back along the main road, hundred and fifty yards or so, take the first exit. Keep going up the track. It's not a proper road. They're at the top of that.' Under his breath he said, 'Dirty buggers.'

'Thank you so much,' Frieda said. She smiled at him, as if thanking a photocopier-room boy for printing off a range of documents, 'That's really very helpful.'

The response was a grunt as the man and his dog walked off.

Tayeb lit a cigarette as he pulled out on to the main road.

'See what I mean, Tayeb? Friendly, aren't they?'

He smiled as they reversed back down the road. Frieda watched a kestrel loop above a large, recently dug field.

'That must be it.' He nodded towards a track that led off the road, then drove on to it, winding for quite a while until, finally, they turned a corner and a panorama of yellow rape-seed fields and rolling hedges lay out before them.

'What's that?' Tayeb said. Frieda looked over. It was a great tall structure of some sort, like a totem pole.

'I fear it's some kind of art sculpture or installation.'

Standing in the middle of the field, about twelve feet high, was a pole decorated with an entwined network of legs, breasts, mouths and other dismembered body parts. The whole creation was painted in chewing-gum pinks and obscene shades of yellow and green.

'Hideous.'

Other art works appeared further along the track. There was an upside-down car with a ladder sticking out of the chassis leading to the sky, or nowhere; a massive fish of rusted iron with a chicken balancing on its fin; more abstract forms mostly made out of disused cars. At last there was a gate, covered with paper flowers and bits of ribbon, bells, wind chimes and peace symbols. Tayeb pulled up the car next to a huge sign that said WELCOME TO THE PRIMA FOUNDATION with three giant ladybirds painted below the lettering. Frieda, with her window wound down, pushed her glasses up to her eyes and squinted at the quote below the ladybirds: *When the knowable, and the knowledge, are both destroyed equally, then there is no second way.*

'Oh my God,' Frieda said, 'we might get forced into a singing workshop. Or worse, a drumming circle.'

He laughed and then looked at her. 'You all right?'

'Of course, why?'

'Well, your mother, you said . . . you have not seen her for a long time.'

'Do you think I'll recognise her?'

Without hesitation he said, 'Of course. No question.' He was sensitive, this stranger from Yemen.

Helping and Teaching: *If anything breaks, it is not necessarily your fault; if anything is insecure, blame no one for not attending to something you should yourself have attended to.*

A Lady Cyclist's Guide to Kashgar – Notes

August 9th

A telegram arrived this morning, delivered by a Hindustani man on horseback:

FROM Mr Steyning – Received your message. Cannot reach you due to riots flaring up. You & E must leave immediately without Millicent. Get to Kucha where I will meet you and bring you to Urumtsi. Millicent expunged from the Mission.

I gave the Hindustani postal man some tea and bread and it wasn't until he left in a dust-whirl that I sat down on the floor with shaking hands. Millicent has been expunged, and I have no idea where she is. Despite my fury at her behaviour I feel her absence terribly and am now torn as to what to do. I had been thinking about going into the city to find her, but now – I don't know. And Kucha? I do not even know where Kucha is.

I am not sure if Father Don Carlo will help us, but there is no one else. I must visit him.

I have been gathering supplies from the garden but we no longer have milk, cream, butter, or meat and this afternoon I tried to talk to Elizabeth. The light sliced through numerous tears in one of the papered windows.

'Lizzie,' I said, 'I believe we are in danger.'

'Job 11:19. Also thou shalt lie down, and none shall make thee afraid; yea, many shall make suit unto thee.' She looked away once she had spoken. I thought about this for a moment.

'What do you mean?'

'There is nothing to fear, Eva.' Her thin neck stretched.

'But, Lizzie –'

She was holding one of Father Don Carlo's calligraphy sheets.

'I shall translate for you: "Be not afraid of sudden fear, neither of the desolation of the wicked, when it cometh" –'

'Lizzie, darling,' I interrupted, 'do you think you could travel?' She turned, slowly, in the kang, her eyes hollowed and pitiful. Her hand shook as it moved towards her lip. She smiled and said, 'Of course.'

'Lizzie, darling.' I tried not to cry.

'As the crow flies.' She pointed at the map on the wall. 'I could reach the other side of the map if I followed the crows.'

'Yes, Lizzie.'

Holding Ai-Lien against me, I climbed up on to Lizzie's kang and lay down at her side. She smelled of something, a sharp, bitter smell and I must have fallen asleep because I woke with a tingling in my arm where Ai-Lien's full weight was resting on it, and my head was full of a dream of my mother who was reprimanding me: it is your duty, Eva, to look after your sister. She is frail, unlike you; she is the one we all love. Unlike you.

August 10th

One's instinct is to pack for a longer journey. Sorting the books, I paused to read Sir Burton's section about the court-yard garden of the mosques being second rate, tawdrily deco-rated with bright-green tiles and flowered carpets and the only admirable features being the stained glass. Wait, I shall write it out: *The scene must be viewed with Moslem bias, and until a man is thoroughly imbued with the spirit of the East, the last place the Rauzah will remind him of, is that which the architect primarily intended it to resemble – a garden.*

It seems pertinent, as I think about this courtyard. Each day it feels less of a garden, more like a prison. Packing, but what on earth sort of luggage must I organise? Then there is my bicycle, old lady, such as she is, dust and mud-covered all the way up to the saddle. All of this is a diversion of course, because I do not know what to do about Lizzie. She acts like a spinster shut up and allowed out only once a year; she is paler and stiller. She says she cannot stand up yet she barely eats. Do I leave her and go to the bazaar to find a carter, return, and then take her to the priest's with me? I cannot send a message any more as the boys have all gone. Oh – why did Lolo leave? I wonder often, was it Lolo who showed Millicent where I keep this journal?

After an examination of the maps I see that Kucha is a long stretch into the Tarim Basin – I do not know if it is the right thing to do to leave Millicent with the natives. I am all upturned, now; the thing to keep in mind is that I am a perfectly able person. I will not be extinguished in this desert dust. Still, oh dear, how to carry Lizzie?

August 11th

At any rate – then, none of that matters.

I brought her a cup of chrysanthemum tea, but when I walked up to her kang there was something wrong. Her hand was unreal in the way it rested and I knew instantly that she was dead. I moved the angel threads of white hair from her face and saw that it looked strange. The bottom half of her face, her chin, mouth and jaw, twisted crookedly as if disconnected from the top, from her nose and eyes. I put my hand on the edge of her chin, pushing slightly, trying to restore her symmetry, but as soon as I released my hand, her chin fell back.

I sat for a moment next to her bed with Ai-Lien asleep against my shoulder, feeling the thud-thud of her heart. Not thinking, letting white spaces fill my mind; keeping still, invisible, as if nothing had happened, nor ever could. This worked for a moment, possibly less than a moment, whatever length of time that might be – then I remembered Mr Mah's warning that Pavilion House has a curse and all who live there have a crooked face and I thought of Lizzie as a crow at school, standing on the wall, arms out to make wings.

Not for the first time, I wished Millicent were here.

In the garden the heat was a noxious bully, fully intending to brutalise. I went to Lizzie's outbuilding, the dusty hovel where she spent much of her time. The entrance was covered by a large blanket. Inside, several of her photographic prints were hanging from a pole that she had fixed from one side of the room to the other. I touched the prints. There was Lizzie lying in grass, a blurred light distorting her so that she was blended into the leaves. A hand with a large ruby ring on an orchid stem. A poplar branch, bleached cleverly into a skeletal arm. Each photograph was a love-letter. On the floor in the corner was a nest of scraps of paper, notes she had written to herself, mostly illegible. I picked them up, straightened them in my palm and tried to read them. Only one was decipherable, written in black ink, her own sweet calligraphy:

– oh to free the soul . . . ######### pigeon-free. – that face that is only for me to read and know, beloved: the other side of your carefully constructed life, the other side of the map: an opposite – yes, I love you that far. That long.

My sister in love, and I think this: Millicent, you are not worth this love, a love that far.

There are more lizards than ever before, slitting through the crevices like a disease. Do not move and it is as if nothing has changed: the baby breathing, her eyes bright-wet, her perfect foot in my hand like a toy and my sister might not be gone. This trickery held up through the night and this ink kept it at bay, but now morning light comes, the spells shudder to an end. With the desert light grief comes up, wrecking me like a wolf.

I shall not think of Mother with her red hair coiled and face full of shame, the shame reflected in the flames burning near her in the grate. I didn't protect her, either of them. I was remiss, busy giving my love to a changeling. I left Lizzie in the storms with the whims and winds all around her head.

Sussex, Present Day

The Prima Foundation

There was a timetable, or schedule, on the wall of the prefab room, outlining a series of activities in pastel-coloured squares: Shakti Chalana Mudra, Mula Bandha, Yoga Mudra. Tayeb accepted water in a green mug from a startlingly attractive young woman with the bright blue eyes of a doll. He stretched his leg and there was an audible crack, a shock inside his calf muscle and the blonde woman looked down at his leg, as did he. He stood up and stamped his foot on the floor, hopping up and down.

'Cramp,' he said. The doll-eyed angel said nothing as he continued stamping. The muscles grew taut inside his calf and correspondingly the dry skin on his back sang out in an itch as if calling 'remember me'. After a minute the pain let up, leaving a ghost of itself underneath his skin and he sat down on the plastic chair again, rubbing his leg and not looking at the woman, embarrassed.

Frieda came back from the toilet and as she walked towards Tayeb she wiped wet hands on her jeans. A very English-woman thing to do, he thought, wiping wet hands outside the toilet. She sat next to Tayeb on an identical red plastic chair. He did not know her very well, this serious, glasses-wearing dark-haired girl, but he could tell she was nervous. From what she had told him, she had not seen her mother since she was small. She was picking at the skin around her nails. The angel offered water to Frieda and Tayeb had an alarming rush of desire for her, this doll-white, tiny woman who said nothing, just smiled. She reminded him of posters of Western women his brothers had on their walls.

'We had prefabs like this at my school,' Frieda said, looking around the room, then up at the ceiling. Tayeb turned to look at Frieda, surprised at his guilt for looking at the other woman. He would like to – he looked out of the small, square window at an awkward, leaning tree – soothe Frieda, if it were possible. He wanted to take a finger and tell her to stop ripping the skin off it. Unlike his scales and cracks, her skin was simple, stretched and sweet and she should leave it alone. Tayeb had a belief about Western women that he had never fully admitted. He was convinced that they required, and, more importantly, wanted someone to tell them what to do; someone (a man) to

266

tell them to stop talking and worrying. It was the one thought he had that his father would approve of.

The pretty woman returned, still saying nothing, not smiling, but this time she pulled out a plastic chair for herself and sat down, looking at them expectantly. Frieda began to talk: I am here to see my mother. She isn't expecting me. There was silence and then the girl opened her bag, pulled out a notebook and a pen and wrote something in bubble-neat schoolgirl handwriting. When she had finished writing she pushed the notebook over towards Frieda.

Welcome to the Prima Foundation Mission. What can we do for you?

'Oh, OK,' Frieda said. 'I'm sorry, I didn't realise.' There was a protracted discussion – verbally by Frieda, written by the girl – to determine who, exactly, her mother was. There were different names it seemed; she was once called Ananda, or Grace and after some discussion they worked out that she was now simply called Amrita.

If you will just excuse me for a moment I will go and find someone to alert them that you are here to see your mother. I won't be long.

She smiled and left the room. Frieda swung around and looked at Tayeb.

'Did you realise she was deaf?'

'No.'

'She must have been lip-reading.'

Tayeb sipped the slightly warm water. On the opposite wall was a poster of a large skull, with the detail of the brain and the interior of the head fully illustrated. A bright yellow line penetrated the top of the brain, coursed the back of the mouth and continued down the throat. Tayeb read the script below it:

This gold line is the symbol for the nadi as it travels through the centre of the tongue. Kechari Mudra is only achieved by the practice of talavya kriya.

'Is it some kind of school do you think?' Frieda said.

'Don't know.' He wanted a cigarette but it didn't look like a room you could smoke in and he was impatient with himself: what am I doing here? He thought of Nidal and his room with the aeroplanes on the wall. Tayeb's right eye began to twitch in its socket. He would never see Nidal again. The door opened and a tall, thin, bald man walked in, followed by the blonde woman. The man had a skeletal head, and the veins in his temples were visible. He walked towards Frieda, and shook her hand.

'Hello,' he said, smiling. 'So, you are Amrita's daughter?'

'That's right.' The handshaking continued for a time.

'My name is Robert Barker. Welcome.' A particularly large vein on his temple stood out now, red–blue, like a tattoo.

'So, Frieda?' He pulled out a plastic chair opposite them, and sat down, nodding at Tayeb, although he did not offer him his hand. 'You have decided to visit your mother?'

'Yes. That's right –'

'And am I correct in thinking that you have had no contact with her for a long time?'

Frieda nodded, then let out a strange, small noise. A half-cough. Brave, this time, Tayeb took hold of her hand and squeezed it. He was relieved that she did not move it from his grip.

'If you don't mind me asking,' Tayeb said, 'are you the . . .' he paused, 'the leader here?'

Robert Barker looked at Tayeb with an expression of monumental boredom.

'*Leader* – huh – no, no, there is no leader here. We are run as a more . . . egalitarian and democratic enterprise.' He turned and faced Frieda again and Tayeb recognised a dismissal. Robert Barker spoke:

'We would love to show you around our Mission and show you the original Victorian kitchen garden. We are trying to find your mother now. She'll need some time to prepare herself before seeing you. Normally, we ask for advance warning, but . . .'

Robert Barker spoke quickly and obviously saw no need for polite small talk. He stood up and turned to the doll-like girl, who was near the door, standing like a guardian angel.

'Can you give them a tour of the residential area, the garden and the farm, and I will go and talk to Amrita?'

The girl nodded and Robert Barker held the door open for them to leave the prefab.

Thin pavements made of slate tiles wound through a complex of identical prefab trailer-style rooms. They were painted bright colours and signs with names hung on the doors,

Bharathi, Gayathri, Hamsini and Kadambari. Another young and beautiful woman stepped out of a doorway just in front of Tayeb. This one had long light brown hair, and an alarming nose piercing – a sharp, aggressive metal point that stuck out from her nostril like a blade.

'Hello,' Tayeb said. She nodded, said nothing, but stared at him directly, then abruptly turned away as if she had assessed enough. Behind the residential area was a wooded section where scrambled clumps of long-established blackberry and raspberry bushes were embedded into clusters of nettles and dock leaves. In a clearing a range of benches made from chopped trees and logs were arranged in rows creating a sort of theatre space. The girl pulled out her notebook and wrote:

This is where we have readings, discussions, music sometimes.

'Where is everyone?'

Working mostly. We have a lot of projects on the go. Some agricultural, some educational. The friend-children are all in the school quarters. A lot of our friends are involved in scholarly work, meditation, mystical questioning. It's hard work. We have many highly intelligent and knowledgeable friends here.

The owl was in the car and suddenly Tayeb worried for it. He thought about going to get it, but did not want to leave Frieda, and anyway, what would he do with it? He trudged behind them for another half an hour of pointing and being shown rows of cabbages and beans climbing up bamboo poles. It was obviously a stalling technique, but on they trudged. Finally, they were taken back to the original prefab room where Robert Barker was waiting for them, sitting on a plastic chair with an array of unappetising biscuits on a yellow plate in front of him.

'Would you wait here please for your mother? She has agreed to see you.'

'Yes. Thank you.'

Tayeb and Frieda were alone in the room. Tayeb had a very strong compulsion to draw. It happened to him sometimes. Draw. Or spray, or paint, or disfigure – basically, to leave his mark – and this place made him irreverent. He took his fountain pen and his small notebook out of his bag and began to draw what he saw immediately in front of him. A line of tins on the windowsill all containing pencils. Beyond them, trees. The motion of making soft marks and lines calmed him. He wanted to scratch his wrists and his back, but he didn't. He would not.

Difficulties to Overcome: No matter what happens, keep it going, the faster the better, until a taste is acquired for the pastime; until the going-forward-forever idea seems to have taken possession of you.

A Lady Cyclist's Guide to Kashgar – Notes

August 12th

Where to start?

With the pink splinters of dawn in the sky as I pushed my bicycle through the Pavilion House gates for the final time? No. Before that, even: I was exhausted after a night of considering what to do with Lizzie. My first thought was to bring her into the sun and let the desert eat her, the insects and the heat. I thought it would be quickest, preferable to festering inside that room. But as I began to move her I remembered the monastery we had visited on the journey here, on the outskirts of Osh's city walls, where the robed monks fed vultures because dealing with human carrion

272

was part of their duties. The thought of beaks ripping Lizzie was –

Well. In the end I covered her with scarves, and sprinkled jasmine and rose petals from the garden on to her hair. For want of any suitable ritual, I dabbed water on her forehead and kissed her. Lost gosling.

Then, movement became my whole intention. I made sure my precious, stolen baby was well fed with Allenbury mix and packed her into a cot, fashioned for her in the basket. I have tied sticks on to the basket and a scarf, devising a method of keeping her shaded from the sun. Precariously balanced and tied behind the seat of the bicycle was the crib-trunk stuffed with the following: the remains of the dried Allenbury food, the Missionary Maps and the Survey Maps; Lizzie's Leica and several of her films with the prints folded into Millicent's Bible; this journal and my books, they have travelled such a distance with me; Mrs Ward's bicycling guide, Burton, Shaw and the pamphlet of Mr Greeves' translated folk stories. There was just room for some clothes and blankets for Ai-Lien. Once these items were strapped into the trunk, I attached, using the rope that used to tether Rebekah, the mimeograph machine. It was heavy, but compacted well into its portable box and could be useful to sell, or use as a bribe.

The bicycle was too heavy to ride, so I pushed, feeling every bump along the ancient river bed that constituted a track and each treacherous turn of the wheel increasing the distance from Lizzie. Ai-Lien seemed content enough on her back looking up at the sky as the light grew pinker and then more yellow. I pushed the bike through the arboreal area where young willows had been grafted on to poplars and it seemed as though my senses were heightened. I have walked this way many times now, but sounds came upon my ears as if in a rush. For the first time I noticed clumps of wild, scraggly lavender and bushes of sage growing at the edges of the track.

I hoped to arrive at the Old Town Citadel before the morning sun was up and blazing in its full fury. The rhythm of the journey took possession of my bones and, to my surprise, rather than Lizzie, I was thinking of Millicent. I should hate her, by rights; one could say she killed my sister, but the powerful sun dissipated hatred. All I could feel was the thud of my feet stepping forward and the turning of the bicycle wheels.

At Kashgar city gates the guards were the worst sort, young and foolish. They looked insolently at me as they checked my papers, even though I could tell they could not read. They looked at Ai-Lien. They smoked several cigarettes, stared again at Ai-Lien, at me and at the bicycle and whispered and smoked more cigarettes. My hair was wrapped in a scarf as best as I could but they continued to leer closely towards my face. I tapped a rhythm on my wrist to keep myself calm until eventually, they let me through. Inside the city wall I asked a benevolent-looking elderly man who had been watching the whole scene if he would take me to the knife souq. It took several efforts of miming to convey my request before he understood: knives.

*　　*　　*

At first I assumed that the priest was out as his room was quiet, but I could smell something recently cooked in oil, and then I heard the cooing and bickering of his restless pigeons. I had no choice but to gather up Ai-Lien and leave my bicycle with all of my possessions in the dubious, awkward-shaped entrance to his house, an entrance that seemed to stand on nothing, the ancient wood beams of its construction looking like a child's game of balance-the-sticks.

I held Ai-Lien against me and we made our way up to his roof. He was at the cages, bent over, feeding the pigeons and at first he did not hear me or realise that I was there, despite me calling him.

'Father, I need your help,' I said, walking towards him. The sun was blinding. I held my scarf over Ai-Lien and squinted at him. He turned around then and did not seem surprised to see me.

'Come out of the sun,' he said. A dove balanced on his arm and his thin face was very red in the brutal heat, his clerical hat filthy and tilted to one side.

'Do you have any news on Millicent, Father?' The priest stroked the neck of the silver-grey dove, kissed its head, then leaned down and put it into one of the cages. He came towards me then.

'They are holding her at the Magistrates' prison,' he said, patting my elbow and nudged me back in the direction of the entrance. 'It is not safe for you here, mi angeli.'

Inside, I attended to Ai-Lien, feeding her and changing her as he poured me some water. Once Ai-Lien was settled

I sat back and was about to tell him about Lizzie when I noticed that on the floor underneath the window, laid out in complex patterns, were tiny scraps of paper. They were arranged in lines, layered across and around each other. As I looked closer I saw that each piece was cut into a star or hexagon shape.

'What is that, Father?'

'Illumination. I have taken the words from the Bible and placed them in the geographical shapes of Islamic Illumination.'

I bent down. An Italian version of the Bible had been cut into thousands and thousands of pieces, some simply words, others whole sections.

'What do you intend to do with them?'

He looked up at me and took a packet of matches from his pocket and lit the match, then picked up one of the scraps of paper.

'Pouff,' he said, 'gone.'

The flame glowed, then he blew it. I watched, mesmerised, as he set fire to scrap after scrap of paper, letting the paper-ash fall from his window, a moment of light, like a firefly. In a sense it was beautiful, the sudden flare and the paper-flakes falling, but the futility of it – him – and of Millicent's Mission, and us here, it was unthinkable.

'They are going to kill her, aren't they?'

Father Don Carlo began to sing softly. Listening to the pipes dangling from the tails of pigeons, dreaming his Islamic spheres, I wondered what exactly it was that the priest was doing here in Kashgar. I repeated myself, 'Aren't they?'

He did not answer but continued to light his flames and I had a strong feeling that he had thoroughly prepared for our meeting. Goodness knows how long the scraps had been on the floor so that he could stage this vision. There was a good chance he had even rehearsed it all, the pause before the strike of the match, the dangle of the flame in the air, the puff-puffs. Along with his pigeons, I saw, it was a cultivation of sorts – a theatrical element – his shabby dress and the felt black hat were all part of his costume. He was less abstract, more fully articulated than I had previously assumed.

'Father,' I said, 'is there anything we can do for Millicent? Do you know what will become of her? You have good contacts, you could help.'

'I asked to see her yesterday, but I was refused.'

'Whom did you seek permission from?' He looked away, and I did not believe him.

'Father, you have spent much time with Millicent, helping her with the translations, you must see that some of the . . .' I paused.

When he had no more matches, he turned the box upside down and looked inside as if surprised that within there was not an extended supply reaching as far as heaven.

'Responsibility lies with you,' I finished.

He turned and looked at me. His bearded face was craggy, but his hands were steady as he took a drink of wine from his dirty cup. In the dull light of his shaded room, and the plum-flesh heat that was upon us, my various impressions of him flickered each second so that at once he was drawn in and up, next peevish and frustrated, then out again, like a pair of bellows expanded and living. Then again came withdrawal and a look of suspicion.

'Responsibility for what?'

'For Millicent, them taking her. What will happen?'

The sigh he emitted was a bitter one, and I could not make it out. He looked despondently at the patterned paper and the ripped-up books. His glance at me was clear, it was one of superiority; he was contemptuous of me, of my existence perhaps, or of my idiocy. This was his kingdom, I now saw, and we were less welcome than we'd presumed.

I busied myself with Ai-Lien and rocking her to sleep, wondering as I did what to do. Millicent, without her eye-glasses, was encased somewhere at the whim of the General. If I went to find her I would presumably be immediately arrested, too. They would take Ai-Lien away. Father Don Carlo clearly could not be relied on to help. Indeed, on the contrary, I had thought him Millicent's ally, but now, I don't know. There was Mr Steyning's telegram insisting that I leave, and the birds, tapping at Lizzie's bones.

The priest was pretending to read a book, turning the pages with elaborate concentration, his manner now entirely super-cilious towards me. Stroking the velvet-down of Ai-Lien's head, hearing the resonance of the cooing birds travel down through the roof timbers, I felt immediately that I must reach Mr Steyning. The only person who might help me get to him was Rami. Or, rather, she was the only other person in this hot, pink city that I knew. Perhaps there was one thing Father

Don Carlo could help me with: his encyclopaedic knowledge of the bazaar.

'Father, all I require is your assistance in helping me find the Inn of Harmonious Brotherhood and then I will be gone.'

The priest and I walked through the narrow streets, I pushing my bicycle, he holding on to his hat. He offered to take Ai-Lien but I declined, and kept her strapped close against me. Although the heat was at its apex it seemed odd that the streets were completely deserted. Previously children had played in doorways, and elderly gentlemen wandered the bazaar's passageways, resilient to the afternoon heat. Now, we were alone.

Slowly, we made our way past the rocky clumps and dust and potholes deeper into the medina, the purposeful web whose full intent is to disorientate a stranger. Each small door led to a hidden courtyard, each passageway led to yet another. Without the priest I would not have found the winding alley nor the sign with the words 'One True Religion'.

I banged for some time at the unassuming door. Ai-Lien was asleep against my body, hot, but peaceful. Finally, there were voices, rumblings, and a small, dark-eyed woman in full abaya opened the door, looked at us and gasped. She closed the door. There was much chattering and shouting inside. The door opened again and it was Rami without her veil, clearly profoundly shocked to see me. She scowled at the priest who bowed, shook my hand and stepped backwards. Then Rami took hold of my wrist and pulled Ai-Lien and myself and the bicycle through the door, quickly closing it behind us before I could even turn to say goodbye to Father Don Carlo. He was not invited in.

'Rami —' I started, 'I am so sorry I did not warn you of my . . .'

Her gesture said, 'Why?'

'I had to come. Things have happened. I had nowhere else.'

Rami answered fast, in Turki, and I couldn't understand what she was saying.

'Slowly, Rami. Please.'

'Revolt.' She said it slowly, giving me time to understand. 'Mohammed is with them. The city is in uprising today. Listen.'

I worked out the words, one by one, then strung them together like silver links on a necklace and listened. Faint, at first, but there it was, a chanting, a drumming and a humming and then several bangs.

'Safe here but a Christian, you killed,' Rami said, slowly, to help me understand. Her face, its ancient beauty-ghosts dancing on the skin, was kind.

'Oh, Rami, I am so sorry. I have brought danger upon your family.'

'Come, come.'

Here was Lamara, the young, beautiful one, and the other women slipping around like minnows and again, the fountain, the rose petals, the soft, sheltering shade of the courtyard garden. We were settled on cushions on top of the coloured rugs and again the small children crawled near us. Rami shooed away the other women who were staring and whispering at Ai-Lien and me.

A slave-girl brought a tray of tea, naan and fruit followed by bowls of leghmen, handmade noodles and beef. Rami pulled Ai-Lien from my arms and sang softly for her, milk was brought. They were kind, I would stay here in this women's quarter for eternity, in the soft fabrics and shade of it, if I could. I cried, and I am crying now, writing this.

August 13th

The drumming is relentless, but despite the uprising that is apparently happening in the city, I feel safe in this inn with its clusters of women. Rami and Lamara help me bathe Ai-Lien, who rolls around, naked, on the divan floors, gurgling. Rami massages her, rubs oils all about her body so that she is relaxed and calm, her little limbs surrendering to the experience of being manipulated by so skilled a handler.

I feel such a thief as I watch my happy baby. She belongs with the brown hands and black eyes of these women and their oils, blended in a way I could never learn how. Their baby-charming tricks passed on mother-to-mother and me, being homeless and rootless, I know nothing. I am a fraud.

They continue to feed me delicious food as if fattening me for a sacrifice: sangza flour dough twists and guxnan lamb pies. We have not mentioned Khadega, or Lizzie, or Millicent. After the pies there is more tea and bread and yoghurt and mint. We get along with scraps of English and Turki and mime.

It's over, as it had to be.

'Eva,' Rami said, waking me up, 'you and Elizabeth must leave. It is very bad for you. Mohammed home soon. I have found a guide to take you.'

'Elizabeth is dead.' As I said those words I had a vision of Lizzie on the kang, and I could not stop myself, I sank to the floor. Rami's eyes were wide but she asked me no questions, she simply helped me to stand up.

'You must leave.'

'Will Mohammed help us?' Rami paused and a moment of despair – an insect suspended in glass, in jelly, held still – and I understood the extent of the risk I had brought to Rami. I have been stupid.

'He would kill me?'

Rami's face, soft and fading into itself, a lost beauty, said a Russian word: *dolg*. I thought of Mohammed in his white thorb, smoking his pipe, and I hunted through my inadequate vocabulary, then miraculously found the word. Yes, it would be his duty.

'He is not here tonight or tomorrow. They attack the Chinese General before dawn.'

'Will he hand me to the General?'

'No. He kill you. All foreigners killed.' Rami pushed her hair behind her ears and disappeared.

'Father Don Carlo? Millicent?'

'Yes.'

I was determined to control the shaking that came in my limbs, and managed it, as far as my hands and legs were concerned, but my right eye would twitch and jump about in its socket. She handed me a small leather pouch. I guessed what was inside. Never had Southsea seemed such a vast, universal distance away from where I stood.

'Please know that Allah is behind you and I am always your friend.'

I was grateful, but had no way of showing her. I desperately wanted to give her a gift in return, but I had nothing.

'Grey lady and priest are bad.'

'Rami, why are they bad? What do you mean?'

She spoke fast but I couldn't understand what she said. *Ezaam.* She then made a show of offering me another meal, but I refused, knowing the risk for her, and said I must leave.

'I have guide for you.'

Outside the inn, it was Mr Mah. His neat hair in plaits, his moustache oiled. He nodded to Rami, but said nothing to me and I looked at her. I did not want to go with him. I have no reason to trust him. A helpless feeling overcame me; it was like being a child again, sent away from the table, sent to bed, sent off, powerless. A resistance, a form of fury came over me, but it quickly died down, I knew there was no choice.

Ai-Lien was wrapped up well and nestled in the bicycle basket. I felt something crooked inside me and realised as I looked at her soft sleeping face that it was love. It was dusk as we left and the guards on the city gate blew their horns to announce the closing of the gates. Rami had conveyed to me that the Moslem army was gathering outside the mosque and an attack on the Chinese section of the town was imminent. She had given me a full abaya and with my face covered I gave the guards a coin from Rami's money and was allowed through quickly, although they saw my bicycle and obviously knew who I was.

Mah travelled by donkey alongside me as I pushed the bicycle. I knew that the journey through the desert at night was a very different thing from a journey by day and I was both disturbed by his presence and glad of it. It was very quickly exceedingly cold. We moved fast, but the temperature continued to drop after sunset and so after several li we stopped near a small farm and Mr Mah negotiated with the farmer for a room.

'Is it safe, Mr Mah?' I wanted to ask him why he was helping me but it was difficult to converse with him; he speaks with a thick, impenetrable accent.

The money Rami gave me is tucked underneath my black satin trousers. The farm room where I now write has a kang covered with a length of blue cloth. For supper we ate pancakes made from flour and oil which we dipped into vinegar. Mah smoked his long-necked pipe and very quickly fell into a deep sleep leaving me to wonder if it is opium that he smokes. At supper I tried to ascertain what he expects.

'I don't know how to thank you.'

He merely smiled, then said, 'You pay me.'

'Of course.'

*　　*　　*

Sleep won't come. Instead, I replay over and over the conversation I had had with Rami before leaving:

'Give baby?' It was a question. 'You have promise she be safe. Mohammed, not know.'

Sitting on the woven patterns and colours, I was holding Ai-Lien to my face; she was dabbing my lips with her fingers. I thought of Khadega, her hair wrapped in stones from the bottom of the river; of Mohammed's other wife, Suheir, wailing, stupidly and hysterically, on the floor with the anguish of wanting to be a mother. I thought of Lolo, of his tenderness towards Ai-Lien, then him disappearing. Part of me thinks that he should have taken her with him. Despite having no mother or father, despite being abandoned, if that is what she was, it is undeniable that, like the frail red poppy I have seen thriving in the harshness of the rocky crevices in the desert, she belongs here. I stroked her face. Rami would certainly look after her. But what would happen to her, a foundling?

'Rami, I –'

Ai-Lien's fingers reached up and pushed against my chin and touched my lips again. At the door Rami put her hand at the small of my back.

'Peace be with you. Allah smiles.'

There are bangs and rumbles in the distance, the drumming continues and I have just realised that the word that Rami had mentioned, *ezaam*, is Arabic for bones.

Sussex, Present Day

A prefab building in the Prima Foundation complex

Badly drawn wings. Aeroplanes. Dragonflies. Butterflies. All hanging from the ceiling. Hot hands. Breath. Outside magpies were rioting, theirs must be the ugliest of all the birdsongs. Tayeb had left earlier with the younger woman and Robert Barker, leaving Frieda alone in the hot headachy room, resonant of distant French lessons. Or, more precisely, her inefficiency at learning French – the shameful sense of being middle-to-lower-middle of the class, befuddled by words in lists and the verbs in lines, none of them adding up to a magical whole in her head – ultimately, the salty-flat memory of failure.

Then, the door opened and in she came. She had dark hair, like Frieda's, though with strands of grey webbed through it. Her face had a dreamy look, as if shaped by the contemplation of rivers and swans and duckweed on water. No smile, but she looked at Frieda as if her eyes could drink her up, as if Frieda were made of milk. There was an awkward pause. Should they shake hands, or kiss? Frieda waited for an indication of which, but there was none and so instead she spoke:

'Hello.'

Still no smile, so Frieda said, 'You look exactly as I remember you. You don't seem to have aged at all.'

Her mother opened a beaded fabric bag whose long handle crossed her body like a safety harness. She pulled out a notebook, the same type that the blonde girl had, red with a black spiral, and wrote on it:

A diet of seaweed and toast keeps me young. You look beautiful.

'Have you lost your hearing?' Frieda stretched her jaw to disguise her shock. Her mother shook her head, and wrote:

So many questions, so much to catch up on. How long are you staying?

'I'm not staying long,' Frieda said, intending to end with the word 'Mum', but didn't. There are things that she missed that a mother shouldn't miss, such as the first spots of blood in her daughter's knickers or a daughter's return from a school disco with the taste of a broken heart in her mouth, but in the end those things did not matter. What did matter, though, was the thumb-print in her brain that Frieda had been left with, a recurring dream: Frieda standing at the bottom of the hill, her mother walking away without looking back, a huge yellow dice rolling over the hill towards Frieda to crush her.

'I really came to ask you a question,' Frieda said.

It was interesting, watching the slight stress-lines gather on her mother's forehead and the eyes narrow. Frieda could see that she thought she was going to ask her why she left. She was trying to think of an answer, knowing that there was no answer other than that she chose herself over Frieda. After all, not all mothers sacrifice themselves for their children. She might have other explanations, clever ones that would clean up the thumb-prints in her head, but that wasn't what Frieda was going to ask.

'Do you know who Irene Guy is?'

Her mother looked surprised, her eyes widening, and then she turned away and coughed, heftily, into her fist. Small bits of phlegm must have landed in her palm, Frieda could tell from the way she cupped her hand and kept it cupped. She needed somewhere to flick them, or wipe them. There she stood with the mucus from her chest in her hand, looking suddenly weary and a little scared. She nodded towards a table and they both sat down, then she took a piece of paper from her notebook, wiped her hand on that and wrote on the next page.

She's my mother.

On the wall was a poster of an Indian man, chubby, surrounded by bright pink lotus flowers and underneath it said, 'I will Establish Peace in the World'. Frieda remembered him from the kitchen as a child, it was the Margarine.

'You told me your mother was dead. Dead before I was born.'

Her mother looked down at the floor, her cheekbones stretched out of her face like the corners of chalk.

'Why can't you speak?'

She picked up her pen. *Serenity resides in silence*.

'I thought it resided in fucking your friends' husbands.'

The words were out and Frieda was immediately sorry. That wasn't why she was here, but there was a swish like the sea in her ears, like the long lug-backwards of a retreating tide through the shingle as everything this woman told her all those years before about love and boundaries rushed through her head. Told, when she was too young to be told any of that. Or, at the very least, if Frieda was going to be indoctrinated into the rites of free love then she should not have then been left behind, like a glove.

Frieda stood up to stop the whirring in her head. She looked around and at the picture of the Indian man. The lotus flowers surrounding the picture frame were browning at the edges and sagged under dust.

'That is Maharaji, I remember him.' A small smile appeared on her mother's face.

'You left me for all of this?' She didn't move, or say anything. 'Is it worth it? Has it brought you what you need?'

Frieda looked up at the ceiling, at the broken wings, thinking of a grandmother in Norwood who owned an owl, their names linked on a database all this time.

'I found this in Irene's flat.' She took the photograph out of her pocket and held it out. She watched her mother look at the photograph for a moment; it was impossible to see from her face what she was thinking as she looked at it.

'I wish I had known I had a grandmother. Well. She's dead now. They sent me a letter about a funeral, but I missed it, I was out of the country. Did they contact you?'

Her mother shook her head, and glanced directly at Frieda this time. She put her hand to her mouth and looked out of the window. Frieda felt ashamed. She should not have been so abrupt about the death like that.

Her mother picked up her pen and began to write, then, urgently, her head down very close to the page, her elbow curled around the notebook like a student in an exam. Frieda slid her feet on the carpeted floor, sliding backwards and forwards watching her mother write fast, in her blue ink, scrawling her own calligraphy across the page, until, finally, she passed Frieda the notebook and sat back. She rubbed her eyes and looked away from Frieda, out of the window at an awkward, leaning tree.

Frieda. Look. I am not going to say sorry for leaving you, because it was the hardest thing I've ever done – you will never know. And I don't expect you to forgive me. I am just going to say this: thank you for coming and telling me about Irene. I would not have known about her death otherwise. It means a lot.

Her mother sat in front of her, like a cat on a wall, composed.

'I wish I'd known,' Frieda said after reading the words, 'that there was someone, other than you and Dad alive. I've always felt . . . adrift.'

The silence was vivid.

'I just have so many questions.' Her mother was looking at the photograph. She tapped it several times with her finger and then picked up her pen.

I was 19 in that photograph, pregnant with you, quite far gone as you can see. I always told you your grandmother was dead, because in truth, she was to me.

'Why can't you speak?' Frieda asked again. It was infuriating, this scribbling. Her mother looked down at the table.

'Why was she dead to you?' Frieda said.

Irene, my mum, lived in Hastings – apart from a short stint in London after the war, a stint that resulted in me – there was no father – I mean, I never met him. Irene had been adopted, and her adopted mother died when I was a baby and so it was just me and her, the two of us on our own and I left as soon as I possibly could. Not because I hated it, she was kind, but – it was claustrophobic. Too closed somehow.

This explains her father's vague responses to Frieda's 'family tree' project.

'I used to ask Dad about my grandparents, but he never knew. I always thought he was lying. I still don't understand why you never spoke to her again.'

Again, the arm curled around the notebook as she wrote.

I ran away with your dad but when I fell pregnant, I suddenly wanted to tell her. I knocked on the door, showed her the bump, told her we were happy and OK. She asked me to come back, said we could look after the baby – you – together and for a moment I was tempted, but she said it was a choice: your father or me.

'You chose him, and then you left him anyway.'

They looked at each other across the table.

'That was the last time you saw her?' She nodded.

It was like I was hypnotised: her standing there, the house full of books and dreams. She talked all the time about learning a language, about travelling. She had maps from all over the world on the walls, inherited mostly from her adopted mother, along with an itch for travel. 'We'll go to India! We'll go to China!' she used to say when I was little, but somehow – she was stuck in Hastings.

'Your mum – Irene Guy – how did she end up in Norwood, then?' Frieda asked. 'If she lived in the house in Hastings?'

Frieda watched as her mother wrote more, each word appearing fast, a blue stain:

I heard through a childhood friend that she moved to London. I had no contact with her by then. I just wanted to be away from her. I got sick of the dreams and plans that came to nothing, in the end, everything she said was meaningless. The reality of her life – renting a seaside house alone, never enough money, looking after me – was so far from her daydreams that I hated the delusions, the way she lied to herself.

A clanging noise came from outside the prefab window, and the sound of someone walking, a crunch of the footfalls.

'So you left and never spoke to her again?' Frieda's leg shook a little so she pressed her foot down to stop the vibrations.

It seemed circular, the sense of repeating mistakes, and the women with the babies and no men. I was terrified that I would get stuck too. That I would end up like her, that any will or plan or dream of mine would be destroyed by these delusions. I ran out of the garden, out of Hastings and when you were old enough I told you that she was dead. I am sorry I lied and that I left. Now, of course, I think of her and you all the time. And I love you, though I know you won't believe me. I left you not because I didn't love you but because I had to.

Frieda pulled at the skin on the back of her hand to give herself a pinching shock. She was about to say – she wanted to say – if that was the case, then why are you hiding here, in this place?

'What shall I do with her things?'

But her mother was retreating already, she could tell, into caves inside her head and suddenly it was awkward again. Frieda was consumed with a familiar feeling, the sadness of being unwanted; of a child waiting on a bench to be picked up by someone who doesn't love her. She stood up and the motion of her doing so clicked her mother out of her hypnotic reverie. She put her hand in her beaded bag, pulled out a folded, printed piece of paper and crushed it into Frieda's palm.

Frieda squinted and repeated, 'Her things – her furniture, books. What shall I do with them?'

Keep them, if you want them.

'Don't you want any of it?'

She shook her head.

'Thank you. I suppose?'

Her mother took Frieda's hand, squeezed it too hard, and then let it drop. After that they did not look at each other, and when it became painful to continue the avoidance of meeting eyes, Frieda closed hers, her mind brewing on the facts she had just absorbed. Her mother stood up while Frieda's eyes were still shut and walked out of the room. Whether she looked back at her, or what exactly the expression in her eyes, Frieda decided not to know. She heard everything acutely, though, the scrape of the chair on the floor, each step, and the hesitation at the door handle. The clunk of the door shutting and the coughing that came from outside, and then nothing.

Back outside, the sky was oppressive, rolled out in strips of grey. Frieda walked on the green and brown–red leaves and the soft mud. A little way down the path Frieda stopped and leaned against a prefab wall and wanted a cigarette. It took a moment for the swishing noise in her head to diminish. She didn't know where Tayeb was, near the car she supposed. She unfolded the paper.

Khechari Mudra

'Kha' means Akasa and 'Chari' means to move. The Yogi moves in the Akasa. The tongue and the mind remain in the Akasa. Hence this is known as Khechari Mudra.

This Mudra can be performed by a man, only if he has undergone the preliminary exercise under the direct guidance of a Guru, who is practising Khechari Mudra. The preliminary portion of this Mudra is in making the tongue so long that the tip of the tongue might touch the space between the two eyebrows.

The Guru will cut the lower tendon of the tongue with a bright, clean knife little by little every week. By sprinkling salt and turmeric powder, the cut edges may not join together again. Cutting the lower tendon of the tongue should be done regularly, once a week, for a period of six months. Rub the tongue with fresh butter and draw it out. Take hold of the tongue with the fingers and move it to and fro. Milking the tongue means taking hold of it and drawing it as the milkman does the udder of a cow during milking. By all these means you can lengthen the tongue to reach the forehead. This is the preliminary portion of Khechari Mudra. Once this is done, there is no reason to speak again.

Then turn the tongue upwards and backwards by sitting in Siddhasana so as to touch the palate and close the posterior nasal openings with the reversed tongue and fix the gaze on the space between the two eye-brows. Now leaving the Ida and Pingala, Prana will move in the Sushumna Nadi. The respiration will stop. The tongue is on the mouth of the well of nectar. This is Khechari Mudra.

By the practice of this Mudra the Yogi is free from fainting, hunger, thirst and laziness. He is free from diseases, decay, old age and death. This Mudra makes one an Oordhvaretas. As the body of the Yogi is filled with nectar, he will not die even by virulent poison. This Mudra gives Siddhis to Yogins. Khechari is the best of all Mudras.

A man with a shaved head and a cotton purple shirt was walking towards her. As he approached her she said, 'Excuse me?'

He smiled.

'Can I ask your name?'

He pulled out a red notebook and wrote on it, '*Tom. And you?*'

'Frieda.'

She held out the handout, and then pointed at his mouth.

'You've cut it?' He nodded, then wrote something: *Vow of eternal silence: true nectar.*

Frieda walked towards the hedge remembering the snip snip snip of the nail scissors in the hotel room. What would the Sheikh think of cutting the tongue? The scissors, the fringe, the Sheikh, all of these melded, and instructions came into her mind at once. She wished she could quieten them by finding Tayeb, but all she could see were leaves and the endless grass.

Breathlessness; Limit Mechanical: *When you dread anything you have undertaken as too difficult of accomplishment, just so much more force is required to overcome that idea. If, mounted on your bicycle, you wheel along in a state of apprehension, you induce a high nervous tension that requires a great reserve of power to resist and supply.*

A Lady Cyclist's Guide to Kashgar – Notes

August 15th

As much as possible we have avoided the villages and mercifully the drumming has faded. I think perhaps I carried the sound with me inside my head for some distance because when I told myself to stop listening the relentless banging vanished. Mah says twenty li more and we will reach Aksu.

Twenty li – it sounds reasonable but this route takes us alongside the edges of Takla Makan desert at the worst possible time of year to travel. We have hired a carter and small pony for me. The carter is a native Kirghiz, I believe, and very young, sulky-faced. His cart carries my bicycle, which I refuse to leave, and all of my possessions. I paid the carter a small amount now, with a promise to pay the full amount at Kucha.

The animals – and indeed we – can only bear to travel at night as the daylight stages are simply too hot and so our rhythm is thus: we rise at three in the morning, travel until the sun has fully risen when we find shelter, usually a hovel or a native cave-home in the ground. I am astounded to discover that villagers here spend the daylight hours underground for protection from the heat at this time of the year. We eat, sleep through the hottest hours, then begin to walk again in the evening. We keep going until midnight, or later if we have the strength. In the hellish afternoon sleeps I dream terrible dreams: of my sister with great black feathers tied to her arms; of Kashgar on fire; of the mosque in flames; of Millicent, sitting in chains in a prison beneath the Magistrates' Court; Lizzie, with the bright red ants one sees here crawling in her hair. I thought I would feel lighter as I move away from Millicent, but it is the converse: I am heavier, inside, and almost choked to death by this heat.

(Few days later) August. I have lost track of the days . . .

We picked up bread this morning from a baker who was baking in a cave-hovel in the ground, ten small loaves, each heavy with oil which helps to keep them fresher. Clearly the riots have not stopped traders. We have met carts from Aksu or Turfan before dawn, piled high with rugs and carpets, or dried

fruits and raw cotton. They stop and talk to Mah and sometimes goods are bought. Yesterday we bought six cucumbers
and ate them under a vineyard trellis of dead poplar wood.
The stretches between the vendor stalls that set up at dusk
and the lonely inns we pass are long and melancholy. I try to
understand the exchange of news: talk of riots and trouble and
uprisings in Herat, Tashkend, Samarkand, Turfan and Barkul.
They point at me, stare at Ai-Lien, Mah says, 'She comes from
England, the other side of Hindustan,' and they all nod, as if
that explains my strangeness.

August

Ai-Lien's bright eyes blink, she sucks her fists. Mah made a stew
from some kind of desert rabbit. Like snakes, we sleep in holes.
The hovels are usually buried into the bottom of the rolling
hills, or dug into the cragged cliff-bases of the moraines. They
have a thin walkway and the rest of the floor is taken up by a
mud kang. The ceilings are a patchwork of hay and filthy grass;
ventilation, if there is any, is simply a number of small holes.
There are no windows, and when the door closes it is as close
as possible to being buried alive. Mah, the carter, Ai-Lien and
I share one room as an economy and each time the door closes
over I have the same thoughts: will Mah and his carter kill me?
Or worse? So far, though, Mah falls into a deep sleep, aided, I
suspect, by a smoke of his opium pipe before coming in, and
the two men snore loudly. It is like lying down in a coffin and

each time I think I cannot bear it, then exhaustion overcomes me and Ai-Lien too. Surprisingly we sleep soundly in the cool black space and I concede that, as I slowly become accustomed to them, these hovels do provide exactly what is required: relief from the sun and protection from thieves.

August

We could not go to Aksu – too dangerous. We are on Nan Lu, the South Road. The merchants and travellers on Nan Lu tell us that blood flows in the streets of Aksu where there have been battles between the Hui and the Turkic men. This means we have not been able to replenish our supplies adequately and we have been forced to hunt out day-time accommodation in the primitive agricultural villages.

Although it barely seems possible, each day appears to be hotter than the last. Sometimes I carry Ai-Lien on my back, sometimes in the basket with the shade contraption erected. I check and re-check the map, I dream of Kucha, where I hope Mr Steyning is waiting. Because we couldn't go down into the city we are forced to drink brackish water. I am making up Ai-Lien's dried food with this same water, too.

Just as the day broke today, we witnessed an astonishing sight: a chain of camels, about fifty of them, being led by their Kirghiz driver riding a donkey at the front. They were crossing a dry stream bed, heading deep into the Takla. Even the carter stood to watch. The bells around their necks gave off a

melancholy sound, evocative, I suppose, of the perils of loneliness and solitude. Without Ai-Lien I should feel unbearably
alone, despite Mah and the carter. The camels moved slowly,
attached to one another with decorated woollen tassels. I
remember Millicent saying, 'Too much mishandling of a camel
and they lose the will to live and simply lie down to die.'

August

Mah remains silent for stretches of time, then when he does
talk, slowly and sonorous-toned, I understand nothing. It
is lonely, to be alongside a person who is an unfathomable
distance away. I am inconsistent in my regard of him. I both
want him to acknowledge me more – I suppose protect me –
and am grateful of his distance. The way he spits his bones
out appals me. This last part of the journey has been terrible:
tents pitched in lonely plains, a series of abandoned villages
now waterless and invaded by sand. The wind brings with it
an almost unbearable sense of desolation and Ai-Lien is sore,
uncomfortable and difficult to console. The skin on my cheeks
is burned and peels and my feet are in agonies. I dare not even
look at them.

The carter is an irritating presence, demanding this and
that, to stop here, to speed up or slow down, always in a state of
agitation like a small puppy and this does not help my nerves.
I have begun hallucinating. Occasionally, a streak of wind is
laced with my sister's voice and often-times I see Millicent,

standing with her hair in its tight bun, just the one or two curls moved outwards, next to a boulder, with a hunting pistol in her hand, looking away. Mr Hatchett, in full dinner dress, waves at me from behind the tamarisk tree mounds and today, amongst the light-shimmers, I saw the entire promenade of Southsea, complete with Clarence pier and the memorial and the bright smell of salt and light, rotting seaweed.

? August

I am a fool.

I conveyed to Mr Mah that I must sleep on an upright kang, not one down under the ground. I must have a proper meal and I must bathe Ai-Lien who, I noticed, had black ridges of dirt behind her ears, and her hair was sticking to her head. I could not stand it one more moment. So, we made a small detour off the Nan Lu to a Moslem village where we took rooms at the Inn of Celestial Friendship. The village, like most Mohammedan towns, was surrounded with a protective wall. The gatekeepers were not friendly. Moreover, they were hostile, and I should have realised that it would be unwise to enter. Through one doorway I saw an elegant, long-stemmed blue iris.

Our room was hot, but clean, and I paid extra for water to bathe myself and Ai-Lien. The cushions and the tea and bread, the glimpses of the colourfully covered women in their bright dresses and white and coloured veils, were restful and it was a relief to be away from Mah who was having tea and smoking with the innkeeper. After I had taken advantage of the peace, and the water, and had settled Ai-Lien, Mah knocked on the door and summoned me. Two military soldiers were arguing with the elderly innkeeper.

At our request, the innkeeper had not informed the authorities of our arrival, and as a result was now being confronted by angry military personnel who had been alerted to our presence. The only way we could calm the situation was to bribe both the innkeeper and the soldiers. I gave Mah half of the money that Rami had given me and told him it was all I had. It was idiocy to have come out of the safety of the wilder part of the desert as my passport is not up-to-date and I do not have the official paperwork that allows me to travel through this region. We were forced to leave immediately, very much lighter of pocket.

Back to the hovels and the road then; and what a turn in my mind, what a mix, with the sun taking off layer after layer of my skin, rinsing it through, sending it off. To make matters worse, the next day, or the day after – I don't know now where we are – led us to an even more sorrowful part of the desert; stony waves crossed an empty plateau. The wind blew constantly, raging my face and I kept Ai-Lien tight against me, wrapped in silk and cotton cloths, but she grumbled and wriggled. In between each raised ridge of rubble and stone and boulder I noticed a raised square, covered with bones. As we passed, I saw that they weren't just cattle bones but also horse skulls. I think these must have been troughs for nomadic animals to feed. I pointed at them, Mah said, 'snow'. The animals must have been caught in sudden snowdrifts, buried at their troughs, where they perished from hunger, or froze to death, I suppose. It is impossible to imagine snow in this dreadful heat. If the weather holds, it is one day to Kucha, the Buddhist city, where I pray Mr Steyning awaits us.

August

Disappointment: he is not here. Instead, a Cingalese servant meets us at the city gates with a message: Mr Steyning is unable to reach Kucha, instead he will be at Korla, the next stage. He will arrange payments with guides when there. We will prepare to cross the mountain pass to Karashahr which will lead us on our way across the Thian-Shan mountains to his home in Urumtsi. It is such an interminable distance. I hold on to sweet Ai-Lien, thankful for the supply of dried food.

August

A group of priests and beggars came along the track towards us today making me think of Lizzie and how she would have liked to photograph them. I was confused; I thought that they meant trouble, but Mah stood talking intensely with one of them, who momentarily pulled back his robes to reveal the usual trousers and it occurred to me that they were scouts, or spies undercover. They invited us to a nearby village, telling us that it was safe. What could I do but trust Mah's judgement? We travelled down and for the first time I saw for myself the evidence that some of the bandits that we have heard of have passed through on the way to Aksu and Kashgar: farmhouses burned down, leaving just scalded timbers; an entire village ransacked, apart from the blacksmith who had been forced to shoe horses and repair endless carts. All bread and resources had been forced over. Mah seems to know everyone on this road but this does not make me feel safer; the opposite in fact, I feel as though I am being marched to meet my maker. Frequently, now, we encounter straggles of weary-looking men and boys, some very young, deserters from the press-gangs. Each day, now, we see one or two of them hiding in the grass. I preferred the isolated stretches.

August – perhaps September?

Mr Steyning was at the camp outside Korla.

My relief was like a plunge into water. We reached him yesterday night at a camp with Kirghiz tents, fresh water and food. The first thing he did was to take Mah and the carter aside and the payment negotiations went on for a good few hours. I attempted to contribute what I could but Mr Steyning refused. I promised to repay him in the future, but he shook his head. When the sum was finalised and handed over, Mah simply mounted his donkey and left, without looking round or saying goodbye. The carter, still grumbling and skipping about like a puppy, demanded a meal.

I attended to Ai-Lien who was in a great need of a proper bath and change of blankets and clothes. Mr Steyning had thought of this and had brought with him clean bedding which I gratefully wrapped around the baby. He also arrived with a generous supply of cow's milk and some bread and Russian jam. Once Ai-Lien was clean and settled we talked.

'Where's your sister?'

I told him. He stood with his Bible in one hand and his other hand on my arm and said sincerely, 'My dear, I am so sorry.'

He elaborated on the situation which I try, despite everything, to understand for my Guide: a defected Chinese General is leading a Moslem uprising and they in turn are being pursued by a Chinese army. Both the Moslem Brigands and the Chinamen are press-ganging local boys into their ranks, attacking villages for supplies and the all-round menace from both sides provokes terror in everyone.

'The main problem,' Mr Steyning said, 'is that they keep poisoning and choking the oasis wells.'

'The scouts I have spoken to suggest that they are moving towards the Gobi,' he said. 'Our route will be across the Celestial Mountains. Once over the pass, we will be safe from all of this trouble.'

I was exhausted and overwrought. Kindly, he wrapped a blanket around me and I even leaned against his shoulder, I was so tired. I fell asleep with my head resting on him. When I awoke this morning I was lying down on a thin mattress and nicely covered; he must have done so himself, gently, without waking me.

September?

After a two-day rest, we are making preparations to go across the Celestial Mountains pass. The mountains stand up in front of us like monumental cathedrals. It cannot be possible to go beyond them; they are of such enormity that there simply cannot be a 'beyond'. I am thus stalled in my preparations. I want to sleep for seven years.

—

Riding horseback with two of Mr Steyning's servants, a Cingelese and a Kirghiz, and I have left my bicycle. It is not feasible to take it up through the mountains, though I cannot imagine motion without it. I remember that Lizzie and Millicent just laughed when I first raised the idea of bringing a bicycle on our journey. Then, when they realised I was serious, Millicent stipulated that I would personally pay any additional expenses for the bicycle.

'Why do you want to bring it?' Lizzie asked, but I don't think I answered her. I did not tell her that it was my shield and my method of escape; or that since the first time I pedalled and felt the freedom of cycling, I've known that it is the closest one can get to flying. It will be left to rust in the desert, then, to become bones, and I am bereft.

—

Ten hours along a terribly narrow path on horseback. The weather, Mr Steyning says, is a blessing – cloudless skies. We have created a sleeping bag from a sack for Ai-Lien and sometimes she is carried on my back, sometimes on one of the servants. As our horses grind on, I become stiff and aching, and to keep my attention from the steep cliffs along one side of the road he tells me the love story of the Tieman Pass: a story from ancient times, of a princess and a commoner who meet and fall in love. The king opposes the union and so the two lovers leap to their death in the Kongque He, the Peacock River. I tried to listen, but I am worried. As we climb higher, Ai-Lien is listless, less rigid in her limbs than usual, and is not really looking around in her bright way. I am trying to make sure that she drinks and drinks, but it is difficult. Holding her limbs up, she seems rather weak.

—

The rocks were cragging, leaning. They rose up above us on all sides. The precipitous narrow road was only a couple of feet wide but the ponies seemed sure-footed. Snow-topped spikes touched the sky, some black, some grey, a Vatican of endless spires. We kept moving as night fell because we could not risk being caught if the weather changes. As we headed upwards I was worried for Ai-Lien. She was breathing, and drinking her milk, but she seemed too still. The smiling Kirghiz boy offered to carry her and I agreed – though I didn't want to let her go – because as we embarked upon an even steeper passage, I could not cope with her weight. Next – there was a terrifying stretch, a grey blank cliff on one side, a sheer drop on the other. I talked to myself to calm the nausea: do not look down. Look ahead, at Mr Steyning, at his back, his steady pony marching, amazingly, up the narrow path.

Fear for Ai-Lien tasted foul.

My legs ached. Occasionally a loose boulder crashed down behind us, dislodged from its timeless place by our presence. Then, just before nightfall, Mr Steyning said, 'Look'. Behind us there was an awe-inspiring panorama: purples, shades of lilac to violet to dusky black, and such impressive beauty in the jagged shapes that my eyes actually devoured the scene before me and the exhaustion and aches and dizziness faded.

But we continued, as the darkness came closer, and at each twist in the path I thought this must be it: the flat pasture area for camp that Mr Steyning said was just beyond. I came to hate the treacherous shadows, and oh dear me, the ache in my legs. There were eternal twists of the road and as dusk engulfed us, various birds of prey, including vultures and at least one eagle, hovered above. We rounded a sharp corner and the pathway dropped, it began to descend but this was worse – the rubble and stones dislodging and rolling around the pony's shaking bumping hooves – on, to another sharp turn until we emerged into the shock of a plain. Vast flat land, with soft grass, so that, if it weren't for the difficulty of breathing properly, one would not think that one was up at such a height, already well on our way up into the Thian-Shan mountains.

—

We are in the inn but it is clear that they do not want foreigners here. This is Karashahr, 'the Black city', once a Buddhist centre but it is now Turkic, very much so.

'I shall just go and see what the disruption is,' Mr Steyning said, leaving Ai-Lien and me here alone in a cluttered, cushioned room.

We entered the city through the Chinese area, which is surrounded by a wall and a ditch. Wanting to keep our presence unknown to the Chinese, we made our way to the primitive gateways. Along the mud wall were Turk-shops and the usual towers, with their pagoda-like roofs and at one of these a number of men watched us. They were young, but they did not look friendly; their faces were glowering and intimidating.

We are very much used to being stared at, but there was something different about the atmosphere here and now, it seems, these men have begun jeering and throwing stones at the innkeeper's windows and doors. It started several hours ago and when Mr Steyning went to unload some of our luggage he returned to report that their number is now approximately twenty.

'Who are they?' I asked Mr Steyning when he came back.

'Young Mohammedans. They resent us being here.'

'Why?'

'This is an ardently Turkic town.' The landlord came at that moment, an elderly man, with hands twisted like sarkaul roots. He peered at us through his watering eyes and spoke fast, in dialect, to Mr Steyning.

'They are throwing bits of earth, shouting. He fears the numbers are growing.'

'We are being hounded?' It seemed unimaginable that they would do this: we had done nothing to them.

'He insists that we leave,' said Mr Steyning. 'Let me talk to him.' He took the ancient innkeeper by the arm and they are in the courtyard, talking now.

Later: there was no choice. We were forced to take the road that leads to the famous freshwater lake, Baghrasch kol, in the early evening and to shelter where we could. In the end, we slept in a cluster of poplars, each of us taking turns to sleep or remain awake. All night I fancied I could hear the crack of a step or see the glimmer of a young man's dagger.

—

We are high in the mountains again, up on a plateau. Today we are in a beautiful, golden camp, in a deep valley. The air is colder, the snow-peaks seem closer, but they are welcome after the intensity of the recent heat. The grass around us is golden, the mountains in the distance are blue–golden and there is even a supply of clear spring water. Still, I cannot enjoy it as Ai-Lien is most definitely ill. She is hot and she cries constantly, only stopping to fall into an unnervingly deep sleep. Mr Steyning examined her but admits he has no medical training. It is his associate in Urumtsi who is medically trained.

'The best thing we can do is get to Urumtsi as quickly as possible.'

'But it is the travelling that is causing the trouble.' I am sure that all she wants to do is sleep, still and calm, rather than being jolted around. Mr Steyning took my hand.

'If you should prefer to stay here,' he said, 'we will do.'

It was kind.

'But we need a doctor,' he said.

My baby: not eating properly, and there was blood in her stools. I held her flat against me, willing her peace, but she did not stop crying for such long periods of time. Then, when exhausted, she fell much too still. Nothing has prepared me for this powerful urge to protect her, and the helplessness I currently feel. I rocked her for hours until Mr Steyning came to me.

'Go and lie down for an hour, we are going to start soon and you have had no sleep. I shall watch her.'

I stretched out on the rug and listened to Mr Steyning as he attempted to soothe Ai-Lien. I had travelled this distance half-believing that Mah would kill me (although I realise now that his desire to be paid would powerfully outweigh his wish to do me harm). The relief of being with Mr Steyning instead is profound. Even in the midst of worrying about Ai-Lien, the sense of security is great. Mr Steyning's company is like being tucked in, covered in blankets, safely. If Lizzie were here I could tell her and I do believe she would understand. There is a calmness to him, a stillness that I have – I realise now – been looking for. Perhaps this is what Lizzie felt with Millicent? It occurred to me that if I were to love a man, then a man like Mr Steyning would be the sort of man I would, indeed, love. This is a confusing thought, and even more, it is tangled with memories of tenderness for my delicate, lost sister. I must have absolute confidence in him. Ai-Lien could not possibly die under his surveillance.

–

Ai-Lien has been crying and vomiting. I have had no more than one hour or so of sleep over the past few nights. When I do sleep there are nightmares: Millicent holding crows, empty suitcases left on platforms, Lizzie lost and looking for me, Mr Hatchett presenting my book proposal to a board of croaking toads, a walnut-cased clock from an elsewhere place called home.

–

We met with a doctor in a tiny native mountain town with hardly any Chinese or Russians. The paths zigzag endlessly up.

It took an age for us to reach the town and it is an unwanted diversion from our course. We saw fires in the distance. As soon as we arrived Mr Steyning went to find some local men about a doctor and soon they arrived with an elderly man and a severe-looking woman who is his daughter. This woman took Ai-Lien in her arms and began to examine her; the old man asked Mr Steyning a lot of questions.

Initially I was hopeful as she pulled down Ai-Lien's lip and stared professionally into her mouth, then peered at her eyes, all the time talking in a harsh yammering clamour, but then she went away and before long returned holding a foul-looking concoction in a bowl. I asked what it was but they would give no answer. I looked at Mr Steyning with frustration. They left and I whispered to him, 'I will not give that poison to her.'

He rubbed his palm against his black beard in a weary manner. It was the first time he had sighed in such a way at me, making clear the extent of my troublesomeness, and instantly the illusion of blankets and safety fell away. I held the concoction closer so that he could see for himself.

'I think you are right.'

'Where have they all gone?' Little Ai-Lien was still and pale, wrapped up in her cottons, though breathing.

'They are organising a ritual now to trick the Gods into not taking her,' he said.

'What?' I said. 'They think she is going to die?'

'It is a possibility.'

'What does this ritual involve?'

He told me: they intend to place Ai-Lien on a funeral pyre

and pretend that she is dead in order to confuse and trick their vile idols. I was flabbergasted and refused immediately, exasperated with all the hocus-pocus, but even Mr Steyning, whom I had taken to be a practical man, simply knelt down to pray as if he had given up on Ai-Lien's survival and wished to ensure she passed to the other side safely.

My anger solidified into a clear state of mind, petrifying thoughts and vision into a brightness. I examined Ai-Lien's pale, sweet face – again, that twist of love; the preciousness of her, delicate sculpture of the finest bone and skin. I decided that practicality must out, that I must be calm and decipher the symptoms. Her stools were bloody and her breath was tight which could possibly mean dysentery. I ploughed through my memory to remember what she would, as a consequence, need and decided: lots of fluids and lots of sleep.

It was difficult, but I managed to frequently get sips of boiled and cooled water into her mouth. I massaged her, remembering Rami's hands – wishing that I had Rami's knowledge now – wishing, in a strange way, that Millicent were here; she might know what to do. I rocked her and sang her to sleep.

–

She was a little brighter when she woke. Mr Steyning did not comment, but smiled and I read in his fingers as they moved over his moustache that he truly believed that his prayers had been answered. His useless prayers! And by the end of the day we agreed to push on to Urumtsi as fast as possible now that Ai-Lien seems slightly better.

I wrapped Ai-Lien tightly into her sleeping bag, put it on to my back and it was a joy to feel her small hands wriggling about, her fingers twining about my hair. I still fear for her, desperately, and too many eagles seem to hover overhead.

—

The roads have been good and flat and yesterday we decided to ride through the night, both anxious to reach Urumtsi as soon as possible. A messenger arrived over the dune, a brown-skinned Kirghiz wearing a decorative coat on a small pony, with news that riots and uprisings have even reached this side of the mountains. He described a group of Moslem soldiers in sheepskin trousers with knives hanging from their belts, looking to avenge their mistreatment. It is very unsafe for us still.

The messenger accompanied Mr Steyning and me as we travelled by moonlight through a pass. The tall cliffs on either side sent eerie shadows across the narrow path and as we rode through I examined the outline of Mr Steyning's back in front of me. He is a big man and his expansive frame brings to mind shelter from storms and unhappy dreams. I have not forgotten his weakness regarding Ai-Lien, but watching his back as he rode ahead was reassuring, but also new and strange and it combined with the unusual atmosphere of the pass through which we travelled.

Thoughts such as these collided – I don't know why – with images of my sister running to the bottom of the garden at Pavilion House and putting her hand on the bark of the handkerchief tree. Thoughts of her come unbidden and leave a stamp of brokenness. Soon, we will reach Urumtsi, the greatest city of Sinkiang. I have been travelling so long to this place that it has taken on an element of the fairytale castle, and unlike Lizzie, I have always disliked fairytales.

Eastbourne, Present Day

Sunnyside View B&B

The water was as hot as it could possibly be. Frieda lowered a
foot and the sting of the heat made her make an involuntary
sound, like zzzzaaaah. Light-headed, she watched her submerged
skin grow bright pink and she pulled her foot out quickly.

She sat on the edge of the bath with her feet balanced at
the opposite side. There were rosebuds on the towels, lilies on
the shower curtains. In fact, most items in the B&B bedroom
were covered in stamen and petals and other elements of floral
reproduction. The steam clouded her glasses so she took them
off and surrendered to the blur. The taps became silver non-
shapes suspended against whiteness.

'She wasn't what you were expecting?' Tayeb had asked, but Frieda didn't answer then. In some ways, yes; some ways, no. The brevity of the meeting was a shock after all those years of wondering and all those endless conversations she had had with her in her mind. There was the raggedness of her mother's hair, black and grey and hanging unwashed and netted. It was curious, the odd mixture of low self-esteem and arrogance that came through her expression. The fact that she had chosen that life, over her, left Frieda with outrage in her chest. No, less than outrage, something duller, more like a stomach ache: none the less it was unwanted.

Steam curled its way around her, easing the nausea that had come when she re-read the pamphlet in the car. The bath water took her down and evaporated thoughts of razor blades on the tiny strand of skin that connects the tongue to the bottom of the mouth. As a child she once told her dad that she wanted to be a mermaid: *I want my feet to bleed from dancing on swords and walking on glass: I want to dissolve into the crack of the froth and foam, to be left to fizz on the edge of the beach until oblivious.* He had answered, 'You don't know what you are saying.'

As Frieda rose noisily out of the water she heard Tayeb open the door and come into the small room. She had left all of her clothes outside the bathroom on the bed and so had no choice but to go out just wrapped in the large pink floral towel. Tayeb placed a takeaway bag on the table and the room immediately smelled of cardamom and grease.

Frieda smiled at him. 'You got curry?'

'Yes.'

She looked down at herself, with a towel wrapped around her, tucked under her arms. Tayeb was looking at her shoulders.

'Curry is a good idea,' she said, grabbing the bag. 'Shall we eat?'

After the food and a glass of beer Frieda lay back and rested against pillows. Tayeb flicked on the portable TV and sat awkwardly next to her. She was conscious of being naked under her towel. She should get dressed. She only ate half of her curry portion, and stood up to go to the bathroom to get some water. As she walked back in, Tayeb was sitting upright on the bed.

'Frieda,' he said, 'your back it's . . . beautiful.'

'Oh.' She felt a blush rising in her neck.

Tayeb put all of the curry wrappings into the brown bag, tying it all up. Then he opened the door and placed the bag in the corridor and immediately the smell began to fade.

'Frieda,' he said again.

'Yes.'

'I would really like to . . .'

She looked at him. The sound of a TV from another room came through the wall, a bang bang bang thumping theme tune to something. Frieda stood in front of Tayeb looking at his face, she rubbed one foot against the other, hyper-aware, suddenly, of her exposed feet, her unlovely, knobbly feet.

'I would really like to draw on you.'

Frieda twisted her head, looked at him. 'Draw?'

'On your back,' he said. She paused for a minute, her mouth

was dry, her eyes were sore. She opened and closed her fist. Why not? She liked the idea, actually.

'OK.'

Tayeb grinned, and went to his bag and pulled something out. 'These are bamboo sticks, for Arabic calligraphy. I will draw on your spine, the ink will stay for a while, but it will come off, eventually. What do you think?'

'OK,' she said again, calm, as if drawing Arabic calligraphy with bamboo was a perfectly normal activity for her and the skin on her back. She lay face-down on the bed and turned her head to the side away from the window, towards the wall. He moved about a bit and then settled on to the bed next to her.

'Once,' Tayeb said, 'calligraphers made their own ink from walnut, mixed with pomegranate skin and water.'

'I like the sound of that.'

Tayeb tugged at the towel gently, and Frieda shifted slightly. He pulled the towel so that the whole of her back was exposed and the air was cool on her skin. His eyes must have been looking at her, but instead of becoming self-conscious or ticklish, she closed her eyes and forced herself to be still. There was a tap-tap, the feeling of a point, and then a tracing of a line along her spine. Tayeb pulled the point away and paused, and then it began again. A long, drawn pressure along her back, pushing quite hard, followed by a sharp, almost ticklish sensation of the nib on her skin and for the next few strokes she flinched at each strike, each line, but by the fifth or sixth her muscles responded, flaring under the skin and then melting down. The TV sang its clanging noises.

'What are you drawing?' she said, mostly into the pillow.

There was a pause before he answered, 'An Arabian Ostrich feather.'

'Oh.'

It seemed to Frieda that each stroke grew more delicate, longer. In a slow voice, with his velvet-Arab accent, he began to tell her about this bird, this Arabian Ostrich.

'It's extinct now.'

'Oh no,' Frieda turned her face so that it was not so squished into the pillow.

Tayeb continued, 'My father used to tell me stories about the desert ostriches,' he said, as the strokes grew even longer and softer on Frieda's back. 'They could run faster than any other beast and their necks were long, like snakes. They were more graceful, more beautiful than any other bird.'

'Did you ever see one of these birds?' she asked.

'No. They became . . . I was born in 1967 and they became extinct sometime before then.' His voice was low, almost like a hum.

'That's very sad.'

'Hmm.' The strokes continued, like rain. 'Nobody bothered to preserve them; where I come from, they kill birds with no consideration of their survival.'

'But I thought you said they were the fastest birds.'

'Not faster than a bullet, sadly.' Frieda pictured the graceful ostriches shot and heaped in a pile.

'I used to believe they were magic,' Tayeb continued, 'and that I could ride on the back of one, fly across huge distances.' As he talked, the pace of his drawing slowed down slightly.

'Now I realise that it was stupid of me to dream of flying away on a bird that cannot fly.'

Frieda opened her eyes. She could feel the weight of him moving around on the bed. He himself had not actually touched her; it was just the bamboo stick tracing his message. Each feather-touch rang through her skin and a soft, sleepiness came over her. Behind her eyelids she saw her mother, with her striped hair and her broken tongue, but then she disappeared again; then Frieda was sinking as if she were taken with Tayeb's skin and he with hers, as if their bones could come together with this delicately drawn tattoo.

She had fallen asleep. She sat up. Tayeb was not in the room; he had gone out somewhere, for a cigarette perhaps. The owl was completely awake now and staring at her. It was looking at her with a distinct expression of expectation and hunger and, for the first time, it called to her, a light hooting noise as she stood up from the bed, naked, and walked into the bathroom, twisting her neck around to look at her back.

There was a beautifully drawn feather along her spine. Its tendrils stretched from the vertebrae and spread along her ribs in a rippled flow. She twisted further to try to see the whole thing but she needed a changing room mirror to see it properly. The ink was drying and as it was doing so it was tickling her skin, a pleasant feeling. She wandered back into the room, looking at the owl, wondering if it were hungry, and thinking that she would like to remain naked for ever, so that the entire world might see her back.

The Art of Wheeling: *The rule for climbing universally recommended reads, 'Pay no attention to hills. Ride them.'*

A Lady Cyclist's Guide to Kashgar – Notes

September 19th

I am blessed to be sitting in an English-style study complete with a fireplace. How we remove ourselves from the elements!

Urumtsi is very Turkic and reminds me of Kashgar with its Moslem area situated a mile in length from the South Gate and the mosques calling their siren-songs to stop the men working at noon.

Mr Steyning's house is simple, but also luxurious, if shelter from the desert is to be counted as luxury – and, to my mind, it very much is. Last night I slept on a bed, an actual bed, imported from Russia, and there was a jug and a basin and the water was clean. We were met at the Outer Gate by another

Cingalese servant who had new animals for us to ride on, and refreshments: brick tea and soft bread. I was surprised because Mr Steyning abruptly left me under the care of the Cingalese and with a slight wave, disappeared. The city is not beautiful but it throbs with life. The roads are filthy and the low buildings unattractive. There seem to be flies everywhere. I was led through the streets and huddles of men and women stood up and openly stared at me. For the first time I could see the influences of Russia: Cyrillic script on walls and signs, and Russian bublikis rolls and black bread displayed on bakers' trays.

We drew up at the Mission House, finally, an almost European-style house with two floors. The house next door also belongs to the Mission, apparently, and houses the servants. Mr Steyning was at the door, fully suited, with shining shoes and black hat – he had changed, specifically to receive Ai-Lien and me to his house, and he looked, I realised, extremely robust, eyes shining, not at all tired from the journey.

I am the first British woman ever to visit Urumtsi. But, more on that later.

September 21st

Trouble with sleep: The moment I close my eyes then I am back in the hovel in the ground, being buried in the dark with Mah who might crush Ai-Lien and me at any moment and outside are the thieves. To assuage this I have been re-reading my books for courage. Dear Richard Burton, how you've watched over me. Dear Maria E. Ward, your wisdom never fails. Millicent's Bible does not bring me solace.

September 25th

Mr Steyning's associate, Mr Greeves, has returned from a research tour to the Outer-Mongolia where he has been recording the speech of the natives on his recording machine. He arrived flanked by a small army of native boys carrying his possessions which included bundles of fabrics and botanical specimens, his recording machine equipment and goodness knows what else.

Let me attempt to draw him here since his arrival has brought a change in the atmosphere: so, a vivid presence, he is small, blue-eyed and simmers with England, despite his obvious ease at being here. He is shimmery, like a Dorset dewpond, all green and blues. His moustache looks much-sculpted and held together with some sort of grease, and he moves in flashes, like a grass snake, rendering Mr Steyning larger in contrast and even more bear-like than usual. Apparently Mr Greeves was a doctor in London. He examined Ai-Lien fully on his return, concluding that apart from dehydration, she is otherwise in full health.

Urumtsi is an unhygienic town not at all helped by the rotting melon that is flung everywhere by its inhabitants, which in turn encourages the flies. Nevertheless, Mr Steyning's accommodation is extremely comfortable. Ai-Lien and I have been given over a whole room and an 'auntie' comes to help look after Ai-Lien. This has freed me some time to write my book, and I sit at Mr Steyning's own personal desk to write it. His room is like the personal study of a Yorkshire squire, full as it is with his collections and artefacts and bits and pieces kept under glass. Mr Steyning is, perhaps, rather the Victorian.

I am fairly stuffed with meals and conversation. We have had entertaining meals most nights so far, with some of Mr Steyning's Russian colleagues and their glamorous wives. This evening, Mr Greeves and Mr Steyning both spoke enthusiastically of my book. After dinner Mr Steyning let me know, in that soft voice of his, that he has written directly to Mr Hatchett on my behalf to assist the arrangement for the transfer of the £150 payment.

I am ashamed to say that I have not yet written to Mother. I do not know how to tell her about Lizzie whose absence echoes, without halt, through my bones. There has been no news of Millicent or the priest. I try to think of other things.

But I must work and here we have it, notes so far, on Urumtsi for the GUIDE:

Historically the site of many battles between Mongols, Mohammedans and Chinese, the ancient city of Urumtsi sits at the cross-roads of four ancient trade routes: a long route from Hami to Kansu; a route connecting it to Ili and Russia; a connection to Mongolia; and a long stretch to Kashgar. Originally called 'Bishbalik', it is the Uighur capital of the Sinkiang kingdom. The Uighurs came from the North of the province, but were forced out and settled on the edges of the Celestial Mountains and even as far down as Hami. The Chinese finally gained power over the Dzungaria province in the mid-eighteenth century. During the Mohammedan Rebellion of 1865 many Chinese were murdered . . .

Yes, oh dear. Too dry.

September 27th

I am the first British woman ever to have visited Urumtsi and as such, I seem to be considered a sort of celebrity. People have been visiting me constantly. I have met the Chinese Governor and his wife, the Qazaq leaders, the leading members of the Russian émigré community, a Persian family bearing long fat, aromatic dates. It brings to mind Burton's comments: *everyone talks, and talking here is always in extremes, either in a whisper, or in a scream.* It is exhausting, but, indeed, what I find more and more is that I want to spend time with Mr Steyning. He is interested in Ai-Lien, I have noticed. He often takes her from the 'auntie' and sings to her and soothes her to sleep.

I have concluded that I must talk to Mr Steyning about my feelings for him although to render into actual words a sensation so private and intimate so that it would be as though a part of me is turned inside-out strikes me as impossible; but, I see no alternative. I cannot remain in this state. We are to have a picnic tomorrow at Tian Chi, the

Heavenly Lake. It is apparently a festive day. I am resolved to say something then.

September 29th

The picnic was next to the most miraculous lake and what an incongruous sight, a European scene, just six hours ride South East from Urumtsi. Snow-topped mountains, cypresses and ferns, it was as if I were transported to my beloved Swiss Alps. The lake is a stunning sapphire-ice blue and around its banks clusters of Kirghiz yurts were set up, their inhabitants clearly in festive mood. There was much smoke from the fires and makeshift stoves, and children rushed in and out of the water, squealing. All in all, it should have been the perfect opportunity to talk to Mr Steyning, but wasn't. There was a low hum and many wasps around and I quickly succumbed to a headache, brought on no doubt by the sharp clear air. In addition, we ate pickled herrings and they supremely disagreed with me. Despite all of this, I convinced myself to continue along my self-appointed course of action.

There was, eventually, a lull in the conversation. Mr Greeves had wandered off to talk to an acquaintance Kirghiz man, Ai-Lien was asleep and as we sat together admiring the shimmer of the lake, I found the courage to ask Mr Steyning if he had ever wanted a wife. As soon as I said it, I was aghast to see that I had embarrassed him greatly.

'Oh, I do not think a Missionary life is what most wives would be looking for,' he said.

I am sure I was blushing hideously but having ventured so far I could not reel myself back: 'It seems to me that it might be a wonderful life.' I looked at the lake rather than at him.

'Well, you are an exceptional woman,' he said. His nose, a proud triangular sharpness, seemed sharper, as if intent on leading its owner to a welcomed exit as he looked at the lake rather than at me, and I was at a loss, almost fainting with the headache and the unknowing. My heart was ready to run and throw itself into the lake of its own accord whilst my head wished to shut up any doors within myself that I had foolishly opened and to rapidly retreat. Still, out they came, the dreadful words, in a high voice as if spoken by a child playing at echoes rather than by me:

'I can't but help think, Mr Steyning, that you need someone to look after you.'

'You think so, Miss English?'

'Yes,' I rolled a piece of bread in my hands, 'I do.' I looked directly at him then. He is indeed a fine-looking man in the raw sunlight. His beard, black and wiry, frames the lower half of his pleasant face and his eyes are intelligent. His largeness emits a lack of pettiness. I am sure that I saw something flicker across his eyes, some understanding. At that moment, of course, Ai-Lien began to cry; I turned and attended to her and when I looked back up, he had stood up and was looking out at the horizon with his hand shielding the sun from his eyes. He did not look down at me again for some minutes. I do believe that my message was clear to him, although I cannot be sure. I am thoroughly inexperienced in the ways of sexual matters. Once we were back at his house again, and he was busy working and I was alone, I began to fret and relive the conversation over and over so that now I cannot know what it means, if anything.

I have hunted through my memory of the afternoon for signs of his response, but, though polite, and warm, as always, there has been nothing as clear as a signal.

October 4th

I have, I realise, been a fool. Life continues as normal. The two gentlemen are gracious, they ask for nothing, no money. They simply say, 'Write your book, Miss English.' I try to get them to call me Evangeline, but although they nod, they forget and always refer to me as Miss English.

Then, today, I came into the room where Mr Greeves was looking over a moth collection which he had laid out across a table. I walked in and looked at the fairylike insects, the lacewings pinned and trapped; their destiny to be gassed and catalogued.

'This one is a hawk moth,' he said, and smiling, he began to talk me through the collection. As he did, his gold clock dangled against his waistcoat, and with his trimmed moustache and neat golden belt clip it occurred to me that he is more elusive than Mr Steyning and more consciously polite. He moved over to the opposite side of the room where the attractive Bilhorn folding harmonium organ rested against the wall.

'How is the book coming along, Miss English?'

'Oh, well, it's coming. I have these ideas, and memories and images, but it's a problem. You know, sorting it into a . . . meaningful whole.'

'Indeed, therein is the craft.' He lifted the lid of the harmonium and began to press a few notes. It was clear that he was not particularly musically inclined.

'Amazing,' he said, 'to think of the distance this harmonium has travelled.'

'Oh?' His fingers pressed a few more notes, a low sound, a flute of air.

'Yes, hauled this way and that. Mongolia, Shanghai.'

'You've seen much of the world, Mr Greeves.'

'Do you mind?' He had taken out a Hatamen and was lighting it, before – I noticed – I had actually agreed. He offered one to me.

'Oh, no,' I said, 'thank you.'

'Of course, I am used to dear Millicent – smokes like a soldier, as you know.'

'You're friends with Millicent?'

'Absolutely, I used to know her in London a long time hence.'

I thought that he might begin to question me about her current status. I suddenly felt rather cautious of Mr Greeves.

'We used to frequent the same . . . circles.' The smoke from his Hatamen spread across his pinned insects.

'Ah,' I said. He let out another long line of smoke and looked me in the eye.

'I should imagine she got her mitts on that sister of yours.' I took a deep breath, shocked at the familiar tone. He was undoubtedly sneering.

'I am not sure I understand, Mr Greeves?'

'She was always one for the younger women and I heard that your sister was a beauty.'

I turned away to hide a moment from what he said. I understood several things: one, that he did not consider me a beauty – that much I knew anyway – but also, something else, that Millicent and he came from a different world, one that, until that moment, hadn't fully occurred to me.

'You know that my sister died, just recently?' I meant it as a reprimand, and to cover my outrage.

'I know. And I am terribly, dreadfully sorry.' With the stealth of a cat, he stepped back neatly into the role of genial doctor, translator and lepidopterist, but I had seen an entirely different person – a different life – and although I did not like it, I suddenly felt compelled to have a frank talk with him.

'Mr Greeves,' I turned to face him fully and he looked at me, his eyes wolf-blue, and again there was that surface of the water shimmer about him. I was about to ask him if he thought there were any possible chance, any chance in the world, that Mr Steyning might marry me. The words were fully formed, but as I was about to say them Mr Steyning himself stepped into the room and looked at us. He hadn't expected me there, clearly, as he was in a slight state of undress, his braces were down and his collar undone.

'Ah, Miss English,' he said, smiling, and then he looked crossly at Mr Greeves.

'Larry! Don't smoke in this room, really.' He made a show of coughing and flapping his hands and walked over to the windows to open one.

'Apologies,' Mr Greeves said. Mr Steyning walked past Mr Greeves and as he did I saw Mr Greeves reach out, take Mr Steyning's hand in his, for a moment, and squeeze it. Mr Steyning pulled his hand away in a snatch, and turned towards me.

'The fresh melons have been delivered, Miss English.'

Having extinguished his cigarette, Mr Greeves gave a small, sarcastic bow, and turned back to his moths, running his finger over the glass casing. I made my excuses, retreated to my room and sat in a heap on a small chair by the window.

Eastbourne, Present Day

Quality Cod! Fish Restaurant

Tayeb would have liked to hold Frieda's hand as they approached the restaurant on the corner of the High Street in Eastbourne. It had just opened. His fingers flickered towards hers, but he moved in front of her instead, going inside and speaking confidently to the fish-fryer.

'Is Nikolai about?'

The fish-fryer was a dark, small man, who frowned at Tayeb and then turned his head to the kitchen and made a whistling noise. After a minute a sulky Eastern European-looking girl popped her head out.

'Get Nikolai,' he said and, without saying anything, she

disappeared. The green gherkins pickling in a jar glimmered in the light, obscene in their fatness, like a giant's fingers. After a couple of minutes' wait, a tall, curly-haired man came out with a dark trace of a beard on his face. He walked straight up to Tayeb and embraced him, then turned to Frieda and shook her hand.

'Upstairs, brother,' he said, 'come upstairs.'

Tayeb believed as a child that dog whiskers were magical. He would crawl through the dust on the floor of their house specifically looking for dog whiskers. Their neighbours thought they were crazy for letting dogs live in their house. Most people in Sana'a would not dream of having a dog for a pet, let alone several great, gangling beasts. But Tayeb's father had spent some time with an English man who worked at the Embassy who was interested in falconry. This man always had dogs with him, and Tayeb's father liked the idea. He had several salukis and they would bark all day at the birds.

When Tayeb first met Nikolai's dog – a flippy, dribbly Boxer – it ran towards him, a whirlwind of dog-claw bounding into his arms, covering Tayeb with a slithery wipe of its filthy tongue and rancid breath. Tayeb laughed. It had been a long time since he had such proximity to a dog, and as he wrestled it to the kitchen floor, Nikolai had laughed too, watching them and smoking a cigarette. Then Tayeb had righted himself, stood up, and shouted at the dog to sit down. It did so, and Nikolai was impressed.

'He won't normally take a command from anyone but me,' he said.

'Well, it's all about the tone with dogs.'

It came back to him now, the memories in a rush. They had been working late. Tayeb remembered Nikolai putting a bottle of whisky on the table and all of the kitchen staff were invited to have a drink and to join in the game. The room was a fug of smoke and cards as the washer-uppers were gambling their wages before pay-day had even arrived. At about quarter past midnight, there was a knock on the door.

Nikolai shouted to ignore it, laying down a king of spades and tipping back the last dregs of glass, but the knocking was insistent. Tayeb stood up and scraped his chair back across the kitchen lino.

'I'll go and see what it is,' he said. He went through into the main area of the restaurant, with Burdock the boxer wriggling at his heels. Burdock barked but Tayeb shushed her. At the door was a woman, very young, about 19, wispy haired, watery blue eyes, looking quite drunk. She had a palm flat against the window of the door and her head was hanging down, as if she had lost the will to live. She was crying.

Tayeb twisted the deadlock and as he did so the girl looked up at him. Mascara had spread below her eyes like spiders. He opened the door.

'I need Nik,' she said.

'Nik?'

'He's here, I know he is, the bastard.'

Tayeb looked at the girl. 'You're drunk, darling. You need to go home.'

'I need to speak to Nikolai.'

'Stay here,' he said. He closed the door again and she slumped against it, her back sliding down the glass. Tayeb walked back into the kitchen where Nikolai was shouting at Seif who had just folded inappropriately. Seif banged his fist on the table in frustration.

Tayeb walked up to Nikolai and leaned over to him, whispered in his ear, 'A drunk girl wants you, don't think she'll go away.'

Nikolai looked up, 'Tell her to go away.'

'Not that easy.'

Nikolai looked round. Everyone was looking at him, listening.

'Young, sort of desperate looking,' Tayeb said.

Nikolai groaned, threw his cigarette into the ashtray and stood up. He disappeared. Tayeb and Seif and the washer-uppers all listened to the sound of the door opening and a girl sobbing. Tayeb closed the door so that the other men in the kitchen wouldn't hear, but they had all mostly turned to the TV screen, anyway, as the commentary for the boxing match was revving up.

Tayeb opened the door to the restaurant and slipped out of the kitchen.

'How could you do this to me?' The girl's face was a mess of tears and mascara. Tayeb stood near the counter and watched. He could see that Nikolai was looking stressed, unusual for him. He tried to pull the girl's arms down but she was furious, flailing. She swiped at a sprig of fake plastic flowers arranged on a table, knocked them on to the floor.

'You told me you'd leave her, you told me you loved me, but you just left me like a bit of rubbish,' she got hold of a chair as if to throw it.

Tayeb looked up and outside of the window saw a car pulling up. It was Nikolai's wife. He shouted to Nikolai:

'The Mondeo's outside.'

Nikolai stood upright. He turned and looked at Tayeb who saw absolute fear in his eyes. The girl had sunk to the ground and was sobbing, stroking the carpet with her right hand. Tayeb walked over, got hold of her by the elbow and gently stood her up.

'Come with me,' he said, pulling her towards himself and she collapsed into him.

'I'm going to be sick.'

He took her to the disabled toilets at the back of the restaurant and locked the door behind them. As soon as she saw the toilet she leaned over to release the remnants of a night's drinking (these English girls drink so much) and above the sounds of the girl retching, he could hear Nikolai arguing with his wife about going home.

'It's the match, Sarah,' he was saying. 'I'll be home as soon as it's over. It's the biggest one of the decade!'

Tayeb heard her voice, shrieking and upset.

'The kids have not seen you for seven days, Nikolai.'

He must have moved her then, outside towards her car, because there was a muffled sound and then finally the reverberations of the engine pulling off. The girl slid to the floor and rested her head on the not-so-clean tiles behind her head.

She looked at Tayeb. 'He's a Greek–Cypriot wanker.' Tayeb offered her a cigarette and she took it.

'True,' he said, lighting one for her and then one for himself. 'I used to smoke in a toilet like this at home,' he said. She looked at him. Like most English people, she did not bother to ask him where home was. She stared at the cigarette in her hand as if it were dynamite, but still continued to smoke it.

'I shouldn't be having this,' she said.

Tayeb looked at her. Her hair, which was dank and sweaty from the exertion of being sick, stuck around her face and half covered her eyes. She had a face that was pretty by virtue of its youth rather than its inherent features. The skin was soft-looking, undisturbed as yet by weather or life; it was a milky face, and her clear eyes were shiny and healthy looking despite the alcohol in her system.

'I'm pregnant, aren't I?' she said.

'It's Nikolai's?'

'Yep.' She began to cry again, less hysterical this time, just like a child.

Tayeb put the toilet seat down, flushed it and pulled her up and sat her on it so that her hair was away from the unsanitary tiles. She really looked very young.

'I shouldn't be drinking either,' she said, 'but I am, I want to stop it, before it grows. You know?' She looked up at him. 'I need some money . . . to get . . . rid of it. Will you ask him for me? He won't talk to me.'

Tayeb nodded, thinking that he should feel more, be gentler

towards her, this girl in distress, but there was something about her that he disliked. Even so, he tried to be polite.

'Why don't you come out here, into the restaurant, and I'll make you a coffee and go and see if I can get Nikolai to talk to you.'

She stood up, staggered a little and almost slipped down again. He caught her by the elbow and opened the door. Sitting her down at a table in the corner of the restaurant he went to find Nikolai who was standing with a glass of whisky in his hand, staring moodily up at the TV on the wall. The kitchen boys were subdued.

'Nik,' Tayeb said. Nikolai turned and walked towards him with a grim face. Tayeb gestured to the restaurant and left Nikolai to walk around and confront the girl.

The next day Nikolai had handed Tayeb a hundred pounds.

'What's that for?' he said.

'For, you know, helping me out, with Sarah and the . . . you know.'

'Yalla, I don't need this,' he handed it back. 'It's that little girl you need to give money to, not me.'

Tayeb looked him in the eye. 'She told me.'

Nikolai made a noise, like a snap with his fingers. A frustrated gesture.

'It's nothing to do with me. Look, it's forgotten.'

Tayeb leaned down and gave Burdock a stroke. 'Good dog.'

'Listen,' Nikolai said, 'you saved me, keeping her out the way of Sarah. I appreciate it. If you ever need help, ever need anything, you come to me? OK?'

'OK.'

'I really mean it.'

'OK.'

Now, here he was, all these years later, needing help, needing Nikolai, having walked in circles for years, getting nowhere like the traces and lines of one of his drawings that were supposed to become a whole but somehow never did. He hoped Nikolai meant what he said.

Breathlessness; Limit Mechanical: *Seated awheel, the bicyclist feels master of the situation. The bicycle obeys the slightest impulse, moving at will, almost without conscious effort, virtually as much a part of the rider, and as easily under control, as hand or foot.*

A Lady Cyclist's Guide to Kashgar – Notes

October 8th

I have informed Mr Steyning that it is time for me to leave and that I must return to England as soon as possible. I insisted that I was suddenly consumed with a terrible guilt regarding my mother – which is not, actually, untrue – and, of course, he did not press me to stay. He simply looked helpful and responsive. What did I expect? I am appalled at my own stupidity.

We have examined the maps together and he has consulted various friends in town. Kindly, he took my hand in his and said, 'The Inland Mission will look after you.'

'You are very kind,' I said, 'but I can support myself. You've already done so much.'

'Nonsense. I will arrange for a colleague to meet you in Moscow and you will be accompanied and assisted with the purchasing of tickets to Warsaw and Berlin, on to Paris. The final part will be the ferry from Calais to Dover.'

Perhaps it was my imagination but I fancy he looked wistful, for a moment, at the memory of Dover.

'It will be an extraordinarily long journey for you, but we shall do our best to make it a pleasant one.'

'I don't know how to thank you.'

'I myself will accompany you to Chuguchak on the border, or, as the Chinese call it, "City of Seagulls".'

I might have cried and as he gave me tea and saw to Ai-Lien, I almost spoke of my great foolishness. I could see clearly, then, that he was simply a good man and that I had misinterpreted all that had transpired between us, but he would never know, I hoped, and for that I am happy.

October 10th

There is much to prepare. The paperwork is endless and protracted. There are vast, difficult visa issues for the complex crossing from this region to Russia. I am waiting for my money from Mr Hatchett to be transferred as it is likely that bribery will be required. It is seven hundred li frum Urumtsi to Chuguchak and it is imperative that we depart soon because a little later and it will be too cold at night-time for this journey, but then, on the other hand, if I leave it too long and spring

starts then the great thaw will occur, making the rivers treacherous and impassable for weeks. Now is just the right time.

There has been much discussion on the issue of Ai-Lien, my
own foundling.

'I intend to take her,' I said to Mr Greeves and Mr Steyning.
'Do you think this is possible?'

'Indeed,' Mr Greeves said, 'I doubt any official here will care
for the cost of her life on their hands, but are you sure?'

Mr Steyning put his hand on mine, 'She was given to you,
Miss English dear, for whatever reason. You belong together
now.'

October 14th

Mr Greeves and Mr Steyning, as a farewell present, have given
me a delightful Chinese toy, complete with opium den, a well
and a market and a curious silver torture scene, all encased in
a glass dome.

'It doesn't appear to be the most practical of presents, I
fear,' Mr Steyning had said, unwrapping it from several sheets
of hessian, 'but when you are back in England, you will look
upon the scene in wonder that you have been here, and lived
this life.'

He wound up the toy, and inside the glass, the figures moved
in time to a clinky-clunky oriental melody. Then he lifted it
up and showed me that underneath, the bottom of the wooden
base slid open to reveal a secret compartment.

'When you get to the border in Siberia, you will not be able to take over any books, letters, papers or photographs. If you hide them in here and claim it is a souvenir, that you are a tourist, then there is a hope that you will be able to make it across the border with a few of your artefacts intact, and indeed, your manuscript.'

The compartment has room for Lizzie's camera, this diary and what I have begun as a manuscript for my Guide. Also, several other travelling companion books, dear Mrs Ward, and Burton. I have also put in Millicent's Bible, some of Lizzie's photographs and, although I cannot say exactly why I want to carry them all this way, some of Father Don Carlo's translations. I have decided, also, to take the mimeograph machine with me. Whether it will make it across the border, I cannot say.

Mr Steyning has also helped me arrange the necessary paperwork for Ai-Lien. She needed to be registered and to have a passport, and so we undertook this.

'You need to anglicise her name,' he said and I tried out a few names. It seems odd to give her an English name, Ai-Lien, Alien. Love Bond. Ai-Lien sounds a little like Irene. Her mother's name we were told that distant day, when we were sitting like buddhas at the Magistrates' Court, had been Giyun. I took the fountain pen and on the passport papers I wrote her name as Irene Guy. Mr Steyning kindly paid the courts here the requisite sum and now she is officially my adopted daughter.

I kiss her all over, pretty little Irene, her face bright and open and sweet and now, such a miracle, she smiles at me.

October 16th

I am tormented by thoughts of Millicent in a jail underneath the Magistrates' Court, her ribs poking through her skin; I think of Father Don Carlo, walking towards the Mohammedan riots in his long black robe, his Bible in his hand; and Lizzie, pecked by birds. Mr Steyning found me at the window of his study, looking down at the sleeping black city, mulling these things over. I told him a little of my troubles.

'Is there a way, Mr Steyning, that we might try to discover Millicent's fate in Kashgar? As the date of departure grows imminent I worry that I should not have left her.'

'You need to look forward, now, Miss English. Move gently forward and it will become easier.'

'I should have buried my sister somehow, Mr Steyning.'

'It was not possible, from what you say.'

'To leave this desert seems a profound betrayal, but if I stayed here, well . . . I do not think I can.'

'I understand,' he said.

October 30th

The first opportunity to write – so, we are travelling by Russian tarantass. It is a Siberian cart, much faster than the smaller spring carts, pulled by Chinese mules. The long trap is fastened to three ponies, each connected by a large hoop that is covered in bells, the jangling of which rings in my head until I might spin into madness.

We did not stay long in the colourful city of Manas where Mr Steyning bought me supplies and provisions to last me the next stage of the journey; we are now fifty li from Chuguchak. These horses are solid beasts. Mr Steyning is firm with our Qazak driver and the journey, so far, passes well.

Ai-Lien is packed sweetly into a pillowcase which fixes either on to my front or back, and from which she can look around or sleep. The roads are fairly well trammelled and there is certainly a lot of traffic, carters and traders, sellers and travellers all on their own journeys, tramping back and forth. We met travellers from Novo Sibersk on their way to Kashgar carrying large quantities of opium (and even attempting to sell some to Mr Steyning!), also cotton traders and Qazak families and travelling vendors selling clusters of ginger, fennel, cardamom and cloves. At one point we encountered a group of Siberian monks who offered us *ikons*.

There are plenty of inns; finding accommodation each night is no trouble. In the interests of speed we survive on tea and bread in the day, then stew or rice or noodles in the evening. We occasionally stop to buy sheep's milk or melon but otherwise we roll on and the edges of the earth have become unsteady and it is as if the desert floor might fall; I cannot understand the difference between the sky and the ground sometimes. Each li takes me further from my lost sister. The only thing that is clear is that, because of this baby, I must continue, onwards to an elsewhere place, though I can't exactly remember why.

November 5th

It lives up to its name: the seagulls are here, flocked and collected. I understand that they have travelled a vast distance along the Irtish river, from the Arctic lands and certainly there is a breath from the Arctic in the air tonight: it is extremely cold, though not quite snow. Seagulls must be great travellers; they do not get bored, they do not sing low, or sad.

Chuguchak is an important border city being the main outlet from Turkestan to Siberia and so endlessly there is the business of providing the temporary passports and visas. The consulates are hustled together in the centre of the city, the most obvious and dominant being the Russian. The whole city is much more Russian than Chinese. Like Urumtsi, there is a large postal centre and telegraph offices and I have telegrammed home to Mother, telling her of Lizzie's death, and my return. Poor Mother.

Ai-Lien – I try out her new name, Irene – and I watch seagulls squawk and squabble with each other. We must wait for the visas and the paperwork to be finished, and this waiting I do not want. It is recognisable, now, the tension between movement and stillness; the feeling that I want to go, but paradoxically, I want to remain. A pause does not help me, it provides time for reflection and reflection leads to sadness. I think of myself, arriving at Kashgar, terrified of the desert, and now – would I go back, if I could, into the vast space of it? I do believe I would. I can see how one wanders, eternally.

Ai-Lien smiles each time she looks at me, bright, sweet black eyes and I think of what I will say to Mother, to explain this baby. It could be that it is a terrible wrong to take Ai-Lien from the desert, but as we watch the seagulls it occurs to me that perhaps I should like to live by the sea, after all.

November 9th

The seagulls drop and dance, finally the paperwork is arranged and tickets are acquired. Trunks packed and I am as ready as it is possible to be for the next part of my journey: a six-day drive to Lake Zaisan, river steamer up the Irtish. The Trans-Siberian railway to Omsk. A week in Moscow and then on, to Berlin and London.

Last night, an attempt – as such – at a goodbye with Mr Steyning, to whom I owe so much, as we ate fine Russian steak and drank thick, coal-black coffee in the dining corner of an inn.

'As I've already said, I simply do not know how to thank you.'

He took my hand, his face thick-spread and sincere.

'My dear. Go home to England, make yourself comfortable and read through your diary and write it into your book.'

'Do you really think I am capable of writing it?'

'Of course.'

I wished that I had a gift to give him, something precious. I said so. 'I will send you a copy, if it ever becomes a real, actual thing. And of being a mother, do you think it will be . . . possible?'

Again he smiled. 'I have arranged for someone to meet you at Victoria Station as long as all goes according to plan and you arrive on the fifteenth January.' Then, taking hold of my hand, he said, 'I shan't tell you who. When you arrive, stand under the great clock in the concourse at Victoria Station at six o'clock on the fifteenth, and you will be found.'

Tomorrow I will be gone, across the border.

The horses will be difficult to restrain, the Qazak driver will jump on the seat. There will be a flurry of movement and horse-breath and then a spring forward and I will wave and Mr Steyning will wave. Lizzie will stand behind him, in her long smock, holding a blue convolvulus from the Pavilion House garden, not waving, just watching. Millicent will be there too, though she will be looking away at something on the other side of the hills.

Eastbourne, Present Day

Quality Cod! Fish Restaurant

She'd had the dream again: in the hotel and the phone not working. Authorities outside, the Sheikh, talking to her – instructing her – regarding the appropriate method for the cutting of tongues. . . Sitting up, she looked around. Nikolai and Tayeb were sitting on a Persian rug, Nikolai was on his phone. Bowls of crisps and nuts were lined between them. Arrangements were clearly being made. They smiled at her. She was on a sofa above a restaurant, and somehow she had nodded off for a second.

Nikolai put his phone on the table, lit a cigarette and explained the decisions: they had one day in Eastbourne

– today – and then that evening, Tayeb would be driven to Harwich in Essex by Nikolai's brother, who had a truck with a false floor for bringing counterfeit goods over on ferries.

Frieda looked at Tayeb; he was scratching his wrist and staring down at the rug. In the B&B she had woken up with her legs in a knot around his, ankle against a calf, and her hand resting on a back. The morning bright light illuminated his skin and she saw that it was covered in scars and sores, as if the skin itself was speaking of troubles. She moved her hand, slowly, over his back. It was not unpleasant, it was just his skin speaking out, sending out its message, just as he had written his message out on her in the night.

'Tayeb,' Frieda said, 'what do you think? Will this plan work for you?'

'My own private compartment,' he said quietly and she couldn't tell whether there was bitterness; she thought perhaps there was.

As these plans were discussed and pistachio nuts eaten, Frieda took the missionary notebook from her bag and gently flipped through the pages, thinking of her mother and of Irene, a woman she never knew. Nikolai sat close to Tayeb and they were murmuring to each other.

She remembered the other items from Irene Guy's flat and stood up, stretching, and went downstairs to the car. In the boot was the holdall with the things she had thrown in from the flat, assuming that she would never be able to visit there again as the week was nearly up. There was the pile of books tied together by the woven fabric, the transcripts, the camera, the Chinese ornament with the peculiar torture scene and the small black Bible. This must have been Millicent's, she realised, examining it. It was well thumbed. She peered at a page that had come loose, A TABLE OF THE MOVEABLE FEASTS FOR FORTY-SIX YEARS 1913–1958. She untied the strip of fabric to look at the books. The first one had a faded blue cover and the lettering was a worn-down gold. Once, presumably, it had a dust jacket. On the inside cover was a frontispiece illustration of a lake in a desert bearing the title 'The Heavenly Lake'. Frieda opened to the front page. The book began:

Travel is, in many ways, an untranslatable experience. For the purposes of writing this book I have drawn heavily upon my diaries and notes, but in essence, they have become as dreamlike and as distant as my memories of the desert which once was so very real to me. This is the problem with the communication of another sphere; in all honesty, adventures – for want of a better word – are inherently personal, and intimate. Even the materiality of the buying of tickets, the alighting of trains, the catching of ferries and all the consequential trifles that go into the organisation of such an endeavour amount, ultimately, to a series of personal moments. Still, this is my attempt to capture something of these travels. Let us hope it is a valiant one.

She looked again at the cover and saw the imprint of the long-faded title: A *Lady Cyclist's Guide to Kashgar*, by Evangeline English. This, she realised, was a published version of the journal she had been reading, and on the inside cover, written in ink, it said *Francis Hatchett*. It was presumably his copy of her book. Frieda returned to the room of chatting, smoking men, holding the blue book and the Bible.

'Right: this is the plan,' Nikolai said, 'we get Tay' into Holland, then he goes straight to Amsterdam.'

'What will you do in Amsterdam?' Frieda asked

'I have an old family friend. He can stay there for a while,' Nikolai answered.

Nikolai offered to pay all of the costs required and give Tayeb enough money to live on for some time. There was much hand shaking and clapping of backs and nodding and smoking throughout these negotiations. Nikolai was gruff, addled, and, Frieda could see, a bit of a bastard, but he obviously cared about Tayeb.

Nikolai arranged whisky glasses on a low table and despite it being not yet eleven in the morning, Frieda sipped the thick, sweet brown liquid and enjoyed its burn-rush in the mouth. She opened the faded book, and flicked through its pages; there were more illustration plates, a photograph of dusty-faced and pigtailed children in exotic clothes, standing in front of a panorama of mountains trailing off to infinity. At the back of the book, sandwiched in the index, was a brown envelope. She pulled it out and opened it. Inside were several letters. The mark at the top of the paper said *Eaton Highlands' Quality Linen Notepaper*.

It was a thrill to rub the thin blue sheets and see the swirl of the ink; she could see straight away that it was Evangeline's handwriting. There were several letters, or parts of letters, and a few telegrams clipped together. Francis Hatchett must have kept them in the book; they were barely creased. She began to read *January 30th, 1924, Acacia House*, but Tayeb was speaking to her.

'What shall we do, then?' Tayeb said, smiling. 'It looks like we have one more day together.'

Frieda moved over to the window and looked out at the seaside street. A sizeable gang of seagulls were clamouring and fighting around the contents of an industrial-sized bin. They were charging each other, wings crooked and beaks orange, racketing and squawking a holy terror of a noise. She folded the letters back into the delicate, thin envelope and replaced them in the index section of the book.

'Let's go out,' she said, 'have a look around.'

Breathlessness; Limit Mechanical: *There is a certain amount you can do, or think you can do; this is one measure of your capacity.*

A Lady Cyclist's Guide to Kashgar – Notes

January 15th, 1924

The sweetness of the ferry crossing and the shock of English voices; a Kentish voice shouting, 'Move along madam, move along.'

Eyes everywhere peered at my queer outfit. Mr Steyning's friend, Herr Schomaker, assisted me in buying a European outfit in Berlin but it was German in flavour, a fur scarf and cloche that looked strange in contrast with the dowdy-coloured wrapover coats that I saw on the women on the train from Dover to London.

At Victoria Station I stepped into the thick tide of London's workers dancing and fighting around me, making their way to wherever they were going. Overwhelmed, I swayed on my feet, fearing that I might faint. I held Ai-Lien to me like a talisman, though it was I who was her guardian. She was asleep in my arms, her face relaxed and her mouth slightly open.

I put my feet as flat as possible to steady us against the pushing and the rushes, standing on the concourse built out of the great gains of Empire. Ai-Lien was a dead weight in my arms and my trunks and bags were behind me. The young porter was waiting expectantly. I looked round for the clock, and was surprised at the change in appearance of the station. The Brighton and South Coast side had been connected to the Chatham side. Southern Railway Company appeared to have even removed the screen wall and the platforms had been re-numbered since my last visit. The clock, however, was still mounted high on the wall in its usual place and I gestured to the porter to follow me as I walked towards it.

There was no one there that I knew, indeed, I thought, well, how could it be that someone were to meet me? Nothing but a pigeon, scuffing on the floor, but I needed a moment to gather myself. My journey was not quite over. There was yet another train to Southsea to be boarded, if I could identify the correct platform and I was not quite ready for that. I paid the porter and watched him scurry into the crowds. I stood, stroking the soft hair on Ai-Lien's head, thinking of Millicent sitting on the divan and Lizzie clicking her Leica camera, and heard the great ticking clock chime out loud as it struck six o'clock.

A voice came up behind me, 'Miss English?'

I turned round. It was Mr Hatchett.

'Oh,' I said, before I could stop myself, and then he stood, a little shyly, in front of me, glancing at Ai-Lien with surprise, but saying nothing. I looked down at Ai-Lien.

'This is Irene,' I said. And then, 'It is really wonderful to see you, Mr Hatchett.'

'Call me Francis.'

His face transformed as he smiled, as if cracking a mask, cheerful underneath, and he stood up straight. There it was, that reddish beard that I remembered and eyes alive and friendly.

'Come,' he said, 'I've got you a room at the Grosvenor, where you can have a hot bath, something to eat.'

I held out my hand towards him and as he took it my bones sang back their own response.

'I imagine that, more than anything, you would like a cup of tea?'

I turned to my luggage so that he could not see the expression on my face. Victoria Station's shuttered roof stretched its cathedral arches above us in great strips and outside I could hear rain drops, clamouring as if wanting to be heard.

'You didn't bring the desert weather with you, then?'

'No, Mr Hatchett – Francis,' I said, turning back to face him, 'I have left the desert weather behind.'

Eastbourne, Present Day

Henry's Café, on the promenade

'It won't survive,' Tayeb said, stirring his tea.

They were sitting on white plastic chairs outside Henry's Café looking out at the sea which was flat and unimpressive. The tide was far out and didn't seem as if it were in a hurry to come in.

Thoughts of Frieda's work, her flat, her life clustered at the edge of the day but she banished them, as much as she could. It was sunny, but with a coolness in the air. They had walked along the neat, refined seafront promenade towards the undistinguished café at the bottom of white, spiked cliffs. Not talking much, but touching each other, lightly all through the day, hand on an arm, an elbow; a stroke of the hair. His hands were rough, and quite small, and she felt she could cherish them, if she were allowed to. When they did talk it was mostly about the fate of the owl. Frieda didn't mention the letters.

'But I do wonder if we should let it go?' It was in Nikolai's lounge at the moment, with a blanket over it. Nikolai had instructed one of his kitchen staff to feed it something raw.

'I tell you Frieda, it won't survive.'

'I'm not sure,' Frieda said. 'Surely it will make its own way, out there in the world? It must have survival instincts.'

'It would be cruel,' he said. 'Freedom would mean it would die.'

Frieda's teeth dug grooves into the rim of her polystyrene cup. 'Is that a euphemism, for you, I mean?' He smiled.

'Keep it,' Tayeb said, 'and if it becomes too much for you take it to a bird sanctuary.'

'You're right,' Frieda said and, surprisingly, it was a relief not to feel she had to free it.

Behind Henry's Café a chalk path ran up to the top of the beginning of the Downs and they made their way up it, slowly. It was the path that led to Beachy Head. The sky was low as if half-lit, odd, but once up on to the flatlands on the top of the Downs, they could see right out to sea. Frieda walked towards the edge of the cliff, hesitantly. Tayeb followed. Once she was a metre or so from the edge, she turned and called to him.

'Be careful, it sometimes crumbles as far back as this.'

Frieda sat down on the grass, feeling a slight wetness rise up through the fabric of her jeans. She knelt forward, on hands and knees, and crawled to the edge of the cliff.

'Come on,' she said.

Tayeb did the same, on hands and knees, and when they were both at the edge they lay down flat on their stomachs, and allowed their heads with stretched necks to lean out over the end of the grass and chalk. It was an endless distance down to the sea where the waves bashed at chalk rocks. A sensation of vertigo shivered through her, but it wasn't unpleasant. How small they were, together, and how together they felt, with their necks stretched over the edge of a cliff, looking down at the smashing, clashing sea on the shingle.

Evening cast a wilderness light over the civilised garden beds along the seafront. Frieda stood next to Tayeb as they watched the sea coming in. The tide had moved up the shore at an incredible rate and with the sound of shingle dragging up, and dragging down, taking away with it all the lies she had been told as a child, the guff about open marriages and love, her mother and her father and the cut tongues. All of it drained away into the gaps around the pebbles and Frieda fancied she could change things. Move, from the city to the sea, perhaps, to another sort of life of less travelling, fewer empty hotel rooms, less continual movement in circles away from herself.

'You could come to Amsterdam, if I make it there?' Tayeb said half to Frieda, half into the wind.

'Perhaps,' she said, 'I could.'

Letters in an envelope, tucked into the index of a book

January 30th, 1924
Acacia House,
17 George Street,
Hastings

Dear Francis,

We are settled in the boarding-house, and we are grateful. It is clean, the landlady cooks well. We shall be comfy here and will venture forth into the New Year nicely. The town is windy, bright and has everything that a seaside place should: cliffs, long stretches of beach, the smell of sea-kale and lavender. There is an old fishing quarter – the Old Town – with alleyways and fisher-man huts and piles of ropes and tackles. There is a coastguard cottage and Irene and I are grateful. Thank you so much, is what I mean to say. When will you be returning?

Yours,

Evangeline.

Next, one page of a letter:

you for the books. They will be useful for distraction purposes. I think that Mother has finally conceded that we will not be return-ing to Southsea, though, she quite rightly points out that there is not much advantage to Hastings over Southsea. I have thought that myself. I am working very hard on the final manuscript; you've strengthened me. I am so grateful for your reassurance. The task of pulling together the remains of my thoughts and memories seems somewhat overwhelming on occasions. Today, for instance, I could hardly set one word after another; it was as if each time I attempted a word a desert-ghost would ambush me – I sound ludicrous, I am aware. Heaven knows, I am sure you don't care a rap about these details, you just want the book finished! How can I ever thank you? Irene gets fatter and happier still.

And the next:

March 30th, 1925
Black Rock House,
Stanley Road,
Hastings

Dearest,

So glorious it looks: real, full of pages, actually here. I am moved – really, you can't imagine how much – to look at it. Its existence is down to you. You perhaps will never quite understand how much I thought of you when in Turkestan; how much your commission meant to me. The fact is, now, you are also my dearest friend. You say that Emily finally understands, that you 'sponsor' Irene? I do hope so, darling. Tell me if there is more I can do? There is a small problem with the nurse, we can discuss when you come.

A peculiar thing: I found Millicent's bible this morning, in my drawer. I hadn't put it there, I am not quite sure how it got there but seeing it stirred up all sorts of impressions of her and it is a curious fact that I think of her more than I do my sister. I can't quite say why that is. She has left a mood, almost a scent on my life.

Yours,
Evangeline.

Frieda flicked through the series of telegrams held together with a clip:

IRENE ILL. DOCTOR HERE. COME.
THURS AT 11 IS BEST. BRING THE PACKAGE.
I WANT TO SEE YOU. E. IRENE KISSES THE PICTURE
AT NIGHT.

October 7th, 1926
Black Rock House,
Stanley Road,
Hastings

Beloved Francis,

Mrs Reckham told Martha that it was 'common knowledge'
all about the town. I admit, at moments like these, I find our
arrangement a little difficult. It is not – my love – that I resent
the making of this 'second home' as you call it. I want to make
the place for you, indeed, I find joy in creating this still place,
away from all the wants of your wife and children and the flib-
bertigibbet of London – I think often of what you said about the
pavements coming up, the heads talking all at once as if full of
demons and the air smelling of cider gone bad – I speak as if I
know London life, when, how could I? Kept as I am, here, with
Irene, at the sea.

I am sorry. I should be happier. Irene is round and happy and loves
Martha as far as I can tell. I mustn't send this letter to you, Darling.
All the worries you have. The work to keep the house a home and
furniture and the fire, the kitchen supplied, all calm for your visits,
in the end, in the night . . . This is just a passing mood. Forgive me.

Bless you and keep you,

Yours,
Eva

June 21st, 1945
Black Rock House,
Stanley Road,
Hastings

Beloved Francis,

Your lovely long letter came and I felt calmed and happy. I'm glad that you have been resting and that Emily, too, is better. Early mornings are best for work; work without looking up until one and then after lunch, relax. It is a much better system than your previous way. Did you get my cable? Irene is due back any day now. She was cross with me for not rallying after VE day and I tried to explain that I felt it inside, a liberation of sorts – or, a dignified sense of weary victory, if one can put it that way – but if I am honest, I merely felt as though I were looking out of my window at a broken piece of glass. I took a walk along the promenade which is covered in barbed wire and hooks, with sandbags propping up the edges, it was dreary; quite empty.

I could not shake an image of Irene in the flat on Regents Park, with her candlesticks in the fireplace as if it were perfectly normal that the windows were knocked out; those dreadful friends: no electric light, no water for her bath. Those things she said to me, 'Eva, I can never reach the places you have been to. How am I supposed to?' She said she found me 'suffocating'. I believe there is a special gentleman somewhere, but she tells me nothing.

She will be coming back to live with me here in Hastings now the war is over. I fear that it might be difficult for us to accommodate each other again after this time apart. I am nervous, darling, but I suppose we shall get along. Perhaps she will not stay for long? I am sure she will travel, go to the places she talks of. One can only hope that the world will open up again now for the young.

This uncanny, brilliant sunshine gets wearing, and I miss you. Ought you not come and meet up with me next month? Meanwhile, all love,

Yours,

Evangeline.

London, Present Day

Victoria Station

Victoria Station was a rush of commuters beating each other to the prime seats. The air was hot, frenetic and Frieda stood, conspicuous with a large birdcage in her hand, waiting on the concourse to take a train to the sea. Her flat was sub-let, her report submitted. She had asked for, and was granted, a sabbatical; a window, a pause, to live by the sea.

'But what are you going to do?' colleagues asked her, after they had together spent two hours in a strategy meeting that resulted in a list of action points that did not resemble or refer to any actual action, or point. She made noises about research and hinted at personal projects but said no more.

'The youth of the Islamic world will simply have to struggle on without you,' they said.

She was rather an expert now at feeding frozen mice to the owl, which, as the print-out warned would happen, had 'attached' itself to her and had taken to hooting through the night, thinking, sadly, of Frieda as its mate. To be friendly, to be a sport, Frieda hoots back. She has left a husband to his discontented wife and their three boys.

She paused for a moment in front of the departure board. The platform numbers flipped and her train came up: platform 19. She made her way on to the train and found an empty seat near the window. She put the cage, covered in a small blanket, on the seat next to her. The moment of disorientation, when it is impossible to tell whether it is the platform moving or the train, when it could just as well be the platform dragging backwards to the past, or the train rushing forward to the future, seemed to last an extended time. She was suspended; but then the sun came through the window, warming Frieda like an old friend. Battersea Power Station sang a goodbye. The tide in the Thames was low, and like her, wending to the sea. There was a card in Frieda's pocket: on the front a picture of a woman in a grey dress leaning out of a window, looking out. On the back, written in beautiful, calligraphic handwriting, *I took the Leica. Come and find me and I shall give it back insh' Allah* and below it, a drawing of a curious-looking bird, with a small beak and long spindly legs. The owl made a rustling movement. Frieda touched the cage, 'We're here,' she said, 'and soon, not long now, we'll be there.'

Acknowledgements

Many, many thanks to friends, colleagues and family who have supported and helped me along the way: Ali Smith, for giving me courage a long time ago; early Goldsmiths readers Tamera Howard, Louise McElvogue, Blake Morrison, Maura Dooley and Stephen Knight; Chris Gribble and Becky Swift (the New Writing Ventures prize and The Literary Consultancy reading gave me the best possible start); Sara Maitland – and Zoe – for timely wit and wisdom; Arts Council England for a research and travel grant which enabled me to visit Kashgar; Gemma Seltzer and Kate Griffin (and thank you Kate for the help with the Serebriakova painting); Tamara Sharp and Beijing-based journalist Paul Mooney for advice on Kashgar, and the anonymous Chinese girl who helped me to leave Xinjiang Province when riots flared up in Urumqi and Kashgar; British Council friends all over the world, in particular Jonathan Barker (a very big thank you), Hannah Henderson, Sinead Russell, Susie Nicklin, Kate Joyce and Vibeke Burke; Elizabeth White for letting me stay in the most beautiful library in Yemen; Cathy Costain for looking after me in Cairo; Tony Calderbank for expert advice on Arabic calligraphy; Laila Hourani for a wonderful friendship (I hope that one day soon you will be able to return to your beautiful Damascus); Emma House for being the best travel companion; Nasser Jarrous for gracious hospitality in Lebanon; Salah Saleh, Amer Rifat and Hussein

Mazeh for kindness in Sana'a; and Peter Clark for a wonderful trip around the Gulf in the footsteps of Ibn Battuta.

Much of my research into Missionary travel writing, diaries and journals was conducted at the China Inland Mission missionary archive at the School of Oriental and African Studies in London. Thank you to the diligent archive staff and likewise staff at the British Library. Thank you to my agent, Rachel Calder, for immense support – both editorially and in life! – and my talented editor Helen Garnons-Williams for enthusiasm and a sharp eye. Erica Jarnes, Alexandra Pringle, Amanda Shipp, Katie Bond and Nigel Newton have all made me feel very welcome at Bloomsbury. Thank you too Bloomsbury USA, in particular my very lovely US editor, Nancy Miller and Michelle Blankenship, George Gibson and Peter Miller for such a warm response to my book; Sarah Greeno for the beautiful cover; and cartographer John Gilkes for Evangeline's map.

I am very grateful to my parents, John and Lynda Joinson, and Dave Joinson, for so much help and support over the years, and to Florence McKinney, Neville Joinson, Jean Joinson (recently passed away) and the rest of my family. Thank you friends of old for your long-term faith: Alice Khimasia, David Parr, Stephanie Cole, Helena Rebecca Howe. Much of this book was written while my children were very tiny and so thank you to Woodrow and Scout for coming along, bringing with you chaos, wonder and love. Above all, thank you to my husband, Ben Nicholls, for everything. I wrote this book for you.